MUTINY ON THE BOUNTY

Books by Charles Nordhoff (1887–1947)

THE FLEDGLING, 1919
THE PEARL LAGOON, 1924
PICARO, 1924
THE DERELICT, 1928

Books by James Norman Hall (1887–1951)

KITCHENER'S MOB, 1916
HIGH ADVENTURE, 1918
ON THE STREAM OF TRAVEL, 1926
MID-PACIFIC, 1928
MOTHER GOOSE LAND, 1930
FLYING WITH CHAUCER, 1930
TALE OF A SHIPWRECK, 1934
THE FRIENDS, 1939
DOCTOR DOGBODY'S LEG, 1940
O, MILLERSVILLE!, 1940
UNDER A THATCHED ROOF, 1942
LOST ISLAND, 1944
A WORD FOR HIS SPONSOR, 1949
THE FAR LANDS, 1950
THE FORGOTTEN ONE
AND OTHER TRUE TALES OF THE SOUTH SEAS, 1952
MY ISLAND HOME, 1952

Books by Charles Nordhoff and James Norman Hall

HISTORY OF THE LAFAYETTE FLYING CORPS, 1920
FAERY LANDS OF THE SOUTH SEAS, 1921
FALCONS OF FRANCE, 1929
MUTINY ON THE BOUNTY, 1932
MEN AGAINST THE SEA, 1934
PITCAIRN'S ISLAND, 1934
THE HURRICANE, 1936
THE DARK RIVER, 1938
NO MORE GAS, 1940
BOTANY BAY, 1941
MEN WITHOUT COUNTRY, 1942
THE HIGH BARBAREE, 1945

MUTINY ON THE BOUNTY

By
CHARLES NORDHOFF
and
JAMES NORMAN HALL

BOSTON

LITTLE, BROWN AND COMPANY

9938528

THE ATLANTIC MONTHLY PRESS BOOKS
ARE PUBLISHED BY
LITTLE, BROWN, AND COMPANY
IN ASSOCIATION WITH
THE ATLANTIC MONTHLY COMPANY

PRINTED IN THE UNITED STATES OF AMERICA

To

Captain Viggo Rasmussen, *Schooner Tiaré Taporo,* Rarotonga

and

Captain Andy Thomson, *Schooner Tagua,* Rarotonga

Old friends who sail the seas the *Bounty* sailed

FOREWORD

They began it as buddies. Nordhoff was a graduate of the Ambulance Service. Norman Hall was a veteran of Kitchener's Army. Just by chance he was in London during the first August days of 1914, and when the mob which went swirling round Nelson's Column to the lilt of "Good-bye, Leicester Square" was hammered into the kernel of an army, he was part of it. Honorably discharged, he reenlisted, this time in the French aviation service, and found the berth he had been fashioned for in the Escadrille Lafayette. Flying was the thing for Charles Nordhoff, too, and when he joined the squadron two contributors to the *Atlantic Monthly* met each other for the first time, and interchanged compliments gracefully given and received. This chance friendship, springing from a common love for letters, was riveted by the comradeship of high adventure. Each found in the other a man whose silence and whose speech delighted and refreshed him. From that day to this, they have shared a common destiny as brothers.

Captain Hall and Lieutenant Nordhoff both distinguished themselves. Were I to lay stress on their military records I should outrage the modesty of both, but somewhere in Nordhoff's trunk under a pile of dungarees you will find a *croix de guerre* with star, and a citation which his children will preserve. As for Hall, I will gratify him by passing over the words that Pétain wrote, but of the dead it is seemly to speak with living praise, and I am justified in recording that during one of his temporary deaths Hall was thus praised in public by the General of the VIIIth Army:

Brillant pilot de chasse, modèle de courage et d'entrain qui a abattu recemment un avion ennemi, a trouvé une mort glorieuse dans un combat contre quatre monoplanes, dont un a été descendu en flammes.

It is pleasant to remember that the writer of this sketch, mourning the same heroic death, was busily occupied in writing a memoir of the sort that might be well worth dying for, when he was interrupted by a cheerful letter from his resurrected hero, who had, it seemed, just made his breakaway from a German camp.

When both men were mustered from the service I saw them again on a memorable occasion. Each wrote to me without the other's knowledge, asking for advice. Both had lived with intensity lives high above the conflict, and to both the stridency and (as they felt) the vulgarity of post-war civilization was past endurance. Each had ambitions, talents, and memories of great price. To transmute these intangibles into three meals *per diem* was the prosaic problem put up to me. How well I remember the day they came to Boston. Reticent and illusive, there was something in each of them that in its pure essence I have not known elsewhere. Conrad called it Romance. When Romance and Chivalry come to refresh my cumbered mind, I see those two young men just as I saw them then.

We talked and we talked, and then we adjourned for counsel to a little Italian restaurant. Those were days when *vino rosso* was a legitimate dressing for a salad to be eaten with an omelette. We ate, drank, and speculated of those places in the world where the dollar or its equivalent is not the sole essential medium of exchange. I called for a geography. We opened it at Mercator's projection, and hardly were the pages pinned down by twin cruets of oil and vinegar, when both the adventurers with a single swoop pointed to the route which Stevenson had taken. I called up Cook for information on prices, and while my companions chatted of palm trees and hibiscus — Loti seasoned with Conrad — I did several sums in addition and multiplication.

We planned with the resolution of genius. Then and there Hall and Nordhoff drew up the rough outline of a miraculous work on the South Seas, and when a day or two later the silent partner took it with him to New York, all the spices of the East were in the chapter headings. One publisher was pitted

against another.   For once in his life the salesman was a credit
to his profession, and when he returned, the respectable firm
of Hall and Nordhoff was incorporated with a capital of
$7,000 — $1,000 paid in.   After all, there is more to literature than pretty words and an agile pen.

Historically, the first work of the firm was the official history of the Lafayette Flying Corps.   Then came, I believe,
the work on the South Seas which, as I have said, I had the
honor to sell.   Nordhoff wrote by himself a capital boy's
story, "The Pearl Lagoon," based on his own early life in
Lower California.   Hall meantime turned out some admirably
individual essays, stories, and poems, but the firm added enor-
mously to its reputation when the story of the Escadrille was
brilliantly retold as fiction under the title, "Falcons of France."
Of all aerial narratives, this, in my judgment, takes the first
place both in its thrilling realism and in that delicate understanding of the co-ordination of mind, body, and spirit which
is at once a flyer's inheritance and his salvation.

A play followed — "The Empty Chair" — accepted for
production on the screen.   Of this I know only at second-
hand, and will not speak, though I cannot but remark how
strange is that conjunction of the planets under whose influence Hall and Nordhoff are reborn in Hollywood.

Now comes the firm's latest and best bid for fame and fortune.   Reader, have you ever heard of the strange history of
His Majesty's Ship *Bounty*?   If ever the sea cast up a saltier
story, I should like to know it.   A chronicle of its events,
clumsy enough in the telling, appeared — Lord, how long
since: "The Pitcairn Islanders," I think was the name of this
particular volume.   Anyway, it was bound in green and
stamped in gold, and for all its heavy-footed style, a boy curled
up on a sofa fifty years ago wore the pages through.   There
was mutiny on the good ship, as the world remembers.
Lieutenant Bligh, the Commander, was lowered into his long
boat to drift, God knows where, and the mutineers cracked on
sail for Tahiti and Fate.   At any rate, that story is of the
primeval stuff Romance is made of, and if Captain Hall and
Lieutenant Nordhoff are not the men to write it, then, thought

I, Providence has been clean wrong in all the games she has played on them from the very beginning. I broached the idea to Hall, or perhaps he mentioned it first to me. Anyway, we both knew this was not a chance to be missed, though one thing we were certain of — that a story so perfect must be told with perfect accuracy. A whole literature has been burgeoning about it for a century, and if the ultimate account is to go into a novel, nothing of the truth must be sacrificed. For Romance is not capricious, it is an attitude of Fate, and Fate, my friends, is greatly to be respected. So on a visit to London in the Spring of 1931 I sought the assistance of Dr. Leslie Hotson, who knows the British Museum as if it were the lining of his trousers pocket. We hit on the perfect record worker, and in due time this lady and I laid hands on every scrap of pertinent evidence. We had photostatic copies of every page of the reports of the court martial of the mutineers, hand written in beautiful copper plate. We assaulted the Admiralty, to which our bountiful thanks are due, for within its sacred precincts Commander E. C. Tufnell of His Majesty's Navy made copies of the deck and rigging plans of the *Bounty*, and in his goodness even made an admirably detailed model of the ship. Meanwhile, booksellers, the mouldier the better, were put on the trail for volumes of the British Navy of the period. Engravers' collections were searched for illustrations of Captain Bligh and of the rascals he set sail with. Item by item, a library unique in the annals of collecting was built, boxed, and shipped to Tahiti. The firm of Hall and Nordhoff hired by way of inspiration the first room that ever they lived in on the Islands. They pinned maps to the walls, stuck up deck and rigging plans, propped photographs of the model on the table in front of them, and, wonder of wonders, in spite of the fascination of their collection, in the face of the perfume blowing in at their windows, in defiance of the Heaven that Idleness is in the tropics, they fell to work!

Here is the book they have written. Read it, and you, too, will know that Romance has come into her own.

ELLERY SEDGWICK

Atlantic office, September 1st, 1932

CONTENTS

CONTENTS

MUTINY ON THE BOUNTY

I

LIEUTENANT BLIGH

THE British are frequently criticized by other nations for their dislike of change, and indeed we love England for those aspects of nature and life which change the least. Here in the West Country, where I was born, men are slow of speech, tenacious of opinion, and averse — beyond their countrymen elsewhere — to innovation of any sort. The houses of my neighbours, the tenants' cottages, the very fishing boats which ply on the Bristol Channel, all conform to the patterns of a simpler age. And an old man, forty of whose three-and-seventy years have been spent afloat, may be pardoned a not unnatural tenderness toward the scenes of his youth, and a satisfaction that these scenes remain so little altered by time.

No men are more conservative than those who design and build ships save those who sail them; and since storms are less frequent at sea than some landsmen suppose, the life of a sailor is principally made up of the daily performance of certain tasks, in certain manners and at certain times. Forty years of this life have made a slave of me, and I continue, almost against my will, to live by the clock. There is no reason why I should rise at seven each morning, yet seven finds me dressing, nevertheless; my copy of the *Times* would reach me even though I failed to order a horse saddled at ten for my ride down to Watchet to meet the post. But habit is too much for me, and habit finds a powerful ally in old Thacker, my housekeeper, whose duties, as I perceive with inward amusement, are lightened by the regularity she does everything to encourage. She will listen to no hint of retirement.   In spite of her years, which must number nearly eighty by now, her step is still brisk and her black eyes snap with a remnant of the old malice. It would give me pleasure to speak with her of the days when my mother was still living, but when I try to draw her into talk she wastes no time in putting me in my place.   Servant and master, with the churchyard only a step ahead!   I am lonely now; when Thacker dies, I shall be lonely indeed.

Seven generations of Byams have lived and died in Withycombe; the name has been known in the region of the Quantock Hills for five hundred years and more.   I am the last of them; it is strange to think that at my death what remains of our blood will flow in the veins of an Indian woman in the South Sea.

If it be true that a man's useful life is over on the day when his thoughts begin to dwell in the past, then I have served little purpose in living since my retirement from His Majesty's Navy fifteen years ago.   The present has lost substance and reality, and I have discovered, with some regret, that contemplation of the future brings neither pleasure nor concern.   But forty years at sea, including the turbulent period of the wars against the Danes, the Dutch, and the French, have left my memory so well stored that I ask no greater delight than to be free to wander in the past.

My study, high up in the north wing of Withycombe, with its tall windows giving on the Bristol Channel and the green distant coast of Wales, is the point of departure for these travels through the past.   The journal I have kept, since I went to sea as a midshipman in 1787, lies at hand in the camphor-wood box beside my chair, and I have only to take up a sheaf of its pages to smell once more the reek of battle smoke, to feel the stinging sleet of a gale in the North Sea, or to enjoy the calm beauty of a tropical night under the constellations of the Southern Hemisphere.

In the evening, when the unimportant duties of an old man's

day are done, and I have supped alone in silence, I feel the pleasant anticipation of a visitor to Town, who on his first evening spends an agreeable half-hour in deciding which theatre he will attend. Shall I fight the old battles over again? Camperdown, Copenhagen, Trafalgar — these names thunder in memory like the booming of great guns. Yet more and more frequently I turn the pages of my journal still further back, to the frayed and blotted log of a midshipman — to an episode I have spent a good part of my life in attempting to forget. Insignificant in the annals of the Navy, and even more so from an historian's point of view, this incident was nevertheless the strangest, the most picturesque, and the most tragic of my career.

It has long been my purpose to follow the example of other retired officers and employ the too abundant leisure of an old man in setting down, with the aid of my journal and in the fullest possible detail, a narrative of some one of the episodes of my life at sea. The decision was made last night; I shall write of my first ship, the *Bounty*, of the mutiny on board, of my long residence on the island of Tahiti in the South Sea, and of how I was conveyed home in irons, to be tried by court-martial and condemned to death. Two natures clashed on the stage of that drama of long ago, two men as strong and enigmatical as any I have known — Fletcher Christian and William Bligh.

When my father died of a pleurisy, early in the spring of 1787, my mother gave few outward signs of grief, though their life together, in an age when the domestic virtues were unfashionable, had been a singularly happy one. Sharing the interest in the natural sciences which had brought my father the honour of a Fellowship in the Royal Society, my mother was a countrywoman at heart, caring more for life at Withycombe than for the artificial distractions of town.

I was to have gone up to Oxford that fall, to Magdalen, my

father's college, and during that first summer of my mother's widowhood I began to know her, not as a parent, but as a most charming companion, of whose company I never wearied. The women of her generation were schooled to reserve their tears for the sufferings of others, and to meet adversity with a smile. A warm heart and an inquiring mind made her conversation entertaining or philosophical as the occasion required; and, unlike the young ladies of the present time, she had been taught that silence can be agreeable when one has nothing to say.

On the morning when Sir Joseph Banks's letter arrived, we were strolling about the garden, scarcely exchanging a word. It was late in July, the sky was blue, and the warm air bore the scent of roses; such a morning as enables us to tolerate our English climate, which foreigners declare, perhaps with some justice, the worst in the world. I was thinking how uncommonly handsome my mother looked in black, with her thick fair hair, fresh colour, and dark blue eyes. Thacker, her new maid, — a black-eyed Devon girl, — came tripping down the path. She dropped my mother a curtsey and held out a letter on a silver tray. My mother took the letter, gave me a glance of apology, and began to read, seating herself on a rustic bench.

"From Sir Joseph," she said, when she had perused the letter at length and laid it down. "You have heard of Lieutenant Bligh, who was with Captain Cook on his last voyage? Sir Joseph writes that he is on leave, stopping with friends near Taunton, and would enjoy an evening with us. Your father thought very highly of him."

I was a rawboned lad of seventeen, lazy in body and mind, with overfast growth, but the words were like a galvanic shock to me. "With Captain Cook!" I exclaimed. "Ask him by all means!"

My mother smiled. "I thought you would be pleased," she said.

The carriage was dispatched in good time with a note for Mr. Bligh, bidding him to dine with us that evening if he could. I remember how I set out, with the son of one of our tenants, to sail my boat at high tide on Bridgwater Bay, and how little I enjoyed the sail. My thoughts were all of our visitor, and the hours till dinner-time seemed to stretch ahead interminably.

I was fonder, perhaps, of reading than most lads of my age and the book I loved best of all was one given me by my fat' on my tenth birthday — Dr. Hawkesworth's account o voyages to the South Sea. I knew the three, heavy, bound volumes almost by heart, and I had read w interest the French narrative of Monsieur de Bougai age. These early accounts of discoveries in the S of the manners and customs of the inhabitants Owhyhee (as those islands were then called), e almost inconceivable to-day. The writing Rousseau, which were to have such lamental results, preached a doctrine which had mac among people of consequence. It became fashi lieve that only among men in a state of nature, free restraints, could true virtue and happiness be found. when Wallis, Byron, Bougainville, and Cook returned fr their voyage of discovery with alluring accounts of the New Cytheræa, whose happy inhabitants, relieved from the curse of Adam, spent their days in song and dance, the doctrines of Rousseau received new impetus. Even my father, so engrossed in his astronomical studies that he had lost touch with the world, listened eagerly to the tales of his friend Sir Joseph Banks, and often discussed with my mother, whose interest was equal to his, the virtues of what he termed "a natural life."

My own interest was less philosophical than adventurous; like other youngsters, I longed to sail unknown seas, to raise uncharted islands, and to trade with gentle Indians who regarded white men as gods. The thought that I was soon to converse with an officer who had accompanied Captain Cook on his last voyage — a mariner, and not a man of science like Sir Joseph — kept me woolgathering all afternoon, and I was not disappointed when the carriage drew up at last and Mr. Bligh stepped out.

Bligh was at that time in the prime of life. He was of middle stature, strongly made and inclining to stoutness, though he carried himself well. His weather-beaten face was broad, with a firm mouth and very fine dark eyes, and his thick powdered hair grew high on his head, above a noble brow. He wore his three-cornered black hat athwartships; his coat was of bright blue broadcloth, trimmed with white, with gold anchor buttons and the long tails of the day. His waistcoat, breeches, and stockings were white. The old-fashioned uniform was one to set off a well-made man. Bligh's voice, strong, vibrant, and a little harsh, gave an impression of uncommon vitality; his bearing showed resolution and courage, and the glance of his eye gave evidence of an assurance such as few men possess. These symptoms of a strong and aggressive nature were tempered by the lofty brow of a man of intellect, and the agreeable and unpretentious manner he assumed ashore.

The carriage, as I said, drew up before our door, the footman sprang down from the box, and Mr. Bligh stepped out. I had been waiting to welcome him; as I made myself known, he gave me a handclasp and a smile.

"Your father's son," he said. "A great loss — he was known, by name at least, to all who practise navigation."

Presently my mother came down and we went in to dinner. Bligh spoke very handsomely of my father's work on the determination of longitude, and after a time the conversation turned to the islands of the South Sea.

"Is it true," my mother asked, "that the Indians of Tahiti are as happy as Captain Cook believed?"

"Ah, ma'am," said our guest, "happiness is a vast word! It is true that they live without great labour, and that nearly all of the light tasks they perform are self-imposed; released from the fear of want and from all salutary discipline, they regard nothing seriously."

"Roger and I," observed my mother, "have been studying the ideas of J. J. Rousseau. As you know, he believes that true happiness can only be enjoyed by man in a state of nature."

Bligh nodded. "I have been told of his ideas," he said, "though unfortunately I left school too young to learn French. But if a rough seaman may express an opinion on a subject more suited to a philosopher, I believe that true happiness can only be enjoyed by a disciplined and enlightened people. As for the Indians of Tahiti, though they are freed from the fear of want, their conduct is regulated by a thousand absurd restrictions, which no civilized man would put up with. These restrictions constitute a kind of unwritten law, called *taboo*, and instead of making for a wholesome discipline they lay down fanciful and unjust rules to control every action of a man's life. A few days among men in a state of nature might have changed Monsieur Rousseau's ideas." He paused and turned to me. "You know French, then?" he asked, as if to include me in the talk.

"Yes, sir," I replied.

"I 'll do him justice, Mr. Bligh," my mother put in; "he has a gift for languages. My son might pass for a native of France or Italy, and is making progress in German now. His Latin won him a prize last year."

"I wish I had his gift! Lord!" Bligh laughed. "I 'd rather face a hurricane than translate a page of Cæsar nowadays! And the task Sir Joseph has set me is worse still! There is no harm in telling you that I shall soon set sail for the South Sea." Perceiving our interest, he went on: —

"I have been in the merchant service since I was paid off four years ago, when peace was signed. Mr. Campbell, the West India merchant, gave me command of his ship, *Britannia*, and during my voyages, when I frequently had planters of consequence as passengers on board, I was many times asked to tell what I knew of the breadfruit, which flourishes in Tahiti and Owhyhee. Considering that the breadfruit might provide a cheap and wholesome food for their negro slaves, several of the West India merchants and planters petitioned the Crown, asking that a vessel be fitted out suitably to convey the breadfruit from Tahiti to the West Indian islands. Sir Joseph Banks thought well of the idea and gave it his support. It is due largely to his interest that the Admiralty is now fitting out a small vessel for the voyage, and at Sir Joseph's suggestion I was recalled to the Service and am to be given command. We should sail before the end of the year."

"Were I a man," said my mother, whose eyes were bright with interest, "I should beg you to take me along; you will need gardeners, no doubt, and I could care for the young plants."

Bligh smiled. "I would ask no better, ma'am," he said gallantly, "though I have been supplied with a botanist — David Nelson, who served in a similar capacity on Captain Cook's last voyage. My ship, the *Bounty,* will be a floating garden fitted with every convenience for the care of the plants, and I have no fear but that we shall be able to carry out the purpose of the voyage. It is the task our good friend Sir Joseph has enjoined on me that presents the greatest difficulty. He has solicited me most earnestly to employ my time in Tahiti in acquiring a greater knowledge of the Indians and their customs, and a more complete vocabulary and grammar of their language, than it has hitherto been possible to gather. He believes that a dictionary of the language, in particular, might prove of the greatest service to mariners in the South Sea. But I know as little of dictionaries as of Greek, and shall have no one on board qualified for such a task."

"How shall you lay your course, sir?" I asked. "About Cape Horn?"

"I shall make the attempt, though the season will be advanced beyond the time of easterly winds. We shall return from Tahiti by way of the East Indies and the Cape of Good Hope."

My mother gave me a glance and we rose as she took leave of us. While he cracked walnuts and sipped my father's Madeira, Bligh questioned me, in the agreeable manner he knew so well how to assume, as to my knowledge of languages. At last he seemed satisfied, finished the wine in his glass, and shook his head at the man who would have filled it. He was moderate in the use of wine, in an age when nearly all the officers of His Majesty's Navy drank to excess. Finally he spoke.

"Young man," he said seriously, "how would you like to sail with me?"

I had been thinking, ever since his first mention of the voyage, that I should like nothing better, but his words took me aback.

"Do you mean it, sir?" I stammered. "Would it be possible?"

"It rests with you and Mrs. Byam to decide. It would be a pleasure to make a place for you among my young gentlemen."

The warm summer evening was as beautiful as the day that had preceded it, and when we had joined my mother in the garden, she and Bligh spoke of the projected voyage. I knew that he was waiting for me to mention his proposal, and presently, during a pause in the talk, I summoned up my courage.

"Mother," I said, "Lieutenant Bligh has been good enough to suggest that I accompany him."

If she felt surprise, she gave no sign of it, but turned calmly to our guest. "You have paid Roger a compliment," she remarked. "Could an inexperienced lad be of use to you on board?"

"He'll make a seaman, ma'am, never fear! I've taken a fancy to the cut of his jib, as the old tars say. And I could put his gift for languages to good use."

"How long shall you be gone?"

"Two years, perhaps."

"He was to have gone up to Oxford, but I suppose that could wait." She turned to me half banteringly. "Well, sir, what do you say?"

"With your permission, there is nothing I would rather do."

She smiled at me in the twilight and gave my hand a little pat. "Then you have it," she said. "I would be the last to stand in the way. A voyage to the South Sea! If I were a lad and Mr. Bligh would have me, I'd run away from home to join his ship!"

Bligh gave one of his short, harsh laughs and looked at my mother admiringly. "You'd have made a rare sailor, ma'am," he remarked — "afraid of nothing, I'll wager."

It was arranged that I should join the *Bounty* at Spithead, but the storing, and victualing, and fitting-out took so long that the autumn was far advanced before she was ready to sail. In October I took leave of my mother and went up to London to order my uniforms, to call on old Mr. Erskine, our solicitor, and to pay my respects to Sir Joseph Banks.

My clearest memory of those days is of an evening at Sir Joseph's house. He was a figure of romance to my eyes — a handsome, florid man of forty-five, President of the Royal Society, companion of the immortal Captain Cook, friend of Indian princesses, and explorer of Labrador, Iceland, and the great South Sea. When we had dined, he led me to his study, hung with strange weapons and ornaments from distant lands. He took up from among the papers on his table a sheaf of manuscript.

"My vocabulary of the Tahitian language," he said. "I have had this copy made. It is short and imperfect, as you will discover, but may prove of some service to you. Please observe that the system of spelling Captain Cook and I adopted should be changed. I have given the matter some thought, and Bligh agrees with me that it will be better and simpler to set down the words as an Italian would spell them — particularly in the case of the vowels. You know Italian, eh?"

"Yes, sir."

"Good!" he went on. "You will be some months in Tahiti, while they are gathering the young breadfruit plants. Bligh will see to it that you are given leisure to devote yourself to the dictionary I hope to publish on your return. Dialects of the Tahitian language are spoken over an immense space of the South Sea, and a dictionary of the commoner words, with some little information as to the grammar, will be in demand among mariners before many years have passed. At present we think of the South Sea as little less remote than the moon, but depend on it, the rich whale fisheries and new lands for planting and settlement will soon attract notice, now that we have lost the American Colonies.

"There are many distractions in Tahiti," he went on after a pause; "take care that you are not misled into wasting your time. And, above all, take care in the selection of your Indian friends. When a ship drops anchor in Matavai Bay the Indians come out in throngs, each eager to choose a friend, or *taio,* from amongst her company. Bide your time, learn something of politics on shore, and choose as your *taio* a man of consideration and authority. Such a man can be of infinite use to you; in return for a few axes, knives, fishhooks, and trinkets for his women, he will keep you supplied with fresh provisions, entertain you at his residence when you step ashore, and do everything in his power to make himself useful. Should you make the mistake of choosing as your *taio* a man of the lower orders, you may find him dull, incurious, and with an imperfect knowledge of the Indian tongue. In my opinion they are not only a different class, but a different race, conquered long ago by those who now rule the land. Persons of consequence in Tahiti are taller, fairer, and vastly more intelligent than the *manahune,* or serfs."

"Then there is no more equality in Tahiti than amongst ourselves?"

Sir Joseph smiled. "Less, I should say. The Indians have a false appearance of equality from the simplicity of their manners and the fact that the employments of all classes are the same. The king may be seen heading a fishing party, or the queen paddling her own canoe, or beating out bark cloth with her women. But of real equality there is none; no action, however meritorious, can raise a man above the position to which he was born. The chiefs alone, believed to be descended from the gods, are thought to have souls." He paused, fingers drumming on the arm of his chair. "You 've everything you will need?" he asked. "Clothing, writing materials, money? Midshipmen's fare is not the best in the world, but when you go on board, one of the master's mates will ask each of you for three or four pounds to lay in a few small luxuries for the berth. Have you a sextant?"

"Yes, sir — one of my father's; I showed it to Mr. Bligh."

"I 'm glad Bligh 's in command; there 's not a better seaman afloat. I am told that he is a bit of a tartar at sea, but better a taut hand than a slack one, any day! He will instruct you in your duties; perform them smartly, and remember — discipline 's the thing!"

I took my leave of Sir Joseph with his last words still ringing in my ears — "Discipline 's the thing!" I was destined to ponder over them deeply, and sometimes bitterly, before we met again.

II

SEA LAW

TOWARD the end of November I joined the *Bounty* at Spithead. It makes me smile to-day to think of the box I brought down on the coach from London, packed with clothing and uniforms on which I had laid out more than a hundred pounds: blue tail-coats lined with white silk, with the white patch on the collar known in those days as a "weekly account"; breeches and waistcoats of white nankeen, and a brace of "scrapers" — smart three-cornered reefer's hats, with gold loops and cockades. For a few days I made a brave show in my finery, but when the *Bounty* sailed it was stowed away for good, and worn no more.

Our ship looked no bigger than a longboat among the tall first-rates and seventy-fours at anchor near by. She had been built for the merchant service, at Hull, three years before, and purchased for two thousand pounds; ninety feet long on deck and with a beam of twenty-four feet, her burthen was little more than two hundred tons. Her name — *Bethia* — had been painted out, and at the suggestion of Sir Joseph Banks she was rechristened *Bounty*. The ship had been many months at Deptford, where the Admiralty had spent more than four thousand pounds in altering and refitting her. The great cabin aft was now rigged as a garden, with innumerable pots standing in racks, and gutters running below to allow the water to be used over and over again. The result was that Lieutenant Bligh and the master, Mr. Fryer, were squeezed into two small cabins on either side of the ladderway, and forced to mess with the surgeon, in a screened-off space of the lower deck, aft of the main hatch. The ship was small to begin with; she carried a heavy cargo of stores and articles for barter with the Indians, and all hands on board were so cramped that I heard mutterings even before we set sail. I believe, in fact, that the discomfort of our life, and the bad humour it brought about, played no small part in the unhappy ending of a voyage which seemed ill-fated from the start.

The *Bounty* was copper-sheathed, a new thing in those days, and with her bluff, heavy hull, short masts, and stout rigging, she looked more like a whaling vessel than an armed transport of His Majesty's Navy. She carried a pair of swivel guns mounted on stocks forward, and six swivels and four four-pounders aft, on the upper deck.

All was new and strange to me on the morning when I presented myself to Lieutenant Bligh, the ship was crowded with women, — the sailors' "wives," — rum seemed to flow like water everywhere, and sharp-faced Jews, in their wherries, hovered alongside, eager to lend money at interest against pay day, or to sell on credit the worthless trinkets on their trays. The cries of the bumboat men, the shrill scolding of the women, and the shouts and curses of the sailors made a pandemonium stunning to a landsman's ears.

Making my way aft, I found Mr. Bligh on the quarter-deck. A tall, swarthy man was just ahead of me.

"I have been to the Portsmouth observatory, sir," he said to the captain; "the timekeeper is one minute fifty-two seconds too fast for mean time, and losing at the rate of one second a day. Mr. Bailey made a note of it in this letter to you."

"Thank you, Mr. Christian," said Bligh shortly, and at that moment, turning his head, he caught sight of me. I uncovered, stepping forward to present myself. "Ah, Mr. Byam," he went on, "this is Mr. Christian, the master's mate; he will show you your berth and instruct you in some of your duties. .. And, by the way, you will dine with me on board the

Tigress; Captain Courtney knew your father and asked me to bring you when he heard that you would be on board." He glanced at his large silver watch. "Be ready in an hour's time."

I bowed in reply to his nod of dismissal and followed Christian to the ladderway. The berth was a screened-off space of the lower deck, on the larboard side, abreast of the main hatch. Its dimensions were scarcely more than eight feet by ten, yet four of us were to make this kennel our home. Three or four boxes stood around the sides, and a scuttle of heavy discoloured glass admitted a dim light. A quadrant hung on a nail driven into the ship's side, and, though she was not long from Deptford, a reek of bilge water hung in the air. A handsome, sulky-looking boy of sixteen, in a uniform like my own, was arranging the gear in his box, and straightened up to give me a contemptuous stare. His name was Hayward, as I learned when Christian introduced us briefly, and he scarcely deigned to take my outstretched hand.

When we regained the upper deck, Christian lost his air of preoccupation, and smiled. "Mr. Hayward has been two years at sea," he remarked; "he knows you for a Johnny Newcomer. But the *Bounty* is a little ship; such airs would be more fitting aboard a first-rate."

He spoke in a cultivated voice, with a trace of the Manx accent, and I could barely hear the words above the racket from the forward part of the ship. It was a calm, bright winter morning, and I studied my companion in the clear sunlight. He was a man to glance at more than once.

Fletcher Christian was at that time in his twenty-fourth year, — a fine figure of a seaman in his plain blue, gold-buttoned frock, — handsomely and strongly built, with thick dark brown hair and a complexion naturally dark, and burned by the sun to a shade rarely seen among the white race. His mouth and chin expressed great resolution of character, and his eyes, black, deep-set, and brilliant, had something of hypnotic power in their far-away gaze. He looked more like a

Spaniard than an Englishman, though his family had been
settled since the fifteenth century on the Isle of Man. Christian was what women call a romantic-looking man; his moods
of gaiety alternated with fits of black depression, and he possessed a fiery temper which he controlled by efforts that brought
the sweat to his brow. Though only a master's mate, a step
above a midshipman, he was of gentle birth — better born than
Bligh and a gentleman in manner and speech.

"Lieutenant Bligh," he said, in his musing, abstracted way,
"desires me to instruct you in some of your duties. Navigation, nautical astronomy, and trigonometry he will teach you
himself, since we have no schoolmaster on board, as on a man-
of-war. And I can assure you that you will not sup till you
have worked out the ship's position each day. You will be
assigned to one of the watches, to keep order when the men
are at the braces or aloft. You will see that the hammocks
are stowed in the morning, and report the men whose hammocks are badly lashed. Never lounge against the guns or
the ship's side, and never walk the deck with your hands in
your pockets. You will be expected to go aloft with the
men to learn how to bend canvas and how to reef and furl
a sail, and when the ship is at anchor you may be placed in
charge of one of the boats. And, last of all, you are the slave
of those tyrants, the master and master's mates."

He gave me a whimsical glance and a smile. We were standing by the gratings abaft the mainmast, and at that moment a
stout elderly man, in a uniform much like Bligh's, came puffing
up the ladderway. His bronzed face was at once kindly and
resolute, and I should have known him for a seaman anywhere.

"Ah, Mr. Christian, there you are!" he exclaimed as he
heaved himself on deck. "What a madhouse! I'd like to
sink the lot of those Jews, and heave the wenches overboard!
Who's this? The new reefer, Mr. Byam, I'll be bound!
Welcome on board, Mr. Byam; your father's name stands high
in our science, eh, Mr. Christian?"

"Mr. Fryer, the master," said Christian in my ear.

"A madhouse," Fryer went on. "Thank God we shall pay off to-morrow night! Wenches everywhere, above decks and below." He turned to Christian. "Go forward and gather a boat's crew for Lieutenant Bligh — there are a few men still sober."

"There's discipline on a man-of-war at sea," he continued; "but give me a merchant ship in port. The captain's clerk is the only sober man below. The surgeon . . . Ah, here he is now!"

Turning to follow Fryer's glance, I saw a head thatched with thick snow-white hair appearing in the ladderway. Our sawbones had a wooden leg and a long equine face, red as the wattles of a turkey cock; even the back of his neck, lined with deep wrinkles like a tortoise's, was of the same fiery red. His twinkling bright blue eyes caught sight of the man beside me. Holding to the ladder with one hand, he waved a half-empty bottle of brandy at us.

"Ahoy there, Mr. Fryer!" he hailed jovially. "Have you seen Nelson, the botanist? I prescribed a drop of brandy for his rheumatic leg; it's time he took his medicine."

"He's gone ashore."

The surgeon shook his head with mock regret. "He'll give his good shillings to some Portsmouth quack, I'll wager. Yet here on board he might enjoy free and gratis the advice of the most enlightened medical opinion. Away with all bark and physic!" He flourished his bottle. "Here is the remedy for nine tenths of human ills. Aye! Drops of brandy! That's it!" Suddenly, in a mellow, husky voice, sweet and true, he began to sing: —

> "And Johnny shall have a new bonnet
> And Johnny shall go to the fair,
> And Johnny shall have a blue ribbon
> To tie up his bonny brown hair."

With a final flourish of his bottle, our surgeon went hopping down the ladderway. Fryer stared after him for a moment before he followed him below. Left to myself in the midst of the uproar on deck, I looked about me curiously.

Lieutenant Bligh, an old hand in the Navy, was nowhere to be seen. On the morrow the men would receive two months' wages in advance, and on the following day we should set sail on a voyage to the other side of the world, facing the hardships and dangers of seas still largely unexplored. The *Bounty* might well be gone two years or more, and now, on the eve of departure, her crew was allowed to relax for a day or two of such amusements as sailors most enjoy.

While I waited for Bligh in the uproar, I diverted myself in studying the rigging of the *Bounty*. Born and brought up on the west coast of England, I had loved the sea from childhood and lived amongst men who spoke of ships and their qualities as men gossip of horses elsewhere. The *Bounty* was ship-rigged, and to a true landsman her rigging would have seemed a veritable maze of ropes. But even in my inexperience I knew enough to name her sails, the different parts of her standing rigging, and most of the complex system of halliards, lifts, braces, sheets, and other ropes for the management of sails and yards. She spread two headsails — foretopmast-staysail and jib; on fore and main masts she carried courses, topsails, topgallants, and royals, and the mizzenmast spread the latter three sails. That American innovation, the crossjack, had not in those days been introduced. The crossjack yard was still, as the French say, a *vergue sèche,* — a barren yard, — and the *Bounty's* driver, though loose at the foot, was of the gaff-headed type, then superseding the clumsy lateen our ships had carried on the mizzen for centuries.

As I mused on the *Bounty's* sails and ropes, asking myself how this order or that would be given, and wondering how I should go about obeying were I told to furl a royal or lend a hand at one of the braces, I felt something of the spell which even the smallest ship casts over me to this day. For a ship is the noblest of all man's works — a cunning fabric of wood, and iron, and hemp, wonderfully propelled by wings of canvas, and seeming at times to have the very breath of life. I was craning my neck to stare aloft when I heard Bligh's voice, harsh and abrupt.

"Mr. Byam!"

I gathered my wits with a start and found Lieutenant Bligh, in full uniform, at my side. He gave a faint quizzing smile and went on: "She's small, eh? But a taut little ship — a taut little ship!" He made me a sign to follow him over the *Bounty's* side.

Our boat's crew, if not strictly sober, were able to row, and put their backs into it with a will. We were soon alongside Captain Courtney's tall seventy-four. The *Tigress* paid Mr. Bligh the compliment of piping the side. Side boys in spotless white stood at attention by the red ropes to the gangway; the boatswain, in full uniform, blew a slow and solemn salute on his silver whistle as Bligh's foot touched the deck. Marine sentries stood at attention, and all was silent save for the mournful piping. We walked aft, saluting the quarterdeck, where Captain Courtney awaited us.

Courtney and Bligh were old acquaintances; he had been with Bligh on the *Belle Poule*, in the stubborn and bloody action of Dogger Bank six years before. Captain Courtney was a member of a great family — a tall, slender officer, with a quizzing glass and a thin-lipped ironic mouth. He greeted us pleasantly, spoke of my father, whom he had known more by reputation than otherwise, and led us to his cabin aft, where a red-coated sentry stood at the bulkhead, a drawn sword in his hand. It was the first time I had been in the cabin of a man-of-war, and I gazed about me curiously. Its floor was the upper gun-deck and its ceiling the poop; so the apartment seemed very lofty for a ship. The ports were glazed, and a door aft gave on the stern-walk, with its carvings and gilded rail, where the captain might take his pleasure undisturbed. But the cabin itself was furnished with Spartan bareness: a long settee under the ports, a heavy fixed table, and a few chairs. A lamp swung in gimbals overhead; there were a telescope in a bracket, a short shelf of books, and a stand of muskets and cutlasses in a rack about the mizzenmast. The table was laid for three.

"A glass of sherry with you, Mr. Bligh," said the captain, as a man handed the glasses on a tray. He smiled at me in his courtly way, and raised his glass. "To the memory of your father, young man! We seamen owe him a lasting debt."

As we drank, I heard a great stir and shuffling of feet on deck, and the distant sound of a drum. Captain Courtney glanced at his watch, finished his wine, and rose from the settee.

"My apologies. They're flogging a man through the fleet, and I hear the boats coming. I must read the sentence at the gangway — a deuced bore. Make yourselves at home; should you wish to be spectators, I can recommend the poop."

Next moment he passed the rigid marine at the bulkhead and was gone. Bligh listened for a moment to the distant drumming, set down his glass, and beckoned me to follow him. From the quarter-deck a short ladder led up to the poop, a high point of vantage from which all that went on was visible. Though the air was crisp, the wind was the merest cat's-paw and the sun shone in a blue and cloudless sky.

The order to turn all hands aft to witness punishment was being piped by the boatswain and shouted by his mates. The marines, with muskets and side-arms, were hastening aft to fall in before us on the poop. Captain Courtney and his lieutenants stood on the weather quarter-deck, and the junior officers were gathered to leeward of them. The doctor and purser stood further to leeward, under the break of the poop, behind the boatswain and his mates. The ship's company was gathered along the lee bulwarks — some, to see better, standing in the boats or on the booms. A tall ninety-eight and a third-rate like the *Tigress* lay at anchor close by, and I saw that their ports and bulwarks were crowded with silent men.

The half-minute bell began to sound, and the noise of drumming grew louder — the doleful tattoo of the rogue's march. Then, around the bows of the *Tigress*, came a procession I shall never forget.

In the lead, rowed slowly in time to the nervous beat of the drum, came the longboat of a near-by ship. Her surgeon and master-at-arms stood beside the drummer; just aft of them a human figure was huddled in a posture I could not make out at first. Behind the longboat, and rowing in time to the same doleful music, came a boat from every ship of the fleet, manned with marines to attend the punishment. I heard an order "Way enough!" and as the rowing ceased the longboat drifted to a halt by the gangway. I glanced down over the rail. My breath seemed to catch in my throat, and without knowing that I spoke, I exclaimed softly, "Oh, my God!" Mr. Bligh gave me a sidelong glance and one of his slight, grim smiles.

The huddled figure in the bows of the boat was that of a powerful man of thirty or thirty-five. He was stripped to his wide sailor's trousers of duck, and his bare arms were bronzed and tattooed. Stockings had been bound around his wrists, which were stoutly lashed to a capstan bar. His thick yellow hair was in disorder and I could not see his face, for his head hung down over his chest. His trousers, the thwart on which he lay huddled, and the frames and planking of the boat on either side of him were blotched and spattered with black blood. Blood I had seen before; it was the man's back that made me catch my breath. From neck to waist the cat-o'-nine-tails had laid the bones bare, and the flesh hung in blackened, tattered strips.

Captain Courtney sauntered placidly across the deck to glance down at the hideous spectacle below. The surgeon in the boat bent over the mutilated, seized-up body, straightened his back, and looked at Courtney by the gangway.

"The man is dead, sir," he said solemnly. A murmur faint as a stir of air in the treetops came from the men crowded on the booms. The Captain of the *Tigress* folded his arms and turned his head slightly with raised eyebrows. He made a gallant figure, with his sword, his rich laced uniform, his cocked hat and powdered queue. In the tense silence which followed he turned to the surgeon again.

"Dead," he said lightly, in his cultivated drawl. "Lucky devil! Master-at-arms!" The warrant officer at the doctor's side sprang to attention and pulled off his hat. "How many are due?"

"Two dozen, sir."

Courtney strolled back to his place on the weather side and took from his first lieutenant's hand a copy of the Articles of War. As he swept off his cocked hat gracefully and held it over his heart, every man on the ship uncovered in respect to the King's commandments. Then, in his clear, drawling voice, the captain read the Article which prescribes the punishment for striking an officer of His Majesty's Navy. One of the boatswain's mates was untying a red baize bag, from which he drew out the red-handled cat, eyeing it uncertainly, with frequent glances to windward. The captain concluded his reading, replaced his hat, and caught the man's eye. Again I heard the faint sighing murmur forward, and again deep silence fell before Courtney's glance. "Do your duty," he ordered calmly; "two dozen, I believe."

"Two dozen it is, sir," said the boatswain's mate in a hollow voice as he walked slowly to the side. There were clenched jaws and gleaming eyes among the men forward, but the silence was so profound that I could hear the faint creak of blocks aloft as the braces swayed in the light air.

I could not turn my eyes away from the boatswain's mate, climbing slowly down the ship's side. If the man had shouted aloud, he could not have expressed more clearly the reluctance he felt.   He stepped into the boat, and as he moved among the men on the thwarts they drew back with set stern faces.   At the capstan bar, he hesitated and looked up uncertainly. Courtney had sauntered to the bulwarks and was gazing down with folded arms.

"Come! Do your duty!" he ordered, with the air of a man whose dinner is growing cold.

The man with the cat drew its tails through the fingers of his left hand, raised his arm, and sent them whistling down on the poor battered corpse.   I turned away, giddy and sick. Bligh stood by the rail, a hand on his hip, watching the scene below as a man might watch a play indifferently performed. The measured blows continued — each breaking the silence like a pistol shot.   I counted them mechanically for what seemed an age, but the end came at last — twenty-two, a pause, twenty-three . . . twenty-four.   I heard a word of command; the marines fell out and trooped down the poop ladder.   Eight bells struck.   There were a stir and bustle on the ship, and I heard the boatswain piping the long-drawn, cheery call to dinner.

When we sat down to dine, Courtney seemed to have dismissed the incident from his mind.   He tossed off a glass of sherry to Bligh's health, and tasted his soup.   "Cold!" he remarked ruefully.   "Hardships of a seaman's life, eh, Bligh?"

His guest took soup with a relish, and sounds better fitted to the forecastle than aft, for his manners at table were coarse.   "Damme!" he said.   "We fared worse aboard the old *Poule!*"

"But not in Tahiti, I'll wager.   I hear you are to pay the Indian ladies of the South Sea another call."

"Aye, and a long one.   We shall be some months in getting our load of breadfruit trees."

"I heard of your voyage in Town.   Cheap food for the West Indian slaves, eh?   I wish I were sailing with you."

"By God, I wish you were! I could promise you some sport."

"Are the Indian women as handsome as Cook painted them?"

"Indeed they are, if you've no prejudice against a brown skin. They are wonderfully clean in person, and have enough sensibility to attract a fastidious man. Witness Sir Joseph; he declares that there are no such women in the world!"

Our host sighed romantically. "Say no more! Say no more! I can see you, like a Bashaw under the palms, in the midst of a harem the Sultan himself might envy!"

Still sickened by what I had seen, I was doing my best to make a pretense of eating, silent while the older men talked. Bligh was the first to mention the flogging.

"What had the man done?" he asked.

Captain Courtney set down his glass of claret and glanced up absently. "Oh, the fellow who was flogged," he said. "He was one of Captain Allison's foretopmen, on the *Unconquerable*. And a smart hand, they say. He was posted for desertion, and then Allison, who remembered his face, saw him stepping out of a public house in Portsmouth. The man tried to spring away and Allison seized him by the arm. Damme! Good topmen don't grow on every hedge! Well, this insolent fellow blacked Allison's eye, just as a file of marines passed. They made him prisoner, and you saw the rest. Odd! We were only the fifth ship; eight dozen did for him. But Allison has a boatswain's mate who's an artist, they say — left-handed, so he lays them on crisscross, and strong as an ox."

Bligh listened with interest to Courtney's words, and nodded approvingly. "Struck his captain, eh?" he remarked. "By God! He deserved all he got, and more! No laws are more just than those governing the conduct of men at sea."

"Is there any need of such cruelty?" I asked, unable to keep silent. "Why did they not hang the poor fellow and have done with it?"

"Poor fellow?" Captain Courtney turned to me with eyebrows raised. "You have much to learn, my lad. A year or two at sea will harden him, eh, Bligh?"

"I'll see to that," said the Captain of the *Bounty*. "No, Mr. Byam, you must waste no sympathy on rascals of that stripe."

"And remember," put in Courtney, with a manner of friendly admonishment, "remember, as Mr. Bligh says, that no laws are more just than those governing the conduct of men at sea. Not only just, but necessary; discipline must be preserved, on a merchantman as well as on a man-of-war, and mutiny and piracy suppressed."

"Yes," said Bligh, "our sea law is stern, but it has the authority of centuries. And it has grown more humane with time," he continued, not without a trace of regret. "Keel-hauling has been abolished, save among the French, and a captain no longer has the right to condemn and put to death one of his crew."

Still agitated by the shock of what I had seen, I ate little and took more wine than was my custom, sitting in silence for the most part, while the two officers gossiped, sailor-like, as to the whereabouts of former friends, and spoke of Admiral Parker, and the fight at Dogger Bank. It was mid-afternoon when Bligh and I were pulled back to the *Bounty*. The tide was low, and I saw a boat aground on a flat some distance off, while a party of men dug a shallow grave in the mud. They were burying the body of the poor fellow who had been flogged through the fleet — burying him below tide mark, in silence, and without religious rites.

OFFICERS AND CREW OF H.M.S. BOUNTY

Lieutenant William Bligh, *Captain*
John Fryer, *Master*
Fletcher Christian, *Master's Mate*
Charles Churchill, *Master-at-Arms*
William Elphinstone, *Master-at-Arm's Mate*
Thomas Huggan, *Surgeon*

Thomas Ledward, *Acting Surgeon*
David Nelson, *Botanist*
William Peckover, *Gunner*
John Mills, *Gunner's Mate*
William Cole, *Boatswain*
James Morrison, *Boatswain's Mate*
William Purcell, *Carpenter*
Charles Norman, *Carpenter's Mate*
Thomas McIntosh, *Carpenter's Crew*
Joseph Coleman, *Armourer*

Roger Byam
Thomas Hayward
John Hallet
Robert Tinkler   } *Midshipmen*
Edward Young
George Stewart

John Norton
Peter Lenkletter } *Quartermasters*

George Simpson, *Quartermaster's Mate*
Lawrence Lebogue, *Sailmaker*
Mr. Samuel, *Clerk*
Robert Lamb, *Butcher*
William Brown, *Gardener*

John Smith
Thomas Hall } *Cooks*

Thomas Burkitt
Matthew Quintal
John Sumner
John Millward
William McCoy
Henry Hillbrandt
Alexander Smith
John Williams   } *Able Seamen*
Thomas Ellison
Isaac Martin
Richard Skinner
Matthew Thompson
William Muspratt
Michael Byrne

III

AT SEA

AT daybreak on the twenty-eighth of November we got sail on the *Bounty* and worked down to St. Helen's, where we dropped anchor. For nearly a month we were detained there and at Spithead by contrary winds; it was not until the twenty-third of December that we set sail down the Channel with a fair wind.

A month sounds an age to be crowded with more than forty other men on board a small vessel at anchor most of the time, but I was making the acquaintance of my shipmates, and so keen on learning my new duties that the days were all too short. The *Bounty* carried six midshipmen, and, since we had no schoolmaster, as is customary on a man-of-war, Lieutenant Bligh and the master divided the duty of instructing us in trigonometry, nautical astronomy, and navigation. I shared with Stewart and Young the advantage of learning navigation under Bligh, and in justice to an officer whose character in other respects was by no means perfect, I must say that there was no finer seaman and navigator afloat at the time. Both of my fellow midshipmen were men grown: George Stewart of a good family in the Orkneys, a young man of twenty-three or four, and a seaman who had made several voyages before this: and Edward Young, a stout, salty-looking fellow, with a handsome face marred by the loss of nearly all his front teeth. Both of them were already very fair navigators, and I was hard put to it not to earn the reputation of a dunce.

The boatswain, Mr. Cole, and his mate, James Morrison, in-

structed me in seamanship.   Cole was an old-style Navy salt,
bronzed, taciturn, and pigtailed, with a profound knowledge of
his work and little other knowledge of any kind.   Morrison
was very different — a man of good birth, he had been a midshipman, and had shipped aboard the *Bounty* because of his
interest in the voyage.   He was a first-rate seaman and navigator; a dark, slender, intelligent man of thirty or thereabouts,
cool in the face of danger, not given to oaths, and far above
his station on board.   Morrison did not thrash the men to
their work, delivering blows impartially in the manner of a
boatswain's mate; he carried a colt, a piece of knotted rope,
to be sure, but it was only used on obvious malingerers, or
when Bligh shouted to him: "Start that man!"

There were much irritation and grumbling at the continued bad weather, but at last, on the evening of the twenty-
second of December, the sky cleared and the wind shifted to
the eastward.   It was still dark next morning when I heard
the boatswain's pipe and Morrison's call: "All hands!   Turn
out and save a clue!   Out or down here!   Rise and shine!
Out or down there!   Lash and carry!"

The stars were bright when I came on deck, and the grey
glimmer of dawn was in the East.   For three weeks we had
had strong southwesterly winds, with rain and fog; now the
air was sharp with frost, and a strong east wind blew in gusts
off the coast of France.   Lieutenant Bligh was on the quarter-
deck with Mr. Fryer, the master; Christian and Elphinstone,
the master's mates, were forward among the men.   There was
a great bustle on deck and the ship rang with the piping of
the bos'n's whistle.   I heard the shouting of the men at the
windlass, and Christian's voice above the din: "Hove short,
sir!"

"Loose the topsails!" came from Fryer, and Christian passed
the order on.   My station was the mizzen-top, and in a
twinkling we had the gaskets off and the small sail sheeted
home.   The knots in the gaskets were stiff with frost, and the

men setting the fore-topsail were slow at their work.   Bligh
glanced aloft impatiently.

"What are you doing there?" he shouted angrily.   "Are
you all asleep, foretop?   The main-topmen are off the yard!
Look alive, you crawling caterpillars!"

The topsails filled and the yards were braced up sharp; the
Bounty broke out her own anchor as she gathered way on the
larboard tack.   She was smartly manned in spite of Bligh's
complaints, but he was on edge, for a thousand critical eyes
watched our departure from the ships at anchor closer inshore.
With a "Yo! Heave ho!" the anchor came up and was catted.

Then it was: "Loose the forecourse!" and presently, as she
began to heel to the gusts: "Get the mainsail on her!"   There
was a thunder of canvas and a wild rattling of blocks.   When
the brace was hove short, Bligh himself roared: "Board the
main tack!"   Little by little, with a mighty chorus at the
windlass: "Heave ho! Heave and pawl! Yo, heave, hearty,
ho!" the weather clew of the sail came down to the waterway.
Heeling well to starboard, the bluff-bowed little ship tore
through the sheltered water, on her way to the open sea.

The sun rose in a cloudless sky — a glorious winter's morning, clear, cold, and sparkling.   I stood by the bulwarks as
we flew down the Solent, my breath trailing off like thin
smoke.   Presently we sped through the Needles and the *Bounty*
headed away to sea, going like a race horse, with topgallants set.

That night the wind increased to a strong gale, with a heavy
sea, but on the following day the weather moderated, permitting us to keep our Christmas cheerfully.   Extra grog was
served out, and the mess cooks were to be heard whistling as
they seeded the raisins for duff, not, as a landsman might suppose, from the prospect of good cheer, but in order to prove
to their messmates that the raisins were not going into their
mouths.

I was still making the acquaintance of my shipmates at

this time. The men of the *Bounty* had been attracted by the prospect of a voyage to the South Sea, or selected for their stations by the master or Bligh himself. Our fourteen able-bodied seamen were true salts, not the scum of the taverns and jails impressed to man so many of His Majesty's ships; the officers were nearly all men of experience and tried character, and even our botanist, Mr. Nelson, had been recommended by Sir Joseph Banks because of his former voyage to Tahiti under Captain Cook. Mr. Bligh might have had a hundred midshipmen had he obliged all those who applied for a place in the *Bounty's* berth; as it was, there were six of us, though the ship's establishment provided for only two. Stewart and Young were seamen and pleasant fellows enough; Hallet was a sickly-looking boy of fifteen with a shifty eye and a weak, peevish mouth; Tinkler, Mr. Fryer's brother-in-law, was a year younger, though he had been to sea before — a monkey of a lad, whose continual scrapes kept him at the masthead half the time. Hayward, the handsome, sulky boy I had met when I first set foot in the berth, was only sixteen, but big and strong for his age. He was something of a bully and aspired to be cock of the berth, since he had been two years at sea aboard a seventy-four.

I shared with Hayward, Stewart, and Young a berth on the lower deck. In this small space the four of us swung our hammocks at night and had our mess, using a chest for a table and other chests for seats. On consideration of a liberal share of our grog, received each Saturday night, Alexander Smith, able-bodied, acted as our hammock man, and for a lesser sum of the same ship's currency, Thomas Ellison, the youngest of the seamen, filled the office of mess boy. Mr. Christian was caterer to the midshipmen's mess; like the others, I had paid him five pounds on joining the ship, and he had laid out the money in a supply of potatoes, onions, Dutch cheeses (for making that midshipman's dish called "crab"), tea, coffee, and sugar, and other small luxuries. These private stores enabled us to live well for several weeks, though a more villainous cook than young Tom Ellison would be impossible to find. As for drink, the ship's allowance was so liberal that Christian made no special provision for us. For a month or more every man aboard received a gallon of beer each day, and when that was gone, a pint of fiery white *mistela* wine from Spain — the wine our seamen love and call affectionately "Miss Taylor." And when the last of the wine was gone we fell back on an ample supply of the sailor's sheet anchor — grog. We had a wondrous fifer on board — a half-blind Irishman named Michael Byrne. He had managed to conceal his blindness till the *Bounty* was at sea, when it became apparent, much to Mr. Bligh's annoyance. But when he struck up "Nancy Dawson" on the first day he piped the men to grog, his blindness was forgotten. He could put more trills and runs into that lively old tune than any man of us had heard before — a cheeriness in keeping with this happiest hour of the seaman's day.

We lost a good part of our beer in a strong easterly gale that overtook the *Bounty* the day after Christmas. Several casks went adrift from their lashings and were washed overboard when a great sea broke over the ship; the same wave stove in all three of our boats and nearly carried them away. I was off watch at the time, and below, diverting myself in the surgeon's cabin on the orlop, aft. It was a close, stinking little den, below the water line — reeking of the bilges and lit by a candle that burned blue for lack of air. But that mattered nothing to Old Bacchus. Our sawbones's name was Thomas Huggan and it was so inscribed on the ship's articles, but he was known as Old Bacchus to all our company. His normal state was what sailors call "in the wind" or "shaking a cloth," and the signal that he had passed his normal state earned him the name by which all hands on the *Bounty* knew him. When he had indiscreetly added a glass of brandy or a tot of grog to the carefully measured supply of spirits demanded at close intervals by a stomach which must have been copper-sheathed, it

was his custom to rise, balancing himself on his starboard leg,
place a hand between the third and fourth buttons of his waistcoat, and recite with comic gravity a verse which begins: —

Bacchus must now his power resign.

With his wooden leg, his fiery face, snow-white hair, and
rakish blue eyes, Old Bacchus seemed the veritable archetype
of naval surgeons.   He had been afloat so long that he could
scarcely recollect the days when he had lived ashore, and viewed
with apprehension the prospect of retirement.   He preferred
salt beef to the finest steak or chop to be obtained ashore, and
confided to me one day that it was almost impossible for him
to sleep in a bed.   A cannon ball had carried away his larboard leg when his ship was exchanging broadsides, yardarm
to yardarm, with the *Ranger,* and he had been made prisoner
by John Paul Jones.

The cronies of Old Bacchus were Mr. Nelson, the botanist,
and Peckover, the *Bounty's* gunner.   The duties of a gunner,
onerous enough on board a man-of-war, were of the very
lightest on our ship, and Peckover — a jovial fellow who loved
a song and a glass dearly — had some leisure for conviviality.
Mr. Nelson was a quiet, elderly man with iron-grey hair.
Though devoted to the study of plants, he seemed to derive
great pleasure from the surgeon's company, and could spin
a yarn with the best when in the mood.   The great event in
his life had been his voyage to the South Sea with Captain
Cook, whose memory he revered.

Mr. Nelson's cabin was forward of the surgeon's, separated
from it by the cabin of Samuel, the captain's clerk, and he was
to be found more often in the surgeon's cabin than in his
own.   All of the cabins were provided with standing bed
places, built in by the carpenters at Deptford, but Bacchus
preferred to sling a hammock at night, and used his bed as a
settee and the capacious locker under it as a private spirit

room. The cabin was scarcely more than six feet by seven; the bed occupied nearly half of this space, and opposite, under the hammock battens, were three small casks of wine, as yet unbroached. On one of them a candle guttered and burned blue.

Another cask served as a seat for me, and Bacchus and Nelson sat side by side on the bed. Each man held a pewter pint of flip — beer strongly laced with rum. The ship was on the larboard tack and making heavy weather of it, so that at times my cask threatened to slide from under me, but the two men on the settee seemed to give the weather no thought.

"A first-rate man, Purcell!" remarked the surgeon, glancing down admiringly at his new wooden leg; "a better ship's carpenter never swung an adze! My other leg was most damnably uncomfortable, but this one's like my own flesh and bone! Mr. Purcell's health!" He took a long pull at the flip and smacked his lips. "You're a lucky man, Nelson! Should anything happen to your underpinning, you've me to saw off the old leg and Purcell to make you a better one!"

Nelson smiled. "Very kind, I'm sure," he said; "but I hope I shall not have to trouble you."

"I hope not, my dear fellow — I hope not! But never dread an amputation. With a pint of rum, a well-stropped razor, and a crosscut saw, I'd have your leg off before you knew it. Paul Jones's American surgeon did the trick for me.

"Let's see — it must have been in seventy-eight. I was on the old *Drake*, Captain Burden, and we were on the lookout for Paul Jones's *Ranger* at the time. Then we learned that she was hove-to off the mouth of Belfast Lough. An extraordinary affair, begad! We actually had sight-seers on board — one of them was an officer of the Inniskilling Fusileers in full uniform. We moved out slowly and came up astern of the American ship. Up went our colours and we hailed: 'What ship is that?' 'American Continental ship *Ranger!*' roared the Yankee master, as his own colours went up. 'Come on —

we're waiting for you!' Next moment both ships let go their broadsides. . . . Good God!"

The *Bounty* staggered with the shock of a great sea which broke into her at that moment. "Up with you, Byam!" ordered the surgeon; and, as I sprang out of his cabin toward the ladderway, I heard, above the creaking and straining of the ship and the roar of angry water, a faint shouting for all hands on deck. Then I found myself in an uproar and confusion very strange after the peace of the surgeon's snuggery.

Bligh stood by the mizzenmast, beside Fryer, who was bawling orders to his mates. They were shortening sail to get the ship hove-to. The men at the clew lines struggled with might and main to hoist the stubborn thundering canvas to the yards.

My own task, with two other midshipmen, was to furl the mizzen topsail — a small sail, but far from easy to subdue at such a time. The men below brailed up the driver and made fast the vangs of its gaff. Presently the *Bounty* was hove-to, all snug on the larboard tack, under reefed fore and main topsails.

The great wave which had boarded us left destruction in its wake. All three of our boats were stove in; the casks of beer which had been lashed on deck were nowhere to be seen; and the stern of the ship so damaged that the cabin was filled with water, which leaked into the bread room below, spoiling a large part of our stock of bread.

In latitude 39°N. the gale abated, the sun shone out, and we made all sail for Teneriffe with a fine northerly wind. On the fourth of January we spoke a French merchant vessel, bound for Mauritius, which let go her topgallant sheets in salute. The next morning we saw the island of Teneriffe to the southwest of us, about twelve leagues distant, but it fell calm near the land and we were a day and a night working up to the road of Santa Cruz, where we anchored in twenty-five fathoms, close to a Spanish packet and an American brig.

For five days we lay at anchor in the road, and it was here that the seeds of discontent, destined to be the ruin of the voyage, were sown among the *Bounty's* people. As there was a great surf on the beach, Lieutenant Bligh bargained with the shore boats to bring off our water and supplies, and kept his own men busy from morning to night repairing the mischief the storm had done our ship. This occasioned much grumbling in the forecastle, as some of the sailors had hoped to be employed in the ship's boats, which would have enabled them at least to set foot on the island and to obtain some of the wine for which it is famous, said to be little inferior to the best London Madeira.

During our sojourn the allowance of salt beef was stopped, and fresh beef, obtained on shore, issued instead. The *Bounty's* salt beef was the worst I have ever met with at sea, but the beef substituted for it in Teneriffe was worse still. The men declared that it had been cut from the carcasses of dead horses or mules, and complained to the master that it was unfit for food. Fryer informed Bligh of the complaint; the captain flew into a passion and swore that the men should eat the fresh beef or nothing at all. The result was that most of it was thrown overboard — a sight which did nothing to soothe Bligh's temper.

I was fortunate enough to have a run ashore, for Bligh took me with him one day to wait upon the governor, the Marquis de Brancheforté. With the governor's permission Mr. Nelson ranged the hills every day in search of plants and natural curiosities, but his friend the surgeon only appeared on deck once during the five days we lay at anchor. Old Bacchus had ordered a monstrous supply of brandy for himself — enough to do the very god of wine, his namesake, for a year. Not trusting the shore boats with such precious freight, he had obtained the captain's permission to send the small cutter to the pier, and when a man went below to inform him that his

brandy was alongside, the surgeon came stumping to the ladderway and clambered on deck.   The cutter was down to the gunwales with her load; as there was a high swell running, Old
Bacchus stood by the bulwarks anxiously.   "Easy with it!"
he ordered with tender solicitude.   "Easy now!   A glass of
grog all around if you break nothing!"   When the last of the
small casks was aboard and had been sent below, the surgeon
heaved a sigh.   I was standing near by and saw him glance
at the land for the first time.   He caught my eye.   "One
island 's as like another as two peas in a pod," he remarked
indifferently, pulling out a handkerchief to mop his fiery
face.

When we sailed from Teneriffe, Bligh divided the people
into three watches, making Christian acting lieutenant, and
giving him charge of the third watch.   Bligh had known him
for some years in the West India trade, and believed himself
to be Christian's friend and benefactor.   His friendship took
the form of inviting Christian to sup or dine one day, and
cursing him in the coarsest manner before the men the next;
but in this case he did him a real service, since it was ten to one
that, if all went well on the voyage, the appointment would
be confirmed by the Admiralty, and Christian would find himself the holder of His Majesty's commission.   He now rated as
a gentleman, with the midshipmen and Bligh; and Fryer was
provided with a grievance both against the captain, and —
such is human nature — against his former subordinate.

Nor were grievances wanting during our passage from
Teneriffe to Cape Horn.   The people's food on British ships
is always bad and always scanty — a fact which in later days
caused so many of our seamen to desert to American vessels.
But on the *Bounty* the food was of poorer quality, and issued
in scantier quantities, than any man of us had seen before.
When Bligh called the ship's company aft to read the order
appointing Christian acting lieutenant, he also informed them
that, as the length of the voyage was uncertain, and the season

so far advanced that it was doubtful whether we should be
able to make our way around Cape Horn, it seemed necessary
to reduce the allowance of bread to two thirds of the usual
amount.   Realizing the need for economy, the men received
this cheerfully, but continued to grumble about the salt beef
and pork.

We carried no purser.   Bligh filled the office himself, assisted
by Samuel, his clerk — a smug, tight-lipped little man, of a
Jewish cast of countenance, who was believed, not without
reason, to be the captain's "narker" or spy among the men.   He
was heartily disliked by all hands, and it was observed that
the man who showed his dislike for Mr. Samuel too openly
was apt to find himself in trouble with Lieutenant Bligh.   It
was Samuel's task to issue the provisions to the cooks of the
messes; each time a cask of salt meat was broached, the choicest
pieces were reserved for the cabin, and the remainder, scarcely
fit for human food, issued out to the messes without being
weighed.   Samuel would call out "Four pounds," and mark
the amount down in his book, when anyone could perceive
that the meat would not have weighed three.

Seamen regard meanness in their own kind with the utmost
contempt, and that great rarity in the Service, a mean officer,
is looked upon with loathing by his men.   They can put up
with a harsh captain, but nothing will drive British seamen to
mutiny faster than a captain suspected of lining his pockets
at their expense.

While the *Bounty* was still in the northeast trades, an incident occurred which gave us reason to suspect Bligh of meanness of this kind.   The weather was fine, and one morning
the main hatch was raised and our stock of cheeses brought up
on deck to air.   Bligh missed no detail of the management of
his ship; he displayed in such matters a smallness of mind
scarcely in accord with his commission.   This unwillingness
to trust those under him to perform their duties is apt to be
the defect of the officer risen from the ranks, — or "come in

through the hawse-hole," as seamen say, — and is the principal reason why such officers are rarely popular with their men.

Bligh stood by Hillbrandt, the cooper, while he started the hoops on our casks of cheese and knocked out the heads. Two cheeses, of about fifty pounds weight, were found to be missing from one of the casks, and Bligh flew into one of his passions of rage.

"Stolen, by God!" he shouted.

"Perhaps you will recollect, sir," Hillbrandt made bold to say, "that while we were in Deptford the cask was opened by your order and the cheeses carried ashore."

"You insolent scoundrel! Hold your tongue!"

Christian and Fryer happened to be on deck at the time, and Bligh included them in the black scowl he gave the men near by. "A damned set of thieves," he went on. "You're all in collusion against me — officers and men. But I'll tame you — by God, I will!" He turned to the cooper. "Another word from you and I'll have you seized up and flogged to the bone." He turned aft on his heel and bawled down the ladderway. "Mr. Samuel! Come on deck this instant."

Samuel came trotting up to his master obsequiously, and Bligh went on: "Two of the cheeses have been stolen. See that the allowance is stopped — from the officers too, mind you — until the deficiency is made good."

I could see that Fryer was deeply offended, though he said nothing at the time; as for Christian, — a man of honour, — his feelings were not difficult to imagine. The men had a pretty clear idea of which way the wind blew by this time, and on the next banyan day, when butter alone was served out, they refused it, saying that to accept butter without cheese would be a tacit acknowledgment of the theft. John Williams, one of the seamen, declared publicly in the forecastle that he had carried the two cheeses to Mr. Bligh's house, with a cask of vinegar and some other things which were sent up in a boat from Long Reach.

As the private stocks of provisions obtained in Spithead now began to run out, all hands went "from grub galore to the King's own," as seamen say. Our bread, which was only beginning to breed maggots, was fairly good, though it needed teeth better than mine to eat the central "reefer's nut"; but our salt meat was unspeakably bad. Meeting Alexander Smith one morning when he was cook to his mess, I was shown a piece of it fresh from the cask — a dark, stony, unwholesome-looking lump, glistening with salt.

"Have a look, Mr. Byam," he said. "What'll it be, I wonder? Not beef or pork, that's certain! I mind one day on the old *Antelope* — two years ago, that was — the cooper found three horseshoes in the bottom of a cask!" He shook his pigtail back over his shoulder and shifted a great quid of tobacco to his starboard cheek. "You've seen the victualing yards in Portsmouth, sir? Pass that way any night, and you'll hear the dogs bark and the horses neigh! And I'll tell you something else you young gentlemen don't know." He glanced up and down the deck cautiously and then whispered: "It's as much as a black man's life is worth to pass that way by night! They'd pop him into a cask like that!" He snapped his fingers impressively.

Smith was a great admirer of Old Bacchus, whom he had known on other ships, and a few days later he handed me a little wooden box. "For the surgeon, sir," he said. "Will you give it to him?"

It was a snuffbox, curiously wrought of some dark, reddish wood, like mahogany, and very neatly fitted with a lid; a handsome bit of work, carved and polished with a seaman's skill. I found leisure to visit the surgeon the same evening.

Christian's watch was on duty at the time. Young Tinkler and I were in Mr. Fryer's watch, and the third watch had been placed in charge of Mr. Peckover, a short, powerful man of forty or forty-five, who could scarcely remember a time when he had not been at sea. His good-humoured face had been blackened by the West Indian sun, and his arms were covered with tattooing.

I found Peckover with the doctor and Nelson — squeezed together on the settee.

"Come in," cried the surgeon. "Wait a bit, my lad — I think I can make a place for you."

He sprang up with surprising agility and pushed a small cask into the doorway. Peckover held the spigot open while the wine poured frothing into a pewter pint. I delivered the snuffbox before I sat down on my cask, pint in hand.

"From Smith, you say?" asked the surgeon. "Very handsome of him! Very handsome indeed! I remember Smith well on the old *Antelope* — eh, Peckover? I have a recollection that I used to treat him to a drop of grog now and then. And why not, I say! A thirsty man goes straight to my heart." He glanced complacently about his cabin, packed to the hammock battens with small casks of spirits and wine. "Thank God that neither I nor my friends shall go thirsty on this voyage!"

Nelson stretched out his hand for the snuffbox and examined it with interest. "I shall always marvel," he remarked, "at the ingenuity of our seamen. This would be a credit to any craftsman ashore, with all the tools of his trade. And a fine bit of wood, handsomely polished, too! Mahogany, no doubt, though the grain seems different."

Bacchus looked at Peckover quizzically, and the gunner returned the look, grinning.

"Wood?" said the surgeon. "Well, I have heard it called that, and worse. Wood that once bellowed — aye, and neighed and barked, if the tales be true. In plain English, my dear Nelson, your mahogany is old junk, more politely called salt beef — His Majesty's own!"

"Good Lord!" exclaimed Nelson, examining the snuffbox in real astonishment.

"Aye, salt beef! Handsome as any mahogany and quite

as durable. Why, it had been proposed to sheathe our West
India frigates with it—a material said to defy the attacks of
the toredo worm!"

I took the little box from Nelson's hand, to inspect it with
a new interest. "Well, I 'm damned!" I thought.

Old Bacchus had rolled up his sleeve and was pouring a train
of snuff along his shaven and polished forearm. With a loud
sniffing sound it disappeared up his nose. He sneezed, blew his
nose violently on an enormous blue handkerchief, and filled
his tankard with *mistela*.

"A glass of wine with you gentlemen!" he remarked, and
poured the entire pint down his throat without taking breath.
Mr. Peckover glanced at his friend admiringly.

"Aye, Peckover," said the surgeon, catching his eye, "nothing
like a nip of salt beef to give a man a thirst. Let the cook
keep his slush. Give me a bit of the lean, well soaked and
boiled, and you can have all the steaks and cutlets ashore.
Begad! Just suppose, now, that we were all wrecked on a
desert island, without a scrap to eat. I 'd pull out my snuffbox
and have one meal, at any rate, while the rest of you went
hungry!"

"So you would, surgeon, so you would," said the gunner
in his rumbling voice, grinning from ear to ear.

IV

TYRANNY

ONE sultry afternoon, before we picked up the southeast trades, Bligh sent his servant to bid me sup with him. Since the great cabin was taken up with our breadfruit garden, the captain messed on the lower deck, in an apartment on the larboard side, extending from the hatch to the bulkhead abaft the mainmast. I dressed myself with some care, and, going aft, found that Christian was my fellow guest. The surgeon and Fryer messed regularly with Bligh, but Old Bacchus had excused himself this evening.

There was a fine show of plate on the captain's table, but when the dishes were uncovered I saw that Bligh fared little better than his men. We had salt beef, in plenty for once, and the pick of the cask, bad butter, and worse cheese, from which the long red worms had been hand-picked, a supply of salted cabbage, believed to prevent scurvy, and a dish heaped with the mashed pease seamen call "dog's body."

Mr. Bligh, though temperate in the use of wine, attacked his food with more relish than most officers would care to display. Fryer was a rough, honest old seaman, but his manners at table put the captain's to shame; yet Christian, who had been a mere master's mate only a few days before, supped fastidiously despite the coarseness of the food. Christian was on the captain's right, Fryer on his left, and I sat opposite, facing him. The talk had turned to the members of the *Bounty's* company.

"Damn them!" said Bligh, his mouth full of beef and pease,

which he continued to chew rapidly as he spoke. "A lazy, incompetent lot of scoundrels! God knows a captain has trials enough without being cursed with such a crew! The dregs of the public houses. . . ." He swallowed violently and filled his mouth once more. "That fellow I had flogged yesterday; what was his name, Mr. Fryer?"

"Burkitt," replied the master, a little red in the face.

"Yes, Burkitt, the insolent hound! And they're all as bad. I'm damned if they know a sheet from a tack!"

"I venture to differ with you, sir," said the master. "I should call Smith, Quintal, and McCoy first-class seamen, and even Burkitt, though he was in the wrong . . ."

"The insolent hound!" repeated Bligh violently, interrupting the master. "At the slightest report of misconduct, I shall have him seized up again. Next time it will be four dozen, instead of two!"

Christian caught my eye as the captain spoke. "If I may express an opinion, Mr. Bligh," he said quietly, "Burkitt's nature is one to tame with kindness rather than with blows."

Bligh's short, harsh laugh rang out grimly. "La-di-da, Mr. Christian! On my word, you should apply for a place as master in a young ladies' seminary! Kindness, indeed! Well, I'm damned!" He took up a glass of the reeking ship's water, rinsing his mouth preparatory to an attack on the sourcrout. "A fine captain you'll make if you don't heave overboard such ridiculous notions. Kindness! Our seamen understand kindness as well as they understand Greek! Fear is what they *do* understand! Without that, mutiny and piracy would be rife on the high seas!"

"Aye," admitted Fryer, as if regretfully. "There is some truth in that."

Christian shook his head. "I cannot agree," he said courteously. "Our seamen do not differ from other Englishmen. Some must be ruled by fear, it is true, but there are others, and finer men, who will follow a kind, just, and fearless officer to the death."

"Have we any such paragons on board?" asked the captain sneeringly.

"In my opinion, sir," said Christian, speaking in his light and courteous manner, "we have, and not a few."

"Now, by God! Name one!"

"Mr. Purcell, the carpenter. He . . ."

This time Bligh laughed long and loud. "Damme!" he exclaimed, "you're a fine judge of men! That stubborn, thick-headed old rogue! Kindness. . . . Ah, that's too good!"

Christian flushed, controlling his hot temper with an effort. "You won't have the carpenter, I see," he said lightly: "then may I suggest Morrison, sir?"

"Suggest to your heart's content," answered Bligh scornfully. "Morrison? The gentlemanly boatswain's mate? The sheep masquerading as a wolf? Kindness? Morrison's too damned kind now!"

"But a fine seaman, sir," put in Fryer gruffly; "he has been a midshipman, and is a gentleman born."

"I know, I know!" said Bligh in his most offensive way; "and no higher in my estimation for all that." He turned to me, with what he meant to be a courteous smile. "Saving your presence, Mr. Byam, damn all midshipmen, I say! There could be no worse schools than the berth for the making of sea officers!" He turned to Christian once more, and his manner changed to an unpleasant truculence.

"As for Morrison, let him take care! I've my eye on him, for I can see that he spares the cat. A boatswain's mate who was not a gentleman would have had half the hide off Burkitt's back. Let him take care, I say! Let him lay on when I give the word or, by God, I'll have him seized up for a lesson from the boatswain himself!"

I perceived, as the meal went on, that the captain's mess was anything but a congenial one. Fryer disliked the captain, and had not forgotten the incident of the cheeses. Bligh made no secret of his dislike for the master, whom he often upbraided before the men on deck; and he felt for Christian a contempt he was at no pains to conceal.

I was not surprised, a few days later, to learn from Old Bacchus that Christian and the master had quitted the captain's mess, leaving Bligh to dine and sup alone. We were south of the line by this time.

At Teneriffe, we had taken on board a large supply of pumpkins, which now began to show symptoms of spoiling under the equatorial sun. As most of them were too large for the use of Bligh's table, Samuel was ordered to issue them to the men in lieu of bread. The rate of exchange — one pound of pumpkin to replace two pounds of bread — was considered unfair by the men, and when Bligh was informed of this he came on deck in a passion and called all hands. Samuel was then ordered to summon the first man of every mess.

"Now," exclaimed Bligh violently, "let me see who will dare to refuse the pumpkins, or anything else I order to be served. You insolent rascals! By God! I'll make you eat grass before I've done with you!"

Everyone now took the pumpkins, not excepting the officers, though the amount was so scanty that it was usually thrown together by the men, the cooks of the different messes drawing lots for the whole. There was some murmuring, particularly among the officers, but the grievance might have ended there had not all hands begun to believe that the casks of beef and pork were short of their weight. This had been suspected for some time, as Samuel could never be prevailed on to weigh the meat when opened, and at last the shortage became so obvious that the people applied to the master, begging that he would examine into the affair and procure them redress. Bligh ordered all hands aft at once.

"So you've complained to Mr. Fryer, eh?" he said, shortly

and harshly. "You're not content! Let me tell you, by God, that you'd better make up your minds to *be* content! Everything that Mr. Samuel does is done by my orders, do you understand? My orders! Waste no more time in complaints, for you will get no redress! I am the only judge of what is right and wrong. Damn your eyes! I'm tired of you and your complaints! The first man to complain from now on will be seized up and flogged."

Perceiving that no redress was to be hoped for before the end of the voyage, the men resolved to bear their sufferings with patience, and neither murmured nor complained from that time. But the officers, though they dared make no open complaints, were less easily satisfied and murmured frequently among themselves of their continual state of hunger, which they thought was due to the fact that the captain and his clerk had profited by the victualing of the ship. Our allowance of food was so scanty that the men quarreled fiercely over the division of it in the galley, and when several men had been hurt it became necessary for the master's mate of the watch to superintend the division of the food.

About a hundred leagues off the coast of Brazil, the wind chopped around to north and northwest, and I realized that we had reached the southern limit of the southeast trades. It was here, in the region of variable westerlies, that the *Bounty* was becalmed for a day or two, and the people employed themselves in fishing, each mess risking a part of its small allowance of salt pork in hopes of catching one of the sharks that swam about the ship.

The landsman turns up his nose at the shark, but, to a sailor craving fresh meat, the flesh of a shark under ten feet in length is a veritable luxury. The larger sharks have a strong rank smell, but the flesh of the small ones, cut into slices like so many beefsteaks, parboiled first and then broiled with plenty of pepper and salt, eats very well indeed, resembling codfish in flavour.

I tasted shark for the first time one evening off the Brazilian coast. It was dead calm; the sails hung slack from the yards, only moving a little when the ship rolled to a gently northerly swell. John Mills, the gunner's mate, stood forward abreast of the windlass, with a heavy line coiled in his hand. He was an old seaman, one of Christian's watch — a man of forty or thereabouts who had served in the West Indies on the *Mediator,* Captain Cuthbert Collingwood. I disliked the man, — a tall, rawboned, dour old salt, — but I watched with interest as he prepared his bait. Two of his messmates stood by, ready to bear a hand — Brown, the assistant botanist, and Norman, the carpenter's mate. The mess had contributed the large piece of salt pork now going over the side; they shared the risk of losing the bait without results, as they would share whatever Mills was fortunate enough to catch. A shark about ten feet long had just passed under the bows. I craned my neck to watch.

Next moment a small striped fish like a mackerel flashed this way and that about the bait. "Pilot fish!" cried Norman. "Take care — here comes the shark!"

"Damn you!" growled Mills. "Don't dance about like a monkey — you'll frighten him off!"

The shark, an ugly yellowish blotch in the blue water, was rising beneath the bait, and all eyes were on him as he turned on his side, opened his jaws, and gulped down the piece of pork. "Hooked, by God!" roared Mills as he hove the line short. "Now, my hearties, on deck with him!" The line was strong and the messmates hove with a will; in an instant the shark came struggling over the bulwarks and thumped down on deck. Mills seized a hatchet and struck the fish a heavy blow on the snout; next moment six or seven men were astride of the quivering carcass, knives out and cutting away for dear life. The spectacle was laughable. Mills, to whom the head belonged by right of capture, was seated at the forward end; each of the others, pushing himself as far aft as possible, to enlarge his cut of shark, was slicing away within an inch of the next man's rump. There were cries of "Mind what you are about, there!" "Take care, else I'll have a slice off your backside!" And in about three minutes' time the poor fish had been severed into as many great slices as there had been men bestriding him.

The deck was washed, and Mills was picking up the several slices into which he had cut his share of the fish, when Mr. Samuel, the captain's clerk, came strolling forward.

"A fine catch, my good man," he remarked in his patronizing way. "I must have a slice, eh?"

In common with all of the *Bounty's* people, Mills disliked Samuel heartily. The clerk drank neither rum nor wine, and it was suspected that he hoarded his ration of spirits for sale ashore.

"So you must have a slice," growled the gunner's mate. "Well, I must have a glass of grog, and a stiff one, too, if you are to eat shark to-day."

"Come! Come! My good man," said Samuel pettishly. "You've enough fish there for a dozen."

"And you've enough grog stowed away for a thousand, by God!"

"It's for the captain's table I want it," said Samuel.

"Then catch him a shark yourself. This is mine. He gets the best of the bread and the pick of the junk cask as it is."

"You forget yourself, Mills! Come, give me a slice — that large one there — and I'll say nothing."

"Say nothing be damned! Here — take your slice!" As he spoke, Mills flung the ten or twelve pounds of raw fish straight at Samuel's face, with the full strength of a brawny, tattooed arm. He turned on his heel to go below, growling under his breath.

Mr. Samuel picked himself up from the deck, not forgetting his slice of shark, and walked slowly aft. The look in his eye boded no good fortune to the gunner's mate.

The news spread over the ship rapidly, and for the first time aboard the *Bounty* Mills found himself a popular man, though there was little hope that he would escape punishment. As Old Bacchus put it that night, "The least he can hope for is a red-checked shirt at the gangway. Samuel's a worm and a dirty worm, but discipline's discipline, begad!"

I believe that a day will come when flogging will be abolished on His Majesty's ships. It is an over-brutal punishment, which destroys a good man's self-respect and makes a bad man worse. Landsmen have little idea of the savagery of a flogging at the gangway. The lashes are laid on with the full strength of a powerful man's arm, with such force that each blow knocks the breath clean out of the delinquent's body. One blow takes off the skin and draws blood where each knot falls. Six blows make the whole back raw. Twelve cut deeply into the flesh and leave it a red mass, horrible to see. Yet six dozen are a common punishment.

As had been predicted, Mills spent the night in irons. The kind hearts of our British seamen were evident next morning when I was told that his messmates had saved their entire allowance of grog for Mills, to fortify him against the flogging they considered inevitable. At six bells Mr. Bligh came on deck, and bade Christian turn the hands aft to witness punishment. The weather had grown cooler, and the *Bounty* was slipping southward with all sail set, before a light northwest breeze. The order was piped and shouted forward; I joined the assembly of officers aft, while the people fell in on the booms and along the ship's side. All were silent.

"Rig the gratings," ordered Mr. Bligh, in his harsh voice.

The carpenter and his mates dragged aft two of the wooden gratings used to cover the hatches. They placed one flat on the deck, and the other upright, secured to the bulwarks by the lee gangway.

"The gratings are rigged, sir," reported Purcell, the carpenter.

"John Mills!" said Bligh. "Step forward!"

Flushed with the rum he had taken, and dressed in his best, Mills stepped out from among his messmates. His unusual smartness was designed to mollify the punishment, yet there was in his bearing a trace of defiance. He was a hard man, and he felt that he had been hardly used.

"Have you anything to say?" asked Bligh of the bare-headed seaman before him.

"No, sir," growled Mills sullenly.

"Strip!" ordered the captain.

Mills tore off his shirt, flung it to one of his messmates, and advanced bare-shouldered to the gratings.

"Seize him up," said Bligh.

Norton and Lenkletter, our quartermasters — old pigtailed seamen who had performed this office scores of times in the past — now advanced with lengths of spun yarn, and lashed Mills's outstretched wrists to the upright grating.

"Seized up, sir!" reported Norton.

Bligh took off his hat, as did every man on the ship, opened a copy of the Articles of War, and read in a solemn voice the article which prescribes the punishments for mutinous conduct. Morrison, the boatswain's mate, was undoing the red baize bag in which he kept the cat.

"Three dozen, Mr. Morrison," said Bligh as he finished reading. "Do your duty!"

Morrison was a kindly, reflective man. I felt for him at that moment, for I knew that he hated flogging on principle, and must feel the injustice of this punishment. Yet he would not dare, under the keen eye of the captain, to lighten the force of his blows. However unwilling, he was Bligh's instrument.

He advanced to the grating, drew the tails of the cat through his fingers, flung his arm back, and struck. Mills winced involuntarily as the cat came whistling down on his bare back, and the breath flew out of his body with a loud "Ugh!" A great red welt sprang out against the white skin, with drops of blood trickling down on one side. Mills was a burly ruffian and he endured the first dozen without crying out, though by that time his back was a red slough from neck to waist.

Bligh watched the punishment with folded arms. "I'll show the man who's captain of this ship," I heard him remark placidly to Christian. "By God, I will!" The eighteenth blow broke the iron of Mills's self-control. He was writhing on the grating, his teeth tightly clenched and the blood pouring down his back. "Oh!" he shouted thickly. "Oh, my God! Oh!"

"Mr. Morrison," called Bligh, sternly and suddenly. "See that you lay on with a will."

Morrison passed the tails of the cat through his fingers to free them of blood and bits of flesh. Under the eye of the captain he delivered the remaining lashes, taking a time that seemed interminable to me. When they cut Mills down he was black in the face and collapsed at once on the deck. Old Bacchus stumped forward and ordered him taken below to the sick bay, to be washed with brine. Bligh sauntered to the ladderway and the men resumed their duties sullenly.

Early in March we were ordered to lay aside our light tropical clothing for warm garments which had been provided for our passage around Cape Horn. The topgallant masts were sent down, new sails bent, and the ship made ready for the heavy winds and seas which lay ahead. The weather grew cooler each day, until I was glad to go below for my occasional evenings with Bacchus and his cronies, or to my mess in the berth. The surgeon messed with us now, as well as Stewart and Hayward, my fellow midshipmen, Morrison, and Mr. Nelson, the botanist. We were all the best of friends, though young Hayward never forgot that I was his junior in service, and plumed himself on a knowledge of seamanship certainly more extensive than my own.

Those were days and nights of misery for every man on board. Sometimes the wind hauled to the southwest, with squalls of snow, forcing us to come about on the larboard tack; sometimes the gale increased to the force of a hurricane and we lay hove-to under a rag of staysail, pitching into the breaking seas. Though our ship was new and sound, her seams opened under the strain and it became necessary to man the pumps every hour. The hatches were constantly battened down, and when the forward deck began to leak, Bligh gave orders that the people should sling their hammocks in the great cabin aft. At last our captain's iron determination gave way, and to the great joy and relief of every man on board he ordered the helm put up to bear away for the Cape of Good Hope.

The fine weather which followed and our rapid passage east did much to raise the spirits of the men on board. We had caught great numbers of sea birds off Cape Horn and penned them in cages provided by the carpenter. The pintado and the albatross were the best; when penned like a Strasburg goose and well stuffed with ground corn for a few days, they seemed to us as good as ducks or geese, and this fresh food did wonders for our invalids.

With the returning cheerfulness on board, the *Bounty's* midshipmen began to play the pranks of their kind the world over, and none of us escaped penance at the masthead — penance that was in general richly deserved. No one was oftener in hot water than young Tinkler, a monkey of a lad, beloved by every man on the ship. Bligh's severity to Tinkler, one cold moonlight night, when we were in the longitude of Tristan da Cunha, was a warning to all of us, and the cause of much murmuring among the men.

Hallet, Hayward, Tinkler, and I were in the larboard berth. The gunner's watch was on duty, and Stewart and Young on deck. We had supped and were passing the time at Able-whackets — a game I have never seen played ashore. It *is* commenced by playing cards, which must be named the Good Books. The table is termed the Board of Green Cloth, the hand the Flipper; the light the Glim, and so on. To call a table a table, or a card a card, brings an instant cry of "Watch," whereupon the delinquent must extend his Flipper to be severely firked with a stocking full of sand by each of the players in turn, who repeat his offense while firking him. Should the pain bring an oath to his lips, as is more than likely, there is another cry of "Watch," and he undergoes a second round of firking by all hands. As will be perceived, the game is a noisy one.

Young Tinkler had inadvertently pronounced the word "table," and Hayward, something of a bully, roared, "Watch!" When he took his turn at the firking, he laid on so hard that the youngster, beside himself with pain, squeaked, "Ouch! Damn your blood!" "Watch!" roared Hayward again, and at the same moment we heard another roar from aft — Mr. Bligh calling angrily for the ship's corporal. Tinkler and Hallet rushed for their berth on the starboard side; Hayward doused the glim in an instant, kicked off his pumps, threw off his jacket, and sprang into his hammock, where he pulled his blanket up to his chin and began to snore, gently and regularly. I wasted no time in doing the same, but young Tinkler, in his anxiety, must have turned in all standing as he was.

Next moment, Churchill, the master-at-arms, came fumbling into the darkened berth. "Come, come, young gentlemen; no shamming, now!" he called. He listened warily to our breathing, and felt us to make sure that our jackets and pumps were off, before he went out, grumbling, to the starboard berth. Hallet had taken the same precautions as ourselves, but poor little Tinkler was caught red-handed — pumps, jacket, and all. "Up with you, Mr. Tinkler," rumbled Churchill. "This 'll mean the masthead, and it 's a bloody cold night. I 'd let you off if I could. You young gentlemen keep half the ship awake with your cursed pranks!" He led him aft, and presently I heard Bligh's harsh voice, raised angrily.

"Damme, Mr. Tinkler! Do you think this ship's a bear garden? By God! I've half a mind to seize you up and give you a taste of the colt! To the masthead with you!"

Next morning at daylight Tinkler was still at the main topgallant crosstrees. The sky was clear, but the strong westsouthwest wind was icy cold. Presently Mr. Bligh came on deck, and, hailing the masthead, desired Tinkler to come down. There was no reply, even when he hailed a second time. At a word from Mr. Christian, one of the topmen sprang into the rigging, reached the crosstrees, and hailed the deck to say that Tinkler seemed to be dying, and that he dared not leave him for fear he would fall. Christian himself then went aloft, sent the topman down into the top for a tailblock, made a whip with the studding-sail halliards, and lowered Tinkler to the deck. The poor lad was blue with cold, unable to stand up or to speak.

We got him into his hammock in the berth, wrapped in warm blankets, and Old Bacchus came stumping forward with a can of his universal remedy. He felt the lad's pulse, propped his head up, and began to feed him neat rum with a spoon. Tinkler coughed and opened his eyes, while a faint colour appeared in his cheeks.

"Aha!" exclaimed the surgeon. "Nothing like rum, my lad! Just a sip, now. That's it! Now a swallow. Begad! Nothing like rum. I'll soon have you right as a trivet! And that reminds me—I'll have just a drop myself. A corpse reviver, eh?"

Coughing as the fiery liquor ran down his throat, Tinkler smiled in spite of himself. Two hours later he was on deck, none the worse for his night aloft.

On the twenty-third of May we dropped anchor in False Bay, near Cape Town. Table Bay is reckoned unsafe riding at this time of year, on account of the strong northwest winds. The ship required to be caulked in every part, for she had become so leaky that we had been obliged to pump every hour during our passage from Cape Horn. Our sails and rigging were in sad need of repair, and the timekeeper was taken ashore to ascertain its rate. On the twenty-ninth of June we sailed out of the bay, saluting the Dutch fort with thirteen guns as we passed.

I have few recollections of the long, cold, and dismal passage from the Cape of Good Hope to Van Diemen's Land. Day after day we scudded before strong westerly to southwesterly winds, carrying only the foresail and close-reefed maintopsail. The seas, which run for thousands of miles in these latitudes, unobstructed by land, were like mountain ridges; twice, when the wind increased to a gale, Bligh almost drove his ship under before we could get the sails clewed up and the *Bounty* hove-to. I observed that as long as the wind held southwest or west-southwest great numbers of birds accompanied us, — pintados, albatross, and blue petrels, — but that when the wind chopped around to the north, even for an hour or two, the birds left us at once. And when they reappeared their presence was always the forerunner of a southerly wind.

On the twentieth of August we sighted the rock called the Mewstone, which lies near the southwest cape of Van Diemen's Land, bearing northeast about six leagues, and two days later we anchored in Adventure Bay. We passed a fortnight here — wooding, watering, and sawing out plank, of which the carpenter was in need. It was a gloomy place, hemmed in by forests of tall straight trees of the eucalyptus kind, many of them a hundred and fifty feet high and rising sixty or eighty feet without a branch. Long strips of bark hung in tatters from their trunks, or decayed on the ground underfoot; few birds sang in the bush; and I saw only one animal — a small creature of the opossum sort, which scuttled into a hollow log. There were men here, but they were timid as wild animals —

black, naked, and uncouth, with hair growing in tufts like peppercorns, and voices like the cackling of geese. I saw small parties of them at different times, but they made off at sight of us.

Mr. Bligh put me in charge of a watering party, giving us the large cutter and instructing me to have the casks filled in a gully at the west end of the beach. Purcell, the carpenter, had rigged his saw pit close to this place, and was busy sawing out plank, with his mates, Norman and McIntosh, and two of the seamen detailed to the task. They had felled two or three of the large eucalyptus trees, but the carpenter, after inspecting the wood, had declared it worthless, and instructed his men to set to work on certain smaller trees of a different kind, with a rough bark and firm reddish wood.

I was superintending the filling of my casks one morning when Bligh appeared, a fowling piece over his arm and accompanied by Mr. Nelson. He glanced toward the saw pit and came to a halt.

"Mr. Purcell!" he called harshly.

"Yes, sir."

The *Bounty*'s carpenter was not unlike her captain in certain respects. Saving the surgeon, he was the oldest man on board, and nearly all of his life had been spent at sea. He knew his trade as well as Bligh understood navigation, and his temper was as arbitrary and his anger as fierce and sudden as Bligh's.

"Damme, Mr. Purcell!" exclaimed the captain. "Those logs are too small for plank. I thought I instructed you to make use of the large trees."

"You did, sir," replied Purcell, whose own temper was rising.

"Obey your orders, then, instead of wasting time."

"I am not wasting time, sir," said the carpenter, very red in the face. "The wood of the large trees is useless, as I discovered when I had cut some of them down."

"Useless? Nonsense. . . . Mr. Nelson, am I not right?"

"I am a botanist, sir," said Nelson, unwilling to take part in the dispute. "I make no pretense to a carpenter's knowledge of woods."

"Aye — that's what a carpenter *does* know," put in old Purcell. "The wood of these large trees will be worthless if sawn into plank."

Bligh's temper now got the better of him. "Do as I tell you, Mr. Purcell," he ordered violently. "I've no mind to argue with you or any other man under my command."

"Very well, sir," said Purcell obstinately. "The large trees it is. But I tell you the plank will be useless. A carpenter knows his business as well as a captain knows *his*."

Bligh had turned away; now he spun about on his heel.

"You mutinous old bastard — you have gone too far! Mr. Norman, take command of the work here. Mr. Purcell, report yourself instantly to Lieutenant Christian for fifteen days in irons."

It was my task to ferry Purcell out to the ship. The old man was flushed with anger; his jaw was set and his fists clenched till the veins stood out on his forearms. "Calls me a bastard," he muttered to no one in particular, "and puts me in irons for doing my duty. He hasn't heard the last of this, by God! Wait till we get to England! I know my rights, I do!"

We were still on the shortest of short rations, and Adventure Bay offered little in the way of refreshment for our invalids, or food for those of us who were well. Though we drew the seine repeatedly, we caught few fish and those of inferior kinds, and the mussels among the rocks, which at first promised a welcome change in our diet, proved poisonous to those who partook of them. While Mr. Bligh feasted on the wild duck his fowling piece brought down, the ship's people were half starved and there was much muttering among the officers.

The whole of our fortnight in Adventure Bay was marred by wrangling and discontent. The carpenter was in irons;

Fryer and Bligh were scarcely on speaking terms, owing to the master's suspicions that the captain had lined his pockets in victualing the ship; and just before our departure, Ned Young, one of the midshipmen, was lashed to a gun on the quarter-deck and given a dozen with a colt.

Young had been sent, with three men and the small cutter, to gather shellfish, crabs, and whatever he might find for our sick, who lived in a tent pitched on the beach. They pulled away in the direction of Cape Frederick Henry and did not return till after dark, when Young reported that Dick Skinner, one of the A. B.'s and the ship's hairdresser, had wandered off into the woods and disappeared.

"Skinner saw a hollow tree," Young told Mr. Bligh, "which, from the bees about it, he believed to contain a store of honey. He asked my permission to smoke the bees out and obtain their honey for our sick, saying that he had kept bees in his youth and understood their ways. I assented readily, knowing that you, sir, would be pleased if we could obtain the honey, and an hour or two later, when we had loaded the cutter with shellfish, we returned to the tree. A fire still smouldered at its foot, but Skinner was nowhere to be seen. We wandered through the woods and hailed till nightfall, but I regret to report, sir, that we could find no trace of the man."

I chanced to know that Bligh had called for the hairdresser, requiring his services that very afternoon, and had been incensed at Young when it was learned that Skinner had accompanied him. Now that the man was reported missing, Mr. Bligh was thoroughly enraged.

"Now damn you and all other midshipmen!" roared the captain. "You're all alike! If you had gotten the honey, you would have eaten it on the spot! Where the devil is Skinner, I say? Take your boat's crew this instant and pull back to where you saw the man last. Aye, and bring him back this time!"

Young was a man grown. He flushed at the captain's

words, but touched his hat respectfully and summoned his men at once. The party did not return till the following forenoon, having been nearly twenty-four hours without food. Skinner was with them this time; he had wandered off in search of another honey tree and become lost in the thick bush.

Bligh paced the quarter-deck angrily as the boat approached. By nature a man who brooded over grudges till they were magnified out of all proportion to reality, the captain was ready to explode the moment Young set foot on deck.

"Come aft, Mr. Young!" he called harshly. "I'm going to teach you to attend to your duty, instead of skylarking about the woods. Mr. Morrison!"

"Yes, sir!"

"Come aft here and seize up Mr. Young on that gun yonder! You're to give him a dozen with a rope's end."

Young was an officer of the ship and rated as a gentleman, a proud, fearless man of gentle birth. Though Bligh was within his powers as captain, the public flogging of such a man was almost without precedent in the Service. Morrison's jaw dropped at the order, which he obeyed with such evidence of reluctance that Bligh shouted at him threateningly, "Look alive, Mr. Morrison! I've my eye on you!"

I shall not speak of the flogging of Young, nor tell how Skinner's back was cut to ribbons with two dozen at the gangway. It is enough to say that Young was a different man from that day on, performing his duties sullenly and in silence, and avoiding the other midshipmen in the berth. He informed me long afterwards that, had events turned out differently, it was his intention to resign from the Service on the ship's arrival in England, and call Bligh to account as man to man.

On the fourth of September, with a fine spanking breeze at northwest, we weighed anchor and sailed out of Adventure Bay. Seven weeks later, after an uneventful passage made miserable by an outbreak of scurvy and the constant state of

starvation to which we were reduced, I saw my first South
Sea island.

We had gotten our easting in the high southern latitudes,
and once in the trade winds we made a long board to the north
on the starboard tack.   We were well into the tropics now and
in the vicinity of land.   Man-of-war hawks hovered overhead, their long forked tails opening and shutting like scissor-
blades; shoals of flying fish rose under the ship's cutwater to
skim away and plunge into the sea like whiffs of grapeshot.
The sea was of the pale turquoise blue only to be seen within
the tropics, shading to purple here and there where clouds
obscured the sun.   The roll of the Pacific from east to west
was broken by the labyrinth of low coral islands to the east
of us, — the vast cluster of half-drowned lands called by the
natives *Paumotu*, — and the *Bounty* sailed a tranquil sea.

I was off watch that afternoon and engaged in sorting over
the articles I had laid in, at the suggestion of Sir Joseph Banks,
for barter with the Indians of Tahiti.   Nails, files, and fishhooks were in great demand, as well as bits of cheap jewelry
for the women and girls.   My mother had given me fifty
pounds for the purchase of these things, and Sir Joseph had
added another fifty to it, advising me that liberality to the
Indians would be amply repaid.   "Never forget," he had remarked, "that in the South Sea the Seven Deadly Sins are com-
pounded into one, and that one is meanness."   I had taken this
advice to heart, and now, as I looked over my store of gifts, I
felt satisfied that I had laid out my hundred pounds to good
effect.   I had been a lover of fishing since childhood, and my
hooks were of all sizes and the best that money could buy.
My sea chest was half filled with other things — coils of brass
wire, cheap rings, bracelets, and necklaces; files, scissors, razors,
a variety of looking-glasses, and a dozen engraved portraits
of King George, which Sir Joseph had procured for me.   And
down in one corner of the chest, safe from the prying eyes of

my messmates, was a velvet-lined box from Maiden Lane. It contained a bracelet and necklace, curiously wrought in a design like the sinnet seamen plait. I was a romantic lad, not without my dreams of some fair barbarian girl who might bestow her favours on me. As I look back over the long procession of years, I cannot but smile at a boy's simplicity, but I would give all my hard-earned worldly wisdom to recapture if only for an hour the mood of those days of my youth. I had returned them to my chest when I heard Mr. Bligh's harsh, vibrant voice. His cabin was scarcely fifteen feet aft of where I sat.

"Mr. Fryer!" he called peremptorily. "Be good enough to step into my cabin."

"Yes, sir," replied the master's voice.

I had no desire to eavesdrop on the conversation that followed, but there was no way to avoid it without leaving my open chest in the berth.

"To-morrow or the day after," said Bligh, "we shall drop anchor in Matavai Bay. I have had Mr. Samuel make an inventory of the stores on hand, which has enabled him to cast up an account of the provisions expended on the voyage so far. I desire you to glance over this book, which requires your signature."

A long silence followed, broken at last by Fryer's voice. "I cannot sign this, sir," he said.

"Cannot sign it? What do you mean, sir?"

"The clerk is mistaken, Mr. Bligh. No such amounts of beef and pork have been issued!"

"You are wrong!" answered the captain angrily. "I know what was taken aboard and what remains. Mr. Samuel is right!"

"I cannot sign, sir," said Fryer obstinately.

"And why the devil not? All that the clerk has done was done by my orders. Sign it instantly! Damme! I am not the most patient man in the world."

"I cannot sign," insisted Fryer, a note of anger in his voice; "not in conscience, sir!"

"But you *can* sign," shouted Bligh in a rage; "and what is more, you *shall!*" He went stamping up the ladderway and on to the deck. "Mr. Christian!" I heard him shout to the officer of the watch. "Call all hands on deck this instant!"

The order was piped and shouted forward and, when we assembled, the captain, flushed with anger, uncovered and read the Articles of War. Mr. Samuel then came forward with his book and a pen and ink.

"Now, sir!" Bligh ordered the master, "sign this book!"

There was a dead silence while Fryer took up the pen reluctantly.

"Mr. Bligh," he said, controlling his temper with difficulty, "the ship's people will bear witness that I sign in obedience to your orders, but please to recollect, sir, that this matter may be reopened later on."

At that moment a long-drawn shout came from the man in the foretop. "Land ho!"

V

TAHITI

THE lookout had sighted Mehetia, a small, high island forty miles to the southeast of Tahiti. I stared ahead, half incredulously, at the tiny motionless projection on the horizon line. The wind died away toward sunset and we were all night working up to the land.

I went off watch at eight bells, but could not sleep; an hour later, perched on the fore-topgallant crosstrees, I watched the new day dawn. The beauty of that sunrise seemed ample compensation for all of the hardships suffered during the voyage: a sunrise such as only the seaman knows, and then only in the regions between the tropics, remote from home. Saving the light, fluffy "fair-weather clouds" just above the vast ring of horizon which encircled us, the sky was clear. The stars paled gradually; as the rosy light grew stronger, the velvet of the heavens faded and turned blue. Then the sun, still below the horizon, began to tint the little clouds in the east with every shade of mother-of-pearl.

An hour later we were skirting the reef, before a light air from the south. For the first time in my life I saw the slender, graceful trunk and green fronds of the far-famed coconut tree, the thatched cottages of the South Sea Islanders, set in their shady groves, and the people themselves, numbers of whom walked along the reef not more than a cable's length away. They waved large pieces of white cloth and shouted what I supposed were invitations to come ashore, though their voices were drowned in the noise of a surf which would have made landing impossible even had Mr. Bligh hove-to and lowered a boat.

Mehetia is high and round in shape, and not more than three miles in its greatest extent.   The village is at the southern end, where there is a tolerably flat shelf of land at the base of the mountain, but elsewhere the green cliffs are steep-to, with the sea breaking at their feet.   The white line of the breakers, the vivid emerald of the tropical vegetation covering the mountains everywhere, the rich foliage of the breadfruit trees in the little valleys, and the plumed tops of the coconut palms growing in clusters here and there, made up a picture which enchanted me.   The island had the air of a little paradise, newly created, all fresh and dewy in the dawn, stocked with everything needful for the comfort and happiness of man.

The men walking along the shelf of reef at the base of the cliffs were too far away for inspection, but they seemed fine stout fellows, taller than Englishmen.   They were dressed in girdles of bark cloth which shone with a dazzling whiteness in the morning sunlight.   They were naked except for these girdles, and they laughed and shouted to one another as they followed us along, clambering with great agility over the rocks.

As we rounded the northern end of the island, Smith hailed me from the top.   "Look, Mr. Byam!" he shouted, pointing ahead eagerly.   There, many leagues away, I saw the outlines of a mighty mountain rising from the sea, — sweeping ridges falling away symmetrically from a tall central peak, — all pale blue and ghostly in the morning light.

The breeze was making up now, and the *Bounty*, heeling a little on the larboard tack, was leaving a broad white wake. When I reached the deck I found Mr. Bligh in a rarely pleasant mood.   I bade him good morning, standing to leeward of him on the quarter-deck, and he saluted me with a clap on the back.

"There it is, young man," he said, pointing to the high

ghostly outlines of the land ahead. "Tahiti! We have made a long passage of it, a long hard passage, but, by God, there is the island at last!"

"It looks a beautiful island, sir," I remarked.

"Indeed it is — none more so. Captain Cook loved it only next to England; were I an old man, with my work done and no family at home, I should ask nothing better than to end my days under its palms! And you will find the people as friendly and hospitable as the land they inhabit. Aye — and some of the Indian girls as beautiful. We have come a long way to visit them! Last night I was computing the distance we have run by log since leaving England. To-morrow morning, when we drop anchor in Matavai Bay, we shall have sailed more than twenty-seven thousand miles!"

Since that morning, so many years ago, I have sailed all the seas of the world and visited most of the islands in them, including the West Indies, and the Asiatic Archipelago. But of all the islands I have seen, none approaches Tahiti in loveliness.

As we drew nearer to the land, with the rising sun behind us, there was not a man on board the *Bounty* who did not gaze ahead with emotions that differed in each case, no doubt, but in which awe and wonder played a part. But I am wrong — there was one. Toward six bells, when we were only a few miles off the southern extremity of the island, Old Bacchus came stumping on deck. Standing by the mizzenmast, with a hand on a swivel-stock, he stared indifferently for a moment at the wooded precipices, the waterfalls and sharp green peaks, now abeam of the ship. Then he shrugged his shoulders.

"They're all the same," he remarked indifferently. "When you've seen one island in the tropics, you've seen the lot."

The surgeon went stumping to the ladderway, and, as he disappeared, Mr. Nelson ceased his pacing of the deck to stand

at my side. The botanist was a believer in exercise and kept
his muscles hard and his colour fresh by walking two or three
miles on deck each morning the weather permitted.

"Well, Byam," he remarked, "I'm glad to be back! Many
a time, since my voyage with Captain Cook, I've dreamed of
revisiting Tahiti, without the faintest hope that the dream
might come true. Yet here we are! I can scarcely wait to
set foot on shore!"

We were skirting the windward coast of Taiarapu, the richest
and loveliest part of the island, and I could not take my eyes
off the land. In the foreground, a mile or more offshore, a
reef of coral broke the roll of the sea, and the calm waters of
the lagoon inside formed a highway on which the Indians
travel back and forth in their canoes. Behind the inner beach
was the narrow belt of flat land where the rustic dwellings of
the people were scattered picturesquely among their neat
plantations of the *ava* and the cloth plant, shaded by groves of
breadfruit and coconut. In the background were the
mountains — rising fantastically in turrets, spires, and precipices, wooded to their very tops. Innumerable waterfalls
plunged over the cliffs and hung like suspended threads of
silver, many of them a thousand feet or more in height and
visible at a great distance against the background of dark green.
Seen for the first time by European eyes, this coast is like
nothing else on our workaday planet; a landscape, rather, of
some fantastic dream.

Nelson was pointing ahead to a break in the line of reef.
"Captain Cook nearly lost his ship yonder," he said, "when the
current set him on the reef during a calm. One of his anchors
lies there to this day — there where the sea breaks high. I
know this part of the island well. As you can see, Tahiti is
made up of two lands, connected by the low isthmus the
Indians call Taravao. This before us is the lesser, called
Taiarapu or Tahiti Iti; the great island yonder they call Tahiti
Nui. Vehiatua is the king of the smaller one — the most

powerful of the Indian princes. His realm is richer and more populous than those of his rivals."

All through the afternoon we skirted the land, passing the low isthmus between the two islands, coasting the rich verdant districts of Faaone and Hitiaa, and toward evening, as the light breeze died away, moving slowly along the rock-bound coast of Tiarei, where the reef ends and the sea thunders at the base of cliffs.

There was little sleeping aboard the *Bounty* that night. The ship lay becalmed about a league off the mouth of the great valley of Papenoo, and the faint land breeze, wandering down from the heights of the interior, and out to sea, brought with it the sweet smell of the land and of growing things. We sniffed it eagerly, our noses grown keen from the long months at sea, detecting the scent of strange flowers, of wood smoke, and of Mother Earth herself — sweetest of all smells to a sailor. The sufferers from scurvy, breathing deep of the land breeze, seemed to draw in new life; their apathy and silence left them as they spoke eagerly of the fruits they hoped to eat on the morrow, fruits they craved as a man dying of thirst craves water.

We sighted Eimeo a little before sunset: the small lofty island which lies to the west of Tahiti, four leagues distant. The sun went down over the spires and pinnacles of Eimeo's sky line, and was followed into the sea by the thin golden crescent of the new moon. There is little twilight in these latitudes and, almost immediately it seemed to me, the stars came out in a cloudless dome of sky. One great planet, low in the west, sent a shimmering track of light over the sea. I saw the Cross and the Magellanic Clouds in the south, and constellations unknown to dwellers in the Northern Hemisphere, all close and warm and golden against the black sky. A faint burst of song came from the surgeon's cabin below, where he was carousing with Peckover; every other man on the ship, I believe, was on deck.

All along shore we could see the flare of innumerable torches, where the Indians went about their fishing or traveled from house to house along the beach.   The men of the *Bounty* stood by the bulwarks or on the booms, speaking in low voices and gazing toward the dark loom of the land.   A change seemed to come over all of us that night: all unhappiness, all discontent, seemed banished, giving way to a tranquil content and the happiest anticipation of what the morrow would bring.   Mr. Bligh himself, walking the deck with Christian, was rarely affable; as they passed me from time to time I overheard snatches of his talk: "Not a bad voyage, eh? . . . Only four down with scurvy, and we'll have them right in a week ashore. . . . The ship's sound as a walnut. . . . Bad anchorage. . . . We'll soon shift out of Matavai Bay. . . . A fine place for refreshments. . . ."

I was in the master's watch, and toward midnight Mr. Fryer chanced to notice me stifling a yawn, for it was many hours since I had slept.

"Take a caulk, Mr. Byam," he said kindly.   "Take a caulk! All's quiet to-night.   I'll see that you are waked if we need you."

I chose a place in the shadow of the bitts, just abaft of the main hatch, and lay down on deck, but, though I yawned with heavy eyes, it was long before sleep came to me.   When I awoke, the grey light of dawn was in the East.

We had drifted some distance to the west during the night, and now the ship lay off the valley of Vaipoopoo, from which runs the river that empties into the sea at the tip of Point Venus, the most northerly point of Tahiti Nui.   It was here that the *Dolphin*, Captain Wallis, had approached the newly discovered land, and here on this long, low point Captain Cook had set up his observatory to study the transit of the planet which gave the place its name.   Far off in the interior of the island, its base framed in the vertical cliffs bordering the valley, rose the tall central mountain called Orohena, a thi

sharp pinnacle of volcanic rock which rises to a height of seven
thousand feet and is perhaps as difficult of ascent as any peak
in the world. Its summit was now touched by the sun, and
as the light of day grew stronger, driving the shadows from
the valley and illuminating the foothills and the rich smiling
coastal land, I fancied that I had never gazed on a scene more
pleasing to the eye. The whole aspect of the coast about
Matavai Bay was open, sunny, and hospitable.

The entrance to the bay bore southwest by west, little more
than a league distant, and a great number of canoes were now
putting out to us. Most of them were small, holding only
four or five persons; strange-looking craft, with an outrigger
on the larboard side and a high stern sweeping up in a shape
almost semicircular. There were two or three double canoes
among them, each holding thirty or more people. The
Indian craft approached us rapidly. Their paddlers took half
a dozen short quick strokes on one side, and then, at a signal
from the man astern, all shifted to the other side. As the
leading canoes drew near, I heard questioning shouts: *"Taio?
Peritane? Rima?"* which is to say: "Friend? British? Lima?"
In the latter case, they were asking whether the *Bounty* was a
Spanish ship from Peru. *"Taio!"* shouted Bligh, who knew
some words of the Tahitian language. *"Taio! Peritane!"*
Next moment the first boatload of Indians came springing
over the bulwarks, and I had my first glimpse at close quarters
of this far-famed race.

Most of our visitors were men — tall, handsome, stalwart
fellows, of a light copper colour. They wore kilts of figured
cloth of their own manufacture, light fringed capes thrown
over their shoulders and joined at the throat, and turbans of
brown cloth on their heads. Some of them, naked from the
waist up, displayed the arms and torsos of veritable giants;
others, instead of turbans, wore on their heads the little
bonnets of freshly plaited coconut leaves they call *taumata*.
Their countenances, like those of children, mirrored every

passing mood, and when they smiled, which was often, I was astonished at the whiteness and perfection of their teeth. The few women who came on board at this time were all of the lower orders of society, and uncommonly diminutive as compared with the men. They wore skirts of white cloth falling in graceful folds, and cloaks of the same material to protect their shoulders from the sun, draped to leave the right arm free, and not unlike the toga of the Romans. Their faces were expressive of good nature, kindness, and mirth, and it was easy to perceive why so many of our seamen in former times had formed attachments among girls who seemed to have all the amiable qualities of their sex.

Mr. Bligh had given orders that the Indians were to be treated with the greatest kindness by everyone on board, though watched closely to prevent the thefts to which the commoners among them were prone. As the morning breeze freshened and we worked in toward the entrance with yards braced up on the larboard tack, the hubbub on the ship was deafening. At least a hundred men and a quarter as many women overran the decks, shouting, laughing, gesticulating, and addressing our people in the most animated manner, as if taking for granted that their unintelligible harangues were understood. The seamen found the feminine portion of our visitors so engaging that we had difficulty in keeping them at their stations. The breeze continued to freshen, and before long we sailed through the narrow passage between the westerly point of the reef before Point Venus and the sunken rock called the Dolphin Bank, on which Captain Wallis so nearly lost his ship. At nine in the forenoon we dropped anchor in Matavai Bay, in thirteen fathoms.

A vast throng of visitors set out immediately from the beach in their canoes, but for some time no persons of consequence came on board. I was joking with a party of girls to whom I had given some trifling gifts, when Mr. Bligh's servant came on deck to tell me that the captain desired to see me below. I found him alone in his cabin, bending over a chart of Matavai Bay.

"Ah, Mr. Byam," he said, motioning me to sit down on his chest. "I want a word with you. We shall probably lie here for several months while Mr. Nelson collects our young breadfruit plants. I am going to release you from further duties on board so that you may be free to carry out the wishes of my worthy friend, Sir Joseph Banks. I have given the matter some thought and believe that you will best accomplish your task by living ashore amongst the natives. Everything now depends on your choice of a *taio*, or friend, and let me advise you to go slowly. Persons of consequence in Tahiti, as elsewhere, do not wear their hearts on their sleeves, and should you make the mistake of choosing a friend among the lower orders of their society, you will find yourself greatly handicapped in your work."

He paused and I said, "I think I understand, sir."

"Yes," he went on. "By all means go slowly. Spend as much time as you wish on shore for a day or two, and when you have found a family to your liking inform me of the fact, so that I may make inquiries as to their standing. Once you have settled on a *taio* you can move your chest and writing materials ashore. After that I expect to see no more of you except when you report your progress to me once each week."

He gave me a curt but friendly nod, and perceiving that the interview was at an end, I rose and took leave of him. On deck, Mr. Fryer, the master, beckoned me to him.

"You have seen Mr. Bligh?" he asked, raising his voice to make the words audible in the din. "He informed me last night that on our arrival here you were to be relieved of duty on board the ship. There is nothing to fear from the Indians. Go ashore at any time you wish. You are free to make gifts of your own things to the Indians, but remember — no trading.

The captain has placed all of the trading in the hands of Mr. Peckover. You are to make a dictionary of the Indian tongue, I understand?"

"Yes, sir — at the desire of Sir Joseph Banks."

"A praiseworthy task — a praiseworthy task! Some slight knowledge of the language will no doubt be of great service to future mariners in this sea. And you're a lucky lad, Mr. Byam, a lucky lad! I envy you, on my word I do!"

At that moment a double canoe, which had brought out a handsome gift of pigs from some chief ashore, cast off from the ship. I was all eagerness to set foot on land. "May I go with those people if they 'll have me?" I asked the master.

"Off with you, by all means. Give them a hail."

I sprang to the bulwarks and shouted to catch the attention of a man in the stern of one of the canoes, who seemed to be in a position of authority. As I caught his eye, I pointed to myself, then to the canoe, and then to the beach a cable's length away. He caught my meaning instantly and shouted some order to his paddlers. They backed water so that the high stern of one of the canoes came close alongside, rising well above the *Bounty's* bulwarks. As I sprang over the rail and slid down the hollowed-out stern into the canoe, the paddlers, glancing back over their shoulders and grinning at me, raised a cheer. The Indian captain gave a shout, a score of paddles dug into the water simultaneously, and the canoe moved away toward the land.

From One Tree Hill to Point Venus a curving beach of black volcanic sand stretches for about a mile and a half. We were heading for a spot about midway between these two boundaries of Matavai Bay, and I saw that a considerable surf was pounding on the steep beach. As we drew near the breakers the man in the stern of the other canoe snatched up a heavy steering paddle and shouted an order which caused the men to cease paddling while four or five waves passed under us. A dense throng of Indians stood on the beach, awaiting our arrival with eagerness. Suddenly the man beside me began to shout, gripping the haft of his steering paddle strongly.

"*A hoe!*" he shouted. "*Teie te are rahi!*" (Paddle! Here is the great wave!) I recollect the words, for I was destined to hear them many times.

The men bent to their work, all shouting together; the canoe shot forward as a wave larger than the others lifted us high in the air and sent us racing for the sands. While the steersman held us stern-on, with efforts that made the muscles of his arms bulge mightily, we sped far up the beach, where a score of willing hands seized our little vessel to hold her against the backwash of the sea. I sprang out as the wave receded and made my way to high-water mark, while rollers were fetched and the double canoe hauled ashore with much shouting and laughter, to be housed under a long thatched shed.

Next moment I was surrounded by a throng so dense that I could scarcely breathe. But the crowd was good-natured and civil as no crowd in England could be; all seemed desirous to welcome me with every sign of pleasure. The clamour was deafening, for all talked and shouted at once. Small children with bright dark eyes clung to their mothers' skirts and stared at me apprehensively, while their mothers and fathers pushed forward to shake my hand, a form of greeting, as I was to learn with some surprise, immemorially old among the Tahitians.

Then, suddenly as the clamour of voices had begun, it ceased. The people fell back deferentially to make way for a tall man of middle age, who was approaching me with an air of easy authority and good-natured assurance. A murmur ran through the crowd: "*O Hitihiti!*"

The newcomer was smooth-shaven, unlike most of the Indian men, who wore short beards. His hair, thick and sprinkled with grey, was close-cropped, and his kilt and short fringed cloak were of the finest workmanship and spotlessly clean. He was well over six feet in height, lighter-skinned than the run of his countrymen, and magnificently proportioned; his face, frank, firm, and humorous, attracted me instantly.

This gentleman — for I recognized at a glance that he was of a class different from any of the Indians I had seen hitherto — approached me with dignity, shook my hand warmly, and then, seizing me by the shoulders, applied his nose to my cheek, giving several loud sniffs as he did so. I was startled by the suddenness and novelty of the greeting, but I realized that this must be what Captain Cook and other navigators had termed "nose-rubbing," though in reality it is a smelling of cheeks, and corresponds to our kiss. On releasing me, my new friend stepped back a pace while a loud murmur of approval went through the crowd. He then pointed to his broad chest and said: "Me Hitihiti! You midshipman! What name?"

I was so taken aback at these words of English that I stared at him for a moment before I replied. The people had evidently been waiting to see what effect the marvelous accomplishment of their compatriot would produce, and my display of astonishment turned out to be precisely what they were hoping for. There were nods and exclamations of satisfaction on all sides, and Hitihiti, now thoroughly pleased with himself and with me, repeated his question, "What name?"

"Byam," I replied; and he said, "Byam! Byam!" nodding violently, while "Byam, Byam, Byam," echoed throughout the crowd.

Hitihiti again pointed to his chest. "Fourteen year now," he said with an air of pride, "me sail Captain Cook!" "*Tuté! Tuté!*" exclaimed a little old man close by, as if afraid that I might not understand.

"Could I have a drink of water?" I asked, for it was long since I had tasted any but the foul water aboard ship. Hitihiti started, and seized my hand.

He shouted an order to the people about us, which sent some of the boys and young men scampering off inland. He then led me up the steep rise behind the beach to a rustic shed where several young women made haste to spread a mat. We sat down side by side, and the crowd, increasing rapidly as parties of Indians arrived from up and down the coast, seated themselves on the grass outside. A dripping gourd, filled to the brim with clear sparkling water from the brook near by, was handed me, and I drank deep, setting it down half empty with a sigh of satisfaction.

I was then given a young coconut to drink — my first taste of this cool, sweet wine of the South Sea — and a broad leaf was spread beside me, on which the young women laid ripe bananas and one or two kinds of fruit I had not seen before. While I set to greedily on these delicacies, I heard a shout go up from the crowd, and saw that the *Bounty's* launch was coming in through the surf, with Bligh in the stern sheets. My host sprang to his feet. *"O Parai!"* he exclaimed, and, as we waited for the boat to land, "You, me, *taio*, eh?"

Hitihiti was the first of the Indians to greet Bligh, whom he seemed to know well. And the captain recognized my friend at once.

"Hitihiti," he said as he shook the Indian's hand, "you've grown little older, my friend, though you've some grey hairs now."

Hitihiti laughed. "Ten year, eh? Plenty long time! By God! Parai, you get fat!"

It was now the captain's turn to laugh, as he touched his waist, by no means small in girth.

"Come ashore," the Indian went on emphatically. "Eat plenty pig! Where Captain Cook? He come Tahiti soon?"

"My father?"

Hitihiti looked at Bligh in astonishment. "Captain Cook your father?" he asked.

"Certainly — didn't you know that?"

For a moment the Indian chief stood in silent amazement; then, with extraordinary animation, he raised a hand for silence and addressed the crowd. The words were unintelligible to me, but I perceived at once that Hitihiti was a trained orator, and I knew that he was telling them that Bligh was the son of Captain Cook. Mr. Bligh stood close beside me as the chief went on with his harangue.

"I have instructed all of the people not to let the Indians know that Captain Cook is dead," he said in a low voice. "And I believe that we shall accomplish our mission the quicker for their belief that I am his son."

While I was somewhat taken aback by this piece of deception, I knew the reverence in which the people of Tahiti held the name of Cook, and perceived that, according to the Jesuitical idea that the end justifies the means, Mr. Bligh was right.

As Hitihiti ceased to speak there was a buzz of excited talk among the Indians, who looked at Bligh with fresh interest, not unmixed with awe. In their eyes, Captain Cook's son was little less than a god. I took the opportunity to inform Mr. Bligh that Hitihiti had offered to become my *taio*, and that with his approval I thought well of the idea, since I should be able to communicate to some extent with my Indian friend.

"Excellent," said the captain with a nod. "He is a chief of consequence on this part of the island, and nearly related to all of the principal families. And, as you say, the English he picked up on board the *Resolution* should be of great assistance to you in your work." He turned to the Indian. "Hitihiti!"

"Yes, Parai."

"Mr. Byam informs me that you and he are to be friends." Hitihiti nodded. "Me, Byam, *taio!*"

"Good!" said Bligh. "Mr. Byam is the son of a chief in his own land. He will have gifts for you, and in return I want you to take him to your house, where he will stop. His work, while we are here, is to learn your language, so that British seamen may be able to converse with your people. Do you understand?"

Hitihiti turned to face me and stretched out an enormous

hand. *"Taio,* eh?" he remarked smilingly, and we shook hands on the bargain.

Presently a canoe was launched to fetch my things from the ship, and that night I slept in the house of my new friend — Hitihiti-Te-Atua-Iri-Hau, chief of Mahina and Ahonu, and hereditary high priest of the temple of Fareroi.

VI

AN INDIAN HOUSEHOLD

I CAN still recall vividly our walk that afternoon — from the landing place to Point Venus, and eastward, behind a second long curving beach of sand, on which the sea broke high, to the house of my *taio*, set on a grassy point, sheltered from the sea by a short stretch of coral reef which supported a beautiful little islet called Motu Au. The islet was not more than half a cable's length from shore; its beaches were of snowy coral sand, contrasting with the rich dark green of the tall trees that grew almost to the water's edge. Between the beach and the islet lay the lagoon — warm blue water, two or three fathoms deep and clear as air.

We walked in constant shade, under groves of breadfruit trees on which the fruit was beginning to ripen. Many of these trees must have been of immense age, from their girth and height; with their broad glossy leaves, smooth bark, and majestic shape, they are among the noblest of all shade trees, and certainly the most useful to mankind. Here and there the slender bole of an old coconut palm rose high in the air; scattered picturesquely, as if at random, among the groves I saw the houses of the Indians, thatched with bright yellow leaves of the palmetto and surrounded by fences of bamboo.

My host, though no more than forty-five, was already many times a grandfather, and as we approached his house, after a walk of little more than half an hour, I heard joyful shouts and saw a dozen sturdy children skipping out to greet him. They halted at sight of me, but soon lost their fear and began to climb up Hitihiti's legs and examine, inquisitively as monkeys, the strange garments I wore. By the time we came to the door the chief had a small boy on each of his shoulders, and his eldest granddaughter was leading me by the hand.

The house was a fine one — sixty feet long by twenty wide, with a lofty, newly thatched roof, and, instead of gables, semicircular extensions at each end, giving the whole an oval shape. Such houses were built only for chiefs. The ends, supported by pillars of old polished coconut wood, were open, and the sides were walled by vertical lathes of bright yellow bamboo, through which the air filtered freely. The floor was of fresh white coral sand, spread with mats at one end on a thick bed of sweet-smelling grass called *aretu*. Of furniture there was scarcely any: small wooden pillows on the family bed, like tiny tables with four short legs; two or three of the seats used only by chiefs, carved from a single log of hard red wood; and a stand of weapons hanging on one of the pillars which supported the ridgepole, including my host's ponderous war club.

Hitihiti's daughter — mother of two of the younger children accompanying us — met us at the door. She was a young woman of twenty-five, with a stately figure and carriage, and the pale golden skin and auburn hair which are not uncommon among this people. These fair Indians were termed *ehu*; I have seen men and women of this strain — unmixed with European blood — whose eyes were blue. My host smiled at his daughter and then at me.

"O Hina," he said in introduction. He said something to her in which I distinguished the word *taio* and my own name. Hina stepped forward with a grave slow smile to shake my hand, and then, taking me by the shoulders as her father had done, she laid her nose to my cheek and sniffed. I reciprocated this Indian kiss, and smelled for the first time the perfume of the scented coconut oil with which the women of Tahiti anoint themselves.

There are perhaps no women in the world — not even the greatest ladies of fashion in Europe — more meticulous in the care of their persons than were the Indian women of the upper class. Each morning and evening they bathed in one of the innumerable clear cool streams, not merely plunging in and out again, but stopping to be scrubbed from head to foot by their serving women with a porous volcanic stone, used as we use pumice in our baths. Their servants then anointed them with *monoi* — coconut oil, perfumed with the petals of the Tahitian gardenia. Their hair was dried and arranged, a task which required an hour or more; their eyebrows were examined in a mirror which consisted of a blackened coconut shell filled with water, and plucked or shaven with a shark's tooth, to make the slender arch which was the fashion among them. A servant then brought a supply of powdered charcoal with which the teeth were scrubbed. When they were ready to dress, the skirt, or *pareu,* which reached from waist to the knees and was of snow-white bark cloth, was adjusted so that each fold hung in a certain fashion. Then came the cloak, which was worn to protect the upper part of the body from sunburn, which the ladies of Tahiti dreaded quite as much as the ladies of the English Court. Each fold of the cloak was arranged just so, and it was ridiculous — to a man, at least — to watch the long efforts of a tirewoman to please her mistress in this respect.

Hina's manners were as handsome as her person. She had the smiling dignity and perfect assurance only to be found among the highest circles of our own race, a poised urbanity, neither forward nor shy. And this is, perhaps, a fitting place to say a word for the Indian ladies, so often and so shamelessly slandered by the different navigators who have visited their island. Captain Cook alone, who knew them best and was their loyal friend, has done them justice, saying that virtue was perhaps as common and as highly prized among them as among our own women at home, and that to form an impression of the ladies of Tahiti from the women who visited his ships would be like judging the virtue of Englishwomen from a study of the nymphs of Spithead. In Tahiti, as in other lands, there are people given over to vice and lewdness, and women of this kind naturally congregated upon the arrival of a ship; but, so far as I know, there was also as great a proportion of faithful wives and affectionate mothers as elsewhere, many of whom were a veritable honour to their sex.

The house which was to be my dwelling for many months stood, as I have said, on a grassy point, about a mile to the eastward of Point Venus. Either by accident or by design, the site was one that commanded in all directions prospects an artist might have traveled many miles to paint. On the northern side were the beach, the lagoon, and the beautiful little island already mentioned; to the south, or directly inland, was the great valley of Vaipoopoo and a distant glimpse of Orohena, framed in the cliffs of the gorge; to the west lay Point Venus, with the sea breaking high on the protecting reefs; and to the east, facing the sunrise, was a magnificent view of the rocky, unprotected coast of Orofara and Faaripoo, where the surges of the Pacific thundered and spouted at the base of stern black cliffs. No doubt because of the beauty of the easterly view at dawn, the name of our point was Hitimahana — the rising of the sun.

A little crowd of the chief's retainers gathered about us, regarding their patron's friend with respectful curiosity, and, while Hina gave some order to the cooks, an exceedingly handsome young girl came out of the house and, at a word from my *taio,* greeted me as his daughter had done. Her name was Maimiti, and she was a niece of my host's — a proud, shy girl of seventeen.

With a nod to Hina my *taio* led me to his rustic dining room — a thatched shed in the shade of a clump of ironwood trees, about a hundred yards distant. The floor of coral sand was spread with mats, on which a dozen of the broad fresh leaves of the plantain served as our tablecloth. The men of Tahiti were uncommonly fond of the company of their women, whose position in society was perhaps as high as that of women anywhere. They were petted, courted, permitted no share in any hard labour, and allowed a liberty such as only our own great ladies enjoy. Yet in spite of all this, the Indians believed that Man was sky-descended, and Woman earth-born: Man *raa*, or holy; Woman *noa*, or common. Women were not permitted to set foot in the temples of the greater gods, and among all classes of society it was forbidden —unthinkable in fact — for the two sexes to sit down to a meal together. I was surprised to find that Hitihiti and I sat down alone to our dinner, and that no woman had a hand either in the cooking or in the serving of the meal.

We sat facing each other across the cloth of fresh green leaves. A pleasant breeze blew freely through the unwalled house, and the breakers on the distant reef made a murmuring undertone of sound. A serving man brought two coconut shells of water, in which we washed our hands and rinsed our mouths. I felt a sharp hunger, augmented by savoury whiffs of roasting pork from the cookhouse not far off.

We were given baked fish with cooked plantains and bananas; pork fresh from the oven, and certain native vegetables which I had never tasted before; and a great pudding to finish with, served with a sauce of rich, sweet coconut cream. I was only a lad, with the appetite of a midshipman, and I had been many months at sea, but though I did my best to maintain the honour of England by eating enough for three men, my host put me to shame. Long after repletion forced me to halt, Hitihiti continued his leisurely meal, devouring quantities of fish, pork, plantains, and pudding I can only describe as fabulous. At last he sighed and called for water to wash his hands.

"First eat — now sleep," he said, as he rose. A wide mat was spread for us under an old branching *purau* tree on the beach

We lay down side by side for the siesta which in Tahiti always follows the midday meal.

This was the beginning of a period of my life on which I look back with nothing but pleasure. I had not a care in the world, save the making of my dictionary, in which I took the keenest interest, and which gave me sufficient occupation to prevent ennui. I lived on the fat of the land, amongst affectionate friends and amid surroundings of the most exquisite beauty. We rose at dawn, plunged into the river which ran within pistol shot of Hitihiti's door, ate a light breakfast of fruits, and went about our occupations until the fishing canoes returned from the sea at eleven or twelve o'clock. Then, while the meal was preparing, I had a bath in the sea, swimming across to the islet or sporting in the high breakers further west. After dinner the whole household slept till three or four in the afternoon, when I frequently joined them in excursions to visit their friends. After sundown, when the strings of candlenuts were lit, we lay about on mats, conversing or telling stories till one after another dropped off to sleep.

During the voyage out from England I had gone through Dr. Johnson's dictionary, which had been provided for me, marking such words as seemed to me in most common usage in everyday speech. I had then set these down alphabetically — nearly seven thousand in all. My present task was to discover and set down their equivalents in the Indian tongue. I have always loved languages; the study of them has been one of the chief interests of my life, and in my younger days I could pick up a new tongue more readily, perhaps, than most men. If I am blessed with any talent, it is the humble one of the gift of tongues.

The language of Tahiti appealed to me from the first, and with the help of my *taio*, his daughter, and young Maimiti, I made rapid progress and was soon able to ask simple questions and to understand the replies. It is a strange language and a beautiful one.   Like the Greek of Homer, it is rich in words descriptive of the moods of Nature and of human emotions; and, like Greek again, it has in certain respects a precision that our English lacks.   To break a bottle is *parari;* to break a rope, *motu;* to break a bone, *fati.*   The Indians distinguish with the greatest nicety between the different kinds of fear: fear of a scolding or of being shamed is *matau;* fear of a dangerous shark or of an assassin, *riaria;* fear of a spectre must be expressed with still another word.   They have innumerable adjectives to express the varying moods of sea and sky.   One word describes the boundless sea without land in sight; another the deep blue sea off soundings; another the sea in a calm with a high oily swell.   They have a word for the glance which passes between a man and a woman planning an assignation, and another word for the look exchanged by two men plotting to assassinate a third.   Their language of the eyes, in fact, is so eloquent and so complete that at times they seem scarcely to need a spoken tongue.   They are masters of the downcast eye, the sidelong glance, the direct glance, the raising of the eyebrow, the lift of the chin, and all the pantomime with which they can communicate without those about them being aware of the fact.

I think I may say, in all truth, that I was the first white man to speak fluently the Tahitian tongue, and the first to make a serious attempt to reduce the language to writing.   Sir Joseph Banks had provided me with a brief vocabulary, compiled from his own notes and from Captain Cook's, but as soon as I heard the Indian tongue spoken I realized that, as he had suggested, a new system of orthography must be devised.   Since my work was to be done for the benefit of mariners, it seemed better to aim at simplicity than at a high degree of academic perfection, so I devised an alphabet of thirteen letters—five vowels and eight consonants—with which the sounds of the language could be set down fairly well.

Hitihiti spoke the Tahitian language as only a chief could, for the lower orders, as in other lands, possessed vocabularies of no more than a few hundred words. He was interested in my work and of infinite use to me, though, as with all his countrymen, mental effort fatigued him if sustained for more than an hour or two. I overcame this difficulty by making myself agreeable to the ladies, and dividing my work into two parts. From Hitihiti I learned the words pertaining to war, religion, navigation, shipbuilding, fishing, agriculture, and other manly pursuits; from Hina and Maimiti I obtained vocabularies concerning the pursuits and amusements of women.

I opened my chest on the day of my arrival at their house and made my host a present of what I thought would please him and the ladies most. This was the seal on our pledged friendship, but though my files, fishhooks, scissors, and trinkets were received with appreciation, I had the satisfaction of learning, as time went on, that the friendship of an Indian like Hitihiti was not for sale. He and his daughter and his niece were sincerely fond of me, I believe, showing their affection in many unmistakable ways. I must have been an infinite nuisance to them, with my pen and ink and endless questions, but their patient good-humour was equal to my demands. Sometimes Maimiti would throw up her hands in mock despair, and exclaim laughingly: "Let me be! I can think no more!" or the old chief, after an hour's patient answering of my questions, would say: "Let us sleep, Byam! Take care, or you will crack your head and mine with too much thinking!" But on the next morning they were always ready to help me once more.

Each Sunday I gathered my manuscript together and reported myself on board the *Bounty* to Mr. Bligh. I must say, in justice to him, that whatever task he undertook was thoroughly performed. He showed the greatest interest in my work, and never failed to run over with me the list of words I had set down during the week. Had his character in other respects been equal to his courage, his energy, and his understanding, Bligh would to-day have his niche in history, among the great seamen of England.

Shortly after the arrival of the *Bounty*, Mr. Bligh had ordered a large tent pitched near the landing place, and Nelson and his assistant, a young gardener named Brown, were now established on shore, with seven men to help them gather and pot the breadfruit plants.

This tree cannot be propagated from seeds, since it produces none. Mr. Nelson informed me that in his opinion the bread-fruit had been cultivated and improved from time immemorial, until—as in the case of the banana—seeds had been entirely eliminated from the fruit. It seems to thrive best when tended by man, and in the neighbourhood of his dwellings. When well grown, the breadfruit tree sends out lateral roots of great length, within a foot or two of the surface of the ground. Should an Indian desire a young tree to plant elsewhere, he has only to dig down and cut one of these roots, which, when separated from the parent tree, immediately sends up a vigorous young plant. When the shoot has reached the height of a man, it is ready to be transplanted, which is done by first cutting it back to a height of about a yard, and then digging down to cut off a small section of the root. Planted in suitable soil and watered from time to time, not one in a hundred of the young trees will fail to grow.

Nelson took long walks daily, scouring the districts of Mahina and Pare for young plants already well grown. The chiefs had ordered their subjects to give Nelson all he asked for, as a present to be sent to King George in return for the gifts the *Bounty* had brought from England.

The *Bounty's* people who remained on board seemed to have forgotten for the time being their captain's severities and the hardships of our long voyage. Discipline was relaxed; the men were allowed to go frequently on shore; and except for the surgeon every man of them had his Indian *taio*, and nearly every one his Indian lass. Tahiti was in those days a veritable paradise to the seaman — one of the richest islands in the world, with a mild and wholesome climate, abounding in every variety of delicious food, and inhabited by a race of gentle and hospitable barbarians. The humblest A. B. in the forecastle might enter any house on shore, assured of a welcome. And as regards the possibilities of dissipation, to which seamen are given in every port, the island could only be described as a Mohammedan paradise.

When I had been about a fortnight at my *taio's* house I was agreeably surprised one morning to receive a visit from some of my shipmates, who came around from Matavai Bay in a double canoe. She was paddled by a dozen or more Indians, and three white men sat in the stern. My host had gone aboard the *Bounty* that day to dine with Bligh, and I stood on the beach as the canoe approached, with Hina, Maimiti, and Hina's husband, a young chief named Tuatau. As the canoe rose on a wave I saw that the two white men facing me were Christian and Peckover, and a moment later I was amazed to see Old Bacchus on the thwart aft of them. A wave reared up behind the little vessel, the Indians dashed their paddles into the water, and the canoe swept forward and ran far up the beach.

The surgeon sprang over the gunwale and came stumping up to greet me, his wooden leg sinking deep into the sand. I had on only a girdle of the native cloth, and my shoulders were burned brown by the sun.

"Well, Byam," said Bacchus as he shook my hand, "damme if I didn't think you an Indian at first! Time I was going ashore, I thought, and where should I go if not to pay you a visit, my lad! So I bottled off a dozen of Teneriffe wine." He turned to the gunner, who stood by the canoe. "Hey, Peckover," he called solicitously, "tell them to be easy with that hamper — should any of the bottles be broken, it would mean another trip to the ship."

Christian gave me a handshake, with a glint of amusement

in his eyes, and we waited while the surgeon and Peckover superintended the unloading of a large hamper of wine. Presently a native came staggering up the beach with it, and I introduced my shipmates to my Indian friends. Hina and her husband led the way to the house, and we followed, Maimiti walking with Christian and me. I had liked Christian from the moment when I first set eyes on him, but it was not until we reached Tahiti that I came to know him well. He was a stalwart, handsome man, and more than once, during the short walk to the house, I saw young Maimiti give him a sidelong glance.

When we were seated on mats on Hitihiti's cool verandah, Old Bacchus motioned the men to set down the hamper of wine. Still panting from the exertion of his walk, he fumbled for his snuffbox, pulled up his sleeve, laid a train of snuff on his polished forearm, and sniffed it up in a twinkling. Then, after a violent sneeze or two and a flourish of his enormous handkerchief, he reached into his coat tails and produced a corkscrew.

He and Peckover were soon well under way on a morning's carouse, and Tuatau loth to leave them while the wine held out, so Christian, Maimiti, Hina, and I walked away up the beach, leaving the preparations of our dinner to Hitihiti's numerous cooks. The morning was warm and calm, and we were glad to walk in the shade of the tall ironwood trees that fringed the sands. A river little larger than an English brook flowed into the sea about a mile east of the house, ending in a clear deep pool close to the beach. Gnarled old hibiscus trees arched together overhead, and the sun, filtering through their foliage, cast changing patterns of light and shade on the still water. The two girls retreated into the underbrush and soon stepped out clad in light girdles of glazed native cloth, which is nearly waterproof. No women in the world are more modest than the ladies of Tahiti, but they bare their breasts as innocently as an Englishwoman shows her face.

Standing beside me on the bank, clad in a native kilt which showed his own stalwart figure to the best advantage, Christian glanced up at them and caught his breath.

"My God, Byam!" he said in a low voice.

Slenderly and strongly made, in the first bloom of young womanhood, and with her magnificent dark hair unbound, Maimiti made a picture worth traveling far to behold. She stood for a moment with a hand on the elder woman's shoulder, and then, gathering her kilt about her, she ran nimbly up a gnarled limb that overhung the deep water. Poising herself for an instant high above the pool, she sprang into the water with a merry shout, and I saw her swimming with slow easy strokes along the bottom, two fathoms deep. Christian, a capital swimmer, went in head first, and Hina followed him with a great splash. For an hour or more we frolicked in the pool, startling shoals of small speckled fish like trout, and making the cool green tunnel overhead echo with laughter.

The Indians of Tahiti rarely bathe in the sea except when a great surf is running. At such times the more daring among the men and women delight in a sport they call *horue* — swimming out among the great breakers with a light board about a fathom long, and choosing their moment to come speeding in, a quarter of a mile or more, on the crest of a high feathering sea. Their daily bathing is done in the clear cool streams which flow down from the mountains everywhere, and though they bathe twice, and often three times each day, they look forward to the next bath as though it were the first in a month. Men, women, and children bathe together with a great hubbub of shouting and merriment, for this is the social hour of their day, when friends are met, courtships carried on, and gossip and news exchanged.

After our bath we dried ourselves in the sun, while the girls combed out their hair with combs of bamboo, curiously carved. Christian was a gentleman, and very far from a rake, though of a warm and susceptible temperament. He lagged behind with young Maimiti while we walked back to the house, and once, turning my head by chance, I saw that the two were walking hand in hand.   They made a handsome couple — the young English seaman and the Indian girl.   The kindly fate which veils the future from us gave me no inkling of what lay in store for these two — destined to face together, hand in hand as I saw them now, long wanderings and suffering, and tragedy. Maimiti cast down her eyes, while a blush suffused her clear olive cheeks with crimson, and strove gently to release her hand; but Christian held her fast, smiling at me.

"Every sailor must have his sweetheart," he said, half lightly and half in earnest, "and I 've found mine.   I 'll stake my life there 's not a truer lass in all these islands!"

Hina smiled gravely and touched my arm as a hint to leave Christian to his courting.   She had liked him at first sight, and knew his rank on board.   And thanks to the uncanny fashion in which news of every sort spreads among the people of Tahiti, she knew that he had had no traffic with the women who infested the ship.

VII

CHRISTIAN AND BLIGH

FROM the day of his meeting with Maimiti, Christian missed no opportunity of visiting us, arriving by day or by night as his duties on board the *Bounty* permitted. The Indians, who felt no need of unbroken sleep, were frequently up and about during the night, and often made a meal at midnight when the fishers returned from the reef. Old Hitihiti oftentimes awakened me merely from a desire to converse, or when he suddenly recollected some word which had escaped his memory during the day. I grew accustomed to this casual and broken sleep, and learned, like my host, to make up during the afternoon for what was lost at night.

Christian was soon accepted by the household as the avowed lover of Maimiti. He seldom came without some little gifts for her and the others, and his visits were anticipated with eager pleasure. He was a man of moods; at sea I had seen him stern, reticent, and almost intimidating for a fortnight at a time. Then all at once he would unbend, shake off his preoccupation, and become the heartiest and gayest of companions. No man knew better how to make himself agreeable to others when he chose; his sincerity, his education, which went beyond that of most sea officers of the time, and the charm of his manner combined to win the respect of men and women alike. And the ardour of his nature, his handsome person and changing moods, made him what women call a romantic man.

One night, when I had been about six weeks at the house of Hitihiti, I was awakened gently in the Indian fashion by a hand on my shoulder.   The flare of a candlenut made a dim light in the house, and I saw Christian standing over me, with his sweetheart at his side.

"Come down to the beach, Byam," he said; "they have built a fire there.   I have something to tell you."

Rubbing the sleep from my eyes, I followed them out of the house, to where a fire of coconut husks burned bright and ruddy.   The night was moonless and the sea so calm that the breakers scarcely whispered on the sand.   Mats were spread around the fire, and Hitihiti's people lay about, conversing in low voices while fish roasted on the coals.

Christian sat down, his back to the bole of a coconut palm and an arm about Maimiti's waist, while I reclined near by. I knew at the first glance that his gaiety of the weeks past had been succeeded by one of his sombre moods.

"I must tell you," he said slowly, at the end of a long silence, "Old Bacchus died last night."

"Good God!" I exclaimed . . .   "What . . ."

"He died, not of drink, as might have been supposed, but of eating a poisonous fish.   We purchased about fifty pounds of fish from a canoe that came in from Tetiaroa, and your mess had a string of them fried for dinner yesterday.   They were of a bright red colour and different from the others.   Hayward, Nelson, and Morrison were close to death for six hours, but they are better now.   The surgeon died at eight bells, four hours ago."

"Good God!" I repeated stupidly and mechanically.

"He will be buried in the morning, and Mr. Bligh bids you to be on hand."

At first the news dazed me and I did not realize the full extent of the loss; little by little the fact that Old Bacchus was no longer of the *Bounty's* company came home to me.

"A drunkard," said Christian musingly, as if to himself, "but beloved by all on board.   We shall be the worse off for his death."

Maimiti turned to me, and in the ruddy firelight I saw glistening in her eyes the easy tears of her race. *"Ua mate te ruau avae hoe,"* she said sorrowfully. (The old man with one leg is dead.)

"I have been many years at sea," Christian went on, "and I can tell you that the welfare of men on shipboard depends on things which seem small. A joke at the right moment, a kind word, or a glass of grog is sometimes more efficacious than the cat-of-nine-tails. With the surgeon gone, life on the *Bounty* will not be what it was."

Christian spoke no more that night, but sat gazing into the fire, a sombre expression in his eyes. Maimiti, a silent girl, laid her head on his shoulder and fell asleep, while he stroked her hair tenderly and absently. I lay awake for a long time, thinking of Old Bacchus and of the trick of fate which had so abruptly closed his career, on a heathen island, twelve thousand miles from England. Perhaps his jovial shade would be well content to haunt the moonlit groves of Tahiti, where the sea he loved was only a pistol shot away — its salt smell in the air and the thunder of its breakers sounding day and night. And he had died on shipboard, as he would have desired, safe from the dreaded years of retirement on shore. Christian was right, I thought; without Old Bacchus, life on the *Bounty* could not be the same.

We buried him on Point Venus, close to where Captain Cook had set up his observatory twenty years before. There was some delay in getting the consent of Teina, the great chief whom the English had believed to be king of Tahiti, and who was the first of the Pomares. At last all was arranged, and the Indians themselves dug the grave, laying it out very exactly east and west. It was not until four o'clock in the afternoon that Old Bacchus was laid to rest, Bligh reading the burial service and a great crowd of Indians — silent, attentive, and respectful — surrounding us. When the captain and the *Bounty's* people had gone on board to see to the auctioning of the dead man's effects, Nelson and Peckover remained on shore, the former still pale and shaken from fish poisoning. The Indians had dispersed, and only the three of us lingered by the new grave, covered with slabs of coral in the Indian style.

Nelson cleared his throat and drew from a bag he carried three glasses and a bottle of Spanish wine. "We were his best friends on board," he said to Peckover, "you and Byam and I. I think it would please him if we added one small ceremony to the burial service Captain Bligh read so well." The botanist cleared his throat once more, handed us the glasses, and uncorked his bottle of wine. Then, baring our heads, we drank in silence to Old Bacchus, and when the bottle was empty we broke our glasses on the grave.

The relaxation of discipline which had followed the hardships of the *Bounty's* long voyage now came to an end as Bligh's harsh and ungovernable temper once more began to assert itself. I saw something of what was going on during my visits to the ship, and learned more from Hitihiti and Christian, who gave me to understand that there was much murmuring on board.

Each man on the ship, as I have said, had his Indian friend, who felt it his duty to send out to his *taio* frequent gifts of food. The seamen quite naturally regarded this as their own property, to be disposed of as they wished, but Bligh soon put an end to such ideas by announcing that all that came on board belonged to the ship, to be disposed of as the captain might direct. It was hard for a seaman whose *taio* had sent out a fine fat hog of two or three hundredweight to see it seized for ship's stores, and to be forced to dine on a small ration of poor pork issued by Mr. Samuel. Even the master's hogs were seized, though Bligh had at the moment forty of his own.

I witnessed unpleasant scenes of this kind one morning when I had gone on board to wait upon Mr. Bligh. The captain had gone ashore and was not expected for some time, so I loitered by the gangway, watching the canoes put out from shore. Young Hallet, the petulant and sickly-looking midshipman whom I liked least of those in the berth, was on duty to see that no provisions were smuggled on board, and he stepped to the gangway as a small canoe, paddled by two men, came alongside. Tom Ellison, the youngest of the seamen and the most popular with all hands, was in the bow of the canoe. He dropped his paddle, clambered up the ship's side, touched his forelock to Hallet, and leaned down to take the gifts his *taio* handed up to him. They were a handful of the Indian apples called *vi*, a fan, with a handle made of a whale's tooth, curiously carved, and a bundle of the native cloth. The Indian grinned up at Ellison, waved his hand, and paddled away. Hallet stooped to take up the apples laid on deck, and began to eat one, saying, "I must have these, Ellison."

"Right, sir," said Ellison, though I could see that he regretted his fruit. "You'll find them sweet!"

"And this fan," said the midshipman, taking it from Ellison's hand. "Will you give it to me?"

"I cannot, sir. It comes from a girl. You've a *taio* of your own."

"He pays me no attention these days. What have you there?"

"A bundle of tapa cloth."

Hallet stooped to feel the thick bundle and gave the seaman an evil smile. "It feels uncommonly like a sucking pig. Shall I call Mr. Samuel?" Ellison flushed and the other went on, without giving him time to reply, "See here! A bargain — the fan's mine, and I say nothing about the pig."

Without a word, the young seaman snatched up his bundle and strode off to the forecastle in a rage, leaving the fan in his superior's hands. I was about to utter angry words when Samuel, the captain's clerk, walked aft. Hallet stopped him. "Do you want a bit of tender pork?" he asked in a low voice.

"Then go to the forecastle.   I suspect that Ellison has a sucking pig wrapped up in a bale of the Indian cloth!"   Samuel gave him a nod and a knowing leer, and passed.   I stepped forward.

"You little swine!" I said to Hallet.

"You 've been spying on me, Byam!" he squeaked.

"And if you were not such a contemptible little sneak, I 'd do more than that!"

The captain's boat was approaching, and, swallowing my anger, I began to prepare the manuscript of my week's work for his inspection.   Half an hour later, when the interview with Bligh was over and we came on deck, I found Christian at the gangway, to receive a gift of provisions and other things sent out by Maimiti, a great landowner in her own right.

There were a brace of fat hogs, as well as taro, plantains, and other vegetables; fine mats, Indian cloaks, and a pair of very handsome pearls from the Low Islands.   Bligh strolled to the gangway, and, seeing the hogs, called for Samuel and ordered him to take them over for ship's stores.   Christian flushed.

"Mr. Bligh," he said, "I meant these hogs for my own mess."

"No!" answered the captain harshly.

He glanced at the mats and cloaks, which Christian was about to send below.   "Mr. Samuel," he went on, "take charge of these Indian curiosities, which may be useful for trading in other groups."

"One moment, sir," protested Christian.   "These things were given me for members of my family in England."

Instead of replying, the captain turned away contemptuously toward the gangway.   Maimiti's servant was handing up to Christian a small package done up in the tapa cloth. "Pearls," said the man in the Indian tongue.   "My mistress sends them to you, to be given your mother in England." Still deeply flushed with anger, Christian took the package from the man's hand.

"Did he say pearls?" put in Bligh. "Come—let me see them!"

Samuel craned his neck and I admit that I did the same. Reluctantly, and in angry silence, Christian unwrapped the small package to display a matched pair of pearls as large as gooseberries, and of the most perfect orient. Samuel, a London Jew, permitted himself an exclamation of astonishment. After a moment's hesitation, Bligh spoke.

"Give them to Mr. Samuel," he ordered. "Pearls are highly prized in the Friendly Islands."

"Surely, sir," exclaimed Christian angrily, "you do not mean to seize these as well! They were given me for my mother!"

"Deliver them to Mr. Samuel," Bligh repeated.

"I refuse!" replied Christian, controlling himself with a great effort.

He turned away abruptly, closing his hand on the pearls, and went below. A glance passed between the captain and his clerk, but though Bligh's hands were clasping and unclasping behind his back, he said no more.

It was not hard to imagine the feelings of the *Bounty's* people at this time—rationed in the midst of plenty, and treated like smugglers each time they returned from shore. There must have been much angry murmuring in the forecastle, for the contrast between life on shore and life on the ship was over-sharp. I had a home and my mother to return to, but the seamen could look forward to nothing in England save the prospect of the press gang, or begging on the Portsmouth streets. It seemed to me that if Mr. Bligh continued as he had begun, we should soon have desertions or worse.

Going on board to report myself one morning in mid-January, I found the captain pacing the quarter-deck in a rage. I stood to leeward of him for some time before he noticed me, and then, catching his eye, I saluted him and said, "Come on board, sir."

"Ah, Mr. Byam," he said, coming to a halt abruptly. "I cannot run over your work to-day; we'll put it off till next week. The ship's corporal and two of the seamen — Muspratt and Millward — have deserted. The ungrateful scoundrels shall suffer for this when I get my hands on them! They took the small cutter and eight stand of arms and ammunition. I have just learned that they left the cutter not far from here and set out for Tetiaroa in a sailing canoe." Mr. Bligh paused, his face set sternly, and seemed to reflect. "Has your *taio* a large canoe?" he asked.

"Yes, sir," I replied.

"In that case I shall put the pursuit in your hands. Ask for Hitihiti's canoe and as many of his men as you think necessary, and sail for Tetiaroa to-day. The wind is fair. Secure the men without using force if you can, but secure them! Churchill may give you some trouble. Should you find that they are not on the island, return to-morrow if the wind permits."

When I had taken leave of the captain, I found Stewart and Tinkler in the berth.

"You've heard the news, of course," said Stewart.

"Yes; Mr. Bligh told me, and I've the task of catching the men."

Stewart laughed. "By God! I don't envy you!"

"How did they make off with the cutter?" I asked.

"Hayward was mate of the watch, and was fool enough to take a caulk. The men stole away with the cutter while he slept. Bligh was like a madman when he learned it. He's put Hayward in irons for a month, and threatens to have him flogged on the day of his release!"

An hour later I found Hitihiti at the house, and told him of my orders and of the captain's request for the loan of his large sailing canoe. He agreed at once to let me have her, with a dozen of his men, and insisted on accompanying the expedition himself.

My host's vessel was of the kind called *va'a motu* — a single sailing canoe, about fifty feet long and two foot beam. On the larboard side, at a distance of about a fathom from the hull, was a long outrigger, or float, made fast to cross booms fore and aft, which crossed the gunwales and were lashed fast to them. Her mast was tall and strongly stayed, and her great sail of closely woven matting was bordered with a light frame of saplings.

I watched idly while Hitihiti's retainers rolled the vessel out from her shed where she was kept, carefully oiled and chocked high above the ground. They fetched the mast and stepped it, and set up the standing rigging all ataut. Then, in their leisurely fashion, the women of the household fetched bunches of newly husked drinking nuts and other provisions for the voyage. The men seemed to look forward eagerly to the expedition — a break in the dreamy monotony of their lives. Counting on taking the deserters by surprise, they seemed to have no fear of the muskets, but Hitihiti asked me with some concern if I were sure that Churchill and his companions had no pistols. When I assured him that the deserters were not provided with pistols, he brightened at once, and began to speak of the voyage.

We sailed at two o'clock in the afternoon, with a fresh easterly breeze on the beam. Tetiaroa lies almost due north of Matavai, about thirty miles distant. It is a cluster of five low coral islands, set here and there on the reef which encircles a lagoon some four miles across, and is the property of what mariners call the royal family — that of the great chief Teina, or Pomare. It is the fashionable watering place for the chiefs of the north end of Tahiti; they repair to its shady groves to recover from the ravages of the *ava* with which they constantly intoxicate themselves, and to live on a light wholesome diet of coconuts and fish. And to Tetiaroa also repair the *pori* — the young girls, one from each district of Tahiti, who are placed on stone platforms at certain times of the year, where they may be admired and compared with their competitors by passers-by. In Tetiaroa, these *pori* are fed on a special diet, kept in the shade to bleach their skins, and constantly rubbed with the perfumed mollifying oil called *monoi;* and I must do the old women who care for them the justice to remark that the whole of Europe might be searched without finding a score of young females lovelier than the *pori* I saw on one small coral island.

As we bore away for Tetiaroa I began to appreciate the qualities of Hitihiti's canoe. Amidships, a long, heavy plank, adzed out of a breadfruit tree, extended from the outrigger float, across the gunwales, and well outboard on the weather side. Four or five of the heaviest men of our crew now took their places on this plank, well out to windward, to prevent us from capsizing in the gusts. Two other men were employed constantly in bailing, as the canoe tore through the waves at a speed of not less than twelve knots. The *Bounty* sailed well, as ships went in those days, but Hitihiti's little vessel would have sailed two miles to her one. The chief and I sat side by side on a seat in her high stern, well above the spray which flew over her bows as she sliced through the waves.

At considerable hazard we ran our canoe over the reef and into the calm waters of the Tetiaroa lagoon. There we were soon surrounded by small canoes and swimmers, all eager to impart some information of importance: the deserters, fearing pursuit, had set sail two or three hours before, some thought for Eimeo, others for the west side of Tahiti. The wind was dying away, as it does toward sunset in this region, and since darkness would soon set in and we had no certain knowledge of Churchill's destination, Hitihiti deemed it best to spend the night on Tetiaroa, and return to Bligh with our news when the morning breeze made up.

I shall not forget the night I spent on the coral island. The Indians of Tahiti are by nature a people given over to levity, passionately devoted to pleasure, and incapable of those

burdens of the white man — worry and care.   And in Tetiaroa,
their watering place, they seemed to cast aside whatever light
cares of family and state they feel when at home, and pass the
time in entertainments of every kind, by night and by day.
Relieved of his mission, which I am convinced he would have
done his utmost to accomplish under other circumstances,
Hitihiti now seemed to forget everything but the prospects of
entertainment ashore, directing his paddlers to make at once
for the nearest islet, called Rimatuu.

Three or four chiefs and their retinues were on the islet at
the time, and, as its area was no more than five hundred acres,
the place seemed densely populated.   We were lodged at the
house of a famous warrior named Poino, whose recent excesses
in drinking the *ava* had nearly cost him his life.   He lay on a
pile of mats, scarcely able to move, his skin scaling off and
green as verdigris, but Hitihiti informed me that in a month
he would be quite restored.   Several of Poino's relatives had
accompanied him to Tetiaroa, and among them was a young
girl, a member of the great Vehiatua family of Taiarapu, in
charge of two old women.   I had a glimpse of her in the distance as we supped, but thought no more of the young lady
till after nightfall, when I was invited to see a *heiva,* or Indian
entertainment.

Strolling with Hitihiti through the groves, we saw the flare
of torchlight some distance ahead, and heard the beating of
the small drums — a hollow, resonant sound with a strange
measure.   My friend's head went up and his step quickened.
Ahead of us, in a large clearing, there was a raised platform of
hewn blocks of coral, about which no less than two or three
hundred spectators were seated on the ground.   The scene was
brightly illuminated by torches of coconut leaves, bound in
long bundles and held aloft by serving men, who lighted fresh
ones as fast as the old burned out.   As we took our places,
two clowns, called *faaata,* were finishing a performance which
raised a gale of laughter, and as they stepped off the platform

six young women, accompanied by four drummers, trooped
on to perform.   These girls were of the lower order of society,
and their dance was believed by the Indians to ensure the fertility of the crops.   The dress of the dancers consisted of no
more than a wreath of flowers and green leaves about their
waists, and the dance itself, in which they stood in two lines
of three, face to face, was of a nature so unbelievably wanton
that no words could convey the least idea of it.   But if the
clowns had raised a gale of laughter, the dance raised a hurricane.   Hitihiti laughed as heartily as the rest — the antics of
one girl, in fact, brought the tears to his eyes and caused him to
slap his thigh resoundingly.   Presently the dance was over
and, in the pause that followed, my *taio* informed me that we
were now to see a dance of a very different kind.

The second group of dancers came through the crowd,
which parted right and left before them, each girl escorted
by two old women and announced by a herald, who shouted
her name and titles as she stepped on to the platform.   All were
dressed alike and very beautifully, in flowing draperies of
snow-white Indian cloth, and the curious headdresses called
tamau.   They carried fans, with handles curiously carved,
and over their breasts they wore plates of pearl shell, polished
till they gleamed like mirrors, and tinted with all the colors
of the rainbow.   Selected for their beauty, nurtured with the
greatest care, kept constantly in the shade, and beautified with
the numerous Indian cosmetics, these girls were of the most
exquisite loveliness.   Poino's young relative, the second to be
announced, caused a murmur of admiration among the spectators.

Like all the Indians of the upper class, she was a full head
taller than the commoners.   Her figure was of the most perfect symmetry, her skin smooth and blooming as an apricot,
and her dark lustrous eyes set wide apart in a face so lovely
that I caught my breath at sight of her.   While the herald
announced her long name, and longer list of titles, she stood

facing us, her eyes cast down proudly and modestly. Judging that the announcement was unintelligible to me, Hitihiti leaned over and whispered the girl's household name.

"Tehani," he announced in my ear, which is to say "The Darling," a name by no means inappropriate, I thought. The *hura* is danced in couples, and next moment Tehani and the first girl began to dance. The measure is slow, stately, and of great beauty, the movements of the arms, in particular, being wonderfully graceful and performed in the most exact time. When Tehani and her companion retired from the stage, amid hearty applause, they were succeeded by a brace of clowns, whose antics kept us laughing till the next pair of girls was ready to dance. But I scarcely noticed the other performers, for I was eager to return to the house, whither I knew Tehani had been led. It was fortunate for my work and my peace of mind, I thought somewhat ruefully, that she was not a member of Hitihiti's household, yet I knew that I would have given anything I possessed to have had her there. But I was not destined to see her again in Tetiaroa, for her two old duennas guarded her closely in a small separate house.

We sailed about two hours after sunrise, with the east wind abeam, and I was able to make my report to Mr. Bligh the same afternoon. The deserters were not apprehended till nearly three weeks later, when they gave themselves up, worn out by guarding against the constant attempts of the Indians to capture them. Churchill was given two dozen lashes, and Muspratt and Millward four dozen each.

The *Bounty* had at this time been shifted to a new anchorage in the harbour of Toaroa, where she was moored close to the shore. It had been Bligh's intention to have Hayward flogged with the deserters, and on the morning of the punishment, happening to be on board, I saw Hayward's *taio*, a chief named Moana, standing on deck with a sullen and gloomy face. But at the last moment the captain changed his mind and ordered Hayward below, to serve out the balance of his month in irons. On the same night an incident occurred which might have caused the loss of the ship and left us marooned among the Indians without the means of returning to England. The wind blew fresh from northwest all night, directly on shore, and at daybreak it was discovered that two strands of the small bower cable had been cut through, and that only one strand was holding the *Bounty* off the rocks. Mr. Bligh made a great to-do about the affair, but it was not till sometime afterwards that I learned the truth of it.

Hitihiti told me that Moana, Hayward's *taio*, was so incensed at the prospect of seeing the midshipman flogged that he had gone aboard that morning with a loaded pistol concealed under his cloak, planning to shoot Mr. Bligh through the heart before the first stroke of the cat could be delivered. Seeing his *taio* escape a flogging, but sent below to be confined, Moana conceived the idea of releasing his friend by wrecking the ship. He sent one of his henchmen to sever the cable under cover of night, and had the man performed his task properly the ship would infallibly have been lost.

I reflected for some time on Hitihiti's words, and finally, considering the incident closed and knowing that the cables were now watched with extra care throughout the night, I came to the conclusion that it was not necessary to inform Mr. Bligh of what I had learned. To tell him would only have increased his harshness to Hayward, and caused trouble with Moana, a powerful chief.

Toward the end of March it became evident to all hands that the *Bounty* would soon set sail. More than a thousand young breadfruit trees, in pots and tubs, had been taken on board, and the great cabin aft resembled a botanical garden with the young plants standing thick in their racks, all in a most flourishing condition, their foliage of the richest dark green. Great quantities of pork had been salted down, under the captain's direction, and a large sea store of yams laid in. Only Mr. Bligh knew when we would sail, but it was clear that the day of departure could not be far off.

I confess that I felt no eagerness to leave Tahiti. No man could have lived with so kind a host as Hitihiti without becoming deeply attached to the old man and his family, and my work on the Indian language interested me more each day. I was now able to carry on ordinary conversations with some fluency, though I knew enough to realize that a real mastery of this complex tongue would require years. The vocabulary I had planned was now complete and had been many times revised as I perceived mistakes, and I had made good progress on the grammar. Leading a life of the most delightful ease and tranquillity, and engaged on a congenial task in which I felt that I was making some headway, it is not to be wondered at that for days at a time I scarcely gave England a thought. Had it not been for my mother, I believe that I might have been content to settle down to a long period of the Indian life, and had I been assured that another vessel would touch at Tahiti within six months or a year, I should certainly have asked Mr. Bligh's permission to stop over and complete my work.

Christian, whom I had grown to know well, disliked the thought of departure as much as I. His attachment to Maimiti was of the tenderest description, and I knew how he must dread the final parting from her. Of the midshipmen, Stewart was as deeply attached to his Indian sweetheart as Christian himself. Young was constantly in the company of a girl called Taurua, the Indian name for the evening star. Stewart called his sweetheart Peggy; she was the daughter of a chief of some consequence on the north end of the island, and devotedly attached to him.

A day or two before the *Bounty* sailed, Christian, Young, and Stewart strolled up the beach to call on me, accompanied by Alexander Smith, my hammock man. Smith had formed an alliance with a short, dark, lively girl of the lower orders, who loved him in the robust fashion of a sailor's lass.   He called her Bal'hadi, which was as close as his honest English tongue could twist itself to Paraha Iti, her true name.

We had been so long in Tahiti, and my shipmates had been so constantly in the company of the natives, that many of them were able to make themselves understood to some extent in the Indian language.   Both Stewart and Ellison spoke it remarkably well, and Young and Smith had likewise made considerable progress in it.   Smith, nevertheless, was of the opinion that, if English were spoken slowly and in a loud voice, it must be a stupid foreigner indeed who could fail to understand.

As my visitors from the *Bounty* approached the house I knew instinctively that Christian had news for me, but he had been so much among the Indians that he had acquired some notion of their ceremonial ideas of politeness, which demand a decent interval of light conversation before any important announcement is made.

Maimiti greeted her lover affectionately, and old Hitihiti had mats spread for us in the shade and ordered drinking coconuts to be fetched.   My host had asked me, as a last favour, to have made for him a model of the *Bounty's* launch, which he admired greatly.   He believed that with the aid of this model his native shipwrights would be able to build a boat, since I had explained to him the process of warping a plank.   I had entrusted the model making to Smith, who had completed the task in less than a week, with every dimension true to scale. He walked behind the others, followed by Bal'hadi, who carried the model on her shoulder.   Hitihiti's face lit up at sight of it.

"Now I shall start my boat," he said to me in the native tongue.   "You have kept your word and I am well content!"

"Let him remember," said Smith, "a foot to the inch and he can't go wrong, I'll warrant!"

He handed the model to Hitihiti, who took it with every sign of pleasure and gave me an order to one of his servants, who soon appeared leading a pair of fine hogs.

"They are for you, Smith," I explained, but my hammock man shook his head regretfully.

"No use, sir," he said. "Mr. Bligh won't let us keep the pigs our *taios* send on board. But if the old chief would give me a sucking pig, me and my lass could cook and eat it in no time." He smacked his lips and gave me a hopeful glance.

Hitihiti smiled with pleasure at the request and directed that Smith should go with one of the Indians to pick out the pig that pleased him best. A few minutes later the seaman passed us, his sweetheart at his side and a squealing young porker under his arm. They disappeared into a thicket near the beach, and presently we heard louder squeals, followed by silence, and saw a column of smoke rising above the trees. I have a fancy that the Indian law which prohibited women from dining with men was broken that day.

Reclining in the shade and drinking the sweet milk of young coconuts, we had been gossiping idly with the girls, and presently Christian glanced up and caught my eye.

"I have news for you, Byam," he said. "We are to set sail on Saturday. Mr. Bligh bids you come on board on Friday night."

As if she understood the words, Maimiti looked at me sorrowfully, took her lover's hand and held it tight. "Bad news for me, at any rate," Christian went on. "I have been very happy here."

"And for me," put in Stewart, with a glance at his Peggy.

Young yawned. "I'm not sentimental," he remarked. "Taurua here will soon find another fancy man." The lively brown-eyed girl at his side understood his words perfectly. She tossed her head in denial and gave him a playful slap on the cheek. Christian smiled.

"Young is right," he said; "when the true seaman leaves one

sweetheart he is already looking forward to the next! But I find it hard to practise what I preach!"

Toward evening our guests left us to return to the ship, and I was forced to follow them the next day. I took leave of Hitihiti and his household with sincere regret, fully convinced that I should never see any one of them again.

I found the *Bounty* crowded with Indians, and loaded with coconuts, plantains, hogs, and goats. The great chief Teina and his wife were the captain's guests and slept on the ship that night. At daybreak we worked out through the narrow Toaroa passage, and stood off and on all day, while Bligh took leave of Teina and made up his parting gifts to the chief. Just before sunset the launch was sent ashore with Teina and Itea, while we manned the ship with all hands and gave them three hearty cheers. An hour later the helm was put up and the *Bounty* stood off shore with all sail set.

VIII

HOMEWARD BOUND

Now that we were at sea again, I had time to observe the change
that had come over the ship's company as a result of our long
island sojourn. In colour we were almost as brown as the
Indians, and most of us were tattooed on various parts of our
bodies with strange designs that added to our exotic appearance. The Tahitians are wonderfully skilled at tattooing, and
although the process of acquiring it is both slow and painful,
there were few of the men who had not been willing to undergo
the torture for the sake of carrying home such evidence of
their adventures in the South Sea. Edward Young was the
most completely decorated of the midshipmen. On either
leg he carried the design of a coconut tree, the trunk beginning at the heel and the foliage spreading out over the fleshy
part of the calf. Encircling the thighs were wide bands of
conventionalized design, and on his back he had the picture
of a breadfruit tree, done with such spirit that one could
all but hear the rustle of the wind through its branches.

In addition to such pictures, there was scarcely a man on
the ship who had not acquired some words and phrases of the
Tahitian language, which they took care to use in their talk
with one another. A few had become remarkably proficient,
and could carry on conversations in which scarcely a word of
English was to be heard. All of them had pieces of the Indian
cloth, and it was a curious sight, in the early mornings when
they were washing down the decks, to see them at their work

dressed only in turbans of tapa, with a strip of the same material about their loins, and jabbering away with great fluency in the Indian tongue. An Englishman fresh from home would hardly have recognized them as fellow countrymen.

There was an inward change as noticeable to any thoughtful observer as these outward ones. Duties were performed as usual, but there was little heartiness displayed, and this applied to some of the officers as well as to the men. Never, I fancy, has one of His Majesty's ships been worked homeward, after long absence, with less enthusiasm.

I was talking of this matter one day with Mr. Nelson, who was always to be found during the daylight hours in the great cabin, looking after his beloved breadfruit plants. I felt vaguely uneasy at this time, and it was always a comforting experience to talk with Mr. Nelson. He was one of those men who are truly called the salt of the earth, and was a rock of peace in our somewhat turbulent ship's company. I confessed that I was disturbed, without knowing exactly why, at the way the ship's work was going on. Nelson thought there was nothing to be concerned about.

"Does it seem strange to you, my dear fellow, that we should all feel a little let down after our idyllic life at Tahiti? I am surprised that the men show as much willingness as they do. My own feelings as I think of England ahead of us and Tahiti behind are decidedly mixed ones. Yours must be, too."

"I admit that they are," I replied.

"Imagine, then, how the men must feel, who have so little to go home to. What have they to expect at the end of the voyage? Before they have been a week ashore most of them may be seized by some press gang as recruits for another of His Majesty's ships. Who knows what the situation may be by the time the *Bounty* reaches England? We may be at war with France, or Spain, or Holland, or heaven knows what power; and in that case, alas for any poor seamen arriving in a home port! They won't even be given the chance to spend their back pay. The sailor leads a dog's life, Byam, and no mistake."

"Do you think war with France is likely?" I asked.

"War with France is always likely," he replied, smiling. "If I were an A.B. I should curse the thought of any war. Think what a paradise Tahiti has been for our men. For once in their lives they have been treated as human beings. They have had abundant food, easy duties, and unlimited opportunities for the sailor's chief distraction, women. I confess that I was surprised, before we left Tahiti, that the lot of them didn't take to the hills. Certainly I should have done so had I been in any of their places."

As the days passed, and we left Tahiti farther and farther astern, the memory of our life there seemed like that of a dream, and gradually, one by one, we fell into the old routine. No unhappy incidents occurred to mar the peace of that period. Captain Bligh took his regular turns on the quarter-deck, but he rarely spoke to anyone, and most of his time was spent in his cabin, where he was busy working on his charts of the islands. So all went quietly enough until the morning of April 23, when we sighted the island of Namuka, in the Friendly Archipelago. Bligh had been here before, with Captain Cook, and it was his intention to replenish our wood and water before proceeding in the direction of Endeavour Straits.

The wind being to the southward, we had some difficulty in making the land, and it was not until late afternoon that we came to anchor in the road, in twenty-three fathoms. The island was much less romantic in appearance than Tahiti or any of the Society Islands that we had seen, but I was conscious of the same feeling of awe and wonder I had experienced elsewhere as I looked upon lands which only a handful of white men had ever seen, and whose very existence, to say nothing of their names, was unknown to people at home.

On the morning of the twenty-fourth we weighed and

worked more to the eastward, and again anchored a mile and
a half from shore, at a more convenient place for our watering
parties.   By this time the arrival of the ship was known far
and wide on shore, and the Indians were arriving not only from
various parts of Namuka, but from neighbouring islands as
well.   We had scarcely come to our new anchorage before
we were surrounded with canoes, and our decks were so filled
with people that we had difficulty in performing our duties.
At first the confusion was great, but order was established when
two chiefs came aboard whom Bligh remembered from his
visit in 1777.   We were able to make them understand that
the decks must be cleared, and they set about it in so resolute
and impetuous a manner that soon all of the Indians, except
those in the chiefs' retinues, were again in their canoes.   Captain Bligh then called me to him to act as interpreter, but I
found that my study of the Tahitian language was of little
service here.   The Friendly Island speech, although it has
points of resemblance, differs greatly from the Tahitian.
However, with the aid of signs and an occasional word or
phrase, we explained our purpose in coming, and, the chiefs
having shouted some orders to their people, most of the canoes
made speedily for shore.

It was Captain Cook who had given the name, "The Friendly
Islands," to this archipelago, but my own impressions of its
inhabitants were far from favourable.   They resembled the
Tahitians in stature, the colour of the skin and hair, and it
was plain that they belonged to the same great family; but
there was an insolent boldness in their behaviour lacking in the
deportment of the Tahitians.   They were thieves of the worst
order and, if offered the slightest opportunity, would seize
whatever loose article lay nearest and leap overboard with it.
Christian was strongly of the opinion that they were not to be
trusted in any respect, and suggested that a strong guard accompany the parties to be sent ashore for wood and water.   Captain Bligh laughed at the notion.

"Surely you're not afraid of the beggars, Mr. Christian?"

"No, sir, but I think we have reason to be cautious in our dealings with them. In my opinion . . ."

He was not permitted to finish.

"And who's asked you for your opinion? Damme! If I haven't an old woman for my second-in-command! Come, Mr. Nelson, we must do something to reassure these timid souls," and he went down the ladder to the cutter that was waiting to row him ashore. Mr. Nelson followed — he was to collect some breadfruit plants to replace several that had died during the voyage — and the party, including the two chiefs, set out for the beach.

This little scene had taken place before many of the ship's company, and I could see that Christian had controlled his temper with difficulty. Mr. Bligh had the unfortunate habit of making such humiliating remarks to his officers, no matter who might be within hearing. It may be said in his defense, perhaps, that, being a thick-skinned man, he had no conception of how galling such remarks could be, particularly to a man like Christian.

As it chanced, nothing unusual happened that day. The fact that Mr. Bligh had gone off with two of the chiefs was a guarantee that his party would not be molested. Later in the day the natives came off to trade, bringing the usual island produce — pigs, fowls, coconuts, yams, and plantains. The afternoon and the whole of the following day were given up to this business, and the third morning the wood and watering parties were sent ashore in Christian's charge. It was then that his distrust of the Indians proved fully justified, for we had no sooner set foot on the beach than they began to make trouble for us. Mr. Bligh had not refused to send a guard with the ship's boats, but he had given strict orders that the arms were not to be used. Hayward was in charge of the cutter and I of the launch, and Christian went with the shore parties. The Indians thronged to the watering place, several hundred

yards from the beach. Every effort was made to keep them
at a distance, but they became increasingly bold as the work
went on, and we had not been half an hour ashore before several
of the sailors, who were cutting wood, had had their axes
snatched from their hands. Christian performed his work
admirably, in the opinion of all the shore party, and it was
thanks to his coolness that we were not rushed and overwhelmed by the savages. They outnumbered us fifty to one.
We managed to get down our wood and water without coming
to a pitched battle, but when we were getting off, toward sundown, they rushed us and managed to make off with the grapnel of the cutter.

When we arrived on board and our losses were reported by
Christian, Captain Bligh flew into a rage, cursing him in language that would have been out of place had he been speaking
to a common sailor.

"You are an incompetent cowardly rascal, sir! Damn me
if you 're not! Are you afraid of a crowd of bloody savages
whilst you have arms in your hands?"

"Of what service are they, sir, when you forbid their use?"
Christian asked quietly. Bligh ignored this question and continued to pour out such a flood of abuse that Christian turned
abruptly and left him, going down to his cabin. When in one
of his rages Bligh seemed insane. I had never before met a
man of this kind, and my conclusion was, having observed
him so often in this state, that he had little recollection, afterward, of what he had said or done. I observed that he frequently worked himself into these passions over matters for
which he was really to blame. Being unwilling to admit a
fault in his own conduct, it seemed necessary to convince himself, through anger, that the blame lay elsewhere.

Usually, after Bligh had given vent to a fit of this sort, we
could promise ourselves several days of calm, during which
time he would have little or nothing to say to us, but it
chanced that the following day a similar incident occurred

which was to have the gravest consequences for all of us. I am no believer in fate. Men's actions, in so far as their relationships with one another are concerned, are largely under their own control; but there are times when malicious powers seem to order our small human affairs for their own amusement, and one of these occasions must surely have been on the twenty-seventh day of April, in the year 1789.

We had sailed from Namuka on the evening of the twenty-sixth and, the wind being light, had made but little progress during the night. All of the following day we were within seven or eight leagues of the land. The supplies we had received from the Indians were being stored away, and the carpenters were making pens for the pigs and crates for the fowls not intended for early use. Mr. Bligh had kept to his cabin all the morning, but early in the afternoon he appeared on deck to give some instructions to Mr. Samuel, who was in charge of the work of sorting over our purchases at Namuka. A great many coconuts had been piled up on the quarter-deck between the guns, and Bligh, who knew to the last ounce how many yams we had purchased, and the exact number of coconuts, discovered that a few of the latter were missing. He may have been told of this by Samuel, but at any rate he knew it.

He ordered all the officers to come on deck immediately, and questioned each of them as to the number of coconuts he had bought on his own account, and whether or not he had seen any one of the men helping himself to those on the quarter-deck. All denied having any such knowledge, and Bligh, doubtless thinking that the officers were shielding the men, became more and more angry. At length he came to Christian.

"Now, Mr. Christian, I wish to know the exact number of coconuts you purchased for your own use."

"I really don't know, sir," Christian replied, "but I hope you don't think me so mean as to be guilty of stealing yours?"

"Yes, you bloody hound! I *do* think so! You must have

stolen some of mine or you would be able to give a better account of your own. You 're damned rascals and thieves, the lot of you! You 'll be stealing my yams next, or have the men steal them for you! But I 'll make you suffer! I 'll teach you to steal, you dogs! I 'll break the spirit of every man of you! You 'll wish you 'd never seen me before we reach Endeavour Straits!"

Of all the humiliating scenes that had taken place up to that time, this was the worst; and yet, considering the nature of the offense committed, there was something meanly comic about it. Christian, however, could not see this side of the matter, and small wonder that he could not. No other captain in His Majesty's service would have made such an accusation against his second-in-command, to say nothing of his other officers. Bligh stamped up and down the quarter-deck, his face distorted with passion, shaking his fists and shouting at us as though we were at the other end of the ship. Of a sudden he stopped.

"Mr. Samuel!"

"Yes, sir," said Samuel, stepping forward.

"You 'll stop the villains' grog until further orders. And instead of a pound of yams per man you 'll issue half a pound to all the messes. Understand?"

"Yes, sir."

"And, by God, I 'll reduce you to a quarter of a pound if I find anything else missing, and make you crawl on your bellies for that!"

He then gave orders that all of the coconuts, belonging to officers and men alike, be carried aft to add to the ship's stores. When this had been done he returned to his cabin.

I never remember the ship to have been more silent than she was that evening. Most of us, doubtless, were thinking of the long voyage ahead. Another year might pass before the *Bounty* could reach England. Meanwhile we should be under the heavy hand of a captain who could do with us as he pleased; against whose tyranny there could be no appeal. My own mess was particularly silent, for at this time Samuel was a member of it, and we knew that anything we might say would be quickly carried to Captain Bligh. Peckover ate his salt junk and his half a pound of yams in a few savage bites, and withdrew. The rest of us were not long in following.

Mr. Fryer's watch came on at eight o'clock. Most of the ship's company were on deck during the early hours, owing to the fineness of the evening. The breeze had been light all day and remained so; we had no more than steerageway, but the air was refreshingly cool. The moon was in its first quarter, and by its light we could dimly see, far ahead, the outline of the island of Tofoa.

Between ten and eleven Bligh came on deck to leave his orders for the night. He paced up and down the quarter-deck for some time, paying no attention to anyone. Presently he stopped near Fryer, who ventured to say: "Sir, I think we shall have a fine breeze by and by. This moon coming on will be fortunate for us when we approach the coast of New Holland."

"Yes, Mr. Fryer, so it will," he replied. A few minutes later he gave his orders as to the course to be steered, and returned to his cabin.

Fryer's prediction of wind was not to be fulfilled. At midnight, when our watch went off duty, the sea was like a mill pond, with a glassy sheen upon the water, reflecting the Southern constellations. Going below, I found it much too hot for sleep. Tinkler and I came on deck together and stood for a while by the rail aft, talking of home and what we would choose for our first meal on shore. Presently, looking around cautiously, he said: "Byam, do you know that I am a double-dyed villain? I stole one of Mr. Bligh's missing coconuts."

"So it's you we have to thank for our dressing-down, you little rascal," I replied.

"Alas, yes. I'm one of the damned rogues and thieves. I could tell you the names of two others, but I forbear. We were thirsty and too lazy to go to the main top for the gun barrel. And there were the coconuts, such a tempting sight, a great heap of them between the guns on the quarter-deck. I wish they were there now; I'd steal another. There's nothing more refreshing than coconut water. Curse old Nelson's breadfruit garden! It keeps a man thirsty all the time."

We were all, in fact, envious of our breadfruit plants. Whatever happened, they had to be watered regularly, and in order to cut down the amount drunk by the ship's company Bligh had thought of a very excellent and ingenious arrangement to prevent us from quenching our thirst too often. Any man who wanted a drink had first to climb to the main top to fetch a gun barrel left there. He then climbed down with this to the scuttle butt, outside the galley, inserted the gun barrel into the bunghole, and, having sucked up his drink, he was required to carry the drinking tube to the main top again. No man, no matter how thirsty he might be, was permitted to make more than two of these gun-barrel climbs during his watch, and a lazy man did without his drink until thirst got the better of him.

"God be thanked! For once I wasn't suspected," Tinkler went on. "How do you explain that? If he had asked me I should have denied, of course, that I'd had anything to do with his rotten coconuts. But I'm afraid my guilty conscience might have given me away this time. I was so damned sorry for Christian."

"Did Christian know that you had taken some of the nuts?"

"Not some—only one, mind you! As I've told you, there were fellow conspirators. Of course he did. In fact, he saw me do it and looked the other way, as any decent officer was bound to do. It wasn't as though we were endangering the safety of the vessel. Four coconuts missing, that's all—I give you my word. Four out of how many thousands? And

I was responsible for only one. Well, if I sleep over my sins, perhaps they won't seem so black to-morrow."

Tinkler was like the ship's cat; he could curl up anywhere for a nap. He now lay down by one of the quarter-deck guns, with his arm for a pillow, and, as I thought, was soon fast asleep.

It was then about one o'clock, and with the exception of the watch there was no one on deck but Tinkler and myself. Mr. Peckover was standing at the rail on the opposite side of the deck. I could make out his form dimly in the starlight. Someone appeared at the after ladderway. It was Christian. After half a dozen turns up and down the deck, he observed me standing between the guns.

"Oh, it's you, Byam?" He came and stood beside me, his elbows on the rail. I had not seen him since the affair of the afternoon.

At length he asked, "Did you know that he had invited me to sup with him? Why? Can you tell me that? After spitting on me, wiping his feet on me, he sent Samuel to ask me to eat at his table!"

"You didn't go?"

"After what had happened? God in heaven, no!"

I had never before seen a man in a mood of such black despair. He seemed at the last extremity of endurance. I was glad to be there, to be of service as a confidant, for it was plain that he was in desperate need of unburdening himself. That Bligh should have asked him to supper was, in truth, all but incredible, after the events of the afternoon. I suggested that it might be taken as evidence of an unsuspected delicacy of conscience in Bligh, but I believed this no more than did Christian himself.

"We're in his power. Officers and men alike, he considers us so many dogs to be kicked or fondled according to his whim. And there can be no relief. None. Not till we reach England. God knows when that will be!"

He was silent for some time, staring gloomily out over the starlit sea.   At length he said, "Byam, there's something I wish you would do for me."

"What is it?"

"The chances are there'll be no occasion, but on a long voyage like this one never knows what may happen.   If, for any reason, I should fail to reach home, I'd like you to see my people in Cumberland.   Would that be too much trouble for you?"

"Not at all," I replied.

"During the last conversation I had with my father, just before I joined the ship, he asked that I make such an arrangement with someone aboard the *Bounty*.   In case anything should happen, he said that it would be a comfort to him to talk with one of my friends.   I promised, and I've let half the voyage pass without fulfilling it.   I feel better now that I have spoken."

"You can count on me," I said, shaking his hand.

"Good!   That's settled, then."

"Well, Mr. Christian!   You're up late."

We turned quickly to find Bligh standing a yard away.   He was barefoot and dressed only in his shirt and trousers.   Neither of us had heard him approach.

"Yes, sir," Christian replied, coldly.

"And you, Mr. Byam.   Can't you sleep?"

"It's very warm below, sir."

"I hadn't noticed it.   A true sailor can sleep in an oven if the case requires.   Or on a cake of ice."

He stood there for a moment as though expecting us to make some reply; then he turned abruptly and walked to the ladderway, halting to glance at the trim of the sails before going below again.   Christian and I talked in desultory fashion for a brief time; then he bade me good-night and went forward somewhere.

Tinkler, who had been lying in deep shadow by one of the guns, sat up and stretched his arms with a deep yawn.

"Go below, Byam, and show that you are a true seaman. Damn you and Christian and your gabble! I was just getting drowsy when he came along."

"Did you hear what he said?" I asked.

"About notifying his father in case anything happened? Yes; I could n't help eavesdropping. My father made no such request of me — which only goes to show that he has no hope of my not coming back. . . . I must have a drink. I 've been thinking of nothing but water this past hour, and I 'm not entitled to one before morning. What would you do, in my case?"

"Mr. Peckover has just gone below for a moment," I said. "You might chance it."

"Has he?" Tinkler leaped to his feet. He ran up the shrouds for the gun barrel and had carried it aloft again before Peckover returned. As we went below together I heard three bells strike, and the far-off call of the lookout in the foretop: "All 's well!" I settled myself in my hammock and was soon asleep.

IX

THE MUTINY

SHORTLY after daybreak I was awakened by someone shaking me roughly by the shoulder, and at the same time I was aware of loud voices, Mr. Bligh's among them, and the heavy trampling of feet on deck. Churchill, the master-at-arms, stood by my hammock with a pistol in his hand, and I saw Thompson, holding a musket with the bayonet fixed, stationed by the arms chest which stood on the gratings of the main hatch. At the same time two men, whose names I do not remember, rushed into the berth, and one of them shouted, "We're with you, Churchill! Give us arms!" They were furnished with muskets by Thompson and hurried on deck again. Stewart, whose hammock was next to mine in the larboard berth, was already up and dressing in great haste. Despite the confused tumult of voices overhead, Young was still asleep.

"Have we been attacked, Churchill?" I asked; for my first thought was that the *Bounty* must have drifted close to one of the islands thereabout, and that we had been boarded by the savages.

"Put on your clothes and lose no time about it, Mr. Byam," he replied. "We have taken the ship and Captain Bligh is a prisoner."

Aroused suddenly from the deepest slumber, I did not even then grasp the meaning of what he said, and for a moment sat gazing stupidly at him.

"They've mutinied, Byam!" said Stewart. "Good God.

Churchill! Are you mad? Have you any conception of what you 're doing?"

"We know very well what we 're doing," he replied. "Bligh has brought all this on himself. Now, by God, we 'll make him suffer!"

Thompson shook his musket in menacing fashion. "We 're going to shoot the dog!" he said; "and don't you try any of your young gentlemen's tricks on us, or we 'll murder some more of you! Seize 'em up, Churchill! They 're not to be trusted."

"Hold your tongue and mind the arms chest," Churchill replied. "Come, Mr. Byam, hurry into your clothes. Quintal, stand fast by the door there! No one 's to come forward without my orders — understand?"

"Aye, aye, sir!"

Turning my head, I saw Matthew Quintal at the rear entrance to the berth. Even as I looked, Samuel appeared behind him, dressed only in his trousers, his thin hair standing awry and his pale face considerably paler than its wont. "Mr. Churchill!" he called.

"Go back, you fat swine, or I 'll run you through the guts!" Quintal shouted.

"Mr. Churchill, sir! Allow me to speak to you," Samuel called again.

"Drive him back," Churchill said, and Quintal made so fierce a gesture with his musket that Samuel vanished without waiting to hear more. "Give him a prod in the backside, Quintal," someone shouted, and, looking up, I saw two more armed men leaning over the hatchway.

Without weapons of any sort, there was nothing that Stewart and I could do but obey Churchill's orders. Both he and Thompson were powerful men and we should have been no match for them even had they been unarmed. I immediately thought of Christian, a man as quick in action as in decision, but I knew there could be no hope of his still being at liberty.

He was the officer of the morning watch and had doubtless been rushed and overwhelmed at the very outset of the mutiny, even before Bligh had been secured. Catching my eye, Stewart shook his head slightly, as much as to say, "It's useless. There's nothing to be done."

We dressed in short order, and Churchill then ordered us to precede him along the passage to the fore ladderway. "Keep the others in the berth, Thompson," he called back. "Leave 'em to me; I'll mind 'em!" Thompson replied. There were several armed guards at the fore-hatch, among them Alexander Smith, my hammock man, whose loyalty in whatever situation I should have thought unquestionable. It was a shock to see him in Churchill's party, but the scene that presented itself as we came on deck made me forget the very existence of Smith.

Captain Bligh, naked except for his shirt, and with his hands tied behind his back, was standing by the mizzenmast. Christian stood before him, holding in one hand the end of the line by which Bligh was bound and in the other a bayonet, and around them were several of the able seamen, fully armed, among whom I recognized John Mills, Isaac Martin, Richard Skinner, and Thomas Burkitt. Churchill then said to us, "Stand by here. We mean no harm to either of you unless you take part against us." He then left us.

Stewart and I had taken it for granted that Churchill was the ringleader of the mutineers. As already related, after his attempted desertion at Tahiti he had been severely punished by Bligh. I knew how deeply he hated him, and it was conceivable that such a man could goad himself even to the point of mutiny. But that Christian could have done so, no matter what the provocation, was beyond anything I could have dreamed of as possible. Stewart's only comment was, "Christian! Good God! Then there's no hope."

The situation looked hopeless indeed. At this time the only unarmed men I saw on deck were Captain Bligh and ourselves. The ship was entirely in the hands of the mutineers. Evidently we had been brought up to divide the party of midshipmen below, thus preventing any opportunity for our taking concerted action. In the confusion we made our way aft a little way, and as we approached the spot where Bligh was standing, I heard Christian say, "Will you hold your tongue, sir, or shall I force you to hold it? I'm master of this ship now, and, by God, I'll stand no more of your abuse!" Sweat was pouring down Bligh's face. He had been making a great outcry, shouting, "Murder! Treason!" at the top of his voice.

"Master of my ship, you mutinous dog!" he yelled. "I'll see you hung! I'll have you flogged to ribbons! I'll . . ."

"*Mamu,* sir! Hold your tongue or you are dead this instant!"

Christian placed the point of his bayonet at Bligh's throat with a look in his eye there was no mistaking. "Slit the dog's gullet!" someone shouted; and there were cries of "Let him have it, Mr. Christian!" "Throw him overboard!" "Feed the bastard to the sharks!" and the like. It was only then, I think, that Captain Bligh realized his true situation. He stood for a moment breathing hard, looking about him with an expression of incredulity on his face.

"Mr. Christian, allow me to speak!" he begged hoarsely. "Think what you do! Release me — lay aside your arms! Let us be friends again, and I give you my word that nothing more shall be said of this matter."

"Your word is of no value, sir," Christian replied. "Had you been a man of honour things would never have come to this pass."

"What do you mean to do with me?"

"Shoot you, you bloody rogue!" cried Burkitt, shaking his musket at him.

"Shooting's too good for him! Seize him up at the gratings, Mr. Christian! Give us a chance at him with the cat!"

"That's it!   Seize him up!   Give him a taste of his own poison!"

"Flay the hide off him!"

"Silence!" Christian called, sternly; and then, to Bligh: "We'll give you justice, sir, which is more than you have ever given us.   We'll take you in irons to England . . ."

A dozen protesting voices interrupted him.

"To England?   Never!   We won't have it, Mr. Christian!"

Immediately the deck was again in an uproar, all the mutineers clamouring against Christian's proposal.   Never was the situation with respect to Bligh so critical as at that moment, and it was to his credit that he showed no sign of flinching.   The men were in a savage mood, and it was touch and go as to whether he would be shot where he stood; but he glared at each of them in turn as though challenging them to do so.   Luckily a diversion was created when Ellison came dashing up flourishing a bayonet.   There was no real harm in this lad, but he loved mischief better than his dinner, and, being thoughtless and high-spirited, he could be counted upon to get himself into trouble whenever the opportunity presented itself.   Evidently he considered joining in a mutiny nothing more than a fine lark, and he now came dancing up to Bligh with such a comical expression upon his face that the tension was relieved at once.   The men broke into cheers. "Hooray, Tommy!   Are you with us, lad?"

"Let me guard him, Mr. Christian!" he cried.   "I'll watch him like a cat!"   He skipped up and down in front of Bligh, brandishing his weapon.   "Oh, you rogue!   You old villain! You'd flog us, would you?   You'd stop our grog, would you?   You'd make us eat grass, would you?"

The men cheered him wildly.   "Lay on, lad!" they shouted. "We'll back you!   Give him a jab in the guts!"

"You and your Mr. Samuel!   A pair of swindlers, that's what you are!   Cheating us out of our food!   You've made a pretty penny between you!   You old thief!   You should be a bumboat man. I'll lay you'd make your fortune in no time!"

It was a bitter experience for Bligh to be baited thus by the least of his seamen, but as a matter of fact nothing more fortunate for him could have happened. His life at that moment hung in the balance, and Ellison, in giving vent to his feelings, relieved the pent-up emotions of men who were not glib of speech and could express their hatred of Bligh only in action. Christian realized this, I think, and permitted Ellison to speak his mind, but he soon cut him short and put him in his place.

"Clear the cutter!" he called. "Mr. Churchill!"

"Aye, aye, sir!"

"Fetch up Mr. Fryer and Mr. Purcell! Burkitt!"

"Here, sir!"

"You and Sumner and Mills and Martin—stand guard here over Mr. Bligh!"

Burkitt took the end of the line in one of his huge hairy fists.

"We'll mind him, sir! I'll lay to that!"

"What's your plan, Mr. Christian? We've a right to know," said Sumner. Christian turned quickly and looked at him. "Mind what you're about, Sumner!" he said quietly. "I'm master of this ship! Lively, men, with the cutter."

Several men climbed into the boat to clear out the yams, sweet potatoes, and other ship's stores which were kept there, while others unlashed it and got ready the tackle for hoisting it over the side. Burkitt stood directly in front of Captain Bligh, holding the point of a bayonet within an inch of his breast. Sumner stood behind him with his musket at ready, and the other men on either side. Thompson excepted, they were the hardest characters among the sailors, and Bligh wisely said nothing to arouse them further. Others of the mutineers were stationed about the decks, and there were three at each of the ladderways. I wondered how the affair had been so well and secretly planned. I searched my memory, but could recall no incident of a character in the least suspicious.

I had been so intent in watching the scene of which Bligh was the centre that I had forgotten Stewart. We had become separated, and while I was searching for him Christian saw me for the first time. He came at once to where I was standing. His voice was calm, but I could see that he was labouring under great excitement.

"Byam, this is my affair," he said. "Not a man shall be hurt, but if any take part against us it will be at the peril of the entire ship's company. Act as you think best."

"What do you mean to do?" I asked.

"I would have carried Bligh to England as a prisoner. That is impossible; the men won't have it. He shall have the cutter to go where he chooses. Mr. Fryer, Hayward, Hallet, and Samuel shall go with him."

There was no time for further talk. Churchill came up with the master and Purcell. The carpenter, as usual, was surly and taciturn. Both he and Fryer were horror-stricken at what had happened, but they were entirely self-possessed. Christian well knew that these two men would seize the first opportunity, if one presented itself, for retaking the ship, and he had them well guarded.

"Mr. Byam, surely you are not concerned in this?" Fryer asked.

"No more than yourself, sir," I replied.

"Mr. Byam has nothing to do with it," said Christian. "Mr. Purcell . . ."

Fryer interrupted him.

"In God's name, Mr. Christian! What is it you do? Do you realize that this means the ruin of everything? Give up this madness, and I promise that we shall all make your interest our own. Only let us reach England . . ."

"It is too late, Mr. Fryer," he replied, coldly. "I have been in hell for weeks past, and I mean to stand it no longer."

"Your difficulties with Captain Bligh give you no right to bring ruin upon the rest of us."

"Hold your tongue, sir," said Christian. "Mr. Purcell, have your men fetch up the thwarts, knees, and gear bolts for the large cutter. Churchill, let the carpenter go below to see to this. Send a guard with him."

Purcell and Churchill went down the forward ladderway.

"Do you mean to set us adrift?" Fryer asked.

"We are no more than nine leagues from the land here," Christian replied. "In so calm a sea Mr. Bligh will have no difficulty in making it."

"I will stay with the ship."

"No, Mr. Fryer; you will go with Captain Bligh. Williams! Take the master to his cabin while he collects his clothes. He is to be kept there until I send word."

Fryer requested earnestly to be allowed to remain with the vessel, but Christian well knew his reason for desiring this and would not hear to the proposal. He put an end to the matter by sending the master below.

Purcell now returned, followed by Norman and McIntosh, his mates, carrying the gear for the cutter. Purcell came up to me at once.

"Mr. Byam, I know that you have no hand in this business. But you are, or have been, a friend to Mr. Christian. Beg him to give Captain Bligh the launch. The cutter is rotten and will never swim to the land."

This, I knew, was the case. The cutter was riddled with worms and leaked so badly as to be almost useless. The carpenters were to have started repairing her that same morning. Purcell would not come with me to speak of the matter, giving as a reason Christian's dislike of him. "He would not care to grant any request of mine," he said. "If the cutter is hoisted out, it will be almost certain death for Captain Bligh and all who are permitted to go with him."

I wasted no time, but went to Christian at once. Several

of the mutineers gathered round to hear what I had to say. Christian agreed at once. "He shall have the launch," he said. "Tell the carpenter to have his men fit her." He then called, "Leave off with the cutter, my lads! Clear the launch."

There were immediate protests, led by Churchill, against this new arrangement.

"The launch, Mr. Christian?"

"Don't let him have it, sir! The old fox 'll get home in her!"

"She's too bloody good for him!"

There was an argument over the matter, but Christian forced his will upon the others. In fact, they made no determined stand. All were eager to be rid of the captain, and they had little reason to fear that he would ever see England again.

The mutineers were in such complete control of the situation that Christian now gave orders for the rest of those who were not of his party to be brought on deck. Samuel, Bligh's clerk, was among the first to appear. He was anything but a favourite with the ship's company, and was greeted with jeers and threats by his particular enemies. I had supposed that he would make a poor showing in such a situation. On the contrary, he acted with spirit and determination. Disregarding the insults of the sailors, he went directly to Captain Bligh to receive his orders. He was permitted to go to Bligh's cabin with John Smith, the captain's servant, to fetch up his clothes. They helped him on with his boots and trousers and laid his coat over his shoulders.

I saw Hayward and Hallet standing aft by the rail. Hallet was crying, and both of them were in a state of great alarm. Someone touched my shoulder and I found Mr. Nelson standing beside me.

"Well, Byam, I'm afraid that we're even farther from home than we thought. Do you know what they plan to do with us?"

I told him the little I knew. He smiled ruefully, glancing toward the island of Tofoa, now a faint blur on the horizon.

"I suppose that Captain Bligh will take us there," he said. "I don't much relish the prospect of meeting any more Friendly Islanders. Their friendliness is of a kind that we can well dispense with."

The carpenter appeared at the ladderway, followed by Robert Lamb, the butcher, who was helping to bring up his tool chest.

"Mr. Nelson," he said, "we know whom we have to thank for this."

"Yes, Mr. Purcell, our unlucky stars," Nelson replied.

"No, sir! We have Captain Bligh to thank for it, and him alone! He has brought it upon us all by his damnable behaviour!"

Purcell had the deepest hatred for Bligh, which was returned with interest. The two men had not spoken for months save when absolutely necessary. Nevertheless, when Mr. Nelson suggested that he might be permitted to stay with the ship if he chose, the carpenter was horrified.

"Stop aboard? With rogues and pirates? Never, sir! I shall follow my commander."

At this moment Churchill, who was everywhere about the decks, caught sight of us.

"What are you about there, Purcell? Damn your blood! You'd steal our tools, would you?"

"Your tools, you scoundrel? They're mine, and they go where I go!"

"You shan't take a nail from the ship if I have my way," Churchill replied. He then called out to Christian, and there was another argument, not only with respect to the tool chest, but as to the carpenter himself. Christian was partly in the mind to keep him on the vessel, knowing his value as a craftsman, but all the others urged against it. Purcell had a violent temper and was regarded by the men as a tyrant second only to Bligh.

"He's a damned old villain, sir!"

"Keep the carpenter's mates, Mr. Christian. They're the men for us."

"Make him go in the boat!"

"Make me go, you pirates?" he cried. "I'd like to see the man who'll *stop* me!"

Unfortunately, Purcell was as thick-headed as he was fearless, and he now so far forgot the interests of Bligh's party as to boast of what we would do as soon as we should be clear of the mutineers.

"Mark my word, you rogues! We'll bring every man of you to justice! We'll build a vessel to carry us home . . ."

"So he will, Mr. Christian, if we give him his tools," several men shouted.

"The old fox could build a ship with a clasp knife!"

Purcell realized too late what he had done. I believe that Christian would have given him many of his tools, of which there were duplicates on board, but having been reminded of what he might do with them, he now ordered the tool chest to be examined, and Purcell was permitted to have nothing but a hand saw, a small axe, a hammer, and a bag of nails. Bligh, who had overhead all that was said, could contain himself no longer. "You infernal idiot!" he roared at Purcell, and was prevented from saying more by Burkitt, who placed a bayonet at his throat.

The decks were now filled with people, but Christian took good care that those not of his party should be prevented from coming together in any numbers. As soon as the launch had been cleared, he ordered the boatswain to swing her out. "And mind yourself, Mr. Cole! If you spring a yard or carry anything away it will go hard with you!" Fifteen or more of us were ordered to assist him, for the mutineers were too canny to lay aside their arms and bear a hand.

"Foresail and mainsail there! All ready?"

"Aye, aye, sir!"

"Let go sheets and tacks!"

"All clear, sir!"

"Clew garnets — up with the clews!"

The breeze was still so light as barely to fill the sails, and the clews of the mainsail and foresail went smoothly up to the quarters of the yards. The yards were now squared and the braces made fast, and with half a dozen men holding the launch inboard she was hoisted, swung out over the bulwarks, and lowered away.

One of the first men ordered into her was Samuel. Hayward and Hallet followed next. Both were shedding tears and crying for mercy, and they were half carried to the gangway. Hayward turned to Christian, clasping his hands imploringly.

"Mr. Christian, what have I ever done that you should treat me so?" he exclaimed. "In God's name, permit me to stay with the ship!"

"We can dispense with your services here," Christian replied, grimly. "Into the boat, the pair of you!"

Purcell went next. He required no urging. I think he would have died rather than remain in the ship now that she had been seized by mutineers. His few tools were handed down to him by the boatswain, who followed. Christian ordered Bligh to be brought to the gangway, and his hands were freed.

"Now, Mr. Bligh, there is your boat, and you are fortunate to have the launch and not the cutter. Go into her at once, sir!"

"Mr. Christian," said Bligh, "for the last time I beg you to reflect! I'll pawn my honour — I pledge you my word never to think of this again if you will desist. Consider my wife and family!"

"No, Mr. Bligh. You should have thought of your family long before this, and we well know what your honour is worth. Go into the boat, sir!"

Seeing that all pleading was useless, Bligh obeyed, and was followed by Mr. Peckover and Norton, the quartermaster.

Christian then handed down a sextant and a book of nautical tables.

"You have your compass, sir. This book is sufficient for every purpose, and the sextant is my own. You know it to be a good one."

With his hands freed and once more in command, though only of his ship's launch, Bligh became his old self again.

"I know you to be a bloody scoundrel!" he shouted, shaking his fist in Christian's direction. "But I'll have vengeance! Mind that, you ungrateful villain! I'll see you swinging at a yardarm before two years have passed! And every traitor with you!"

Fortunately for Bligh, Christian's attention was engaged elsewhere, but several of the mutineers at the bulwarks replied to him in language as forceful as the captain's, and it was a near thing that he was not fired upon.

In the confusion I had lost sight of Stewart. We had been hauling together at one of the braces when the launch was hoisted out, but now I could find him nowhere. It soon became clear that many were to be allowed to go with Bligh, and Mr. Nelson and I, who had been standing together by the bulwarks, were hastening toward the after ladderway when we were stopped by Christian.

"Mr. Nelson, you and Mr. Byam may stay with the ship if you choose," he said.

"I have sympathy with you for the wrongs you have suffered, Mr. Christian," Nelson replied, "but none whatever with this action to redress them."

"And when have I asked you for sympathy, sir? Mr. Byam, what is your decision?"

"I shall go with Captain Bligh."

"Then make haste, both of you."

"Have we permission to fetch our clothes?" Nelson asked.

"Yes, but look sharp!"

Nelson's cabin was on the orlop deck directly below that of

Fryer. Two guards stood by the ladderway on the lower
deck. We parted there and I went to the midshipmen's
berth, where Thompson was still on guard over the arms chest.
I had seen nothing of Tinkler and Elphinstone, and was about
to look into the starboard berth to see if they were still there.
Thompson prevented me.

"Never you mind the starboard berth," he said. "Get your
clothes and clear out!"

The berth was screened off from the main hatchway by a
canvas-covered framework. To my surprise, I found Young
still asleep in his hammock. He had been on watch from
twelve to four, and this was his customary time for rest, but
it was strange that he could have slept through such a turmoil.
I tried to rouse him, but he was a notoriously heavy sleeper.
Finding the matter hopeless, I left off and began to ransack my
chest for things I should most need. Stacked in the corner of
the berth were several Friendly Island war clubs that we had
obtained from the savages of Namuka. They had been carved
from the *toa*, or ironwood tree, which well deserved its name,
for in weight and texture the wood was indeed like iron. At
the sight of them the thought flashed into my mind, "Could
I strike Thompson down with one of these?" I glanced
quickly out the doorway. Thompson was now seated on the
arms chest with his musket between his knees, facing the
passageway leading aft. But he saw me thrust out my head
and, with an oath, ordered me to "look sharp and clear out
of there."

At this moment Morrison came along the passageway, and
as luck would have it Thompson's attention was attracted by
someone calling him from above. I beckoned Morrison into
the berth, and he dodged in without having been seen. There
was no need for words. I handed him one of the war clubs
and took another for myself; then, together, we made a last
effort to waken Young. Not daring to speak, we nearly shook
him out of his hammock, but we might have spared ourselves

the trouble. I heard Thompson call out, "He's getting his
clothes, sir. I'll have him up at once." Morrison drew back
by the door and raised his club, and I stood at ready on the
other side, for we both expected Thompson to come in for me.
Instead of that he shouted, "Out of there, Byam, and be quick
about it!"

"I'm coming," I called, and again looked out of the doorway. My heart sank as I saw Burkitt and McCoy coming along
from the fore hatchway. They stopped by the arms chest to
speak to Thompson. Both had muskets, of course. Our
chance to get at Thompson and the arms chest was lost unless
they should pass on. Fortune was against us. We waited for
at least two minutes longer and the men remained where they
were. I heard Nelson's voice calling down the hatchway:
"Byam! Lively there, lad, or you'll be left behind!" And
Tinkler's: "For God's sake, hasten, Byam!"

It was a bitter moment for Morrison and me. The opportunity had been a poor one at best, but had there been time
something might have come of it. We quickly put the war
clubs aside and rushed out, colliding with Thompson, who
was coming to see what I was about.

"Damn your blood, Morrison! What are you doing here?"

We didn't wait to explain, but ran along the passage to the
ladderway. Morrison preceded me, and in my haste to reach
the deck, cumbered as I was with my bag of clothes, I slipped
and fell halfway down the ladder, giving my shoulder a wrench
as I struck the gratings. I clambered up again and was rushing
toward the gangway when Churchill seized me. "You're too
late, Byam," he said. "You can't go." "Can't go? By
God, I *will!*" I exclaimed, giving him a shove which loosened
his hold and all but toppled him over. I was frantic, for I
saw the launch being veered astern, one of the mutineers carrying the painter aft. Burkitt and Quintal were holding Coleman, the armourer, who was begging to go into the boat, and
Morrison was struggling with several men who were keeping

him back from the gangway. We were, in fact, too late; the launch was loaded almost to the point of foundering, and I heard Bligh shouting: "I can take no more of you, lads! I'll do you justice if ever we reach England!"

When the launch had drifted astern, the man holding the painter took a turn with it around the rail and threw the free end to someone in the boat. Those left in the ship now crowded along the rail, and I had difficulty in finding a place where I could look over the side. I was sick at heart, and appalled at the realization that I was, indeed, to be left behind among the mutineers. Norton was in the bow of the launch holding the end of the painter. Bligh was standing on a thwart, astern. Of the others, some were seated and some were standing, and the boat was so heavily loaded as to have no more than seven or eight inches of freeboard. There was a great deal of shouting back and forth, and Bligh was contributing his full share to the tumult by bellowing out orders to those in the boat, and curses and imprecations against Christian and his men.

Some of the mutineers looked on silently and thoughtfully, but others were jeering at Bligh, and I heard one of them shout: "Go and see if you can live on half a pound of yams a day, you bloody villain!" Fryer called out, "In God's name, Mr. Christian, give us arms and ammunition! Think where we go! Let us have a chance to defend our lives!" Others, the boatswain among them, joined earnestly in this plea.

"Arms be damned!" someone shouted back.

"You don't need 'em."

"Old Bligh loves the savages. He'll take care of you!"

"Use your rattan on 'em, boatswain!"

Coleman and I sought out Christian, who was standing by one of the cabin gratings, out of sight of the launch. We begged him to let Bligh have some muskets and ammunition.

"Never!" he said. "They shall have no firearms."

"Then give them some cutlasses at least, Mr. Christian,"

Coleman urged, "unless you wish them to be murdered the moment they set foot on shore. Think of our experience at Namuka!"

Christian consented to this. He ordered Churchill to fetch some cutlasses from the arms chest, and a moment later he returned with four, which were handed into the boat. Meanwhile, Morrison had taken advantage of this opportunity to run below for some additional provisions for the launch. He and John Millward brought up a mess kid filled with pieces of salt pork, several calabashes of water, and some additional bottles of wine and spirits, which they lowered into the boat.

"You cowards!" Purcell shouted, as the cutlasses were handed in. "Will you give us nothing but these?"

"Shall we lower the arms chest, carpenter?" Isaac Martin asked, jeeringly. McCoy threatened him with his musket. "You'll get a bellyful of lead in a minute," he shouted.

"Bear off and turn one of the swivels on 'em!" someone else called. "Give 'em a whiff of grape!"

Burkitt now raised his musket and pointed it at Bligh. Alexander Smith, who was standing beside him, seized the barrel of the musket and thrust it up. I am convinced that Burkitt meant to shoot Bligh, but Christian, observing this, ordered him to be dragged back, deprived of his arms, and placed under guard. He made a terrific struggle, and it required four men to disarm him.

Meanwhile, Fryer and others were urging Bligh to cast off lest they should all be murdered. This Bligh now ordered to be done, and the launch dropped slowly astern. The oars were gotten out, and the boat, so low in the water that she seemed on the point of foundering, was headed toward the island of Tofoa, which bore northeast, about ten leagues distant. Twelve men made a good load for the launch. She now carried nineteen, to say nothing of the food and water and the gear of the men.

"Thank God we were too late to go with her, Byam!"

Morrison was standing beside me.

"Do you mean that?" I asked.

He was silent for a moment, as though considering the matter carefully. Then he said, "No, I don't. I would willingly have taken my chance in her — but it's a slim chance indeed. They'll never see England again."

Tinkler was sitting on a thwart. Mr. Nelson, and Peckover, Norton, Elphinstone, the master's mate, Ledward, the acting surgeon — all were as good as dead, more than a thousand miles from any port where they might expect help. About them were islands filled with the cruellest of savages, who could be held at bay only by men well armed. Granted that some might escape death at the hands of the Indians, what chance had so tiny a boat, so appallingly loaded, to reach any civilized port? The possibility was so remote as to be not worth considering.

Sick at heart, I turned away from the sight of the frail craft, looking so small, so helpless, on that great waste of waters. There had been a cheer from some of the mutineers: "Huzza for Tahiti!" as Christian had ordered, "Get sail on her!" Ellison, McCoy, and Williams had run aloft to loose the fore-topgallant sail. Afterward a silence had fallen over the ship, and the men stood by the bulwarks, gazing at the launch growing smaller and smaller as we drew away from her. Christian, too, was watching, standing where I had last seen him, by the cabin grating. What his thoughts were at this time it would be impossible to say. His sense of the wrongs he had suffered at Bligh's hands was so deep and overpowering as to dominate, I believe, every other feeling. In the course of a long life I have met no others of his kind. I knew him, I suppose, as well as anyone could be said to know him, and yet I never felt that I truly understood the workings of his mind and heart. Men of such passionate nature, when goaded by injustice into action, lose all sense of anything save their own misery. They neither know nor care, until it is too late, what ruin they make of the lives of others.

It was getting on toward eight o'clock when the launch had been cast off. Shortly afterward the breeze, from the northeast, freshened, and the *Bounty* gathered way quietly, slipping through the water with a slight hiss of foam. The launch became a mere speck, seen momentarily as she rose to the swell or as the sunlight flashed from her oars. Within half an hour she had vanished as though swallowed up by the sea. Our course was west-northwest.

X

FLETCHER CHRISTIAN

OUR company was divided, and, though linked together by a common disaster, we were not to share a common fate. I doubt whether a ship has ever sailed from England whose numbers, during the course of her voyage, were to be so widely scattered over the face of the earth, and whose individual members were to meet ends so strange and, in many cases, so tragic.

There had gone with Bligh, in the launch: —

John Fryer, *Master*
Thomas Ledward, *Acting Surgeon*
David Nelson, *Botanist*
William Peckover, *Gunner*
William Cole, *Boatswain*
William Elphinstone, *Master's Mate*
William Purcell, *Carpenter*

Thomas Hayward }
John Hallet   } *Midshipmen*
Robert Tinkler }

John Norton   } *Quartermasters*
Peter Lenkletter }

George Simpson, *Quartermaster's Mate*
Lawrence Lebogue, *Sailmaker*
Mr. Samuel, *Clerk*
Robert Lamb, *Butcher*

John Smith } *Cooks*
Thomas Hall }

Of those who remained in the *Bounty,* the following had taken an active part in the mutiny: —

Fletcher Christian, *Acting Lieutenant*
John Mills, *Gunner's Mate*
Charles Churchill, *Master-at-Arms*
William Brown, *Gardener*

Thomas Burkitt
Matthew Quintal
John Sumner
John Millward
William McCoy
Henry Hillbrandt
Alexander Smith   } *Able Seamen*
John Williams
Thomas Ellison
Isaac Martin
Richard Skinner
Matthew Thompson

Those in the *Bounty* with, but not of, Christian's party, were: —

Edward Young   } *Midshipmen*
George Stewart

James Morrison, *Boatswain's Mate*
Joseph Coleman, *Armourer*
Charles Norman, *Carpenter's Mate*
Thomas McIntosh, *Carpenter's Crew*
William Muspratt, *Able Seaman*

Also Michael Byrne, the half-blind seaman, and myself.   William Muspratt had, for a moment, pretended to be of the mutineers' party and had accepted a musket offered to him by Churchill.   He had overheard Fryer say that he hoped to form a party to retake the vessel, and I am certain he had taken the musket for no other reason than to assist Fryer. When he saw that the matter was hopeless, he immediately laid aside his arms.   Coleman, Norman, and McIntosh had been prevented from going in the launch because the mutineers had need of their services as artificers. Smiths and carpenters can no more be dispensed with on a ship at sea than can seamen themselves.

It was but natural that those who had taken no part in the mutiny should be looked upon with suspicion by those who had. Most of the seamen, however, showed no active hostility against us. Churchill ordered us to remain on deck, but forward of the mizzenmast, and there we awaited Christian's pleasure. Burkitt, who had been deprived of his musket and placed under arms, lest he should shoot Captain Bligh, was again set at liberty. He and Thompson now began baiting and jeering at us, and McCoy and John Williams joined with them. For a moment it seemed likely that there would be a pitched battle between us, and there is no doubt that the non-mutineers would have had the worst of it. Fortunately for us, Christian soon restored order. He came forward, his eyes blazing with anger.

"Get about your work, Thompson," he ordered. "Burkitt, if I have any more trouble from you, I'll put you in irons and keep you there!"

"That's how it is to be, is it?" Thompson replied. "Well, we won't have it, Mr. Christian. We ain't mutinied to have you come the Captain Bligh over us!"

"No, by God, we haven't!" Martin added; "and that you'll find!"

Christian looked at them for a moment without speaking, and there was that in his eyes to relieve any apprehensions one might have had as to his ability to cope with the situation. The four turbulent men dropped their glances sullenly. Several of the seamen were standing by, Alexander Smith among them. "Order all hands aft, Smith," said Christian. He returned to the quarter-deck and paced up and down while the men collected. Then he turned and faced them.

"There is one matter we will decide once for all," he began, quietly, "and that is who is to be captain of this ship. I have taken her with your help, in order to be rid of a tyrant who has made life a burden to all of us. Make no mistake about our status from this time on. We are mutineers, and if we should be discovered and taken by one of His Majesty's vessels, not a man of us but will suffer death. That possibility is not so remote as some of you may think. Should Mr. Bligh succeed in reaching England, immediately upon his arrival there a ship of war will be sent in search of us. Should the *Bounty* not be reported in a year's time, or, at the latest, two years, a ship will be sent, nevertheless, to discover, if possible, the reason for her disappearance. Bear this in mind, all of you. We are not only mutineers but pirates as well, for we have run away with one of His Majesty's armed vessels. We are cut off from England forever, except as prisoners whose fate, if taken home, is certain.

"The Pacific is wide, and still so little known that we need never be taken except as the result of our own folly. In our situation a leader is essential, one whose will is to be obeyed without question. It should be needless to tell British seamen that no ship, whether manned by mutineers or not, can be handled without discipline. If I am to command the *Bounty* I mean to be obeyed. There shall be no injustice here. I shall punish no man without good cause, but I will have no man question my authority.

"I am willing that you shall decide who is to command the *Bounty*. If there is some man most of you prefer in my place, name him, and I will resign my authority. If you wish me to lead you, mind what I have said. I mean to be obeyed."

Churchill was the first to speak. "Well, men, what have you to say?"

"I'm for Mr. Christian!" Smith called out.

There was an immediate hearty agreement with Smith on the part of all the mutineers with the exception of Thompson and Martin; but when Christian called for a show of hands, even these two raised theirs with the others.

"We have another matter to decide," Christian went on.

"There are a number of men with us who took no part in seizing the vessel. They would have gone with Mr. Bligh had opportunity permitted . . ."

"Put 'em in irons, sir," Mills called out. "They'll do us a mischief if they can."

"On this ship, there shall be no putting of anyone in irons without good cause," Christian replied. "These men are not to be blamed for taking no part with us. They decided as seemed best to them, and I respect their decisions; but I shall know how to act if they show toward us any sign of treachery. It is for them to decide now what their treatment with us shall be."

He then called each of us in turn, beginning with Young, and asked whether he could count upon our coöperation, as members of the ship's company, so long as we remained in the *Bounty*. Young decided, then and there, to throw in his lot with the mutineers.

"Chance has decided this matter for me, Mr. Christian," he said. "I will not say that I would have helped you take the ship had I been awake at the time of the mutiny, but now that you have taken her, I am content that it should be so. I have no great desire to see England again. Wherever you may go you can count on me to go with you."

Of the neutral party, he was alone in this decision. The rest of us promised to obey orders, to assist in every way in working the ship, and to refrain from all treachery so long as we should remain aboard of her. Our numbers being what they were, this was the only thing we could do. Christian neither asked, nor, I think, expected, that we should not desert if an opportunity presented itself.

"That is sufficient," he said when he had heard us out. "I require from you no more than that. But you will understand that I must protect myself and these men from capture. In doing so I shall consider our interests before your own. You could not expect me to do otherwise."

He then appointed his officers. Young was made master,

Stewart the master's mate, myself quartermaster, Morrison boatswain, and Alexander Smith boatswain's mate. Churchill was master-at-arms, as before. Burkitt and Hillbrandt were appointed quartermaster's mates. Millward and Byrne were to be the cooks. We were divided into three watches.

These matters being decided, we went about our duties. A part of the great cabin was fitted up as Christian's quarters, and as soon as they were ready the arms chest was removed there. He used it for his bed, and kept the keys always on his own person. One of the mutineers stood on guard, day and night, at the doorway to the cabin. As for Christian himself, he messed alone, and rarely spoke to anyone except to give an order. The captain of a vessel lives, of necessity, a solitary existence, but never could there have been one more lonely than Fletcher Christian. Despite the bitterness I felt toward him at this time, my heart softened as I watched him pacing the quarter-deck hour after hour, by day and by night. All the gaiety had gone out of him; there was never the hint of a smile on his face — only an expression of sombre melancholy.

Stewart, Young, and I messed together, as usual, but our meals were not the jolly affairs they had so often been in the past. It was impossible to become accustomed to the emptiness and silence of the ship. We avoided speaking of those who had gone in the launch, as one avoids speaking of the recently dead, but we were reminded of them at every turn; and the thought of their probable fate, and our own, put a damp upon our spirits hard to overcome. But this applied to Stewart and me rather than to Young. He seemed to have few regrets for the turn our fortunes had taken; indeed, he looked forward with pleasure, rather than otherwise, to the prospect of spending the remainder of his life on some island in the South Sea.

"We may as well make the best of it, lads," he said one evening when we were discussing the future. "It's far from a bad best, if you look at the matter sensibly. I've always wanted a life of ease. Ever since reading Captain Wallis's and Captain Cook's accounts of their discoveries in the Pacific, I've dreamed of nothing but tropical islands. When the chance came to ship with the *Bounty* I was the happiest man in England. I'm willing to confess now that, had it been possible, I would have deserted the ship at Tahiti."

"We shall never see Tahiti again, that is certain," said Stewart, gloomily. "It will be the last place Mr. Christian will consider as a refuge. He knows only too well that a ship of war will turn up there, sooner or later, in search of us."

"What does it matter?" asked Young. "There are scores, hundreds of other islands where we can live as happily. I advise the pair of you to put all thoughts of home out of your minds. The chances of your ever seeing England again are very remote. Make the most of what life offers you here."

Remote indeed they seemed then. After parting with the launch we had followed the course the ship was then on, west-northwest, until well into the afternoon; then we bore off to the eastward, since which time our general course had been east by south. We were now in unknown seas, in so far as I knew, off the track of any ship that had explored the Pacific. It was clear that Christian was in search of undiscovered islands, for we hove-to at night lest we should pass any in the darkness. Those days and nights were as peaceful as any that I remember. The absence of Bligh was a godsend to all of us, mutineers and non-mutineers alike. There was no more of the continual feeling of tension, of uncertainty as to what would happen, whenever the captain appeared upon deck. Christian maintained the strictest discipline, but no one had cause to complain of his justice. He was a born leader of men, and knew how to rule them without the perpetual floggings and abuse which Bligh considered so essential. After the turbulent events of the mutiny the men seemed glad of the tranquillity which had settled over the

ship.   The breeze blew steadily from the northeast, and the
Bounty nosed her way quietly along as though she had mastered
the task of sailing herself and required no further help from
us.   The moon waxed and was on the wane when, one morning
shortly after sunrise, land was descried bearing west by
north.

Late in the afternoon we approached to within a mile of the
reef which seemed to enclose the island, forming a shallow
lagoon where we saw many canoes plying back and forth.
The island appeared to be about eight miles long.   The interior was mountainous like that of Tahiti, although the land
was not so high, and the lowlands surrounding it were covered
with the same luxuriance of vegetation.   As in most of the
islands in that part of the Pacific, deep water came directly up
to the reef, and we coasted along, close inshore.   Several
canoes, with ten or a dozen men in each, put off from the beach
and soon came up with us.   The Indians resembled the Tahitians in colour, stature, and the manner of their dress, and it
was evident that they had never seen a European vessel before.   We tried to persuade them to come alongside, and at
last one of them paddled abreast of us at a distance of about
thirty yards.

The men were strongly made, with handsome features and
well-formed bodies.   At Christian's order I spoke to them in
the Tahitian language, asking them the name of their land.
This they understood, and replied that it was Rarotonga.
They seemed utterly astonished at my words.   One of them
replied at some length, but his speech was largely unintelligible.
For all our friendly gestures we could not persuade them to
approach more closely.   Some trinkets Christian wished to
give them were wrapped in a cloth and lowered over the side on
a piece of planking.   When we had let this drift well astern,
they approached and took the parcel and the plank as well,
which they put into their canoe without unwrapping the cloth
to see what it contained.

Having failed in our efforts to persuade any of them to come on board, Christian gave orders to make sail, much to the regret of all of us, for this island was scarcely less beautiful than Tahiti, and, judging by the actions of the men in the canoes, the people would not have opposed our landing. It has always remained a puzzle to me why Christian did not choose this island as his hiding-place; for Rarotonga lies nearly seven hundred miles southwest of Tahiti, and at this time he had no reason to believe that its existence was known to any Europeans save ourselves. His reason may have been that, in coasting the entire length of one side of the island, no possible anchorage was to be seen; or perhaps, at this time, he was so disturbed in mind as to have no definite plans for the future.

One evening, greatly to my surprise, he sent for me to sup with him. The afterpart of the great cabin had been partitioned off for his use, and there I found him, seated at his table, with a copy of one of Captain Cook's charts outspread before him. He greeted me with formal politeness, but when he had dismissed the sentinel stationed outside and had closed the door, he fell back into the old friendly manner customary between us before the mutiny.

"I have asked you to sup with me, Byam," he said, "but you need not accept unless you choose."

I responded, against my inclination, to his friendly overtures. I had come to resent bitterly the ruin he had brought upon us all; but under the influence of his appealing kindly manner I found my indignation melting away. I stood before Fletcher Christian, my friend, not the mutineer who had cast nineteen men adrift in a small boat thousands of miles from home. To those who blame me I can merely say that they never knew the man.

He was in great need of someone to whom he could unburden his thoughts, and I had not been five minutes in his cabin before he was speaking of the mutiny.

"When I think of Bligh," he said, "I have no regrets. None

whatever. I have suffered too much at his hands ever to care
what his fate may be.   But for those who went with him . . ."

He shut his eyes tightly and pressed his knuckles against
them, as though to blot from his mind the picture of the small
open boat, filled, almost to the point of foundering, with
innocent men. Such desolation of heart was apparent in his
voice and the expression on his face that I pitied him deeply.
I knew that he would never know peace again — never until
his last day.   He begged me to profit by his example and never
act upon impulse, and for all my sympathy I could not avoid
saying that a mutiny so carefully and secretly planned could
hardly be called an act of impulse.

"Good God!" he exclaimed. "Did you think it was
planned?   Ten minutes before Bligh was seized I had no more
thought of mutiny than you yourself.   Had it been an act of
deliberation . . . Is it possible that you could have believed
it?"

"What else could I think?" I replied.   "It happened in your
watch.   When I was awakened by Churchill I found you in
complete possession of the ship, with armed men stationed at
the hatchways and all about the decks.   It is inconceivable to
me that all this could have happened without prearrangement."

"And yet it did," Christian replied, earnestly.   "It was all
the work of five minutes. Let me tell you. . . .   Do you
remember the talk we had the night before, during Peckover's
watch?"

"Perfectly."

"I asked that, in case anything happened to me during the
voyage home, you would explain the circumstances to my
people when you reached England. My reason for speaking
of this matter was that I planned to leave the ship before the
morning watch.   I had taken no one into my confidence except
the quartermaster, John Norton, a man whom I knew I could
trust.   I was not willing that you should know.   I wanted
to spare your feelings until I had gone, and it was certain that

you would have tried to dissuade me. Norton had managed to make, secretly, a tiny raft upon which I hoped to reach the island of Tofoa. With the sea as calm as it was, I had every reason to think that I could make the land."

"You really meant to cut yourself off for all time from home and friends?"

"Yes. I was in hell, Byam! I had suffered from Bligh's tyranny to the limit of my endurance. When he accused me, that same afternoon, with stealing his coconuts, I felt that I could bear no more."

"I know," I said; "you were sorely tried, but we were all in the same sorry situation with you."

"I did n't think of that. I thought only of the shame of the accusation; of the contemptible, sordid meanness of the man who could bring such a charge against his officers. I thought as well of the long voyage ahead of us, and I knew that I could not and would not endure another year of such torment.

"But luck was against me. The calmness and beauty of the night, so favourable otherwise to my purpose, were against me. As you know, most of the ship's company were on deck and, almost becalmed as we were, it would have been impossible to slip away unseen. At last I decided that the plan would have to be abandoned, temporarily at least. I should have to wait until we passed some other island farther to the westward.

"Even at four o'clock, when I took charge of the deck from Peckover, the thought of mutiny had not occurred to me. Believe this; I assure you that it is true. I paced up and down for some time, brooding over the repeated insults I had received from Bligh. I don't defend myself; I merely relate the facts. I was in a mood to kill the man. Yes, that thought crossed my mind more than once: why not murder him and be done with it? The temptation was all but overpowering. This will give you an indication of the state of my feelings at that time. I was, in sober truth, out of my mind.

"As you know, Hayward was the mate of my watch. In order to regain control of myself I went in search of him, and found him stretched out in the lee of the cutter, asleep. At another time such neglect of duty would have aroused my anger. We were in unknown waters, and Bligh had rightly given orders that the strictest watch should be kept, no matter how far we might be from land. Hayward was in charge of the forward deck, and three of the men, taking their cue from him, were asleep. I stood for a moment looking down at Hayward, and then, as plainly as though they had been spoken, I heard the words, 'Seize the ship.'

"From that moment my brain worked with the utmost clearness and precision. It appeared to function outside of me; I had only to obey its commands. I realized what an opportunity had presented itself, but not at all the wrong I should be doing the rest of you. Burkitt was awake, standing in the waist by the bulwarks on the larboard side. He had been frequently punished by Bligh and I knew that I could count on his help, but I didn't reveal my plan then — for I now had a plan. I asked him to come below with me and waken Churchhill, Martin, Thompson, and Quintal, without disturbing anyone else, and to tell them I wanted to see them at the fore ladderway. Meanwhile I went to Coleman's hammock, roused him quietly, and asked for the key to the arms chest, saying that I wanted a musket to shoot a shark. He gave it to me, turned over in his hammock, and fell asleep again.

"I found Hallet asleep on the arms chest. As he was also of my watch, I roused him with a show of anger and set him on deck by the after ladderway. He was badly frightened at being caught, and begged me in a low voice to say nothing of the matter to Captain Bligh. Burkitt and the men he had awakened were awaiting me. They fell in at once with my plan. We provided ourselves with muskets and pistols, and I placed Thompson sentinel over the arms chest. We then roused McCoy, Williams, Alexander Smith, and others, every man of them promising his hearty support. They were given arms, and when I had placed sentinels at the hatchways we went to Bligh's cabin. The rest you know."

He fell silent and sat for some time with his head in his hands, staring at the deck between his feet. At length I forced myself to say, "What chance do you think Bligh has of reaching England?"

"Little enough. Timor is the nearest place where they could expect help. It is twelve hundred leagues from the place where the launch was cast adrift. . . . When I seized the ship my only thought was that I would carry Bligh home in irons. The men wouldn't have it; you saw that for yourself. I was forced to give way on that point. Then came the question of who was to go with him. My plan was, at first, to send only Fryer, Samuel, Hallet, and Hayward, but I could not refuse to let any others go with him who wished to; in fact, not to have done so would have been highly dangerous. Fryer, Purcell, Cole, and Peckover would, I knew, make every effort to form a party for retaking the ship, if kept with us. . . . Well, enough of this. What is done can't be undone. I now have to think of the men who are with me. The least I can do is to prevent them from being taken."

"And what of the rest of us?"

"I have been expecting that question. You have every right to ask it. I can't hope that any of you will give up all thoughts and hope of home and throw in your lot with us as Young has done. My predicament is only less hard than the one I have brought you into."

He rose and stood by one of the stern ports, looking out to westward, where the sun had just set. Presently he turned to me again.

"If I should take you to Tahiti and allow you to part company from us, none of you would feel bound to keep silence about the mutiny. For the present, much as I regret it, I must keep you with us.   I can say no more.   You must be content with that."

Of his immediate plans Christian said nothing, although he gave me to understand that we should be making land within a few days.   On the morning of May 28, precisely four weeks after the mutiny, an island was seen dead to windward, distant about six leagues.   We spent most of that day in beating up to it, and were becalmed toward nightfall about three miles off the western end.   At dawn, when the trade wind made up again, we coasted along the barrier reef which lay a great way offshore, in places as far as two miles.   Stewart, who had a perfect memory for latitudes and longitudes and for any chart he had seen, was convinced that this island was Tupuai, which had been discovered by Captain Cook.   After nearly two months at sea, the place seemed a Garden of Eden to all of us and, mutineers and nonmutineers alike, we were eager to go ashore.   There were various small islands scattered along the reef, and between them, across the lagoons, we had entrancing glimpses of the main island.   All along the coast we saw evidences of a numerous population.

Christian now informed us that there was a pass through the reef into the lagoon, and that he meant to take the ship inside; but when we came abreast of the entrance we found a formidable array of Indians awaiting us.   The entire male population of the island must have gathered there.   We estimated their numbers at eight or nine hundred.   All were armed with spears, clubs, and canoe loads of stones for repelling our entrance.   There was no doubt of the hostility of their intentions; they would have none of our friendly overtures, but brandished their spears and sent such showers of stones on our decks from their slings that several of our men were hurt.   We were forced to draw off the land, and from the masthead it was clear that the passage into the lagoon and the lagoon itself were scattered with coral shoals which would make navigation of the ship difficult, even granted that we were unmolested by the Indians.   With them in opposition all hope of a landing had to be abandoned.   Some of the mutineers were for turning the guns on the Indians, and had we done so we could have killed hundreds of them and brought the remainder under subjection; but Christian would have none of this plan.   He was resolved that, wherever we went, we would make a peaceful settlement or none at all.

He now called a conference on the quarter-deck of the men of his own party, and the rest of us, with the exception of Young, were sent forward, out of hearing.   At the end of a quarter of an hour the men dispersed to their duties, and it was plain that some decision had been reached pleasing to all of them.   The ship was headed north.

Young was bound to say nothing of what had taken place at the meeting, and we refrained from asking him embarrassing questions.   But, knowing our position, we also knew that north, if that course were to be held for several days, could mean only one thing: our destination was Tahiti.   Morrison, Stewart, and I talked in whispers in the berth that evening. We scarcely dared hope for such good fortune as a return to Tahiti.   There, if anywhere, we stood some chance of meeting any vessel that might be sent out to search for the *Bounty*.   We might have to wait for several years, but a vessel was certain to come at last.   We resolved that, if the *Bounty* called there, we would never come away in her.   We would escape, somehow, and conceal ourselves until the ship had put to sea again.

XI

THE LAST OF THE BOUNTY

On the day following our decision to escape, should the ship put in at Tahiti, Christian sent for me once more. I found him with Churchill in his cabin, and when he had motioned me to the settee he dismissed the sentinel and closed the door. Christian looked stern, sad, and careworn, but Churchill, who stood by the door with folded arms, greeted me with a smile. He was a tall, powerful fellow, in middle life, with cold blue eyes and a determined reckless face.

"I have sent for you, Mr. Byam," said Christian formally, "to acquaint you with our decision regarding you and your companions who had no hand in the taking of the ship. We bear you no ill-will, yet circumstances oblige us to take every precaution for our own safety. We are now steering for Tahiti, where we shall stop for a week or more while we load livestock and stores."

My face must have betrayed my thoughts, for Christian shook his head. "My first thought," he went on, "was to leave you there, where sooner or later you might hope for a ship to take you home. But the men would have none of it, and I fear that they are right."

He glanced at Churchill, who nodded, still standing with folded arms. "No, Mr. Byam," said the master-at-arms, "we had it out in the forecastle last night — a regular Dover-court. Not a man on the ship but wishes you well, but we can't allow it."

"They are right," said Christian gloomily; "we can neither

leave you on Tahiti nor let you set foot on shore.   The men were for keeping the lot of you below decks, under guard, but I persuaded them that if you and Mr. Stewart and Mr. Morrison would give parole not to mention the mutiny to the Indians, nor to say anything which might prejudice our interests, we might safely permit you to come on deck while we are at anchor in Matavai."

"I think I understand, sir," I replied, "though I must admit that we had hoped to be left in Tahiti, whither we supposed the ship to be bound."

"Impossible!" Christian said.   "I hate to carry you away against your will, but it is essential to the safety of your ship-mates.   None of us will ever see England again — we must make up our minds to that.   You may tell the others that it is my intention to search out one of the many unknown islands in this sea, land our stores and livestock, destroy the ship, and settle there for good, hoping never again to see a strange white face."

"Aye, Mr. Christian," put in Churchill approvingly.   "It is the only way."

Christian stood up, to notify me that the interview was at an end, and I went on deck with a sinking heart.   With the fresh east wind abeam, the *Bounty* was sailing fast on the starboard tack, rolling slowly and regularly to the lift of the swell.   I stood by the lee gangway, watching the blue water swirl past the ship's side, and striving to collect my thoughts. Stewart and I had often discussed in privacy our hopes and fears for the future, and now, unless we found means to escape during the ship's sojourn in Matavai, our hopes seemed destined to come to naught.   It was true that the parole demanded of us, if we were to be allowed on deck, contained no mention of escape, but I had no doubt that we should be closely watched. And even if we were lucky enough to escape, I realized that the chances were a hundred to one we should be retaken. Christian would have invented some plausible tale to account for the absence of Bligh and the others, and, as captain of the ship, the chiefs would be on his side. For the reward of a musket or two, they would have the mountains and valleys of the interior scoured by men certain to find us, no matter how distant and secret our hiding-place. Our only chance — a slender one, indeed — would be to get possession of a fast sailing canoe and make for the islands to leeward of Tahiti, whither the authority of Teina and the other great chiefs of north Tahiti did not extend. Once there, even though Christian learned our destination and gave pursuit, we might be able to dodge from island to island till he wearied of the chase.

To leave the ship under the eyes of the mutineers would be hard indeed; to set sail at once, in a fast and seaworthy canoe, watered and provisioned for a voyage across the open sea, would be harder still. Yet hardest of all was the thought of the alternative: "England — home, lost to us forever."

As I stood by the gangway, deep in these disquieting reflections, Stewart touched my arm. "Look," he said; "they are throwing the plants overboard!" Directed by Young, a line of men had formed on the ladderway, and they were beginning to pass the pots from hand to hand. A man by the rail, aft, pulled up each young plant by the roots and flung it overboard, while others emptied the earth into the sea and carried the pots to the forehatch. We carried more than a thousand young breadfruit trees, all in flourishing condition, and now the *Bounty* left a wake of their rich green foliage tossing on the blue swell. They had been gathered and cared for with infinite pains; to obtain them we had suffered hardships, braved unknown seas, and sailed more than twenty-seven thousand miles, in fair weather and foul. And now the plants, eagerly awaited in the West Indies, were going overboard like so much unwanted ballast.

"Waste!" remarked Stewart presently. "Futility and waste! And, like a good Scot, I hate both!"

It was sad to reflect on the results of the expedition: the plants thrown overboard; Bligh and his companions probably drowned or killed by savages; the mutineers, desperate and unhappy, planning to hide away forever from the face of mankind; ourselves forced to share the same hard fate.

Later, in the privacy of the berth, I told Stewart of my interview with Christian and of the gloomy prospect ahead of us. "We must tell Morrison as soon as possible," he said.

He was silent for some time, his thin, bronzed face expressionless. At last he looked up. "At least I'll see Peggy."

"That's certain, if you give your parole."

"I'd give that, and more, for a glimpse of her!" He rose abruptly and began to pace back and forth nervously. I said nothing, and presently he went on in a low voice: "Forgive me for inflicting my thoughts on you — seamen are sentimental, and I have been long at sea. But Peggy might be the means of effecting our escape — I can think of no other."

"That she might!" I exclaimed, for I had given the subject much anxious thought. "She could obtain a canoe for us — a favour we could ask of no other person in Matavai. Since we must give our parole we cannot make known the true state of affairs, nor why we desire to leave the ship. You will have to tell Peggy that we are planning to desert, as Churchill and the others deserted, in order to live among the Indians after the ship is gone. The chiefs alone own vessels large enough to take us to the Leeward Islands, and both Teina and Hitihiti feel themselves too much indebted to the friendship of King George to take part in what they would regard as a conspiracy against him. Peggy's father is under no such obligation."

Stewart seated himself once more. His mind was quicker than my own, and he had perceived in an instant what had taken me some time to puzzle out.

"Precisely," he said. "Peggy is our only chance. I could arrange everything in ten minutes alone with her. It must be on a night when the wind holds from the east. The canoe will be paddled past the ship as if outbound on one of their night passages to Tetiaroa, and her crew must make some disturbance which will draw the men of the watch to that side of the *Bounty*.   We can then slip overboard on the other side and swim to Peggy's vessel, which will lie hove-to while they get sail on her.   With good luck, no one will observe us in the dark."

"By God, Stewart!   I believe it can be done!"

"Must be done, rather!   Morrison and I are Navy men, and we have our careers to think of.   But there have been many times when I have longed to stay here."

On the evening of the fifth of June we raised the highlands of Tahiti, far ahead and ghostly among the clouds, and on the following afternoon we sailed into Matavai Bay and dropped anchor close to Point Venus.   Every man on board had been instructed what to tell the Indians of his acquaintance who might make inquiries: at Aitutaki we had fallen in with Captain Cook, Bligh's father, who was forming an English settlement on that island.   Bligh, Nelson, and others of the *Bounty's* crew had been taken aboard Cook's ship, and he had ordered the *Bounty* to leave the breadfruit plants with him, and return to Tahiti to trade for further stores and whatever livestock it might be possible to obtain.   The ship was then to set sail in search of another island suitable for settlement.

The Indians flocked out to the ship — Teina, Hitihiti, and the other chiefs curious to know why we had returned so soon and what had become of the absent members of the ship's company.   The story invented by Christian satisfied them completely, and since he was popular — much more so than Bligh — the natives promised to furnish everything we desired, and the trading was friendly and brisk.

I dined with Christian that evening; his sweetheart and old Hitihiti, my *taio*, were the other guests.   With the girl — who would eat nothing — at his side, Christian seemed to have

shaken off for the moment the sombre mood from which he
had not emerged since the mutiny.   He raised his glass and
smiled at me across the table.

"To our sweethearts," he said lightly.   "You can drink to
mine, Byam, since you have none of your own."   Maimiti
smiled gravely and touched the glass with her lips, but my
taio drained his wine at a gulp.

"Stop ashore my house, Byam," he said.

I could feel Christian's eyes on me as I replied.   "I'm sorry,"
I said; "but we shall be here only a few days, and Mr. Christian
has informed me that I shall be needed on board."

Hitihiti was evidently surprised at this.   He turned to
Christian, who nodded.

"Yes," he said.   "He will be needed on board during the
whole time we are at anchor here."   The old chief understood
enough of discipline on a British ship to let the subject drop.

Peggy had come on board during the afternoon, and when
I went on deck after dinner I saw the couple seated by the
mainmast, in the shadow of the pumps.   Stewart's arm was
about her waist and they were speaking together in the Indian
tongue.   When she had gone ashore, Stewart, Morrison, and I
met by agreement on the main hatch.   Young was the officer
of the watch, and since we were at anchor and the night was
calm, he had given his men permission to sleep on deck.   He
was a carefree, unsuspicious fellow, and now he lolled on the
poop, his head turned toward the dark loom of the land.
Taurua, his Indian sweetheart, kept the watch with him — a
slender ghostly figure, shrouded in white tapa.   The night
was chilly, for it was winter in Tahiti, and Matavai Bay was a
black mirror to reflect the stars.

"I have talked with Peggy," said Stewart in a low voice,
"and explained our determination to desert the ship.   She
thinks that I am leaving for her sake — a half-truth, at least.
As for you two, she believes that you are enamoured of the
Indian life, or of some of the young ladies on shore.   Peggy

will aid us with her whole heart. Unfortunately, the only large canoe her family possesses is at Tetiaroa. She will send a small vessel to fetch it to-morrow if the wind is fair."

"Then let us pray for a fair wind," said Morrison seriously.

"I wish we could take the others," I said.

"There will be no chance of that," Morrison replied. "Christian means to keep them confined below till the ship sails."

"In any case there would be too many," said Stewart. "Their very numbers would make escape impossible."

Morrison shrugged his shoulders. "No — we can think only of ourselves. I have only one desire, one thought — to return to England. A ship will come, you may count on that, though we may have to wait two or three years for her. We shall have to be patient, that is all."

"Patient?" Stewart remarked. "Well, I could put up with three years here — or with four or five! And Byam is a lover of the Indian life."

"Damn the Indian life," said Morrison without a smile. "Who knows what wars are going on, what chances for prize-money and promotion we are missing!"

I went to sleep with a light heart that night, for our escape seemed a certainty, and the prospect of a year or two among the Indians was far from displeasing. At dawn I saw Peggy's light double canoe, paddled by half-a-dozen stalwart fellows, set out for Tetiaroa, and all through the forenoon I watched every sign of the weather anxiously. Nature herself now took a hand against us. The day turned chilly and films of cloud began to stream seaward off the mountains. We were in the lee of the high land, and Matavai Bay remained still as a lake, but the wind had chopped around to the south and was blowing up one of the boisterous southerly storms the Indians call *maraai*. Gazing out to sea, I perceived the line of white-caps at the end of the lee, and knew that as long as the south wind held, no canoe would even attempt to return from the island north of us.

Day after day the strong south wind blew, while we traded for our strange cargo. Hogs, fowls, dogs, and cats came on board till the ship resembled a menagerie, and finally the bull and the cow left on Tahiti by Captain Cook. Goats skipped about comically on deck, among mounds of taro, sweet potatoes, and yams. And little by little our hope, which had run so high, began to change to fear. There were signs that Christian was nearly ready to sail, and Peggy's face, when she visited her lover on board, grew haggard with anxiety. I shall not dwell on our suspense. It is enough to say that on the ninth day the wind shifted to northeast and brought our sailing canoe in, four hours after the shift. This was at noon and all was arranged for our escape the same night, but now at the last moment fate turned against us once more. At two o'clock in the afternoon Christian ordered the anchor up and, close-hauled on the starboard tack, the *Bounty* sailed out of Matavai Bay.

The months from June to September of that year, 1789, are a nightmare in my memory, and since they have little to do with the main thread of this narrative, I shall give them no more space than they deserve.

In spite of our hostile reception when we first visited Tupuai, Christian had determined to settle on that island. We were now southbound, like modern Noahs on our Ark, with livestock of various kinds to increase and multiply on the island, and even a few Indian Eves to become the grandmothers of a new race — half white, half brown. Christian's Maimiti was on board, and Young's Taurua; and Alexander Smith, distrustful of the ladies of Tupuai, had persuaded Bal'hadi to accompany him. Nor was any great degree of persuasion necessary, for the Indians were passionately fond of travel and adventure of any sort. Long after Tahiti had disappeared below the horizon north of us, it was discovered that we had on board nine Indian men, twelve women, and eight boys, most of them stowaways.

Our reception on Tupuai was at first friendly, owing to the Tahitian passengers, who explained our desire to settle on the island. With incredible labour we hauled the ship up on land and built thatched shelters to protect her decks from the sun. We then built a fort, on a point of land purchased from one of the chiefs, and surrounded it with a moat twenty feet deep and twice as wide, all hands, including Christian himself, taking part in the work. The men murmured much at this truly Herculean labour, but Christian's foresight was soon evident. Our goats, loosed to increase among the mountains of the interior, descended on the taro gardens of the Indians, which they cultivate and water with infinite pains. Unable to capture or kill the wary animals, the people came to us, asking us to shoot them with our muskets. When we refused, explaining that the progeny of the marauders would provide an important supply of food, the Indians at first murmured and then broke out in open hostility, declaring that they would never cease their efforts until we were either exterminated or driven from the island for good. Time after time they attacked our fortress furiously, only to be driven off by the fire of our four-pounders and swivels, and before long it became impossible to venture outside save in strong parties, heavily armed. Our lives grew insupportable; even the hardiest among us wearied of the constant fighting, and early in September, perceiving that all hands were heartily sick of the place, Christian assembled the lot of us and called for a show of hands. All were for leaving Tupuai; sixteen expressed a desire to be left on Tahiti, and the rest wished to sail away with the *Bounty* to search for some uninhabited island where they might settle in peace. On being informed of our decision to leave Tupuai, the Indians agreed to cease hostilities while we launched and watered the ship, and after a week of labour such as falls to the lot of few men, we got the *Bounty* launched, her sails bent, and water and stores aboard. At the last moment, on the verge of leaving this ill-omened place, we nearly lost the ship in a tremendous squall which made up unperceived during the night. As it was, we lost the spare gaff of the driver and all our spare topgallant yards.

At daybreak, with a fresh breeze at east, we weighed and sailed out through the narrow passage, heartily glad to be clear of a place where we had met with nothing but misfortune and strife, and five days later, after an agreeable voyage, we were at anchor once more in Matavai Bay. The following men had decided to remain on the ship: — Fletcher Christian, Acting Lieutenant; John Mills, Gunner's Mate; Edward Young, Midshipman; William Brown, Gardener; Isaac Martin, William McCoy, John Williams, Matthew Quintal, and Alexander Smith, Able Seamen.

The rest of the *Bounty's* company had elected to remain on Tahiti. I was overjoyed at this sudden change in my fortunes, as were Stewart and Morrison. My old friend Hitihiti was among the first of the Indians to come off to us, and when I informed him that I hoped to go ashore and make my home at his house, his face beamed with smiles. As he had come out in a double canoe large enough to freight all my belongings ashore, I lost no time in asking Christian's permission to leave the ship. I found him at the main hatch, superintending the division of the muskets, cutlasses, pistols, and ammunition, of which each man was to have his share.

"By all means," he said, looking up from the paper in his hand. "Go ashore whenever you like. And take a musket with you and a supply of lead to mould bullets. We are so short of powder that I can give only a few charges to each man. You will stop with Hitihiti, of course?"

"That is my intention, sir."

"I shall see you to-night, then. I wish to speak to you and

to Stewart — I shall ask him to be there an hour after sundown."

My hammock man and his lusty Indian wench lent me a hand to get my things out of the berth, and after a farewell glance about the *Bounty's* decks, and a silent handshake with Edward Young, I followed my belongings into Hitihiti's canoe.

It was like a homecoming to return once more to the house of my *taio*, to greet Hina and her husband, and to see Hitihiti's grandchildren running to welcome me. I had lived so long among these kind people that they seemed joined to me by ties closer than those of mere friendship.

When I had stowed my belongings and precious manuscript I became at once the centre of a circle of all ages, eager to hear the story of our adventures. I recounted at length, in the Indian tongue, the history of our attempt to settle on Tupuai, and ended by expressing some sympathy with the people of that island, who, after all, had done no more than repel what they considered an invasion of their home. Hina shook her head indignantly.

"No!" she exclaimed; "you are wrong. I have seen some of those people, who came here in a large canoe five years ago. They are savages! You should have killed them all and taken their island!"

"You are fierce, Hina," I said with a smile. "Why should we kill innocent men, whose only fault was love of their land? Had we desired to kill them, Christian would not have allowed it."

"He was foolish, then. Did they not try to kill him, and you? But what will you do, now that you have returned? Shall you be long among us?"

"To-morrow or the day after, Christian and eight of the others will set sail for Aitutaki to rejoin Captain Cook. The rest of us, who love your island, have permission to settle here."

All of us who were to be left on Tahiti had given our words

to tell the same story, and, little as I liked the task, I lied with a brazen face. Hina leaned towards me and seized me in a strong embrace, smelling at my cheek affectionately.

"Ah, Byam," she said, "we are delighted, all of us! The house has been empty since you sailed away!"

"Aye," said her husband heartily. "You are one of us, and we shall not let you go!"

Early in the evening Stewart appeared on the path from Matavai, accompanied by Peggy and her father, old Tipau. Hitihiti had returned to the ship, to fetch Christian and his niece. I walked down to the beach with Stewart and his sweetheart, leaving the old chief to gossip with the others in the house.

The calm Pacific nuzzled lazily at the sands, and we sat quietly, as if the beauty of the evening had cast upon us a spell of silence and immobility.

Twilight was fading to night when Stewart started slightly and gazed out to sea. "There they come!" he said. Rising and falling on the gentle swell outside the reef, I saw the double canoe—a moving shadow on the waters. She came on rapidly, and before long her prows grounded on the sand and Christian sprang out, turning to help Maimiti over the high gunwale. He nodded to us, saying only, "Wait for me here," and followed Hitihiti to the house to take leave of his sweetheart's family. At a word from Stewart, Peggy followed him.

The sight of Christian on the twilit beach had moved me deeply. It was not hard to imagine his feelings on the eve of this final departure from Tahiti. Presently I heard a rustle in the bushes behind us, and his step falling softly on the sand. We rose, but he motioned us to seat ourselves, and sank down cross-legged beside us, casting aside his hat and running his fingers through his thick dark hair.

"This is the last time I shall see you," he said abruptly, after a long silence. "We shall sail in the morning, as soon as the wind makes up.

"I have told you the story of the mutiny," he went on; "remember that I, and I alone, am responsible. In all probability, Bligh and those with him are long since dead — drowned or killed by savages. In the case of Bligh, I have no regrets; the thought of the others, innocent men, lies heavy on my conscience. You know the circumstances; they may explain, even to some extent excuse, the action I took, but they can never exonerate me. I am a mutineer and, since I made off with one of His Majesty's ships, a pirate as well. It is my duty to guide and protect those who have chosen to follow me. You know my plans. This is the greatest ocean in the world, set with innumerable islands. On one of them — north, or south, or east, or west of here — we shall settle, and destroy the ship. You shall see us no more — I promise you that."

Again silence fell upon us. The stillness of the night was broken only by the faint lap and wash of the sea, and far down the beach, where a fire of coconut husks made a ruddy point of light, I heard the wail of an awakening child.

"Sooner or later," Christian went on, after a long pause, "a British man-of-war will drop anchor here. If Bligh, or any of his men, succeed in reaching England, the Admiralty will dispatch a ship at once, to apprehend the mutineers. If, as I fear, all those in the *Bounty's* launch are lost, a vessel will be sent out, after a reasonable period of waiting, in search of us. When she comes, I desire you earnestly to go out to her at once and give yourselves up to the officer in command — you two, and the others who had no hand in the mutiny. You are innocent, and no harm can come to you. As for the others, let them behave as they think best. Since they refuse to follow me, I am forced to wash my hands of them.

"Once before, Byam, in a moment of desperation, I requested you to communicate with my father, in the event of my not reaching home. Fate was against me that night! Had I succeeded in leaving the ship . . . My father is Charles

Christian, of Mairlandclere, in Cumberland. Will one of you, the first to reach England, go to him and explain the circumstances of the mutiny? Tell him the story as I have told it to you, and explain particularly that my design was only to relieve Bligh of his command and take him home in irons. A full acquaintance with the truth may extenuate in my father's eyes, though never justify, the crime I have committed. Will you do this for me?"

Christian stood up and Stewart and I sprang to our feet. I was the first to seize Christian's hand.

"Yes," I said, too moved for further speech.

A moment later Christian turned to hail the house. "Maimiti!" he called, in his strong seaman's voice. She must have been awaiting the call, for she appeared almost instantly, a slender white figure flitting under the palms. The paddlers followed her, seized the canoe, and dragged it into the wash of the sea. The Indian girl came to me without a word and embraced me tenderly in the fashion of her people. Still in silence she embraced Stewart, and sprang into the canoe. Christian shook our hands for the last time. "God bless you both!" he said.

We stood on the beach, watching the double canoe fade into the night. At dawn, when I walked out of the house for a plunge in the sea, the *Bounty* was standing offshore with all sail set, heading north, with the light easterly breeze abeam.

XII

TEHANI

THOUGH I had reason to congratulate myself on my present situation, the week following the *Bounty's* departure was an unhappy time for me. For the first time in my life, I think, I began to question the doctrines of the Church in which I had been brought up, and to ask myself whether human destiny was ordered by divine law or ruled by chance. If God were all-powerful and good, I thought, with a lad's simplicity, why had He permitted one man, in a moment of not unrighteous anger against oppression and injustice, to ruin his own life and the lives of so many others? Many a good and innocent man had accompanied Bligh in the launch: where were they now? The majority of the mutineers themselves were simple fellows with a grievance that might have led better men to revolt. Held in subjection by the iron law of the sea, they had endured with little complaint the hardships of the long voyage and the temper of a man considered brutal in a brutal age. Had Bligh not goaded his junior officer beyond endurance, no other man on the ship would have raised the cry of mutiny, and the voyage would have been completed peacefully. But one moment of passion had changed everything. Out of the whole ship's company, only seven of us — those who had had no hand in the mutiny and were now awaiting the first English ship — had come out of the affair scot-free. And our fate could scarcely be termed enviable — marooned for an indefinite time among Indians, on an island at the very ends of the earth. As for the mutineers who had chosen to remain on Tahiti, 1 knew only too well what their fate was likely to be. Young Ellison, who had been our mess boy, was often in my thoughts at this time. He had no realization of the gravity of the part he had played. Yet I knew that unless he quitted Tahiti before the arrival of a British man-of-war, our sea law would infallibly condemn him to death.

During those days of doubt and depression at Hitihiti's house, when Hina strove to divert my thoughts and my good old *taio* tried fruitlessly to cheer me up, I ceased to be a boy and became a man. Morrison was settled with Poino, the famous warrior who lived not far off, and Stewart was living with Peggy, in the house of Tipau, at the foot of One Tree Hill. I went frequently to pass the time of day with these two friends, and from their example learned to be ashamed of my fruitless depression. Morrison and Millward, who lived with Stewart at Poino's house, were already planning the little schooner they eventually built, and in which, without awaiting the arrival of a ship from home, they hoped to sail to Batavia, whence they might get passage to England. Stewart, who loved gardening, worked daily at beautifying the grounds about the new house old Tipau was building for him. When I mentioned my thoughts to him, he only smiled and said: "Never worry about what you cannot change," and went on with his digging, and planting, and laying out of paths. Perceiving at last that hard work was the remedy for my greensickness, I set to once more on my dictionary and was soon absorbed in the task.

One morning, about ten days after the departure of the *Bounty*, I found myself unable to sleep and set out for a walk on the long curving beach that led to Point Venus. It was still an hour before dawn, but the stars were bright and the northerly breeze blowing from the region of the equator made the air warm and mild. A dog barked at me as I passed an encampment of fishermen asleep on the sands under blankets of bark cloth.   Their great net, hung on stakes to dry, stretched for a quarter of a mile along my path.   At the very tip of the point, sheltered by the reef and provided with a deep, safe entrance, lies one of the most beautiful little harbours on the island, resorted to by travelers in sailing canoes who wish to pass the night on shore.   The water is always calm and beautifully clear, and a good-sized vessel can be moored so close inshore that a man may leap from her stern to the beach.

The point was a favourite resort of mine at this hour, for the view up the coast at sunrise was one I loved.   I was pleased to find the cove deserted, and, settling myself comfortably on one of the high sand dunes, I gazed eastward, where the first faint flush of dawn was beginning to appear.   At that moment a slight sound caught my ear, and, glancing seaward, I perceived that a large sailing canoe was stealing in through the passage. Her great brown sails of matting were ghostly blots on the sea, and presently I could hear the low commands of the man at the masthead, conning her in.   She came on fast under her press of sail, rounded-to smartly inside, and dropped her stone anchor with a resounding plunge.   The sails were furled while paddlers brought her stern to the land, and a man sprang ashore to make fast her stern-line to a coconut stump.

From the size of the vessel and the number of her crew, I judged that she carried passengers of consequence, but whoever they were, they still slept under the little thatched awning aft. Several of the crew came on land to build a fire of coconut husks and prepare food for the morning meal, and I saw two women helped ashore, who strolled away westward along the point and disappeared.

It was full daylight, with the rim of the sun just above the horizon, when I rose, unperceived by the travelers, and walked across to the large river which emptied into the sea on the west side of the point.   It was called Vaipoopoo, and close to the mouth there was a long reach of deep clear water in which I

loved to swim — a quiet and beautiful spot, distant from the
habitations of the Indians. The water was a good twenty
yards across and so deep that a boat of twelve tons burthen
might have entered to a distance of a quarter of a mile. Tall
old *mape* trees arched overhead, their buttressed roots forming
many a rustic seat along the banks.

I had long since chosen such a seat for myself, high above the
still water and at a distance of about a cable's length from the
beach. Frequently in the late afternoon I spent an hour or
two alone at this place, listening to the rustling of the trees
high overhead, and watching the small speckled fresh-water
fish as they rose for their evening meal of flies. In my fancy
I had named this spot Withycombe, after our home in England,
for indeed there were moments when the place seemed English
to the core, when I fancied myself in the warm summer twilight
at home, watching the trout rise in one of our West Country
streams.

To Withycombe, then, I repaired for my morning bath. I
threw off the light mantle of Indian cloth from my shoulders
and girded up the kilt about my waist. Next moment I
slipped into the deep clear water and swam leisurely downstream, drifting with the gentle flow of the current. High in
a tree overhead a bird was singing — an *omaomao,* whose song
is sweeter than that of our English nightingale.

As I drifted downstream I perceived suddenly, seated among
the buttressed roots of an old tree, a young girl lovely as a
water-sprite. I must have made some slight splashing sound,
for she turned her head with a little start and gazed full into
my eyes. I recognized her at once — she was Tehani, whom
I had seen in Tetiaroa long before. She gave no sign of shyness
or embarrassment, for a girl of her position had in those days
nothing to fear by day or by night, alone or in company. A
rude word to her would have been the cause of instant death to
the offender; an act of violence to her person might easily have
brought on a devastating war. This sense of security imparted

to the girls of Tehani's class an innocent assurance of manner which was by no means the least of their charms.

"May you live!" I said, Indian-fashion, rounding-to against the current.

"And you!" replied Tehani, with a smile. "I know who you are! You are Byam, the *taio* of Hitihiti!"

"True," said I, eager to prolong the conversation. "Shall I tell you who *you* are? You are Tehani, Poino's relative! I saw you in Tetiaroa, when you danced there."

She laughed aloud at this. "Ah, you saw me? Did I dance well?"

"So beautifully that I have never forgotten that night!"

"*Arero mona!*" she exclaimed mockingly, for the Indians call a flatterer "sweet tongue."

"So beautifully," I went on as if I had not heard, "that I said to Hitihiti: 'Who is yonder girl, lovelier than any girl in Tahiti, who might be the young goddess of the dance herself?'"

"*Arero mona!*" she mocked again, but I could see the blush mantling her smooth cheeks. She had just come out of the river and her brown hair lay in damp ringlets on her shoulders. "Come — let us see which can swim further under water, you or I!" Tehani slipped into the stream, and dived so smoothly that she scarcely rippled the still water. Clinging to the great root which had been her seat, I watched for what seemed an interminable time. The river turned in a bend about fifty yards below me, and at last, from out of sight beyond the bend, I heard Tehani's voice. "Come," she called gaily. "It is your turn to try!"

I dove at the words and began to swim downstream, about a fathom deep. The water was clear as air and I could see the shoals of small bright fish scatter before me and seek refuge among the shadowy boulders below. On and on I went, determined that no girl should excel me in the water, an element I have always loved. Aided by the current, my

progress was swift, and finally, when my lungs would endure
no more and I felt satisfied that I had won, I came to the surface
with a gasp. A chuckle musical as the murmur of the stream
greeted me, and shaking the water from my eyes I saw the
girl seated on a long root, flush with the water, a full ten yards
beyond.

"You came up there?" I asked in some chagrin.

"I have not cheated."

"Let us rest for a little while, and then I shall try again."

Tehani patted the root beside her. "Come and rest here,"
she said.

I pulled myself up beside her, shaking the wet hair back from
my eyes. Moved by common impulse, our two heads turned,
and Tehani's clear brown eyes smiled into mine. She turned
away suddenly and all at once I felt my heart beating fast.
Her hand was close to mine on the rough gnarled root; I took
it gently, and since it was not withdrawn I locked my fingers
in hers. She bent her head to gaze into the clear water, and for
a long time neither of us spoke.

I gazed, not at the water, but at the beautiful girl at my side.
She wore only a light kilt of white cloth, and her bare shoulder
and arm, turned to me, were smooth as satin and of the most
exquisite proportions. Her feet and hands, small and
delicately made, might have been envied by a princess, and
Phidias himself could have produced in cold marble nothing
one half so lovely as her young breasts, bared in all innocence.
In her face I saw sweetness and strength.

"Tehani!" I said, and took her hand in both of mine.

She made no answer, but raised her head slowly and turned
to me. Then all at once, and without a word between us, she
was in my arms. The faint perfume of her hair intoxicated
me, and for a time the beating of my heart made speech impossible. It was the girl who spoke first.

"Byam," she asked, stroking my wet hair caressingly, "have
you no wife?"

"No," I replied.

"I have no husband," said the girl.

At that moment I heard a woman's voice calling from downstream: "Tehani! Tehani O!" The girl hailed back, bidding the caller to wait, and turned to me.

"It is only my servant who came ashore with me. I bade her wait at the mouth of the stream while I bathed."

"You came from Tetiaroa?" I asked, with her head on my shoulder and my arm about her waist.

"No, I have been to Raiatea with my uncle. We have been two days and two nights at sea."

"Who is your uncle?"

The girl turned to me in real astonishment. "You do not know?" she said incredulously.

"No."

"Yet you speak our tongue like one of us! Strange men, you English — I have never talked with one of you before. My uncle is Vehiatua, of course, high chief of Taiarapu."

"I have often heard of him."

"Are you a chief in your own land?"

"A very small one, perhaps."

"I knew it! Knew it the moment I laid eyes on you! Hitihiti would not take as his *taio* a common man."

Again we fell silent, both conscious that our words reflected only the surface of our minds. "Tehani!" I said.

"Yes."

She raised her head and I kissed her in the English fashion, full on the lips. We walked back to the cove hand in hand, while the servant followed us, her eyes round with wonder.

Vehiatua had come ashore and was at breakfast when we came to the cove. He was a nobly proportioned old man, with thick gray hair and a manner of cheerful, good-natured dignity. His retainers were grouped about him as he ate, serving him with breadfruit, grilled fish fresh from the coals, and bananas

from a great bunch they had brought ashore. The old chief's
tattooing, which covered every portion of his body save his
face, was the most beautiful and intricate I have ever seen. I
was glad that I wore only my kilt, for it is discourteous to
approach the great Indian chiefs with covered shoulders.
Vehiatua gave no sign of surprise at sight of me.

"Eh, Tehani," he called out affectionately to his niece.
"Your breakfast is ready for you on board. And who is the
young man with you?"

"The *taio* of Hitihiti — Byam is his name."

"I have heard of him." And then, turning to me courteously, Vehiatua asked me to join him at his meal. I sat down
beside him, nothing loth, and answered his questions regarding
Hitihiti and the *Bounty*, of which he had heard much. He
expressed surprise at my knowledge of the Indian tongue, and
I told him of my mission and how my *taio* had aided me.

"And now you and the others are settling on Tahiti to remain among us?" Vehiatua asked.

"For a long time, at any rate," I replied. "It is possible
that when the next British ship arrives, in two years or three,
King George may send word that one or all of us must go
home."

"Aye," said the old aristocrat, "one must obey one's king!"

Presently Tehani came ashore, her breakfast over and her
toilet made, very different from the young tomboy who had
beaten me at diving so short a time before. Her beautiful
hair, dried in the sun, combed out and perfumed, was dressed
in the Grecian fashion, low on the nape of her neck. Her
mantle of snow-white cloth was draped in classic folds, and she
walked ahead of her little band of women with an air of
dignity few English girls of sixteen could have assumed.
The chief gave me a nod and rose to his feet.

"Let us go to the house of my kinsman," he said.

A stout muscular fellow crouched before Vehiatua, hands
braced on his knees. The chief vaulted to his shoulders with

the ease of long practice, and the human horse stood upright with a grunt. Vehiatua, Teina, and two or three other great chiefs of those days were never permitted to walk, for the touch of their feet rendered a commoner's land theirs. Wherever they went, save in their own domains, they were borne on the backs of men trained to the task.

With Tehani at my side, I followed her uncle down the beach, walking on the hard moist sand at the water's edge. As we passed the encampment of fishermen they hastened to throw off the mantles from their shoulders and seat themselves on the sand. To remain standing while a high chief passed would have been the greatest of insults.

"*Maeva te arii!*" was their greeting. (Hail to the chief!)

"May you live," said Vehiatua affably; "and may your fishing prosper!"

Old Hitihiti met us before his door, throwing off his mantle and stepping forward with bare shoulders to greet his friend. A meal was being prepared, and though our visitor had just eaten a prodigious quantity of food, he expressed his willingness to share in a second breakfast. Tehani and Hina knew each other well and seemed to have much to talk over. From the glances Hina cast at me from time to time, I suspected that Tehani was telling her of our meeting in the stream.

Toward noon, when the others had sought out shady places in which to spread their mats for a nap, I found my *taio* awake. He was alone, under his favourite hibiscus tree close to the beach, and I told him of my meeting with the girl, and that I loved her too dearly for my peace of mind.

"Why not marry her, if she is willing?" asked Hitihiti, when I had done.

"I think she might be willing, but what would her parents say?"

"She has none; both are dead."

"Vehiatua then."

"He likes you."

"Very well. But suppose we were married, and an English ship came with orders that I must go home."

My *taio* shrugged his great shoulders in despair. "You English are all alike," he said impatiently; "you make yourselves miserable by thinking of what may never happen! Is not to-day enough, that you must think of to-morrow and the day after that? The thought of an English ship makes you hesitate to marry the girl you fancy! And ten years, or twenty, might pass before another ship arrives! Enough of such talk! Yesterday is gone; you have to-day; to-morrow may never come!"

I could not help smiling at my old friend's philosophic outburst, not without its grain of sound common sense — called "common" because it is so rare. Worry over the future is without doubt the white man's greatest strength and greatest weakness in his quest of happiness — the only conceivable object in life. To the people of Tahiti, worry over the future was unknown; their language indeed contained no word with which to express such an idea.

No doubt Hitihiti was right, I reflected; since I was destined to live a long time among the Indians, I was justified in adopting their point of view. "You are my *taio*," I said. "Will you intercede for me with Vehiatua? Tell him that I love his niece dearly, and desire to marry her?"

The old chief clapped me on the back. "With all my heart!" he exclaimed. "You have been too long without a wife! Now let me sleep."

Tehani was awake before the others had finished their siesta, and I found her strolling on the beach. We were alone, and she came to me swiftly. "Sweetheart," I said, "I have spoken to my *taio*, and he has promised to ask Vehiatua for your hand. I have not done wrong?"

"I spoke to my uncle before he lay down to sleep," Tehani replied, smiling. "I told him I wanted you for my husband and must have you. He asked if you were willing, and I said that I must have you, willing or not! 'Do you want me to make war on Hitihiti and kidnap his friend?' he asked. 'Yes,' said I, 'if it comes to that!' He looked at me affectionately and then said: 'Have I ever denied you anything, my little pigeon, since your mother died? This Byam of yours is English, but he is a man nevertheless, and no man could resist you!' Tell me, do you think that is true?"

"I am sure of it!" I answered, pressing her hand.

When we returned to the house the sun was low, and the two chiefs, who had dismissed their followers, were conversing earnestly. "Here they are!" said Vehiatua, as we came in hand in hand.

"And well content with one another," remarked my *taio* smilingly.

"Vehiatua gives his consent to the marriage," he went on to me. "But he makes one condition — you are to spend most of your time in Tautira. He cannot bear to be separated from his niece. You will sympathize with him, Byam, and I too can understand. But you must come often to visit old Hitihiti, you two!"

"You are to be married at once, Tehani says, and in my house," said the chief of Taiarapu. "You can sail with me to-morrow, and Hitihiti and Hina will follow in their single canoe. They will represent your family at the temple. You two may consider yourselves betrothed."

I rose at these words and went into the house to open my box. When I returned, I carried the bracelet and the necklace purchased in London so long before. I showed them first to Vehiatua, who turned them admiringly in his hands.

"My gift to Tehani," I explained. "With your permission."

"She should be happy, for no girl in these islands possesses such things. I have seen gold, and know that it is very precious and does not rust like iron. A royal gift, Byam! What may we give you in return?"

"This!" I said, clasping the necklace about Tehani's neck, and taking her by the shoulders as if I would carry her off.

Vehiatua chuckled approvingly. "Well answered!" he said. "A royal gift in truth. For three and seventy generations she can count her ancestors back to the gods! Look at her! Where in all these islands will you find her like?"

Early the next morning, Vehiatua's men carried my belongings to the cove, and presently we went on board and the paddlers drove the vessel out through the passage, in the morning calm. She was the finest of all the Indian ships I had seen—her twin hulls each well over a hundred feet long, and twelve feet deep in the holds. Her two masts, well stayed and fitted with ratlines up which the sailors could run, spread huge sails of matting, edged with light frames of wood. On the platform between the two hulls was the small house in which the chief and his women slept, and it was here, sheltered from the rays of the sun, that I was invited to recline during our forty-mile voyage.

We paddled westward, skirting the long reefs of Pare, till the wind made up, and then, spreading our sails, we raced down the channel between Tahiti and Eimeo, with a fresh breeze at north-northeast. Toward noon, when we were off the point of Maraa, the wind died away and presently made up strong from the southeast, so that we were obliged to make a long board out to sea. I perceived at this time that the large Indian canoes, like Vehiatua's, could outpoint and outfoot any European vessel of their day. With the wind abeam they would have left our best frigates hull-down in no time, and, close-hauled, they would lay incredibly close to the wind.

The sea was rough off shore, and nearly all of the women on board were sick, but I was delighted to observe that Tehani was as good a sailor as I. She was *tapatai*, as the Indians said —fearless of wind and sea. As we approached the southern coast of Tahiti Nui, she pointed out to me the principal landmarks on shore, and on Taiarapu, beyond the low isthmus toward which we were steering. The southeast wind fell away an hour before sunset, as we were entering a wide passage through the reefs. The sails were furled and, with a score of paddlers on each side, we rowed into a magnificent landlocked bay, where the fleets of all the nations of Europe might have cast anchor, secure from any storm. This bay is on the south side of the Isthmus of Taravao, and is one of the finest and most beautiful harbours in the world.

The isthmus was uninhabited and overgrown with jungle, for the Indians believed it to be the haunt of evil spirits and unfit to be inhabited by men. We slept on board Vehiatua's vessel that night, and next morning — since the passage around the southeast extremity of Taiarapu was judged dangerous, owing to the violent currents and sunken reefs extending far out to sea — our vessel was dragged on rollers across the isthmus, a distance of about a mile and a half, by a great company of people from the near-by district of Vairao, summoned for the purpose. The principal chiefs and landowners of Tahiti, on their voyages around the island, always have their canoes dragged across this low land, and in the course of centuries a deep smooth path has been worn in the soil. The Vairao people performed their task with remarkable order and cheerfulness, and in less than three hours' time our vessel was launched on the north side. At Pueu we entered a passage through the reef and traveled the rest of the distance in the smooth sheltered water close along shore. It was mid-afternoon when we reached Tautira, where Vehiatua resided most of the time.

The chief was received ceremoniously by the members of his household, by the priest of the temple, who offered up a long prayer of thanks that Vehiatua had been preserved from the dangers of the sea, and by a vast throng of his subjects, to whom his justice and good nature had endeared him.

A meal had been prepared, for news of our coming had preceded us, and when Vehiatua, Taomi, the old priest, Tuahu, Tehani's elder brother, and I sat down to eat on the great semicircular verandah of the house, I caught my breath at the magnificence of the prospect. The house, shaded by old breadfruit trees, stood on high land, close to the deep clear river of Vaitepiha. To the east, the blue plain of the Pacific stretched away to the horizon; to the north and west, across ten miles of calm sea, Tahiti Nui swept up in all its grandeur to the central peaks; and to the west I gazed into the heart of the great valley of Vaitepiha, where cascades hung from cliffs smothered in vegetation of the richest green, and ridges like knife-blades ran up to peaks like turrets and spires. No man in the world, perhaps, save Vehiatua, possessed a house commanding such a view.

Hitihiti and his daughter arrived next day, and the ceremonies of my marriage with Tehani began on the day following. Vehiatua's first act was to present me with a fine new house, on the beach, about a cable's length distant from his own. It had been built for the under chief of the district, a famous warrior. This good-natured personage moved out cheerfully when informed that Vehiatua desired the house for his son-in-law — for so he was kind enough to consider me.

Into my new house I moved at once, with Hitihiti, his daughter, her husband, and the people of their household who had accompanied them from Matavai. Early in the morning my party and I set out for Vehiatua's house, carrying with us numerous gifts. These were termed the o — which is to say, with truly extraordinary brevity, "insurance of welcome." When these presents had been formally received, both families joined in a slow and stately parade to my house, while servants in the rear brought the bride's gifts — livestock, cloth, mats, furniture, and other things which would be useful to the new household. A throng of Vehiatua's subjects lined the path, and a band of strolling players caused constant laughter with their antics and songs.

In the house, Hina, who represented the female side of my "family," spread a large new mat, and on it a sheet of new white cloth. Vehiatua was a widower, and his older sister, a thin, white-haired old lady, straight and active as a girl, acted for his clan. Her name was Tetuanui, and she now spread upon Hina's cloth, half overlapping it, a snow-white sheet of her own. This symbolized the union of the two families, and Tehani and I were at once ordered to seat ourselves on the cloth, side by side. To the right and left of us were arrayed a great quantity of gifts — mats, capes, and wreaths of bright featherwork. We were then enjoined to accept these gifts in formal phrases, and when we had done so Hina and Tetuanui called for their *paoniho*. Every Indian woman was provided with one of these barbarous little implements — a short stick of polished wood, set with a shark's tooth keen as any razor. They were used to gash the head, causing the blood to flow down copiously over the face, on occasions of mourning and of rejoicing. While the spectators gazed at them in admiration, the two ladies now did us the honour of cutting their heads till they bled in a manner which made me long to protest. Taomi, the priest, took them by the hands and led them around and around us, so that the blood dripped and mingled on the sheet on which we sat. We were then directed to rise, and the sheet, stained with the mingled blood of the two families, was carefully folded up and preserved.

Vehiatua had dispatched to the mountains, the night before, a brace of his *piimato*, or climbers of cliffs. The office of these men was hereditary, and every chief kept one or two of them to fetch the skulls of his ancestors when required for some religious ceremony, and to return them afterwards to the secret caves, high up on the cliffs, where they were kept secure from desecration by hostile hands. The *piimato* carried in each hand a short pointed stick of ironwood, and with the aid of these they climbed up and down vertical walls of rock to which a lizard could scarcely cling. The skulls of Vehiatua's ancestors were to be witnesses of the religious ceremony presently to take place.

When the ceremony of the bride's reception in my house was over, we paraded slowly back to the house of Vehiatua, and went through a precisely similar ceremony there, even to the bloodletting and the folded sheets. This marked my reception into the house of Tehani's family. We next sat down to a feast, the men apart from the women, which lasted till mid-afternoon.

The social part of the marriage was now over; the religious remained. It was performed in Vehiatua's family *marae*, or temple, on the point not far from his house. Old Taomi, the priest, led the solemn procession. The temple was a walled enclosure, shaded by huge banyan trees and paved with flat stones. Along one side a pyramid thirty yards long and twenty wide rose in four steps to a height of about forty feet, and on top of it I perceived the effigy of a bird, curiously carved in wood. Accompanied by Hitihiti and his daughter, I was led to one corner of the enclosure, while Tehani, with Vehiatua and other relatives, took her place opposite me. The old priest then approached me solemnly and asked: —

"You desire to take this woman for your wife; will not your affection for her cool?"

"No," I replied.

Taomi next walked slowly across to where my young bride awaited him, and put the same question to her, and when she answered, "No," he made a sign to the others, who advanced from their respective corners of the *marae* and unfolded the two sheets of white cloth, on which the blood of the two families was mingled. Other priests now came forward, bearing very reverently the skulls of Vehiatua's ancestors, some of them so old that they seemed ready to crumble at a touch. These silent witnesses to the ceremony were placed carefully in a line on the pavement, so that their sightless eyes might behold the marriage of their remote descendant.

The girl and I were told to seat ourselves on the bloodstained sheets of cloth, hand in hand, while our relatives grouped themselves on either side. The priest then called upon the mighty chiefs and warriors whose skulls stood before us, giving each man his full name and resounding titles, and calling upon him to witness and to bless the union of Tehani with the white man from beyond the sea. When this was done, old Taomi turned to me.

"This woman will soon be your wife," he said seriously. "Remember that she is a woman, and weak. A commoner may strike his wife in anger, but not a chief. Be kind to her, be considerate of her." He paused, gazing down at me, and then addressed Tehani: "This man will soon be your husband. Bridle your tongue in anger; be patient; be thoughtful of his welfare. If he falls ill, care for him; if he is wounded in battle, heal his wounds. Love is the food of marriage; let not yours starve." He paused again and concluded, addressing us both: "*E maitai ia mai te mea ra e e na reira orua!*" This set phrase might be translated: "It will be well, if thus it be with you two!"

The solemnity of old Taomi's words and manner impressed the girl beside me so deeply that her hand trembled in mine, and, turning my head, I saw that there were tears in her eyes. In the dead silence following his words of admonition, the priest began a long prayer to Taaroa, the god of the Vehiatua clan, beseeching him to bless our union and to keep us in bonds of mutual affection. At last he finished, paused, and then called suddenly: "Bring the *tapoi!*"

A neophyte came running from the rear of the temple, carrying a great sheet of the sacred brown cloth made by men. The priest seized it, spread it wide, and flung it over us, covering Tehani and me completely. Next moment it was flung aside and we were told to rise. The marriage was over, and we were now embraced in the Indian fashion by the members of both clans. Of the days of feasting and merrymaking that followed our wedding there is no need to speak.

XIII

THE MOON OF PIPIRI

IT means little to say that I was happy with Tehani. It may mean more to state that only two women have left their mark on my life — my mother and the Indian girl. Long before the birth of our daughter I had resigned myself to the prospect of a life of tranquil happiness in Tautira; the sense of my immense remoteness from England grew stronger with the passage of time, and the hope that a ship might come faded into the background of my thoughts. Had it not been for my mother, who alone seemed to lend reality to memories of England, I am by no means certain that the arrival of a ship would have been welcome to me. And since I felt assured that neither Bligh nor any of those with him in the launch would ever reach home, I knew that my mother would be in no distress on my account until it became evident that the *Bounty* was long overdue. Adopting old Hitihiti's tropical philosophy, I put the past and the future out of mind, and for eighteen months — the happiest period of my entire life — I enjoyed each day to the full.

With her marriage, Tehani seemed to take on a new dignity and seriousness, though in the privacy of our home she showed at times that she was still the same wild tomboy who had beaten me at swimming in Matavai. I was working on my dictionary every day, and Sir Joseph Banks himself could not have entered into these labours with greater enthusiasm than did my wife. She directed our household with a firmness and skill that surprised me in so young a girl, leaving me free to do my writing and to divert myself with fishing parties, or with hunting wild boars in the hills. But I preferred excursions in which Tehani could accompany me, and missed many a boar hunt in order to take my wife on short voyages in our sailing canoe.

About a month after our marriage, Tehani and I sailed down to Matavai for a visit to my *taio*. I was eager to see old Hitihiti, as well as Stewart, Morrison, and other friends among the *Bounty's* people settled there. The distance is about fifty miles, and with the strong trade wind abaft the beam we made the passage in less than five hours, arriving early in the afternoon.

"Your friends are building a ship," Hitihiti informed me as we dined. "Morrison and Millward, the man with him at the house of Poino, are directing the task, and several others are helping. They have laid the keel and made fast the stem and stern. They are working on the point, not far from the sea."

Toward evening we strolled across to the little shipyard — Hina, her father, Tehani, and I. Morrison had chosen a glade about a hundred yards from the beach, an open grassy spot shaded by tall breadfruit trees. A crowd of Indians sat about on the grass, watching the white men at work. Their interest was intense, and in return for the privilege of being spectators they kept the shipbuilders more than supplied with food. The great chief Teina, to whom the land belonged, was there, with his wife Itea. They greeted us affably, and at that moment Morrison glanced up and caught my eye. He laid down his adze, wiped the sweat from his eyes, and took my hand heartily.

"We have heard of your marriage," he said. "Let me wish you happiness."

I made him known to Tehani, and as he pressed her hand young Tom Ellison came up to me. "What do you think of our ship, Mr. Byam?" he asked. "She's only thirty feet long, but Mr. Morrison hopes to sail her to Batavia. We 've christened her already: *Resolution 's* to be her name. By God, it takes resolution to build a ship without nails, or proper tools, or sawn-out plank!"

I shook hands with old Coleman, the *Bounty's* armourer, and with the German cooper, Hillbrandt. Norman and McIntosh, the carpenter's mates, were there, and Dick Skinner, the hairdresser who had been flogged in Adventure Bay. All worked with a will, under Morrison's direction; some impelled by a desire to reach England, others, conscious of their guilt, by the fear that a British ship might take them before their little vessel could set sail.

At sunset the shipwrights laid down their tools, and, leaving Tehani to return to the house with Hina and my *taio*, I accompanied Morrison to his residence at the foot of One Tree Hill. He and Millward lived with the warrior Poino, their friend, a stone's throw from Stewart's house.

I found Stewart pottering about his garden in the dusk. He had made Tipau's wild glen a place of ordered beauty, with paths leading this way and that, bordered with flowering shrubs, and shaded rockeries where he had planted many kinds of ferns. He made me welcome, straightening his back and shaking the earth from his hands.

"Byam, you 'll stop to sup, of course? And you too, Morrison?"

Ellison passed us at that moment on his way over the hill, for he lived in Pare, a mile to the west. Stewart liked the lad and called out to him: "I say, Tom! Won't you stop the night? It will be like old times."

"With all my heart, Mr. Stewart!" he said, grinning. "I 'm half afraid to go home, anyhow."

"What 's wrong?" asked Morrison.

"That wench of mine again. Last night she caught me giving her sister a kiss. I swear there was no harm intended, but do you think she would listen to reason? She knocked her sister down with a tapa mallet, and would have done the same for me if I had not run for it."

Stewart laughed. "I've no doubt you deserved it."

Peggy was calling us into the house, and half an hour later we sat down to our evening meal, served by old Tipau's slaves. Stewart's dining room was a large thatched house open to the air, and decorated with hanging baskets of ferns. A man stood at one end, holding aloft a torch which illuminated the place with a flickering glare. Peggy had gone off to sup with her women, and Tipau preferred to eat his meal alone.

"How long will it take you to complete your vessel?" I asked Morrison.

"Six months or more. The work goes slowly with so few tools."

"You hope to reach Batavia in her?"

"Yes. From there we can get passage home on a Dutch ship. Five of us are to make the attempt — Norman, McIntosh, Muspratt, Byrne, and I. Stewart and Coleman prefer to wait here for an English ship."

"I feel the same," I remarked. "I am happy in Tautira, and glad of the chance to work on my Indian dictionary."

"As for me," said Stewart, "I find Tahiti a pleasant place enough. And I have no desire to be drowned!"

"Drowned be damned!" exclaimed Morrison impatiently. "Our little schooner will be staunch enough to sail around the world!"

"You have n't told Mr. Byam about *us*," put in Ellison. "We are going to start a little kingdom of our own. Desperate characters we are — not one but would swing at the yardarm if taken by a British ship! Mr. Morrison has promised to set us down on some island west of here."

"It is the best thing they can do," said Morrison. "I shall try to find an island where the people are friendly. Tom is coming, as are Millward, Burkitt, Hillbrandt, and Sumner. Churchill intends to stay here, though he's certain to be taken and hanged.   Dick Skinner believes it his duty to give himself up and suffer for his crime.   As for Thompson, he is more of a beast than a man, and I would not have him on board."

"Where is Burkitt?" I asked.

"He and Muspratt are living in Papara," said Stewart, "with the chief of the Teva clan."

"They offered to join us in the work," Morrison added, "but neither man has any skill."

I was glad to have news of the *Bounty's* people, most of whom I liked.   We talked late into the night, while Tipau's man lit torch after torch from the bundle at his side.   The moon was rising when I took leave of my friends and trudged home along the deserted beach.

I had occasion, the next morning, to recall what Morrison had said of Thompson, the most stupid and brutal of the *Bounty's* crew.   He and Churchill had struck up an oddly assorted friendship, and spent most of their time sailing about the island in a small canoe, fitted with a sail of canvas. Thompson disliked the Indians as much as he distrusted them, and on shore was never without a loaded musket in his hand.

Going down to the beach for an early bath in the sea, I found the pair encamped by their canoe, with a sucking pig roasting on the coals near by.   "Come — join us at breakfast, Mr. Byam," called Churchill, hospitably.

Thompson looked up, scowling.   "Damn you, Churchill," he growled — "Let him find his own grub.   We 've no more than enough for ourselves."

Churchill flushed.   "Hold your tongue, Matt," he exclaimed, "Mr. Byam 's my friend!   Go and learn manners from the Indians, before I knock them into your head!"

Thompson rose and stalked off to a sandhill, where he seated himself sulkily, his musket between his knees.   I had already breakfasted, and as I turned away I saw a dozen men pulling a large sailing canoe up on the beach, and the owner and his wife approaching us. The man carried in his arms a child of three or four years. They stopped by Churchill's canoe to admire its sail of canvas, and turned to wish us good day. The Indian woman leaned over the boom to examine the stitching of the bolt rope, and at that moment I heard Thompson's harsh voice.

"Get out of it!" he ordered abruptly.

The Indians glanced up courteously, not understanding the words, and Thompson shouted again: "Grease off, damn you!" The Indian couple glanced at us in bewilderment, and Churchill was opening his mouth to speak when suddenly, without further warning, the seaman leveled his musket and fired. The ball passed through the child and through the father's chest; both fell dying on the beach, staining the sand with their blood. The woman shrieked and people began to run toward us from the house.

Churchill sprang to his feet and bounded to where Thompson sat, with the smoking musket in his hand. One blow of his fist stretched the murderer on the sand; he snatched up the musket, seized Thompson's limp body under the arms, and ran, dragging him, to where the canoe lay in the wash of the sea. Setting the musket carefully against a thwart, he tossed his companion into the bilges as if he had been a dead pig, then sprang into the canoe, pushing off as he did so. Next moment he had sail on her; the little vessel was making off swiftly to the west before the gathering crowd understood what had occurred.

I rushed to the dying father and his small daughter, but perceived at once that there was nothing to be done for them. Within five minutes both expired. The moment it was ascertained that they were dead the frantic mother seized her *paoniho* and gashed her head in a shocking manner, while blood covered her face and shoulders. The crew of her vessel armed themselves with large stones and were beginning to gather about me threateningly when Hitihiti appeared. He grasped

the situation, and the sullen murmur of the people died away
as he held up an arm for silence.

"This man is my *taio*," he said; "he is as innocent as yourselves! Why do you stand there chattering like women?
You have weapons! Launch your canoe! I know the man
who killed your master; he is an evil-smelling dog, and not one
of the Englishmen will lift a hand to protect him!"

They set off at once in pursuit, but, as I learned afterwards,
they were unable to come up with the fugitives. The dead
were buried the same night, and Hina and Tehani did their
best to comfort the poor woman, whose home was on the neighbouring island of Eimeo. The sequel to this tragedy came a
fortnight later, when Tehani and I returned to our home.

Fearing to land on the west side of Tahiti, and wishing to put
the greatest possible distance between themselves and Matavai,
Churchill had steered his canoe through the dangerous reefs
at the south end of Taiarapu and sailed on to Tautira,
where Vehiatua, supposing him to be one of my friends, had
welcomed him. But Thompson's reputation had preceded
him, and he found himself shunned and abhorred by all.
Churchill was by this time heartily sick of his companion
and desired nothing better than to be rid of him. He told
me as much when he came to my house on the evening of our
arrival, musket in hand.

"I've half a mind to shoot the fellow!" he remarked.
"Hanging's too good for him! But damn me if I can shoot
a man in cold blood! I was a fool not to leave him to be dealt
with by the Indians in Matavai!"

"They'd have made short work of him," I said.

"And a bloody good job! I'm done with him. I told him
to-day he could have the canoe if he'd get out of here and
not come back."

"Leave him to the Indians," I suggested. "They'd have
killed him long since had he not been with you."

"Aye. Look — there he is now."

Thompson was seated alone on the beach, half a cable's length from us, with the air of a man brooding over his wrongs, as he nursed the musket between his knees.

"The man's half mad," growled Churchill. "You've a musket, Byam; best load it and keep it handy till he's gone."

"Are you planning to stop in Tautira?" I asked after a pause.

"Yes. I like the old chief—your father-in-law, whatever he is—and he seems to like me. He's a fighting man, and so is the other chief, Atuanui. We were planning a bit of a war last night. He says if I'll help him he'll give me a piece of land, with a fine young wife thrown in. But come—it is time we went to his house."

Vehiatua had bidden us to witness a *heiva* that evening—a night dance of the kind I had seen in Tetiaroa long before. We found the grounds bright with torchlight and thronged with spectators, and when we had greeted our friends, Tehani and I seated ourselves with Churchill on the grass, on the outer fringe of the audience.

The drums had scarcely struck up when I heard an Indian shout warningly behind us, followed instantly by the report of a musket. Churchill attempted to spring to his feet, but sank down coughing beside me, the musket dropping from his nerveless hand. Women were shrieking and men shouting on all sides, and I heard Vehiatua's voice boom out above the uproar: "Aye! Kill him! Kill him!" In the flickering torchlight I saw Thompson break away from the scuffle behind me and begin to run toward the beach with ungainly bounds, still clinging to his musket. Atuanui, the warrior chief, snatched up a great stone and hurled it with his giant's arm. It struck the murderer between the shoulders, and sent him sprawling. Next moment the Indian warrior was upon him, beating out his brains with the same stone that had brought him down. When I returned to the house, Churchill was dead.

Since the Indians made war, and abandoned plans for war, for reasons which struck me as frivolous in the extreme, the loss of Churchill was accepted as an unfavourable omen by Vehiatua's priests, and the expedition planned against the people of the south coast of Eimeo was given up. I was secretly glad to be freed from the duty of taking up arms against men to whom I bore no ill-will, and settled down with relief to a tranquil domestic life and my studies of the Indian tongue.

I shall not cumber this narrative with my observations on the life and customs of the Indians — their religion, their intricate system of *tapu*, their manner of making war, their *arioi* society, and their arts and sciences, all of which have been fully described by Cook, Bougainville, and other early visitors to Tahiti. But I shall do the people of Tahiti the justice to mention two of their customs, shocking in themselves, but less so when the reasons for them are made clear. I allude to infanticide and human sacrifice.

Nowhere in the world are children cherished more tenderly than in the South Sea, yet infanticide was considered by the Indians a praiseworthy act of self-sacrifice. The object of the *arioi* society — the strolling players whose chiefs were of the most considerable families in Tahiti — was to set an example both to chiefs and to commoners, as a warning against over-populating the island. Should a member of the society give birth to a female child, it was killed at once, in the quickest and most painless manner, and their greatest term of contempt was *vahine fanaunau* — a fertile woman. The Indians had a perfect understanding of the dangers of overpopulation, and guarded against them by making large families unfashionable. Cruel as the method seems, it should not be criticized without reflecting that men increase, while the amount of habitable land on a small island remains the same.

As for human sacrifice, the ceremony was rarely performed, and then only on the altar of Oro, god of war. The victim was taken unaware and killed mercifully, by a sudden blow from behind, and he was without exception a man who, in the opinion of the chiefs, deserved death for the public good. In a land where courts, judges, and executioners were unknown, the prospect of being sacrificed to the god of war restrained many a man from crimes against society.

The people of Tahiti were fortunate in many respects — the climate, the fertility of their island, and the abundance of food to be obtained with little effort; yet they were still more fortunate, perhaps, in their lack of money or any other general medium of exchange.   Hogs, mats, or bark cloth might be given as a reward for building a house or the tattooing of a young chief, but such property was perishable, and considered a gift rather than an exchange.   Since there was nothing that a miser might hoard, avarice, that most contemptible of human failings, was unknown, and there was little incentive to greed. To be accused of meanness was dreaded by chief and commoner alike, for a mean man was considered an object of ridicule.   By our introduction of iron, and inculcation of the principles of barter, there is no doubt that we have worked the Indians infinite harm.

On the fifteenth of August, 1790, our daughter Helen was born.   The child was given Tehani's name and long title, which in truth I cannot recollect, but I gave her my mother's name as well.   She was a lovely little creature, with strange and beautiful eyes, dark blue as the sea, and since she was our first-born, or *matahiapo*, her birth was the occasion for ceremonies religious and political.

A large enclosure had been fenced on the sacred ground behind Vehiatua's family temple, and three small houses built within.   The first was called "The House of Sweet Fern," in which the mother was to be delivered of her child; the second was known as "The House of the Weak," where mother and child would pass a fortnight afterwards; the third was called "The Common House" and had been built to shelter Tehani's attendants. For six days after our little Helen was born, silence reigned on sea and land along the coast of Tiarapu; all of the commoners retiring into the mountain fastnesses, where they might converse, build fires for their cooking, and live in comfort till the restriction was over.

On the seventh day I was admitted into the House of the Weak, and saw my daughter for the first time. Vehiatua and I went together, for no man save Taomi, the priest, had set foot within the enclosure till that time. It was dark in the house, and for a moment I could scarcely make out Tehani on her couch of soft mats and tapa, nor the tiny newcomer, waving chubby fists at me.

Our child was three months old when Stewart and Peggy sailed around the island to visit us. They had a small daughter of their own, as I had learned some time before, and the two young mothers found in their children an inexhaustible subject of conversation. Stewart spent a week with us, and one day of the seven stands out in my memory.

It was still dark when I rose that morning, but when I emerged from my plunge into the river the fowls were beginning to flutter down from the trees. As I stood on the bank, breathing deep of the cool morning air, I felt a touch on my shoulder and found my wife beside me.

"They are still asleep," she said; "you should see Helen and little Peggy, side by side! Look, there is not a cloud in the sky! Let us take a small canoe and paddle to Fenua Ino — the four of us, and the children, and Tuahu."

We had often spoken of spending a day on the islet of Fenua Ino, a place I had never visited, and, knowing that Stewart would enjoy the trip, I assented readily. We chose a single canoe, stocked her with provisions and drinking-nuts, and installed the two sleeping babies on soft tapa, side by side in the shell of a large sea-turtle, well polished and cleaned, and shaded with green coconut fronds. Tuahu, my brother-in-law, was a tall, powerful young man, a year older than I, and as pleasant a companion as I have ever known. He took his place in the stern, to steer us through the reefs, and set us a lively stroke. Stewart and I had long since become accomplished hands in a canoe, and our wives were strong active girls, able to wield a paddle with any man.

For five miles south from Tautira, the coast is sheltered by a reef at some distance from the land, and is perhaps the richest and most densely populated district in all Tahiti. This was the coast I had seen when the *Bounty* first approached the island, so long before. Then the reef ceases, and the Pacific thunders against the tall green cliffs called Te Pari — a wild region, uninhabited and believed to be the haunt of evil spirits. At the beginning of the cliffs, where the reef ended, was the small coral island, about half a mile from shore, where we planned to spend the day.

We spread our mats in the shade of a great unfamiliar tree, and Tuahu fetched our lunch and the turtle shell. Stewart called to his wife: "Bring the children, Peggy. Byam and I will keep an eye on them, and have a yarn while you and Tehani explore the island."

Stewart and I stretched ourselves out comfortably in the shade. Our daughters slept in their odd cradle, starting a little from time to time as babies do, but never opening an eye.

"Byam, what do you suppose has become of Christian?" Stewart asked. "Sometimes I think that he may have killed himself."

"Never! He felt too deeply his responsibility toward the others."

"Perhaps you are right. By this time they must have settled on some island — I wonder where!"

"I have often puzzled over that question," I replied. "They might have gone to one of the Navigators' Islands, or to any of the coral islands we passed on the voyage north."

Stewart shook his head. "I think not," he said; "those places are too well known. There must be scores of rich islands still uncharted in this part of the sea. Christian would be more apt to search for some such place, where he would be safer from pursuit."

I made no reply and for a long time we lay sprawled in the shade, our hands behind our heads. I felt deeply the lonely peace and beauty of the islet. Beyond the long white curve of the reef, a northerly breeze ruffled the Pacific gently. I groped in memory for a phrase of Greek and at last it came to me — "wine-dark sea." Stewart spoke, half to himself, as if putting his thoughts into words: "What a place for a hermit's meditations!"

"Would you like to live here?" I asked.

"Perhaps. But I would miss the sight of English faces. You, Byam, living alone among the Indians, do you never miss your own kind?"

I thought for a moment before I replied: "Not thus far."

Stewart smiled. "You are half Indian already. Dearly as I love Peggy, I would be less happy at Matavai without Ellison. I've grown fond of the lad, and he spends half his time at our house. It's a damned shame he had to meddle in the mutiny."

"There's not an ounce of harm in the young idiot," I said; "and now he must sail away with Morrison and pass the rest of his days in hiding, on some cannibal island to the west. All for the pleasure of waving a bayonet under Bligh's nose!"

"They'll be launching the *Resolution* in another six weeks," remarked Stewart. "Morrison has done wonders! She's a staunch little ship, fit to weather anything."

Our wives were approaching us, followed by Tuahu, who carried a mass of sweet-scented flowers which they had woven into wreaths for us.

One flower in particular, in long sprays and wonderfully fragrant took my fancy. It was unknown on Tahiti, and our companions were trying to recall its name.

"It is common in the low islands east of here, where the people eat man," said Tuahu; "I saw hundreds of the trees in Anaa, when I was there last year. They have a name for it in their language, as we have in ours, but I forget both."

"*Tafano!*" exclaimed Tehani, suddenly.

"Aye, that's it!" said her brother, and I made a note of the word for my dictionary.

We fetched the baskets of food for the girls, and retired to a little distance, Indian fashion, to eat our own lunch. When it was over and we were together once more, in the shade, Tuahu recounted the legend of the islet.

"Shall I tell you why no men live here?" he began. "It is because of the danger at night. Several times in the past men have tried to sleep here, out of bravado, or because they did not know. All have crossed to Tahiti in the morning silent and dejected, and died soon after, raving mad. Since the very beginning, a woman has come here each night when the sun has set. She is more lovely than any mortal, with a melodious voice, long shining hair, and eyes no man can resist. Her pleasure is to seduce mortal men, knowing that her embraces mean madness and death."

Stewart winked at me. He plucked two blades of coarse grass, a long and a short, and held them out. "Come," he said banteringly, with a glance at the girls, "we'll draw to see who stops the night."

But Tehani snatched the grass from his hand. "Stop the night if you like," she said to Stewart, "but Byam goes ashore! I want no demon-woman for him, nor mortal girls who would swim out to impersonate her!"

Stewart sailed for Matavai on the day after our picnic, and four months passed before I saw him again. Yet as I review those months in memory, they seem no longer than so many weeks. It has often been observed — with a justice for which I can vouch — that in the South Sea men lose their sense of the passage of time. In a climate where perpetual summer reigns and there is little to distinguish one week from another, the days slip by imperceptibly.

That year of 1790 was the happiest and seemed the shortest of my entire life. And 1791 began happily enough; January passed, and February, and toward the middle of March Tehani sailed with Vehiatua to the other side of the island, to take part in some religious ceremony. The Indian ceremonies of this nature were wearisome to me, and I decided to remain in Tautira, with my brother-in-law. My wife had been gone a week or more when the ship came.

Tuahu and I had been amusing ourselves at a *heiva* the night before, and, returning late to bed, I slept till the sun was up. Tuahu woke me with a hand on my shoulder. "Byam!" he said in a voice breathless with excitement. "Wake up! A ship! A ship!"

Rubbing the sleep from my eyes, I followed him to the beach, where numbers of people were already gathering. All were staring out to the east, into the dazzling light of the morning sun. There was a light breeze at east by north, and far offshore, so far that she was hull-down and her courses hidden by the curve of the world, I saw a European ship. Topsails, topgallants, and royals — looking small, dark, and weatherbeaten in the level light — were visible, though the distance was still too great to guess at her nationality. The Indians were in great excitement.

"If a Spanish ship," I heard one man say, "she will put in here."

"And if French, she will go to Hitiaa!"

"British ships always go to Matavai," said Tuahu, glancing at me for confirmation.

"Do you think she is British?" asked Tetuanui, my wife's old aunt.

I shrugged my shoulders, and an Indian said: "She is not Spanish, anyway. They are standing off too far."

The vessel was approaching the land on the starboard tack, and it was clear that she was not steering for the Spanish anchorage at Pueu.   She might have been a French frigate making for Bougainville's harbour, or a British vessel bound for Matavai. We seated ourselves on the grass, and presently, as she drew slightly nearer and the light increased, I was all but convinced, from the shape of her topsails, that she was British.   I sprang to my feet.

"Tuahu," I said, "I believe she's British!   Let us take your small sailing canoe and run down to Matavai."

My brother-in-law sprang up eagerly.   "We shall beat them there by hours," he exclaimed; "this wind always blows strongest close to land.   They will be becalmed offshore."

We made a hasty breakfast on cold pork and yams, left over from the night before, had the canoe well stocked with provisions and drinking nuts, and set sail within the hour, accompanied by one man.   As Tuahu had predicted, the wind blew strong alongshore, while the vessel four or five miles distant lay almost becalmed.   With the fresh breeze abeam, our canoe tore through the sheltered water within the reefs, headed out into the open sea at Pueu, and sailed past Hitiaa and Tiarei. It was mid-afternoon when we ran through the gentle breakers before Hitihiti's house.   The place was deserted, for news of the ship had preceded us, and my *taio*, with all his household, had repaired to the lookout point on One Tree Hill.

XIV

THE PANDORA

THROUGHOUT the day the Indians had been coming to Matavai in great numbers, and many canoes were drawn up on the beach, belonging to those who had arrived from remote parts of the island. When I climbed One Tree Hill, late in the afternoon, I found it thronged with people keeping a lookout for the vessel. The excitement was intense. It was such a scene as must have presented itself twenty-four years earlier when Captain Wallis arrived in the *Dolphin*, the first European vessel to visit the island. The crowd was so great that I had difficulty in finding Stewart. Presently I spied him with some of the Matavai people, standing near the ancient flowering tree which gave the hill its name. He made his way to me at once.

"I've been expecting you all day, Byam," he said. "What can you tell me of the ship? You must have seen her as you were coming round the coast."

"Yes," I replied. "She's an English frigate, I should say."

"I thought as much," he replied, sadly. "I suppose I should be glad. In one sense, I am, of course. But fate has played a sorry trick upon us. You must feel that, too?"

I did feel it, profoundly. The first sight of the vessel had given me a moment of keen happiness. I knew that it meant home; but after all these months Tahiti was home as well, and I realized that I was bound to the island by ties no less strong than those which drew me from it. Either to go or to stay seemed a cruel choice; but we well knew that there would be

no choice.   Our duty was plain.   We should have to go aboard
as soon as the ship came to anchor and report the mutiny.

We had little doubt that the vessel had been sent out in
search of the *Bounty*.   The Indians, of course, had no inkling
of this.   They believed that the awaited ship probably belonged to Captain Cook, coming for additional supplies of
young breadfruit trees, and that Captain Bligh, his supposed
son, would be with him.   While Stewart and I were talking,
a messenger from Teina was sent in search of us.   He wished to
see us at his house.   We sent back word that we would come
shortly.

"What of our wives and children?" Stewart asked gloomily.
"It may seem strange to you, Byam, but the truth is that I
have never before realized that we should have to go.   England seems so far away, as though it were on another planet."

"I know," I replied.   "My feeling has been the same."

He shook his head mournfully.   "Let's not talk of it.
You are certain the ship is English?"

"All but certain."

"In that case, I'm sorry for poor Morrison.   He left in the
schooner four days ago.   They may be well on their way westward by this time."

Morrison's plans, he told me, had not changed.   All the
mutineers remaining on Tahiti, with the exception of Skinner,
had decided to go with him in the *Resolution*.   They had
agreed among themselves to go ashore at some island to the
westward where there would be little chance of their ever
being discovered.   Morrison, Norman, McIntosh, Byrne, and
Muspratt would then try to make their way to Batavia, on the
island of Java, where they hoped to sell the schooner and take
passage in some ship bound to Europe.

"It's a desperate venture for all of them," Stewart continued.   "There are Ellison, Hillbrandt, Burkitt, Millward,
and Sumner to be left at some island yet to be decided upon.
God knows what their fate will be!   They have firearms and

think they will be able to defend themselves until they can establish friendly relations with the people. But what can five men do against hundreds of savages? We know what the islanders to the westward are like; our experiences at Namuka taught us that. They are as good as dead, in my opinion."

"They will have a fighting chance at least," I said. "In any event it will be better than being taken home to be hung."

"Yes, they were wise to go, no doubt. What chance do you think Morrison has of reaching Batavia?"

We discussed the matter at length. Morrison was an excellent navigator, and five men were ample to work the little schooner. They were provided with a compass and one of Captain Bligh's charts of the passage through Endeavour Straits; but looked at in the most hopeful light, it seemed doubtful indeed that the *Resolution* would ever reach Batavia. Stewart told me that the schooner had first gone to the district of Papara, on the southern side of Tahiti, to pick up McIntosh, Hillbrandt, and Millward. It was possible, he thought, that the schooner might still be there.

Presently a great shout went up from the watchers on the hill. The frigate had been sighted as she emerged from behind a distant headland. She was four or five miles offshore, and the dying wind was so light that we knew she could not make the land before dark. Evidently her captain realized this, for shortly afterward the ship hove-to under her topsails.

Some of the Indians remained on the hill, but most of them, seeing that the vessel did not intend to come in that night, descended with us. On our way to Teina's house we met Skinner and Coleman, who had been on an excursion into the mountains and had only just heard the news of the frigate. Coleman was deeply moved when I told him that the ship was, almost certainly, English. More than any of us, with the exception of Morrison, had he longed for home. He had a wife and children there and had formed no alliance with any of the Tahitian women. Tears of joy dimmed his eyes, and without waiting for further information he rushed up the hill for a sight of the vessel that would take him to England.

Stewart and I were concerned for Skinner. He had long since repented of the part he had taken in the mutiny, and was, in fact, the only one of the mutineers who had done so. His sense of guilt had grown stronger as the months had passed. A deeply religious man, he had brooded over his disloyalty to the Crown and was determined to give himself up at the first opportunity. We knew that repentance, however sincere, would have no weight with a court-martial. His doom was certain if he surrendered himself. Guilty though he undoubtedly was, we had no desire to see the poor fellow clapped into irons and taken to England to be hung. But he would not listen to our suggestions that he try to hide himself while there was yet time.

"I have no wish to escape," he said. "I know what will happen when I surrender myself, but my death will be a warning to others who may be tempted to mutiny."

We pleaded with him for some time, but it was useless, so we left him and proceeded to Teina's house. We found the chief at supper, which he asked us to share with him, and while we ate he plied us with questions concerning the vessel. How many guns was she likely to carry? How many men? Would King George be aboard? And the like. All the Tahitians had a great desire to see the King of England, and Bligh, as well as the British captains who had visited the island before him, had played upon their credulity to the extent of giving them reason to hope that the King might some day visit Tahiti.

We explained to Teina that King George had great dominions, and was so occupied with affairs at home, particularly in wars with neighboring nations, that he had little opportunity for voyaging to such far places.

"But Tuté will come," Teina said, with conviction. (Tuté was the universal name for Captain Cook, the nearest they could come to the sound of it; and Bligh was called Parai.)

"Parai promised that Tuté would come. This must be his ship." He went on to conjecture what the purpose of this visit might be. He believed that Cook and Bligh, if the latter chanced to be with him, would now decide to remain permanently at Tahiti. He would urge them to do so, and would set aside great tracts of land for their use and provide them with as many servants as they might want. With their help he would bring the whole of Tahiti under subjection; then we would all proceed to the island of Eimeo, and on to Raiatea and Bora Bora, conquering each of these islands in turn. And he promised that Stewart and I should be made great chiefs, and that our children should grow in power after us.

It must have been well past midnight when we left Teina's house, but none of the people there or elsewhere thought of sleep that night. Those who had come from distant parts were encamped along the beach and among the groves inland, and the light of their fires illuminated the entire circle of the bay. Canoes were still arriving, most of them small craft containing ten or a dozen men, bringing island produce to be bartered for the trade goods of the vessel. As we walked down the beach we saw one huge canoe, containing fifty or more paddlers, just entering the bay. Her men were singing as they urged her forward, and the blades of the paddles flashed in the firelight as they approached. It was an interesting sight to watch them berth her. With her great curved stern rising high above the water, she looked like some strange sea monster. She was heavily loaded and grounded at some distance from the beach, whereupon all the men leaped out and brought her farther along. There must have been one hundred people in her, to say nothing of the cargo of pigs and fowls. When these had been unloaded, rollers were placed under her keel, and with twenty or thirty men on each side she was quickly run up the long slope of the beach to level ground.

We went to Stewart's house, which stood just under One Tree Hill, on the western side of the bay. Here, too, everyone was astir. Peggy, Stewart's wife, with their little daughter asleep on the mat beside her, was sorting over great rolls of tapa cloth, selecting the finest pieces as gifts for her husband's friends on the ship. She took it for granted that we must know everyone aboard, and it was plain that she had no suspicion of what the arrival of the vessel might mean to us both. Presently I went off to seek Tuahu and my other friends from Tautira who were encamped near by. By this time dawn was not far off, and Tuahu suggested that we should take a canoe and paddle out to sea to meet the vessel.

"If it is a strange ship, Byam, the captain will be glad of a pilot into the bay. But I think it is Parai coming back to see us. We shall be the first to meet him."

I agreed to the proposal at once, and taking old Paoto, Tuahu's servant, with us, we hauled our canoe to the water, and a few moments later had rounded Point Venus and were well out to sea.

Tahiti had never seemed so beautiful as on that morning, in the faint light of dawn. The stars were shining brightly when we set out, but they faded gradually, and the island stood out in clear, cold silhouette against the sky. We paddled steadily for half an hour before we caught sight of the ship, and then drifted to wait for her to come up with us. The breeze was of the lightest, and an hour later she was still at a considerable distance. She was a frigate of twenty-four guns, and, although I was convinced that she was British, my heart leaped when at last I saw the English colours.

In my first eagerness to go off to her, I had forgotten that I was dressed as an Indian and not as an English midshipman. My only remaining uniform had come to grief at Tautira. I had not worn it from the day I left the *Bounty*, but had kept it carefully wrapped in a piece of tapa cloth hanging from a rafter in my house. Thinking it safe there, I had not examined the parcel in many months, and when at last I did so I found that it had been nearly devoured by rats, and was past all hope of repair. This mattered nothing then, for I had long since adopted the Tahitian costume, and for the most part wore nothing but a girdle of tapa and a turban of the same material. Reminded now of my half-naked condition, I was tempted to turn back, but it was too late to reconsider. The vessel was only a few hundred yards distant and had altered her course to pick us up.

The larboard bulwarks were crowded with men, and I saw the captain on the quarter-deck with his spyglass leveled at us, and a group of officers standing behind him. As the ship came alongside we paddled with her, and a line was thrown to us from the gangway. I clambered aboard and Tuahu after me. Paoto remained in the canoe, which was veered astern and towed after us.

My skin was as brown as that of the Indians themselves, and, with my arms covered with tattooing, it is not strange that I should have been mistaken for a Tahitian. A lieutenant stood at the gangway, and as we reached the deck sailors and marines alike crowded close for a better view. The lieutenant smiled ingratiatingly and patted Tuahu on the shoulder. "Maitai! Maitai!" (Good! Good!) he said. This was evidently the only Indian word he knew.

"You can address him in English, sir," I said, smiling. "He understands it very well. My name is Byam, Roger Byam, late midshipman of His Majesty's ship *Bounty*. If you like, I shall be glad to pilot you in to the anchorage."

The expression on the lieutenant's face altered at once. Without replying he glanced me up and down, from head to foot.

"Corporal of marines!" he called.

The corporal advanced and saluted.

"Fall in a guard and take this man aft."

To my astonishment four men with muskets and bayonets fixed were told off, and I was placed in the midst of them, and in this manner marched to the captain, who awaited us on the quarter-deck. The lieutenant preceded us. "Here's one of the pirates, sir," he said.

"That I am not, sir!" I replied. "No more than you yourself!"

"Silence!" the captain ordered. He regarded me with an expression of cold hostility, but I was too incensed at the accusation to hold my tongue.

"Allow me to speak, sir," I said. "I am not one of the mutineers. My name is . . ."

"Did you hear me, you scoundrel? I ordered you to be silent!"

I was hot with shame and anger, but I had self-possession enough not to give way further to it, and I was certain that the misunderstanding with respect to me would soon be cleared up. I saw Tuahu regarding me with an expression of utter amazement. I was not permitted to speak to him.

The most humiliating treatment was yet to come. The armourer was sent for, and a few moments later handcuff were placed upon me and I was taken under guard to the captain's cabin, there to await his pleasure. Two hours passed, during which time I was kept standing by the door. I saw no one except the guards, who refused to speak to me. Meanwhile the ship had been worked into Matavai Bay and came to anchor at the same spot where the *Bounty* had lain upon her arrival nearly three years earlier. Through the ports I could see the throngs of Indians along the shore and canoes putting off to the frigate. In one of the first of these were Coleman and Stewart. Stewart was dressed in his midshipman's uniform, and Coleman in an old jacket and a pair of trousers patched with pieces of tapa cloth, all that remained of his European clothing. Their canoes passed under the counter and I saw no more of them for some time.

The frigate was called the *Pandora*, and she was commanded by Captain Edward Edwards, a tall spare man with cold blue eyes and pale bony hands and face. As soon as the ship was safely anchored he came to his cabin, followed by one of his lieutenants, Mr. Parkin. He seated himself at his table and ordered me to be brought before him. I protested at once against the treatment I had received, but he ordered me to be silent, and sat for some time regarding me as though I were a curiosity brought to him for examination. Having finished his scrutiny, he leaned back in his chair and gazed sternly at my face.

"What is your name?"

"Roger Byam."

"You were a midshipman on His Majesty's armed vessel, the *Bounty*?"

"Yes, sir."

"How many of the *Bounty's* company are now on the island of Tahiti?"

"Three, I believe, not counting myself."

"Who are they?"

I gave him their names.

"Where is Fletcher Christian, and where is the *Bounty*?"

I told him of Christian's departure with eight of the mutineers, and of all the events that had taken place at Tahiti since that time. I told him of the building of the schooner, under Morrison's supervision, and of Morrison's intention to sail with her to Batavia, where he hoped to find a homeward-bound ship.

"A likely story!" he said grimly. "In that case, why did not you go with him?"

"Because the schooner was not well found for so long a voyage. It seemed to me wiser to wait here for the arrival of an English ship."

"Which you never expected to see, no doubt. You will be surprised to learn that Captain Bligh, and the men who were driven from his ship with him, have succeeded in reaching England?"

"I am profoundly glad to hear it, sir."

"And you will be equally surprised to learn that all the facts of the mutiny, including that of your own villainy, are known."

"My villainy, sir?   I am as free from guilt in that affair as any member of your own ship's company!"

"You dare to deny that you plotted with Christian to seize the *Bounty?*"

"Surely, sir, you must know that some of us who were left in the ship were compelled to remain for lack of accommodation in the launch?   There were nine of us who took no part whatever in the mutiny.   The launch was so overloaded that Captain Bligh himself begged that no more men should be sent into her; and he promised, if ever he reached England, to do justice to those of us who were forced to remain behind. Why, then, am I treated as though I were a pirate?   If Captain Bligh were here . . ."

Edwards cut me short.

"That will do," he said.   "You will meet Captain Bligh in good time, when you have been taken to England to suffer the punishment you so richly merit.   Now then, will you or will you not tell me where the *Bounty* is to be found?"

"I have told you all that I know, sir."

"I shall find her and those who went with her, be sure of that.   And I promise that neither you nor they shall gain by an attempt to shield them."

I was too angry and sick at heart to reply.   Never, during all the months that had passed since the mutiny, had I suspected that I might be considered a member of Christian's party.   Although I had not been able to speak with Bligh on the morning the ship was seized, Nelson, and others who went in the launch, knew of my loyalty and of my intention to leave with them.   I had supposed that Bligh himself must have known, and I could not imagine what might have happened to cause me to be listed among the mutineers.   I was eager to know the fate of those who had gone with Bligh, and how many of them had reached England safely, but Edwards would not permit me to inquire.

"You are here to be questioned, not I," he said.   "You still refuse to tell me where Christian is?"

"I know no more than you do, sir," I replied.

He turned to the lieutenant.

"Mr. Parkin, have this man sent below, and see to it that he has no communication with anyone. . . .   Wait a moment.   Ask Mr. Hayward to step in."

My surprise at the mention of Hayward's name must have been apparent.   A moment later the door opened, and Thomas Hayward, my former messmate on the *Bounty*, appeared. Forgetting my shackles, I stepped forward to greet him, but he gazed at me with a look of contempt, at the same time putting his hands behind his back.

"You know this man, Mr. Hayward?"

"Yes, sir.   He is Roger Byam, a former midshipman on the *Bounty*."

"That will do," said Edwards.   With another cool glance at me, Hayward went out, and I was taken by the guard to the orlop deck, to a place evidently prepared for prisoners, next to the bread room.   It was a foul situation, below the water line, and nauseating with the stench of the bilges.   The only means of ventilation was a ladderway some distance forward. Irons were now placed on my legs as well as on my wrists, and here I was left, with two guards outside the door at either end of the compartment.   About an hour later, Stewart, Coleman, and Skinner were brought down and ironed in the same manner.   No one, save the guard who brought our food, was permitted to enter the place, and we were forbidden to speak to each other.   There we lay the whole of that interminable day, as wretched in mind and body as men could well be.

XV

DOCTOR HAMILTON

DURING the next four days, Stewart, Coleman, Skinner, and I were conscious of little save our own misery. A frigate's orlop deck is a foul place in which to be confined at any time, and with the ship at anchor, in the lee of a tropical island, the heat and stench were scarcely to be endured. Our sentinels were changed every two hours, and I remember with what longing we watched the departing guard returning to the freshness of the open air. Food was brought to us morning and evening, and only thus were we able to distinguish night from day, for no sunlight penetrated to our quarters. Our victuals were the rancid salt beef and hard bread which the *Pandora* had carried all the way from England, with never an addition of the fresh meat, fruit, and vegetables which the island furnished in such abundance. But more than food we craved fresh air and the luxury of movement. Our leg irons were made fast to ringbolts in the planking, and although we could rise to our feet, we could take no more than one short step in either direction.

On the fifth morning of our confinement, the corporal of marines appeared with an extra guard. My leg irons were removed and I was taken up the ladderway and aft along the gundeck to a cabin on the starboard side of the vessel. It was the surgeon's cabin, and the surgeon himself, Dr. Hamilton, was awaiting me there. He dismissed the guard and then, observing that I was in handcuffs, recalled the corporal and requested that these be removed. The man was reluctant to comply.

"Lieutenant Parkin's orders were . . ."

"Nonsense," the doctor interrupted. "Take them off. I'll answer for this man's safety." The irons were then removed and once more the corporal retired. The surgeon turned the key in the lock, smiling as he did so.

"I'm not taking this precaution against yourself, Mr. Byam," he said. "I wish our conversation to be uninterrupted. Please to be seated."

He was a sturdily built man of forty, or thereabout, with a pleasant voice and manner. He looked like a ship's surgeon and a capable one. I felt drawn to him immediately. After the treatment accorded us by Edwards and Parkin, mere courtesy seemed, by contrast, the highest of virtues. I seated myself on his clothes chest and waited for him to speak.

"First," he said, "about your studies of the Tahitian language. You will wonder how I know of them. Of that, presently. Have you continued them during your sojourn here?"

"I have, sir," I replied. "Not a day has passed that I have not added to my dictionary. I have also compiled a grammar for the use of those who may wish to study the language hereafter."

"Good! Sir Joseph Banks was not mistaken, I see, in the confidence he placed in you."

"Sir Joseph! You know him, sir?" I asked, eagerly.

"Not as intimately as I could wish. In fact, I met him only shortly before the *Pandora* sailed; but he is an esteemed friend of friends of mine."

"Then you can tell me whether he believes me guilty in this affair of the mutiny. Do you yourself, sir, think I could have been so mad as to have joined it? And yet I have been treated by Captain Edwards as though I were one of the ringleaders."

The surgeon regarded me gravely for a moment.

"I will say this, Mr. Byam, if it will afford you comfort. You have not the look of a guilty man. As for Sir Joseph, despite all that has been said against you, he still believes in your innocence. . . .

"Wait! Allow me to continue," he went on as I was about to interrupt him. "I am as ready to hear what you have to say as you are to speak; but let me first inform you how serious the charges laid against you seem to be. I have been informed on this matter by Sir Joseph, who has not only talked with Captain Bligh, but has read the sworn statement concerning the mutiny which he has furnished to the Admiralty. I will not give the details. One will suffice to show how deeply you are implicated. On the night before the *Bounty* was seized, Captain Bligh himself, coming on deck during the middle watch, surprised you and Mr. Christian in earnest conversation. And Captain Bligh, so he insists, overheard you say to Mr. Christian: 'You can count on me, sir,' or words to that precise effect."

I was so taken aback as to be speechless for a moment. However strange it may seem, although I had the clearest recollection of the conversation with Christian, this vastly important detail had quite slipped from memory. The excitement of the events immediately following had, I suppose, driven it from my mind. Now that it had been recalled to me, I realized at once how black the appearances against me must be, and that Bligh was justified in placing the most damning construction upon what I had said. What could he have believed except that I was pledging my allegiance to Christian in his plan to seize the ship?

Dr. Hamilton sat with his hands clasped, his elbows on the arms of his chair, waiting for me to speak.

"It is plain from your manner, Mr. Byam, that you have a recollection of such a conversation."

"I have, sir. I said those very words to Mr. Christian, and under the circumstances described by Captain Bligh." I then proceeded to tell him the whole story of the mutiny, omitting nothing. He heard me through without comment. When I had finished he gazed at me keenly; then he said, "My boy, you have convinced me, and here's my hand on it!" I shook it warmly. "But I must tell you that my conviction is due to your manner rather than to the matter you have related. You must see for yourself that the very plausibility of your story is against it."

"How is that, sir?" I asked.

"Understand — I believe you; but put yourself in the place of the ships' captains who will sit at the court-martial. Your sincerity of manner in telling the story will have weight with them too, but they will be justified in ascribing this to your longing to escape death. As to the story, could you blame them for thinking it a little too perfect to fit the facts? It meets your necessities so well. The damning words to Christian are completely explained. And your going below, on the morning of the mutiny, just before the launch was cast off, is perfectly explained as well. There is not one of those captains who will not say to himself: 'This is such a tale as one would expect an intelligent midshipman, eager to save his life, to invent.'"

"But, as I have told you, sir, Robert Tinkler overheard the conversation with Christian. He can corroborate every word of my testimony."

"Yes; Tinkler, I think, saves you. Your life is in his hands. He reached England safely with the rest of Captain Bligh's party. To return to your story, you see how difficult it will be to convince a court-martial that Mr. Christian, presumably a man of intelligence and one capable of reflection, would have considered the mad plan of casting himself adrift on a tiny raft, for the purpose of making his way, alone, to an island peopled with savages?"

"It would not seem improbable if they knew Christian's character and the abuse he had received from Captain Bligh."

"But these officers will know nothing of Christian's character, and their sympathies will all be with Captain Bligh. You will have to prove your story of that conversation beyond the shadow of a doubt. Was there no one at that time to whom he revealed his plan to leave the ship? Such a man would be a most important witness for you."

"Yes; John Norton, one of the quartermasters. He prepared the raft for Christian."

The surgeon opened a drawer in his table and brought forth a paper.

"I have here a list of the men who went with Captain Bligh in the launch. Twelve of the party survived to reach England."

He glanced down the list, and then looked at me gravely.

"Norton, I am sorry to say, is not one of them. According to this record he was killed by the savages on the island of Tofoa."

It was a shock to me to learn of Norton's death, and I realized what a misfortune the lack of his evidence would be for me. Mr. Nelson, too, was dead, having succumbed to a fever when the party reached Coupang. Mr. Nelson was not only my friend; he was also a witness who could have vouched for my intention to leave the ship. With these two gone, my chance for acquittal seemed much less hopeful. Dr. Hamilton took a more encouraging view of the situation.

"You must not be disheartened," he said. "Tinkler's evidence is vastly more important to you than that of Norton and Mr. Nelson, and you may be sure that he will be summoned. Sir Joseph Banks will see to it that every scrap of evidence in your favour is brought to bear. No, take my word for it, your case is far from hopeless."

His quiet confident manner reassured me, and for the time I put aside all thought of what my fate might be. Mr. Hamilton then related, briefly, what I was most eager to hear: the story of what had happened to Bligh and his party after the launch had been cast adrift. They had first called at the island of

Tofoa, for water and other refreshment, but the savages, seeing that the party lacked the means of defending themselves, attacked them in such numbers that a massacre of the entire company was barely averted.   As it happened, Norton was the only man to be killed.   Their subsequent adventures made up a record of appalling hardships, and had any one but Bligh been in command, there is little doubt that the launch would never have been heard of again.   On the fourteenth of June, forty-seven days after the mutiny, they reached the Dutch settlement at Coupang Bay, on the island of Timor, a distance of more than twelve hundred leagues from Tofoa.   After recuperating for two months among the kindly inhabitants of Coupang, a small schooner was purchased and fitted out for the voyage to Batavia, where they arrived on October 1, 1789. Here three more of the party died: Elphinstone, Lenkletter, the remaining quartermaster, and Thomas Hall, a seaman.   Ledward, the acting surgeon, was left behind at Batavia, and the rest of the party embarked in ships of the Dutch East India Company for the voyage home.   Robert Lamb, the butcher, died on the passage, leaving but twelve of the nineteen men who had set out from the *Bounty's* side.

"In all the annals of our maritime history there has never been such an open-boat voyage as this," Dr. Hamilton continued.   "You will understand the excitement and interest aroused when Bligh reached England.   I was then in London, and for weeks the story of the mutiny and the voyage of the launch were the chief topics of conversation everywhere.   The whole country rang with Bligh's praises, and the sympathy for him is universal.   It would be useless to deny the fact, Mr. Byam — those who remained in the *Bounty* are all considered scoundrels of the blackest description."

"But did Captain Bligh say nothing," I asked, "of the men who were kept against their inclination?   I fully understand, now, his bitterness toward me, but there are others whom he knows to be innocent, and he pledged himself to do them justice if ever he reached England. Stewart and Coleman are in irons at this moment, as you may know. They are as guiltless as any of those who went with Captain Bligh."

"I have read the instructions furnished to Captain Edwards by the Admiralty," he replied. "They contain a list of the names of those who remained in the *Bounty*, and you are all considered mutineers. No distinction is made amongst you, and Captain Edwards is instructed to keep you so closely confined as to preclude all possibility of escape."

"Does this mean that we shall be confined where we are now until the *Pandora* reaches England?"

"Not if Captain Edwards will follow my advice. His instructions also say that, in confining you, he is to have a proper regard for the preservation of your lives. In this matter I am equally responsible with him, and I would not answer for the life of a pig kept for months on end on the orlop deck. I shall do my best to persuade him to remove you to more healthful quarters."

"And if possible, sir," I urged, "persuade him to permit us to speak with one another."

"God bless my soul! Do you tell me that he has denied you that small privilege?" The surgeon regarded me with a grim smile. "Captain Edwards is a just man, Mr. Byam. You will understand, perhaps, what I mean by this? He will carry out his instructions to the letter, and if ever he errs, it will not be on the side of leniency. But I think that I can promise you relief in some small matters. At any rate, be assured that I shall try. To return to the matter of your studies: you have your manuscripts at your house, I presume?"

All of my personal belongings had been left at Tautira. I told the surgeon of my friend, Tuahu, and that, if I might send him word, he would bring my chest to the ship. Dr. Hamilton asked that I write his name on a slip of paper.

"I will find him," he said. "Sir Joseph is extremely anxious that these manuscripts of yours should not be lost."

"It would be a godsend to me, sir, if I might continue my work on the voyage home."

"Sir Joseph had requested this very thing, in case you should be found," the surgeon replied. "Captain Edwards will, I believe, grant permission."

This news cheered me greatly. I should have an occupation that would suffice to make the long confinement endurable, and as Stewart, Coleman, and Skinner were all proficient in the Indian tongue, if we were permitted to converse my studies could be carried on with their help.

Mr. Hamilton glanced at his timepiece.

"I must send you below soon," he said. "I had Captain Edward's consent to this interview that I might question you with respect to the manuscripts. He is ashore this morning. I have taken advantage of the fact to enlarge upon my privilege."

He rose, unlocked the door of his cabin, glanced out, and closed it again.

"I shall enlarge upon it still more," he said. "Sir Joseph has charged me with another commission. In case you could be found, he asked me to deliver this letter to you."

Dr. Hamilton busied himself with some papers of his own while I read my letter. It was from my mother, of course. I still have it to this day, but I need not consult it to refresh my memory. For all the years that have passed, I can recall it, word for word: —

My dear Son: —

I have only just learned that I may have this precious opportunity to write to you. I must make every moment count, and waste none in unnecessary words.

When Captain Bligh returned with the news of the dreadful fate of the *Bounty*, I wrote to him at once, and received from him the letter which I enclose. What may have happened to turn him against you, I cannot conceive. After the receipt of so cruel a message I did not again write to him, but you must not believe that

I have been greatly distressed. I know you too well, dear Roger, to have the least doubt of your innocence.

I know what your anxiety, on my account, will be upon the arrival of the *Pandora*, when you learn that you are counted among the mutineers. Imagine then, dear son, that you have been able to write to me, explaining fully the circumstances, and imagine that your letter has reached me. I am as certain as though I had this letter before me that events over which you had no control caused you to remain in the *Bounty*, and I await with perfect confidence your homecoming and the clearing of your name from this infamous charge.

My only concern for you is at the thought of the hardships you may have to suffer as a prisoner on the long voyage to England. But they can be borne, and remember, my son, that home is beyond them.

Sir Joseph has talked with Captain Bligh, and you will be gratified to know that he does not share Mr. Bligh's belief that you were one of his enemies. I have not been told upon what ground you are charged with conspiracy, but in closing his letter to me, Sir Joseph said: 'I confidently expect that the proof of your son's innocence only awaits the day when the *Pandora* returns and all the facts shall be known.' I not only expect it. I am as sure of it as I am of the light of to-morrow's sun.

Good-bye, my dear Roger. I may not write more. The *Pandora* is to sail within three or four days, and my letter must go to London by this night's coach. God bless you, my son, and bring you safely home! Believe me, my dear boy, I can smile at the thought of the preposterous charge against you. May England breed many such villains as you are supposed to be.

Dr. Hamilton was kindness itself. Our quarters on the orlop deck were as dark as a cave and I could never have read my letter there. He permitted me to go over it again and again in his cabin until I knew it by heart. The enclosed letter from Bligh to my mother was, surely, the most cruel and heartless message that has ever been sent to the mother of an absent son: —

LONDON, *April 2nd,* 1790.

MADAME: —

I received your letter this day, and feel for you very much, being perfectly sensible of the extreme distress you must suffer from the conduct of your son, Roger Byam. His baseness is beyond all description, but I hope you will endeavour to prevent the loss of him, heavy as the misfortune is, from affecting you too severely. I imagine he is, with the rest of the mutineers, returned to Otaheite.

I am, Madame,
WILLIAM BLIGH.

I returned to our dark hole in a vastly different frame of mind than when I left it. As we passed along the lower deck I caught glimpses through the scuttles of the Matavai beach, and the canoes and the boats from the frigate plying back and forth between the ship and the shore. Those brief bright glimpses brought home to me the preciousness of freedom, the inestimable boon of being merely alive and at liberty. I made no attempt to compute the length of time that must pass before it could be mine again.

XVI

THE ROUNDHOUSE

The following morning our prison was cleaned for the first time since we had been confined there, and lighted with two additional candles. A bucket of sea water was then furnished us and we were permitted to wash our hands and faces. We were in a truly deplorable condition, only less filthy than the prison itself, and we begged the master-at-arms to allow us a complete bath.

"I have been ordered to give you one bucket of water and no more," he said. "Make haste, for the captain is coming directly."

We had no sooner finished our hurried toilet than Captain Edwards entered, followed by Lieutenant Parkin. The master-at-arms called out, "Prisoners! Stand!" We rose to our feet, and Edwards glanced around the compartment and from one to another of us. The stench of the place was frightful, and our naked bodies gleamed with sweat in the dim light. From the appearance of my fellow prisoners I knew what a disgusting appearance I myself must present. My intention had been to protest against the inhumanity of such a place of confinement; but believing that conditions would speak eloquently enough for themselves, I decided to say nothing. Edwards turned to the master-at-arms.

"Command them to hold out their hands," he said.

"Prisoners, hold out your hands!"

We obeyed, and Edwards examined our handcuffs and leg

irons. It chanced that Stewart's manacles fitted somewhat loosely to his wrists, and Edwards noticed this.

"Mr. Parkin, see to it that the armourer inspects all of these irons," he said. "I shall hold him responsible if any prisoner shall be able to free himself."

"I shall attend to the matter immediately, sir," Parkin replied.

Edwards continued to regard us coldly for a moment or two.

"Inform the prisoners that, in future, they may converse with one another. But let them understand this: they shall speak only in English. If I hear of as much as a single word passing between them in the Indian language, the permission I have granted shall be withdrawn."

This information was conveyed to us through the proper channel.

"And under no circumstances whatever is any prisoner to speak to a sentinel or to any member of the ship's company except Mr. Parkin or the corporal in charge of the guard. I shall severely punish any infringement of this order."

Parkin was in general charge of us. I felt an instinctive aversion for this man. He was short, thickset, and excessively hairy, with eyebrows that met in an irregular line over his nose. The vice of cruelty was written plain on his face, and we had not been long in discovering the character of the man in whose power we were. Thus far he had displayed it in various small ways, but Edwards had now given him the kind of opportunity he craved. No sooner had the captain left us than Parkin himself made an inspection of our irons, beginning with Stewart, whom he ordered to lie down and stretch up his hands. He then grasped the chain connecting the handcuffs, and, placing his foot against Stewart's chest, he strained and tugged with all his strength, succeeding at length in wrenching off the irons, taking the skin from Stewart's knuckles and the backs of both hands as he did so. As the handcuffs came away he nearly fell over backward. In his anger, Stewart forgot his helpless posi-

tion.   He sprang to his feet, and had Parkin been within reach
Stewart would have knocked him down.

"You filthy beast!" he said.   "Do you call yourself an officer?"

Parkin had a high soft voice, almost feminine in quality, in
strange contrast to his swarthy, hairy appearance.

"What did you say?" he asked.   "Repeat that."

"I called you a filthy beast," said Stewart, "and so you are!"

He was as near to Parkin as his irons would permit him to go.
The lieutenant took care to keep beyond reach.

"You will regret that," he said.   "I promise that you will
repent of it more than once before you're hung."

I am unable to say whether he would have tried the irons of
the rest of us in the same manner.   I was resolved that he
should not test mine in that fashion; but at that moment the
armourer appeared and Parkin ordered him to carry on the
examination.   It would have been impossible for any of us to
have freed ourselves from the leg irons, but Parkin ordered all
the handcuffs to be altered so that they should fit more tightly.
When they had been repaired and brought back, it was only
with great difficulty that they could be fastened upon us.

Meanwhile, I told the others of my conversation with the
surgeon.   We forgot our wretched situation in the pleasure of
being permitted to converse again, and the day passed more
rapidly than the previous five had done.   Realizing now that
we had nothing to hope for until we reached England, we
resolved to make the best of things, and to devise methods of
passing the time.   Of the four of us, Skinner alone had nothing
to hope for, and yet he was the most cheerful of us all.   I
began to suspect, at this time, that the man was not wholly
right in his mind.   He said more than once that, if the decision were again to be made, he would give himself up to justice as he had done, and he seemed to look forward with pleasure to the day when he would be hung.

We were careful to obey Edwards's order with respect to

the sentinels. We had no desire to make trouble for them, and Parkin was spying about at all hours. But there was a seaman, James Good, whose name was an indication of his kindly nature. He was the man usually sent with our food, and he never failed to whisper to us welcome bits of news as he handed round our plates. "Mr. Parkin's gone ashore, sir," he would say; "you won't be bothered this morning." Or, "I'll fetch you a bit of fresh meat for your supper." Whenever possible he would bring us morsels of fresh pork or breadfruit or sweet potatoes wrapped in a handkerchief inside his blouse. This he did with the connivance of the cooks. Had any of these men been discovered, they would have been severely flogged, and yet they cheerfully ran the risk in order to lighten the misery of our situation.

But never had Good brought us such welcome news as on the evening when he informed us that we were to be moved to other quarters.

"Have you heard the knockin' and 'ammerin' on deck, sir?" he whispered to me. "The carpenters are makin' a proper 'ouse for you up there."

We had heard, at times, the sounds of hammering, and now that we knew it concerned us, it was music to our ears. The following day we were unshackled from the filthy planking of cur dungeon, marched up the ladderway, along the lower deck, and up a second ladderway to the pure air of the upper deck. At first our eyes were so dazzled by the brilliance of the sunshine that we could scarcely see, and so lost half the pleasure of our moment in the open. It was, in fact, no more than a moment. Edwards was present, and the master-at-arms ordered us into our new prison at once. We mounted the ladder to the top of the box, which stood on the quarter-deck. There was a scuttle about eighteen inches square through which we descended inside.

This place was to be our prison for as long as we remained on the *Pandora*. It was called "the roundhouse," but more often we prisoners referred to it as "Pandora's Box." It was eleven feet long at the deck and eighteen feet wide at the bulkhead. There were two scuttles, nine inches square, in the bulkhead, and these, with the one in the roof, were heavily barred and gave us what light we had. Across the deck midway between the walls was a line of fourteen heavy ringbolts to which the leg irons were to be attached. We were now made fast in the corners of the compartment, Stewart and Skinner next the bulkhead, and Coleman and I on the after side. Our leg irons were cylindrical bands three inches wide with a twelve-inch length of chain which passed through a ringbolt. One key unlocked all the leg irons and another the handcuffs. The keys were carried by the master-at-arms.

As in our former prison, we could stand up and move half a pace in either direction, and we had full headroom. The floor was the deck itself, and on either side were small scupper holes. In fair weather the roof scuttle was left open save for the iron grating, and two sentries continually paced the roof. The monotonous, everlasting tread of their feet so close overhead became a sound as wearisome to us as the clinking of our chains through the ringbolts.

We could not suppose that so large a prison had been prepared for four men, and by each of the unoccupied ringbolts lay a pair of leg irons ready for use. Evidently Captain Edwards had reason to believe that he would soon take others of the *Bounty's* company. That Christian and his party had returned was so improbable as not to be worth considering. The only remaining possibility was that the departure of the *Resolution* from Papara had been delayed, and that she was either captured or about to be. We were not long kept in doubt. Two days later, the grating over the roof scuttle was raised, and Morrison, Norman, and Ellison were brought down and chained beside us.

This was a meeting such as none of us had hoped for. Morrison and Norman had not yet recovered from their astonish-

ment at being treated as pirates. Ellison was the same scatter-
brained youngster he had always been. Excitement in any
form was the breath of life to him, and to be considered a
desperate character, chained up like a wild beast, was his conception of a lark. Fortunately he had no sense of the gravity
of his situation, and we did nothing to remind him of it. Of
all those who had taken part in the mutiny, he was the one I
most hoped would escape capture.

The armourer, supervised by Parkin, fitted handcuffs to the
new captives, and Ellison being no more than a boy, Parkin
tried upon him the same measures he had used with Stewart.
Ordering him to lie down, he placed one foot on his chest and
tried to draw the handcuffs over his hands. For a moment
Ellison endured this treatment in silence; then he said, smiling,
"Leave off, sir. I'll give you these things if you want them,
but you can't get them that way."

Parkin's only reply was to let go the chain so suddenly that
Ellison fell back, striking his head heavily on the deck. Parkin's eyes shone with delight as Ellison sat up, rubbing his
head. He ordered him to stretch up his hands again, but this
time Ellison was prepared, and when Parkin let go the chain
the boy fell back on one shoulder and avoided striking his
head.

"That's one for me, sir," he said with a grin.

The lieutenant was breathing heavily, not so much from
exertion as from emotion. The fact that a common seaman
and a mutineer beside had dared to speak to him was more than
he could endure.

"Lie down!" he ordered.

A look of fear came into Ellison's eyes as he obeyed. He
stretched up his arms, expecting Parkin to grasp the chain
again. Instead of that he kicked Ellison in the side, as cruel a
blow as was ever given a defenseless man.

"That will teach you how to speak to an officer," he said, in
his soft bland voice. The armourer was a witness of this foul

proceeding. "Good God, sir!" he exclaimed in spite of himself. By a happy chance Parkin stood within reach of Morrison, who drew back his manacled fists and gave him a blow which sent him staggering in my direction. I had barely time to fetch him another that knocked him off his balance, and as he fell he struck his head against one of the ringbolts. He got up slowly and looked from one to another of us without speaking. Presently he turned to the armourer.

"You may go, Jackson," he said. "I shall know how to deal with this." The armourer went up the ladder, and Parkin stood looking down at Ellison, who was lying on his belly with his hands pressed against his side.

"Oh, you dogs!" he exclaimed softly, as though speaking to himself. "I could have you flogged to death for this. But I'm to see you hung! Remember that—I'm to see you hung!" He then went up the ladder, the grating was lifted for him, and he climbed out.

Had not the armourer witnessed the brutal assault upon Ellison, I have no doubt that we should have suffered for our rebellious conduct. But evidently Parkin feared that the truth would come out if complaint should be made to the captain. At any rate, no action was taken, and for several days we saw no more of the man. Ellison suffered great pain, but youth and natural toughness of body were in his favour, and he quickly recovered.

As soon as we were alone again, Morrison gave us an account of the taking of the schooner. Having called at Papara to pick up McIntosh, Hillbrandt, and Millward, they had decided to take advantage of the fine weather to salt down some extra casks of pork. Several days were spent in this work, and on the morning of what was to have been their last day on the island, most of the men made an excursion far up the Papara Valley for a supply of mountain plantains. Morrison, Ellison, and Norman remained with the schooner, and toward noon word reached the district of the arrival of a vessel at Matavai.

Before any action could be taken, a ship's launch filled with marines appeared.

"Norman and I could have danced for joy at sight of the English uniforms," Morrison went on; "but when we thought of the others we felt less happy. They were certain of capture now and I had no time to send them warning. The launch was upon us five minutes after she had rounded the point. She came alongside and you can imagine our astonishment when we saw that Thomas Hayward, in a lieutenant's uniform, was in charge of her."

"I suppose you fell on each other's necks, Morrison," Stewart put in.

"He did n't condescend to speak to me, but ordered his men to clap me in irons. He remained with the schooner with most of the marines. We were sent back with the launch."

"Mr. Hayward is in a difficult position; we must remember that," said Coleman.

"In a position that precisely suits the little cad," said Stewart, hotly. "He knows that we are as innocent as he himself."

"Do you remember how he whimpered when Christian ordered him into the launch?" asked Morrison.

"So he did, Coleman," said Norman. "Him and Mr. Hallet both begged to stay with the ship, and that 's something none of us was guilty of."

Hayward's superior, contemptuous attitude was naturally resented by all of us who had taken no part in the mutiny. Making all possible allowances for him, we still found it inexcusable.

The other men were soon brought in from Papara. There were seven of them: McIntosh, Hillbrandt, Burkitt, Millward, Sumner, Muspratt, and Byrne. The roundhouse was none too large, now, for our accommodation. Eight men were chained so that they slept with their heads at the bulkhead, and six on the opposite side. I was in the corner, on the starboard side aft, with Muspratt on my left. I had reason to be grateful for my chance position in the roundhouse. Two or three days after we had been confined there, I discovered in one of the wall planks a knot that had become loosened as the green lumber dried in the sun. I tried for several nights, without success, to draw it out. James Good, our steward, came to my assistance. He pushed the knot in to me, and thereafter I had a tiny window through which I had a glimpse of the bay and the shore line beyond. Sometimes, as the *Pandora* shifted her position with the current, I had Stewart's house directly opposite my window, and although we were too far distant to enable me to distinguish the people moving about there, I could easily imagine who they were.

I watched canoes and the ship's boats coming and going. Many of the people in the canoes I knew; they were old friends of one or another of us. As they approached, I could see them more and more distinctly until they were cut off from view by the side of the vessel. Several times I saw Peggy, Stewart's wife, being paddled around the ship by her father or one of her brothers. With what longing she gazed in our direction! Her father, wisely, never brought her within earshot. She would have been certain to cry out to her husband had she thought him within hearing, only adding to the misery of them both. I said nothing to Stewart of the matter. I had no desire to harrow his feelings any more than was already the case with him.

One morning while I was standing on lookout, Muspratt, who was keeping watch for me, gave the warning, "Hatchway!" and I had barely time to thrust in the knot before the master-at-arms descended the ladder, followed by Edwards. It was an unexpected visit, the first we had had from the captain since our confinement in the roundhouse. Our prison had not been cleaned in all that time, and I will say no more of its condition than that fourteen chained men were obliged to obey the calls of nature in that close-walled space.

Edwards halted at the foot of the ladder.

"Master-at-arms, why is this place in such a filthy state?"

"Mr. Parkin's orders were that it was to be cleaned once a week, sir."

"Have it washed out immediately, and report to me when it is done."

"Very good, sir."

Edwards lost no time in leaving the place; then, to our great joy, swabs were handed down to us, and bucket after bucket of salt water. When we had scoured our quarters thoroughly, passing the swabs from hand to hand, we scrubbed each other. To be clean once more had a wonderful effect upon our spirits. Some of the men sang and whistled at the work, sounds that contrasted strangely with the clinking of manacles, but these cheerful noises were cut short by a curt order from the master-at-arms. In half an hour we had the place as clean as salt water and good will could make it, whereupon the master-at-arms returned, followed, this time, by Dr. Hamilton. The surgeon threw a quick glance in my direction, and there was a friendly glint in his eyes; otherwise he gave no indication that we had met before. He passed along the line, glancing over our bodies in a professional manner, and stopped before Muspratt.

"That needs attention, my man," he said, indicating a great boil on Muspratt's knee. "Have him sent to the sick-bay at ten, Mr. Jackson."

"Yes, sir."

Dr. Hamilton had fully as much dignity as the captain, but he did not feel it necessary to address us through an inferior officer.

"Are any of the rest of you suffering from boils or other humours?" he asked. "If so, speak up, and I'll attend to you at the same time. Remember, it is my duty to care for your health as well as that of the ship's company. You must not hesitate to inform me when you need my services."

"May I speak, sir?" Stewart asked.

"Certainly."

"Would it be possible, while the ship remains here, for us to be supplied now and then with fresh food?"

Morrison eagerly seconded this request.

"We have friends among the Indians, sir, who would be only too glad to send us fruit and cooked vegetables if this could be permitted."

"And it would save the ship's stores, sir," Coleman added.

Dr. Hamilton glanced from one to another of us.

"But you're having fresh food," he said.

"No, sir, begging your pardon," said Coleman. "Only salt beef and hard bread."

Dr. Hamilton looked at the master-at-arms.

"That's been their victuals, sir. Mr. Parkin's orders."

"I see," the surgeon replied. "I'll look into the matter. Perhaps it can be arranged."

We thanked him warmly, and he went on deck again.

It was plain from the events of that morning that Parkin's treatment of us had been without the knowledge of the captain or of Dr. Hamilton. Edwards was willing to be ignorant of the lieutenant's cruelty, but from that day forth Dr. Hamilton made us frequent visits. We were never again compelled to lie in our own filth, and our food was the same as that given to the seamen of the *Pandora*.

XVII

THE SEARCH FOR THE BOUNTY

ONE morning early in May, Stewart and I were freed from our leg irons and conducted to the place used as the sick-bay on the lower deck. We found Dr. Hamilton awaiting us in the passageway outside. He said nothing, but motioned us to enter. We went in, not knowing what to expect, and the door was closed behind us. Tehani and Peggy were there, with our little daughters.

Tehani came close and put her arms around me, speaking in a low voice directly into my ear, lest she should be heard by those outside.

"Listen, Byam. I have no time for weeping. I must speak quickly. Atuanui is here with three hundred Tautira men, his best warriors. They have been coming around the coast from both sides, five or ten each time. For many days I have been trying to see you. There was no chance. At last it comes. They will attack the ship at night. In the darkness the great guns will do us little harm. What we fear is that you may be killed by the soldiers before we can reach you. That is why the attack has not yet been made. Are you all in the house they have built on the deck? Are you chained? Atuanui wishes to know how you are guarded there."

I was so overcome with joy at seeing Tehani and our little daughter that I was unable to speak for a moment.

"Tell me, Byam, quickly! We shall not have long to speak."

"How long have you been at Matavai, Tehani?"

"Three days after you left Tautira, I came.   Did you think I would desert you?   It is Atuanui and I who have made this plan.   All of your friends are eager to attack."

"Tehani," I said, "you must tell Atuanui that there is no chance to save us.   He and all of his men would be killed."

"No, no, Byam!   We will club them to death before they can use their guns.   We will save you from these evil men. Atuanui wishes to attack to-morrow night.   There is no moon. It must be done quickly, for the ship is soon to go."

It was useless trying to explain to Tehani the reason for our imprisonment.   She could not understand; and, indeed, we had only ourselves to blame, for, as already related, the fact of the mutiny had been kept a secret from all the Tahitians.

"We know.   That captain, Etuati, has told Hitihiti that you are bad men.   He says he must take you to England to be punished.   Hitihiti does not believe this.   No one believes it."

Meanwhile, Stewart's wife had told him what Tehani had told me.   There was but one way of preventing an attack upon the frigate.   We explained that all of the prisoners were chained, hand and foot; that we were entirely helpless and would undoubtedly be killed before the ship could be taken. I told Tehani, which was true, that Captain Edwards was prepared for such an attack, and our guards under orders to shoot us at the first sign of any attempt at rescue on the part of our friends on shore.   We succeeded at last in convincing our wives of the hopelessness of the plan.

Until this moment Tehani and Peggy had kept their emotions under control.   Realizing now that nothing could be done, Peggy broke down in a flood of passionate weeping heart-rending to see.   Stewart tried in vain to comfort her.   Tehani sat on the floor at my feet, her head buried in her arms, making no sound.   Had she wept I would have been better able to bear it.   I knelt beside her with our child in my arms.   For the first time in my life I tasted to the full the bitterness of true misery.

Presently Stewart could endure no more.   He opened the
door.   Dr. Hamilton and the guards were waiting outside.
He motioned them to come in.   Peggy clung to him desperately, and it was only with the greatest difficulty that he could
disengage her fingers.   Had it not been for Tehani she would
have had to be carried from the ship.   Tehani's grief was beyond tears, as mine was.   We held each other close, for a moment, without speaking.   Then she lifted up Peggy, and
supported her as we went out.   Stewart and I followed, carrying our children.   At the gangway we gave them to the servants who had come with our wives.   Stewart begged to be
taken to the roundhouse at once.   I was conducted to Dr.
Hamilton's cabin and was deeply grateful for the privilege he
gave me of being alone there for a few moments.   Through
the port I saw the canoe, with my friend Tuahu and Tipau,
Peggy's father, at the paddles, leave the side of the ship.   One
of the servants held Peggy's child.   Tehani sat on a thwart in
the bow, holding our little Helen in her arms.   I watched the
canoe growing smaller and smaller, with such despair in my
heart as I had never known till then.

I was still standing at the port when Dr. Hamilton entered.
"Sit down, my boy," he said.   His eyes were moist as he
looked at me.   "I persuaded Captain Edwards to consent to
this meeting.   My intentions were of the best, but I didn't
realize how cruel a trial it would be for all of you."

"I can speak for Stewart as well as for myself, sir.   We are
deeply grateful to you."

"Would you mind telling me your wife's name?"

"Tehani.   She is the niece of Vehiatua, the chief of Taiarapu."

"She is a noble woman, Mr. Byam.   I was greatly impressed
by her dignity and poise.   I don't mind confessing that my
ideas of the Indian women have altered greatly, now that I
have seen them.   My conception had been gained from the
stories about them that circulate in England.   I had supposed

them all wanton little creatures without character or depth of feeling. I see more clearly every day how mistaken this conception was. We call these people savages! I realize now that in many respects we are the savages, not they."

"You have not seen my wife before?" I asked.

"On the contrary, I have seen her every day this past month. She has been moving heaven and earth in her attempts to see you. Stewart's wife has been doing the same. Until yesterday, Captain Edwards refused all requests of the Indians for permission to visit the prisoners. He fears that they may attempt to rescue you."

"He has reason to fear it, sir."

"Reason to fear it? How is that?"

I would gladly have avoided speaking of what Tehani had told me, and could I have been certain that Atuanui would abandon his plan, I would have said nothing. But I knew his fearless impetuous nature, and neither he nor Tehani had any conception of the murderous effect of great guns loaded with grape. They had never seen them fired, and it was more than possible that Atuanui might yet be persuaded of the feasibility of his plan. Therefore I told the surgeon of the plan to attack the frigate, and of what I had done to prevent its being carried out. He was astonished at the news.

"We have had no suspicion that anything of the sort was afoot," he said. "You have done well to tell me of this. An attack would mean the death of scores, if not hundreds, of the Indians."

"Captain Edwards can easily avoid all danger," I said. "He will have only to keep a strong guard on shore and to prohibit any gathering of canoes near the ship."

The surgeon then told me that he had received from Tuahu the manuscripts of my dictionary and grammar.

"I have your private Journal as well," he added. "Would you permit me to look into this latter sometime, or does it contain matters which you wish no one to see?"

I told him that it contained nothing but a day-to-day account of my experiences from the time of leaving England until the arrival of the *Pandora*, which he was welcome to read, if he chose.

"I shall appreciate that privilege," he replied.   "Your Journal will be of great value to you in later years.   If you like, I will take care of all these papers for you.   They can go into the bottom of my small medicine chest, and there they will be certain of reaching England safely.   With respect to the dictionary, Captain Edwards knows of the great interest Sir Joseph Banks takes in it, and you are to be permitted to work on it during the passage home."

This was a welcome assurance indeed.   I had looked forward with dread to our long voyage.   I now mentioned the captain's prohibition against our speaking in Tahitian among ourselves.   "If this could be removed, sir, I could be given much help by the other prisoners, and perform a service to them at the same time, by giving them something to occupy their minds."

The surgeon promised to intercede with the captain on this account, and as soon as the *Pandora* sailed the permission was granted.

All the next day the ship's boats were kept busy bringing off provisions, and the tents and implements of the carpenters and armourers which had been set up on the beach near our anchorage.   Our steward, James Good, told us that the frigate was to sail within twenty-four hours.   Edwards had gained no information with respect to Christian and the *Bounty*, and apparently had come to the conclusion that we had told the truth in saying that we knew nothing of Christian's possible destination.   All that day I gazed my fill at the green land where I had been so happy, and during the night I heard every bell strike, followed by the clear calls of the sentinels in various parts of the ship.   Fortunately, no attempt was made to seize the frigate.   At dawn we were under way.   At ten o'clock, looking from my knot-hole window, I saw nothing but empty sea.

There followed a weary time for the fourteen men confined in "Pandora's Box." My dictionary proved a blessing to nearly all of us. On our second day at sea it was brought to me by Dr. Hamilton himself, together with writing materials, and the surgeon had had the carpenter make me a small table which rested on the floor across my lap as I sat in my corner. The green island timber of which the roundhouse had been made was beginning to shrink in the hot sun, and sufficient light streamed through the cracks between the planks to enable me to write without straining my eyes greatly. The prohibition against speaking in the Indian tongue was lifted, and the other men entered with pleasure into my studies. Stewart, Morrison, and Ellison were accomplished linguists, only a little less proficient in Tahitian than in English. Ellison surprised me. He spoke the language with a purer accent than any of us, and seemed to have absorbed his knowledge of it without the least effort. He pointed out many fine distinctions between words that had escaped me. This poor lad had never known who his parents were. He had been kicked from larboard to starboard ever since he could remember, and it had never occurred to him that he had a good mind. It saddened me to think that such a youngster, with an excellent capacity for education, had received none, while many a dull-witted son of wealthy parents was offered advantages he was not equipped to profit by.

There were grey days of continual violent squalls when it was impossible to work on the dictionary. The frigate laboured heavily through the seas, rolling and pitching, and we rolled with her, each man clinging to his ringbolt in an attempt to maintain his position. Often we were thrown to the extent of our chains, and our wrists and ankles were terribly galled by the bands of iron around them. To add to our misery in seasons of bad weather, the rain trickled down upon us day and night through the uncaulked seams in the roof of our prison, and we slept, or, better, tried to sleep, on boards slimy wet.

We had been several days at sea when we learned that the *Pandora* was not alone on this voyage. She was accompanied by the *Resolution,* the little schooner which Morrison and the others had built. Edwards had fitted her out as a tender to the frigate, and she was commanded by Mr. Oliver, the master's mate of the *Pandora,* with a crew of a midshipman, a quartermaster, and six seamen. She was a beautiful little craft and outsailed the frigate in any kind of weather. Many and many a time poor Morrison, and the men who were to have gone with him in the *Resolution,* had occasion to lament their fate in being captured at Papara. Whatever hardships they might have suffered would have seemed light indeed compared with the misery of existence in "Pandora's Box."

Henry Hillbrandt soon began to show signs of breaking under the strain of confinement. By nature he was a man of brooding, melancholy disposition, and it was evident that thoughts of the court-martial ahead of us were preying upon his mind. I remember well the evening when he first gave evidence of this. The sea was dead calm, but a fine cold rain had been falling since morning, and we were cold, wet, and miserable. It must have been toward midnight that I was wakened from a doze by the sound of Hillbrandt's voice. It was pitch-dark in the roundhouse. Hillbrandt was praying in low monotonous tones that went on interminably. Seamen, however irreverent some of them may be, invariably respect those of a religious temperament, and rarely interfere with another man's prayers. Although I could see nothing in the darkness, I knew that the other men were awake, listening to Hillbrandt. He continued for at least half an hour, praying God to save him from being hanged. It was the same

thing over and over again. At last I heard Millward's voice:
"Hillbrandt! For God's sake, *mamu!*" (Be quiet!)

Hillbrandt broke off.

"Who was that? Was it you, Millward?"

"Yes. We want no more of your praying."

"No," someone else put in. "Pray to yourself if you must,
Hillbrandt, but give us a rest."

Of a sudden Hillbrandt broke out in a violent fit of sobbing. "We're doomed, men," he said; "doomed, every one
of us! We're to be hanged, think of that! Choked to death
at the end of a rope!"

"Damn your blood! Hold your tongue, will you?" I
heard Burkitt say. "Choke him off, Sumner, if he says another word!"

Sumner was chained next to Hillbrandt. "That I will!" he
replied. "I'll save the hangman one dirty job if he don't
let up!"

One topic, our possible fate when we reached England, was
never mentioned in the roundhouse. With the exception of
Hillbrandt and Skinner, present misery was enough for all
of us, without anticipating events to come.

The events of that dreary time are only less unpleasant to
recall than they were to endure. We had no knowledge of
whither we were bound, except that it was in the general direction of home. James Good, our only source of information,
told us that Captain Edwards was making a zigzag course to
westward, calling at every island raised, in search of the
Bounty. We had to form our own conclusions as to where
we were from the little I could see through my knothole window. Some of the others could also see something of what was
taking place outside through the cracks that began to appear
in the walls as the planking shrunk under the tropical sun. I
kept a record of the days. We left Tahiti on May 9, 1791.
On the nineteenth of May we sighted an island which all who
could view it recognized at once. It was Aitutaki, discovered

by Captain Bligh after the departure of the *Bounty* from Tahiti, and shortly before the mutiny.   There was great excitement in the roundhouse that morning.   The ship came close inshore and hove-to on the larboard tack while the cutter was being lowered.   We saw one of the lieutenants and fifteen men go off in the boat.

"We'll have Christian and the others here before nightfall; I'll venture my day's rations on it," said Coleman.

"Nonsense, Coleman," said Stewart.   "Christian would never be so foolish as to choose any hiding-place known to Captain Bligh."

"What of Tupuai, Mr. Stewart?" Norman asked.   "Christian would have stayed there if the Indians had been friendly, and that island was known to Captain Bligh."

"What do you think, Byam?" Stewart asked.

My opinion was, and Morrison and most of the others agreed, that Christian would never again seek an asylum on a known island, more particularly on any island that Bligh had visited. Nevertheless, we waited with impatience for the return of the cutter.   The frigate stood off and on all day, and toward sunset we saw the cutter putting off from shore.   I had an excellent view of her as she approached, and when I could say, with certainty, that none of Christian's party was in her, Ellison gave a cheer, and clapped his manacled hands together.   We all felt as he did: we wanted Christian and the men with him to escape.   As soon as the cutter was hoisted on board we stood out to sea, and that is the last we saw of Aitutaki.

Every day or two we had glimpses of the *Resolution* and knew that she was following us from island to island.   She came up with us again when we were within sight of a low island, or atoll, which consisted of a number of small islands connected by long stretches of barren reef, the whole enclosing a lagoon of considerable extent.   We saw the schooner being revictualed from the frigate, and then she stood in for shore with a cutter and one of the yawls in tow. The schooner was proving of great service to Edwards in his search. Owing to her light draft, she could examine, close inshore, the various islands at which we touched. The following day James Good brought us most interesting news. The boats' crews had gone ashore at the atoll, and had discovered on the beach of one of the islands a spar marked "Bounty's Driver Gaff."

This discovery caused no less excitement in the roundhouse than it did, presumably, in Captain Edwards's cabin. The captain evidently considered the find as proof that the *Bounty* had called at this island, or had passed near it. We knew better, but we took good care to keep the information to ourselves. This driver gaff was, unquestionably, one of the missing spars that had gone adrift at Tupuai, and had been carried by winds and currents these many miles to leeward.

During the next two months we cruised north and south among the island of the Union Group, the Navigator and the Friendly Archipelagoes, still searching for some trace of the *Bounty*. On the twenty-first of June, in a night of very thick weather, we lost the *Resolution*. The frigate cruised about in that vicinity for several days, but the schooner was seen no more, whereupon Captain Edwards proceeded to Namuka, in the Friendly Islands, the appointed place of rendezvous in case the vessels should become separated. Namuka, it will be remembered, was the island where the *Bounty* had put in for refreshment only a few days before the mutiny. The *Pandora* anchored where the *Bounty* had lain, and from my knot-hole I could see the familiar scene: the scattered thatched houses of the Indians among the groves, the watering place where the grapnel had been stolen, and the same throngs of thieving savages crowding about the ship in their canoes.

The *Pandora* remained here from July 28 until the second of August, waiting for the *Resolution,* and during that time the Indians proved as troublesome to the frigate's watering parties as they had to those of the *Bounty*. The schooner having failed to appear, she was given up as lost, and Captain Edwards now decided to proceed on the homeward voyage without further loss of time. Accordingly, we sailed from Namuka, and the following afternoon passed within view of the island of Tofoa, and within a few miles of the very spot where the mutiny had taken place so many months before. The interest of the men in the roundhouse, as we peered through the cracks at the blue outline of Tofoa, may be imagined. To me, the events of that melancholy morning, and all that had since passed, seemed unreal, and our present misfortunes the experiences of a nightmare from which I should wake, presently, to find myself still at home, in England. I had the strange feeling that I had traveled backward in time and was living again through the events of the night preceding the mutiny.

XVIII

THE LAST OF THE PANDORA

I WILL pass briefly over the events of August. They were, no doubt, interesting enough to the members of the *Pandora's* company. To the prisoners in the roundhouse they passed with interminable slowness. Islands were raised and left behind as we proceeded toward Endeavour Straits. We were sailing much the same course as that followed by Captain Bligh in his open-boat voyage to Timor, and as we ploughed through that vast ocean scattered with islands and shoals all but unknown to white men, I gained a truer conception of the remarkable nature of Bligh's achievement. That he should have succeeded in bringing seventeen men, without arms, and so meagrely provided with food and water, through fair weather and foul, to a destination nearly four thousand miles from his point of departure seemed in the nature of a miracle. This achievement was our principal topic of conversation in the roundhouse. Whatever our personal feelings toward Bligh, there was not one of us who did not feel proud, as Englishmen, of his voyage in the *Bounty's* launch.

We saw little of Edwards. Three or four times, perhaps, in the course of the voyage thus far, he had made an official inspection, merely stopping at the foot of the ladder, glancing coldly from one to another of us, and going out again. We were at the mercy of Parkin, who made existence as wretched for us as he dared. As we approached Endeavour Straits even Parkin ceased to visit us, this duty being left to the master-at-arms. The lieutenants as well as the captain himself were continually occupied with the navigation of the ship. Every day one, and sometimes two, of the ship's boats were sent out in advance of the frigate, for we had now reached the northern extremity of the Great Barrier Reef which extends along the eastern coast of Australia, as treacherous an extent of shoal-infested ocean as any on the surface of the globe. Our course was extremely tortuous, among reefs and sand-bars innumerable, and all day long we could hear the calls of the men heaving the lead as we worked our way slowly along. Not even the prisoners suffered from boredom at this time. Those of us who could see something of what was taking place outside kept constant watch, reporting to others the dangers sighted or passed.

The twenty-eighth of August was a dismal day of alternate calms and black squalls which greatly increased the dangers of navigation. Looking from my knot-hole at dawn, I saw that we were in the midst of a labyrinth of reefs and shoals upon which the sea broke with great violence. The frigate had been hove-to during the night, and now one of the boats, with Lieutenant Corner in command, had gone ahead to seek for a possible passage. We could see little of what was taking place, but the orders continually shouted from the quarter-deck indicated only too clearly the difficulties in which the ship found herself. Once, as we wore about, we passed within half a cable's length of as villainous a reef as ever brought a sailor's heart into his mouth.

So it went all that day, and as evening drew on it was apparent that we were in greater danger than we had been at dawn. The launch was still far in advance of us, and a gun was fired as a signal for her to return. Darkness fell swiftly. False fires were burned and muskets fired to indicate our position to the launch. The musket fire was answered from the launch, and as the reports became more distinct we knew that she was slowly approaching. All this while the leadsmen were continually sounding, finding no bottom at one hundred and ten fathoms; but soon we heard them calling depths again: fifty fathoms, forty, thirty-six, twenty-two. Immediately upon calling this latter depth the ship was put about, but before the tacks were hauled on board and the sails trimmed, the frigate struck, and every man in the roundhouse was thrown sprawling to the length of his chain.

Before we could recover ourselves the ship struck again, with such force that we thought the masts would come down. It was now pitch-dark, and to make matters worse another heavy squall bore down upon us. Above the roaring of the wind we could hear the voices of the men, sounding faint and thin as orders were shouted. Every effort was made to get the ship free by means of the sails, but, this failing, they were furled and the other boats put over the side for the purpose of carrying out an anchor. The squall passed as suddenly as it had come, and we now heard distinctly the musket shots of the men in the returning launch.

The violence of the shocks we had received left no doubt in our minds that the ship had been badly damaged. I heard Edwards's voice: "How does she do, Mr. Roberts?" and Roberts's reply: "She's making water fast, sir. There's nearly three feet in the hold."

The effect upon the prisoners of this dreadful news may be imagined. Hillbrandt and Michael Byrne began to cry aloud in piteous voices, begging those outside to release us from our irons. All our efforts to quiet them were useless, and the clamour they made, with the tumult of shouting outside and the thunder of the surf on the reef where we lay, added to the terror and gloom of the situation.

Hands were immediately turned to the pumps, and orders were given that other men should bail at the hatchways. Presently the grating over the roundhouse scuttle was unlocked and the master-at-arms entered with a lantern. He quickly unshackled Coleman, Norman, and McIntosh, and ordered them on deck to lend a hand. We begged the master-at-arms to release all of us, but he gave no heed, and when he had gone out with the three men the iron grating was replaced and locked as before.

Some of the prisoners now began to rave and curse like madmen, wrenching at their chains in the vain effort to break them. At this time Edwards appeared at the scuttle and sternly ordered us to be silent.

"For God's sake, unshackle us, sir!" Muspratt called. "Give us a chance for our lives!"

"Silence! Do you hear me?" Edwards replied; then, to the master-at-arms, who stood beside him by the scuttle: "Mr. Jackson, I hold you responsible for the prisoners. They are not to be loosed without my orders."

"Let us bear a hand at the pumps, sir," Morrison called, earnestly.

"Silence, you villains!" Edwards called, and with that he left us.

Realizing now that pleading was useless, the men quieted down, and we resigned ourselves to the situation in that mood of hopeless apathy that comes over men powerless to help themselves. Within an hour another tempest of wind and rain struck us, and again the frigate was lifted by the seas and battered with awful violence on the reef. These repeated shocks threw us from side to side and against the walls and each other, so that we were dreadfully cut and bruised. As nearly as we could judge, the ship was being carried farther and farther across the reef. At length she lay quiet, down by the head, and we heard Lieutenant Corner's voice: "She's clear, sir!"

It must then have been about ten o'clock. The second squall had passed, and in the silence that followed the screaming of the wind we could plainly hear the orders being given. The guns were being heaved over the side, and the men who could be spared from bailing and pumping were employed in thrumbing a topsail to haul under the ship's bottom, in an endeavor to fother her.   But the leak gained so fast that this plan had to be abandoned, and every man on board, with the exception of our guards and ourselves, fell to bailing and pumping.

Edwards's conduct toward us is neither to be explained nor excused.   The reef upon which the *Pandora* had struck was leagues distant from any land, with the exception of a few small sand-bars and stretches of barren rock.   Had we been free, there would have been no possibility of escape; and yet Edwards doubled the guard over the roundhouse and gave orders to the master-at-arms to keep us chained hand and foot. Fortunately, we did not realize the imminence of our danger. The roundhouse being on the quarter-deck, we were high above the water, and while we knew that the ship was doomed, we did not know that the leak was gaining so rapidly.   It was, in fact, a race between the sea and daylight, and had the frigate gone down in the night, every man on board of her must have perished.

In the first grey light of dawn, we realized that the end was a matter, not of hours, but of minutes.   The frigate's stern was now high out of water, and the pitch of the deck made it impossible to stand.   The boats were lying close by, and the officers were busy getting supplies into them.   In the forward part of the vessel the water was fast approaching the gunports.   Men swarmed on top of the roundhouse and were going into the boats by the stern ladders.   We called to those outside, begging and pleading that we might not be forgotten, and some of the men began wrenching at their leg irons with the fury of despair.   What the orders respecting us were, or whether any had been given, I know not, but our entreaties must have been heard by those outside.   Joseph Hodges, the armourer's mate, came down to us and removed the irons of Byrne, Muspratt, and Skinner; but Skinner, in his eagerness to get out, was hauled up with his handcuffs on, the two other men following close behind.   Then the scuttle was closed and

barred again. This was done, I believe, by the order of Lieutenant Parkin, for a moment before I had seen him peering
down at us.

Hodges had not noticed that the scuttle had been closed. He
was unlocking our irons as rapidly as possible when the ship
gave a lurch and there was a general cry of "There she goes!"
Men were leaping into the water from the stern, for the boats
had pushed off at the first appearance of motion in the ship.
We shouted with all our strength, for the water was beginning
to flow in upon us. That we were not all drowned was due to
the humanity of James Moulter, the boatswain's mate. He
had scrambled up on the roof of the roundhouse in order to
leap into the sea, and, hearing our cries, he replied that he
would either set us free or go to the bottom with us. He
drew out the bars that fastened the scuttle to the coamings,
and heaved the scuttle overboard. "Hasten, lads!" he cried,
and then himself leaped into the sea.

In his excitement and fear, the armourer's mate had ne-
glected to remove the handcuffs of Burkitt and Hillbrandt,
although they were free of their leg irons. We scrambled out,
helping each other, and not a moment too soon. The ship
was under water as far as the mainmast, and I saw Captain
Edwards swimming toward the pinnace, which was at a considerable distance. I leaped from the stern and had all I could
do to clear myself from the driver boom before the ship went
down. I swam with all my strength and was able to keep
beyond the suction of the water as the stern of the frigate
rose perpendicularly and slid into the sea. Few seamen know
how to swim, and the cries of drowning men were awful beyond the power of words to describe. All hatch covers, spare
booms, the coops for fowls, and the like, had been cut loose,
and some of the men had succeeded in reaching floating
articles; but others went down almost within reach of planks
or booms that might have saved them. I swam to one of
the hatch covers and found Muspratt at the other end. He

was unable to swim, but told me that he could hang on until he should be picked up. I swam to a short plank, and, with this to buoy me, started in the direction of one of the boats. I had been in the water nearly an hour before I was taken up by the blue yawl. Of the prisoners, Ellison and Byrne had been rescued by this boat, which was now filled with men, and we set out for a small sandy key on the reef at a distance of about three miles from where the ship went down. This was the only bit of land above water anywhere about, although there were shoals on every side near enough to the surface for the sea to break over them.

There was quiet water at the key, which was nearly encircled by reef, and we had no difficulty in landing. As soon as the men were disembarked, with such provision as the boat contained, the yawl was sent back to the scene of the wreck. Ellison, Byrne, and I were kept at the oars, and Bowling, the master's mate, was at the tiller. We made a wide search among floating wreckage, and so strong were the currents thereabout that we took up men as far as three miles from the reef where the ship had struck. We rescued twelve in all, among them Burkitt, clinging to a spar with his handcuffs still on his wrists.

It was nearly midday before we returned to the key, and by that time the other boats had assembled there. The sandbar, for it was no more than that, was about thirty paces long by twenty wide. Nothing grew there — not a sprig of green to relieve the eyes from the blinding glare of the sun. Captain Edwards ordered a muster of the survivors, and it was found that thirty-three of the ship's company and four of the prisoners had been drowned. Of the prisoners, Stewart, Sumner, Hillbrandt, and Skinner were missing.

Morrison told me that he had seen Stewart go down. He had not been able to get clear of the ship as she foundered. A heavy spar had shot up from the broken water, and as it fell Stewart was struck on the head and sank instantly. Of all the events that had happened since the *Bounty* left England, excepting only my parting from my wife and little daughter, Stewart's death was the one that cast the deepest gloom upon my spirit. A better companion and a truer friend, in good fortune and bad, never lived.

Captain Edwards ordered tents to be erected with the sails from the ship's boats, one for the officers and one for the men. We prisoners were sent to the windward end of the sand-bar, and, as there was no possibility of escape, we were not guarded in the daytime; but two sentinels were placed over us at night, lest ten of us should attack a ship's company nearly ten times our strength. Nor were we permitted to speak to anyone save each other. During our five months' confinement in the frigate, our bodies, which had become inured to tropical sunlight at the time of our capture, had bleached, and were almost as white as that of any counting-house clerk in London. Most of us were stark naked, and our skin was soon terribly blistered by the sun. We begged to be allowed to erect a shelter for ourselves with one of the sails not in use, but Edwards was so lacking in humanity as to refuse this request. Our only recourse was to wet the burning sand at the water's edge and bury ourselves in it up to the neck.

The suffering from thirst was scarcely to be endured. Nearly all of us had swallowed quantities of salt water before we had been rescued by the boats, which added to our torture. The provision that had been saved was so scanty that each man's allowance on the first day spent on the key was two musket-balls' weight of bread and a gill of wine. No water was issued that day. Lieutenant Corner made a fire with some bits of driftwood, placed a copper kettle over it, and, by saving the drops of steam condensed in the cover, got about a wineglass full of water, which was issued to the ship's company, a teaspoonful per man, until the supply was exhausted. One of the seamen, a man named Connell, went out of his senses from drinking salt water.

We prisoners were far too miserable to converse. We lay by the water's edge, covered by sand and longing for darkness; and when it came we were only a little less wretched than before. Our raging thirst and our burned and blistered bodies made sleep impossible. The following morning the *Pandora's* master was sent in the pinnance to the scene of the wreck to learn whether anything else might be recovered from it. He returned with a part of the topgallant masts which were above water, and with a cat which he had found perched on the crosstrees. This poor animal was saved only to be sacrificed to the needs of shipwrecked seamen. It was cooked and eaten that same day, and a cap was made from its fur to cover the bald head of one of the officers who had lost his wig.

The following day was a repetition of the preceding one. In the early morning a search was made in the shallow water along the sandbar for shellfish, and a number of giant cockles were discovered; but the thirst of every man was so great that these could not be eaten and had to be thrown away. The carpenters were employed in preparing the boats for the long voyage ahead of us. The floor boards were cut into uprights which were fastened to the gunwales, and around these canvas was stretched to prevent the sea from breaking into the boats, for they would all be so heavily loaded as to leave very little freeboard.

On the morning of August 31, the repairs to the boats having been completed, Captain Edwards mustered the company. We prisoners were herded together, under guard, a little to one side of the others. Officers, seamen, and prisoners alike, we were as gaunt and woebegone a crowd as had ever been cast ashore from a shipwrecked vessel. Edwards was clad in his shirt, trousers, and pumps, without stockings. Dr. Hamilton was in a like costume except that he had lost his shoes; but he had saved his medicine chest, and he took an opportunity to whisper to me that my Journal and manuscripts had been saved with it. Most of the sailors were naked to the waist, but had managed to come ashore in their trousers, and, with the exception of three or four, wore turbans made of large red or yellow handkerchiefs twisted about their heads, a common article of dress among the men at sea. Of the prisoners, four of us were stark naked, and the others had only rags of pulpy Indian bark cloth about their waists. We were all without hats and our bodies were seared and blistered by the sun. Muspratt in particular suffered terribly from his burns. Our condition spoke eloquently for us, but Edwards would have done nothing had it not been that Dr. Hamilton urged him to allow the naked men to have some remnants of canvas. It was owing to the surgeon that they had some slight covering from the pitiless sun.

Edwards walked up and down in front of the company for some time. We were gathered in a half-circle before the boats, which were ready to be launched. The sky was cloudless and the sea of the deepest blue, save where it broke over the reefs and shoals that stretched away before us. We waited in silence for the captain to speak. Presently he turned and faced us.

"Men," he said, "we have a long and dangerous voyage ahead of us. The nearest port at which we can expect help is the Dutch settlement on the island of Timor, between four and five hundred leagues from this place. We shall pass various islands on our way, but they are inhabited by savages from whom we have nothing to expect but the barbarity common to such people. Our supply of provision is so scant that each man's allowance will be small indeed; but it will be sufficient to maintain life even though we are unable to add to it during the passage. Each of us, officers, men, and prisoners alike, will receive the following allowance, which will be issued each day at noon: two ounces of bread, half an ounce of portable soup, half an ounce of essence of malt, two small glasses of water, and one of wine. It is to be hoped that we shall be able to add to our supplies during the voyage, but this cannot be counted upon.

"With favouring winds and weather we may be able to reach Timor in fourteen or fifteen days, but I must warn you that we can scarcely expect such good fortune. But within three weeks, if we meet with no accidents on the way, we shall be approaching our destination. Most of our provision must be carried in the launch, and for this reason, as well as for support and defense, the boats must keep together.

"I expect implicit obedience from every man, and cheerful and immediate compliance with the orders issued by your officers. Our safety depends upon this, and any infringement of discipline will be severely dealt with.

"Captain William Bligh, in a boat laden more deeply than any of ours, and with provision even more scanty, has made the same voyage that we are to make. He must have passed near this spot, and at that time he and his men had sailed and rowed their boat between six and seven hundred leagues. And he arrived at Timor with the loss of only one man. What he has done, we can do."

Edwards now turned to us.

"As for you," he continued, "you are not to forget that you are pirates and mutineers being taken to England to suffer the punishment you so richly merit. I am ordered by His Majesty's Government to have a proper regard for the preservation of your lives. This duty I shall continue to fulfill."

This was the first, indeed the only time he condescended to address us directly.

The boats were now dragged into the water, and our company was distributed among them. Morrison, Ellison, and I were assigned to the captain's pinnace.

We were delayed in starting owing to the condition of the seaman Connell, the man who had drunk salt water to allay his thirst. All through the previous night he had been raving mad, and it was plain that he had only a few hours to live.

In his condition it was impossible to take him into any of the boats. His sufferings were horrible, and offered an object lesson to anyone who might have been tempted to follow his example. Death came mercifully at about ten o'clock in the morning, and in his haste to embark Edwards read no burial service over the body. A shallow grave was scooped in the sand, and it was the work of no more than five minutes to bury him there. A lump of sun-blackened coral was placed as a headstone. No British seaman, I imagine, has had a lonelier grave.

We now quickly embarked, and, with the pinnace in the van, set out on our voyage to Timor.

XIX

TEN WEARY MONTHS

We had a fair wind and a calm sea, and the sail was hoisted directly we left the key. Edwards sat at the tiller. He looked as gaunt and ill-kempt as any of his men, but his lips were set in their usual thin line, and from the expression on his face he might have been walking the quarter-deck of the *Pandora*. One of the men cried, "Ho for Timor, lads!" but there was no response. We were so tortured by thirst that scarcely a word passed among the company.

Morrison, Ellison, and I had been placed in the bow of the pinnace. Her burden of twenty-four men brought her low in the water and made it impossible for Edwards to separate us from the seamen; but lest we should somehow contaminate them, he took the precaution of placing Hayward, and Rickards, the master's mate, next to us. When it was necessary for either of them to take the tiller, Packer, the gunner or Edmonds, the captain's clerk, took his place. When the wind failed we took our turns at the oars with the others, but we were never permitted to forget that we were pirates on the way to a rope's end on some ship of war in Portsmouth Harbour. Hayward evidently felt the awkwardness of his situation in being placed directly beside us in a small boat; but under Edwards's watchful eye he managed to maintain toward us his usual manner of contemptuous aloofness.

The calm sea was less than half a dozen miles in extent; then we found ourselves, as before the wreck, in the midst of a maze of sand-bars and half-drowned reefs, leagues distant from any land. The currents and tide-rips were as strong as they were treacherous, and it was necessary to take in sail and trust to the oars; but with the boat so heavily laden it was heartbreaking work keeping clear of the shoals. The floor of the sea was a miracle of vivid colouring, but its beauty became hateful to us, and I remember with what longing we looked ahead for the deep blue water that meant safety.

At midday our allowance of food and water was issued. Edwards had devised a pair of scales, using two musket balls for weights, and the water and wine were measured in a small glass. We had but two of these glasses, and it was necessary for each man to drink his allowance at once so that others might be served; but later we provided ourselves with clam shells which enabled us to sip as slowly as we pleased.

All the morning the four boats had kept within a mile of one another, and the work at the oars had increased our thirst to the point of agony. Most of us were without hats, and the heat of the tropical sun was like a heavy weight upon the brain. The only relief from it was to wet such garments as we had and place them on our heads, and many sponged their bodies, as well, with sea water, but the absorption through the skin of the salts in the water increased thirst and gave a nauseating taste to the saliva. Some of the men, made reckless by suffering, begged or demanded an increased allowance of water, and one of them, in the launch, after he had drunk his own allowance, tried to seize the glass of another as it was being passed from hand to hand, and the precious liquid was spilled. The man was immediately knocked senseless by Bowling, one of the master's mates, who clubbed him over the head with an emptied bottle. Under the circumstances, it was a well-deserved punishment. Edwards now spoke to the company.

"It is my purpose," he said, "to bring every man of you safe to Timor; but if we have another incident of this kind, the one responsible for it shall be shot. Let each man remember that his sufferings are shared by all of the others. To-morrow we shall be close in with the coast of Australia. Somewhere along that coast we shall undoubtedly find water; I promise that we shall not leave it until we do. Meanwhile, bear in mind what I have said."

From the condition of my own parched lips and swollen tongue, I was able to appreciate what an effort it must have cost Edwards to make even so brief an address to the company. We proceeded on our way, the four boats keeping within view of each other during the afternoon, and before sunset we had passed through the worst of the reefs and had more open water before us. The pinnace, which was still in the van, lay-to to allow the other boats to come up with her, and we made fast, bow and stern, lest we should become separated during the night. Never, I imagine, have men welcomed the coming of darkness more gratefully. The breeze was cool, and carried us smoothly on the way we would go. Oars were laid over the thwarts, and by this means we were able to stow two tiers of men, which gave us room to stretch our limbs a little.

At dawn the lines were again cast off, and each boat proceeded as best it could. We were now close in with the northernmost coast of Australia, but whether it was the continent itself or one of the innumerable islands adjoining it, no one of us knew. The land had an arid look, and we gazed at it with hopeless eyes, for it seemed unlikely that we should find water there. The pinnace and the red yawl were close together at this time. For several hours we coasted along within half a mile of the shore. We saw no signs of man or beast, and the vegetation was nothing more than scattered trees and hardy shrubs that looked as tortured with thirst as ourselves.

We came to an inlet that deeply indented the coast. The breeze died down, the oars were gotten out, and we rowed into the bay. Here the water was like a sheet of glass, reflecting the sky and the brown shore line. It was about three miles to the head of the bay, but, eager though we were to reach it, we made but slow progress in our enfeebled condition. As we approached we saw a narrow valley where the vegetation was of a much richer green, which made it all but certain that water was to be found there. At last we brought up within wading distance of the beach, and in their eagerness some of the men leaped into the water; but Edwards ordered them back until a guard had been told off in each of the boats to watch over the prisoners. The rest of the company were then permitted to go ashore, and we watched with feverish eyes as they spread out along the bay and proceeded inland. Then a shout was heard, and all of them rushed like madmen to one spot. An excellent spring had been found within fifty yards of the beach. It was all that our guards could do to prevent themselves from rushing after the others.

The delay was torture, but our turn came at last. We drank and drank and drank again until we could hold no more. Nothing mattered now. Having been relieved from the most terrible of all man's bodily sufferings, we were content. Those whose thirst was quenched crawled into the shade of the trees and fell asleep at once. They lay sprawled like dead men, around the spring. Edwards would gladly have remained here, but the launch and the blue yawl had, somehow, missed the bay and, shut in by land as we were, it was impossible to signal them. Therefore the men were kicked or buffeted awake by the officers, and having filled our small keg, the teakettle, two bottles, and even a pair of water-tight boots belonging to the gunner, we reëmbarked. Several of the seamen were so exhausted that it was impossible to waken them. They were carried aboard and dropped into the bottom of the boats.

When we had emerged from the bay we saw the launch and the blue yawl far ahead of us. We made all haste to come up with them and signaled by musket fire; but the signals were not heard, and it was not until mid-afternoon that we managed to get abreast of them. They had found no water and we were now too far to leeward to permit them to return to the bay where the spring was. Edwards issued three wineglasses of water to each man in the two boats, and we made sail again.

At daybreak the following morning we were not far from an island that proved to be inhabited. It looked much less desolate than the mainland. The white sandy beach soon gave way to rising ground where there was abundant vegetation. We searched eagerly for a landing place; but we had been seen from afar, and as we proceeded the Indians gathered in ever greater numbers, following us along the beach. They were jet-black in colour and stark naked, and armed with spears and bows and arrows. Finding a break in the reef, we entered a narrow lagoon and approached to within half a cable's length of the shore. In a moment the place was thronged with savages in a state of great excitement, and it was evident that they had never before seen white men. We made signs to them that we wanted water, and after much persuasion half a dozen of them were coaxed near enough to the boats to enable us to give them some buttons cut from various articles of clothing. They took the keg of the pinnace, the only container of any size that we had for water, and presently returned with it filled. The eager, desperate haste with which we drank would have offered a pitiful sight to any civilized observer, but the savages laughed and yelled with delight as they watched us. The keg was soon emptied and again given to them, but upon bringing it back a second time they placed it on the beach and made signs for us to come and fetch it. This Edwards would not allow to be done, suspecting treachery, and he ordered the boats to push off to a safer distance. At this sign of timidity on our part the natives rushed forward to the water's edge and discharged a shower of arrows at us. Fortunately no one was hit, although there were many narrow escapes. One arrow struck a thwart in our boat, piercing an oak plank an inch thick. A volley was then fired over their heads, and the sound and the smoke so frightened them that all ran for their lives, and in an instant the beach was deserted. The pinnace pushed in to recover the keg. We got it, and none too soon, for the savages rushed out again, but we made off before any harm was done.

The savages were so numerous and so hostile that Edwards abandoned hope of refreshment here. Other islands were in view at this time, and rather than risk the loss of any of the company, we were ordered to proceed to the nearest of these. About two o'clock in the morning we entered a small bay which I still remember with the keenest pleasure. It was a cool cloudless night, with a late moon casting a glamorous light over the glassy surface of the water. The four boats entered in complete silence as a precaution against the presence of savages. We disembarked upon a beach of coral sand, packed hard and firm, and delightfully cool to our bare feet. The prisoners were taken aside under a guard, and two parties were told off to make an exploration of the place. The rest of the company remained by the boats with their arms in readiness. In about an hour's time the search parties returned with the welcome news that the place was deserted, and that they had found water. Every man had his thirst quenched that night. Sentinels were then posted, and all of the others stretched out on the cool sand for the sleep so desperately needed.

I awoke shortly after dawn, feeling completely refreshed and very hungry. The bay was still in shadow, but the light was streaming up from behind the green hills enclosing it. Morrison was awake, but the rest of the prisoners, as well as the *Pandora's* company, were sleeping as though they would never have done. Edwards let them have their sleep out, but as the men awakened they were sent out in small parties to search for food. A pleasanter refuge than this bay afforded could scarcely have been found, except for the fact that no food-bearing trees could be discovered, nor did those searching the shallows of the bay have any better success. Mor-

rison and I proposed to the master-at-arms that the prisoners
be permitted to forage for the ship's company. The request
was carried to Edwards, who granted it with great reluctance.
To be indebted to a group of pirates and mutineers for benefits
of any kind was opposed to all his ideas of fitness; but, his
own men having failed to discover anything save a few sea
snails, we were sent out, well guarded, to see what we could do.

We made fishlines of bark cut into thin strips and braided,
and we devised fish hooks with some nails furnished us by
the carpenter. With other nails and long slender poles cut
from the bush, we made fish spears, and, thus provided, we
set out with the ever-present marines accompanying us in one
of the ship's boats.

During our long sojourn at Tahiti we had learned how
and where to search for shellfish, and within two hours we
returned with the boat loaded with fish, lobsters, mussels, and
the like, enough for two good meals for the whole company.
We received no word of thanks from Edwards, and immediately we had returned we had the guard round us as before;
but it was enough for us to see with what relish all hands
partook of the meal.

We remained at this place, which Edwards named "Laforey's
Island," all of that day and the following night. We found
no Indians, but it was plainly used by them as a place of frequent resort. The ground in the vicinity of the spring was
much footworn, and two or three well-used paths led over the
hills toward the interior. Near the shore we found some heaps
of sun-bleached human bones which gave us reason to believe
that the people were cannibals. On the morning of September 2 we again embarked, greatly refreshed, and before nightfall had reached the open sea beyond Endeavour Straits.

For all the years that have passed, I still have a clear recollection of the feeling of horror and gloom that, at this time,
seized the greater part of the men in the pinnace. Timor was

still a thousand miles distant, and not many of us had more than a dim hope of reaching it. We had far more than our share of faint-hearts, for the *Pandora's* crew had been made up largely of landsmen, with no sense of the traditions of the sea, unaccustomed to the dangers and hardships which sailors take as a matter of course. Above all, they were ignorant of what a good ship's boat can do when ably handled. Luckily, most of the *Pandora's* officers were thorough seamen, and there was a saving leaven of the same type among the men.

Now that we were once more in the open sea, new dangers presented themselves. There was a heavy westerly swell running, and with our boats so deep in the water we were kept bailing constantly. Our only vessels were some giant mussel shells we had found at Laforey's Island, and they were heavy and ill-adapted to the purpose. During the first day we had not a moment of rest. The wind had come round to the east and, running counter to the swell, made a dangerous sea. There were times when every man of us was bailing who could be spared for the purpose, and at midday it was only with great difficulty that the food and water could be issued.

At nightfall the boats were again fastened to each other, but the towlines broke repeatedly, and we were in such danger of being dashed to pieces against each other that we were obliged to cast off and trust to Providence that we should be able to keep together. Muskets were fired in each of the boats at two-hour intervals, but these signals could not always be made, owing to our powder being wetted. At dawn we found ourselves widely scattered, and the blue yawl was so far to windward that for an hour or two we thought we had lost her; but at last we caught sight of her masthead as she rose to the crest of a sea.

By midday we had again assembled, and the meagre allowance of food and water was passed around. Those noonday meetings have left a series of indelible pictures in my mind. I see the blue yawl or the launch slowly approaching, looking inconceivably small and lonely, now lost to view in the trough of the sea, now clearly outlined against the sky as it rose to the swell.   At last it is near enough so that we can make out the figures of the men, bailing, bailing, bailing, without respite. Now we are within half a cable's length of each other, and I see the faces, gaunt and hollow-eyed, and the expression of unutterable weariness upon each of them.   We would stare at each other like so many spectres.   Sometimes Edwards would call across to one of his officers: "How do you prosper, Mr. Corner?" or, "Is it well with your company, Mr. Passmore?"   And the reply would come back, "We're not doing badly, sir."   Then we would approach each other as closely as we dared while the precious food and water were being passed from boat to boat.

Dr. Hamilton was a tower of strength to the men in the red yawl.   He suffered as much as the rest of us, but he heartened and encouraged everyone at these midday meetings.   I was glad for the sake of Muspratt and Burkitt that the surgeon was with them, for Parkin was in charge of the red yawl, and he would have found the means to increase the misery of the prisoners had it not been for the doctor.

A curious incident occurred in the pinnace at one of these noonday assemblies.   An elderly sailor named Thompson had carried with him from the wreck of the *Pandora* a small bag of dollars, his savings during many years.   When the day's allowance of water was being issued, a wineglass was passed to the man sitting next him, a Scot named McPherson. Prompted by his raging thirst, Thompson offered the whole of his savings for this small glass of water.   McPherson's struggle was a bitter one.   His desire for the dollars — and it was a goodly sum, sewed up in a canvas bag — was almost equally balanced by his desire for the two or three mouthfuls of water the glass contained.   The rest of us forgot our misery for a moment as we waited to see the result.   Presently the master's mate said: "Do one thing or the other and be quick about it."

"Give me the bag," said McPherson, but while Thompson was loosening the cord which held it to his waist, the Scot thought better of the matter and drank his allowance of water at a gulp.

The sufferings of the older men were, naturally, greater than those of the younger ones. A midshipman, who was no more than a boy, sold his allowance of water two days running for another man's allowance of bread. So terrible is thirst that several of the men drank their own urine. They died, without exception, in the sequel of the voyage.

We again attempted to keep the boats together by towing, during the nights of the fifth and sixth of September, but the lines broke as usual, and the strain on the boats was so great that we were obliged to abandon this method of keeping together during the night. Edwards had given his officers the exact latitude of Timor, and the longitude by the timekeeper on that date. This in case we should become separated. Fortunately, we managed to keep within sight of each other during the whole of the following week. In the pinnace we caught one booby, and the blood and flesh were divided into twenty-four shares and distributed in the old seaman's manner of "Who shall have this?" This good fortune came on the eleventh of September, at a time when we were sorely in need of it.

On the morning of the thirteenth land was sighted, a faint bluish blur on the Western horizon. At first we could not believe it possible that Timor was within view, but as the morning wore on even the skeptics were convinced that it was land and not cloud that we saw. We were so wretched in mind and body that we could not even summon up the strength to cheer when Rickards said, "It's Timor, lads. No doubt of it."

To add to our misery, it fell dead calm about the middle of the afternoon. The oars were gotten out and we proceeded wearily on. The boats now separated, each one being in haste to make the land. Some of the older men in the pinnace were by now so helpless that they lacked the strength to sit up-right. They lay huddled in the bottom of the boat, moaning and crying out for water.

By noon of the following day we were close in with the land. The other boats were not in sight. The torture of thirst had become so great that Edwards decided to pass out our remaining supply of water, which came to half a bottle per man. This greatly refreshed us and we proceeded along the coast, seeking a possible landing place.

I remember nothing of the hinterlands of Timor. I have in mind only a dim picture of green hills and distant mountains. Every man's gaze, like my own, was fixed on the foreshore. There was a high surf running, and for several hours we found no place at which a boat could be landed without risk of its being dashed to pieces. Toward sunset we came to a more sheltered part of the coast, and two of the sailors swam ashore with bottles fastened about their necks. They proceeded along the beach, the boat following, until it was almost dark, without finding so much as a muddy creek where we might have re-freshed ourselves. Having taken them aboard again, we stood off the land. We had the breeze again and made good progress during the night. The next morning we found an excellent landing place, and near it the water so urgently needed. I doubt whether some of the men could have survived another day without it, for we had been upon short rations so long that all the bodily juices were dried up.

About twelve o'clock on the night of September 15, the pinnace came to a grapnel off the float by the fort in Coupang Bay. It was a calm night with the sky ablaze with stars. The settlement was asleep. A ship was anchored not far from where we lay, and two or three smaller craft, but in the dark-ness we were unable to see whether any of the other boats of the *Pandora* had arrived. The night was profoundly still. On the high rampart of the fort a dog stood, barking mourn-fully. That was our welcome to Coupang. Worn out with our long journey, we remained where we were until daylight, sleeping huddled in our places, and never, I imagine, have men slept more soundly.

I shall give only a brief account of our experiences from the morning of our arrival at Coupang until the day when we sighted the cliffs of Old England. Captain Edwards and his men doubtless enjoyed the stay at Coupang, where they were the guests of the Dutch East India Company. As for the prisoners, we were guests of another sort. We were taken at once to the fort and placed in stocks in the guardroom, a dreary place with a bare stone floor, and lighted by two small barred windows high in the wall. Parkin took charge of us again, and he saw to it that we lacked even the most primitive means for comfort. Edwards never once visited us, but we were not forgotten by Dr. Hamilton. During the first week at Timor, he was kept busy attending the *Pandora's* sick, several of whom died within a few days of our arrival; but as soon as he was free to do so he paid us a visit, accompanied by the Dutch surgeon of the place. So foul was our prison by that time that before they could enter it the place had to be scrubbed out by slaves, and ourselves with it. We begged Dr. Hamilton to use his influence so that Lieutenant Corner might be placed in charge of us; but Corner being a decent and humane man, Edwards would not consent to this. We remained in Parkin's care, and he made our life so wretched that we wished ourselves dead a dozen times over before we reached the Cape of Good Hope.

On October 6 the entire company was embarked on the *Rembang*, a Dutch East India ship, for the passage to Batavia, on the island of Java. The *Rembang* was an ancient vessel, and leaked so badly that it was necessary to work the pumps every hour in the twenty-four. We prisoners were kept at this work, and, exhausting though it was, we preferred it to confinement below decks. Near the island of Flores a great storm arose, which struck us so suddenly that every sail on the ship was torn to ribbons. The Dutch sailors believed the vessel lost, and there was reason to think so, for the pumps became choked and useless at the time when we most needed them, and the ship was fast driving on a lee shore only seven miles distant. It was due to Edwards, who took command, and the exertion of some of our British tars, that we weathered the storm.

We arrived at Samarang on October 30, and here, to the amazement and delight of everyone, we found the schooner *Resolution*, from which we had become separated among the Navigators' Islands four months earlier. After losing sight of the *Pandora*, Oliver, the master's mate in charge of the *Resolution*, had cruised about for several days in search of us, and had then proceeded to the Friendly Islands. Namuka was the island appointed for a rendezvous in case of such an emergency, but Oliver had gone to Tofoa, mistaking this island for Namuka, and so had missed us. He and his crew of nine had undergone dangers and hardships equal to, if not greater than, our own. Upon reaching the great reef that stretches between New Guinea and the coast of Australia, they had searched in vain for an opening, and then formed the desperate resolve of running over the reef on the crest of a sea. It was a chance in a hundred, but they succeeded, and were later saved from death by thirst when they met a small Dutch vessel beyond Endeavour Straits. Having been supplied with food and water, they pursued their voyage to Samarang, where we found them.

Edwards sold the *Resolution* at Samarang, and the money was divided among the *Pandora's* crew for the purchase of clothing and other necessities. This seemed hard upon Morrison and the other prisoners who had built the schooner. Not a shilling did they receive, but they at least had the satisfaction of knowing that they had built a staunch little ship, as good as any turned out by the shipwrights of England. After her sale at Samarang she had a long and honourable career in the western Pacific, and made the record passage between China and the Sandwich Islands.

At Samarang the *Rembang* was reconditioned and we proceeded to Batavia, where the company was divided and transshipped to four vessels of the Dutch East India Company for the long voyage to Holland. Captain Edwards, with Lieutenant Parkin, the master, purser, gunner, clerk, two midshipmen, and the ten prisoners from the *Bounty*, embarked on the *Vreedenburg*, and on January 15, 1792, we arrived at the Cape of Good Hope, where we found *H.M.S. Gorgon* awaiting orders for England. Edwards therefore left the *Vreedenburg* and took passage for all of his party on the *Gorgon*. We remained at the Cape for nearly three months, during which time we were confined on the *Gorgon*. Mr. Gardner, first lieutenant of that vessel, treated us with great humanity. We were chained by one leg only, instead of having both feet and both hands in irons as heretofore, and we were given an old sail to lie upon at night, a luxury we had not enjoyed during the previous twelve months. On the long passage to England we were permitted to remain on deck for several hours each day to enjoy the fresh air. This circumstance was galling to Edwards, who would have kept us below during all that weary time; but as the ship was not his, he was not in a position to protest.

On the nineteenth of June we arrived off Spithead, and before dark had anchored in Portsmouth Harbour. Four years and six months had passed since the *Bounty's* departure from England, during which time we had spent nearly fifteen months in irons.

XX

SIR JOSEPH BANKS

Every vessel in Portsmouth Harbour knew of the arrival of the *Gorgon*, and that she had brought home with her some of the notorious *Bounty* mutineers. The harbour was crowded with shipping at this time, merchant vessels and ships of war. Among the latter was H.M.S. *Hector*, and on the morning of June 21, 1792, we were transferred to this vessel to await court-martial. It was a cloudy day, threatening rain, with a fresh breeze blowing, and the choppy waves slapped briskly against the bow of the boat. As we passed ship after ship we saw rows of heads looking down at us from the high decks, and groups of men crowded at the gun-ports for a view of us. We knew only too well what they were thinking and saying to each other: "Thank God I'm not in any of those men's boots!"

We were received with impressive solemnity on board the *Hector*. A double line of marines with fixed bayonets were drawn up on either side of the gangway. There was a deep silence as we passed between them and down to the lower gun-deck. No doubt we looked like pirates in our nondescript clothing acquired here and there all the way from Timor to England. Some of us were without hats, others without shoes, and none of us had anything resembling a uniform. The rags that we wore consisted of cast-off garments given us by various kind-hearted English sailors at Batavia and at Table Bay, — chiefly by men of the *Gorgon*, — and they were in a wretched state indeed by the time we reached home. We were conducted to the gun room which lay right aft, and it was a great relief to find that the treatment to which Edwards had so long accustomed us was now a thing of the past. We were regarded, not as condemned men, but as prisoners awaiting trial, and what a world of difference this made can be appreciated only by men who have been placed in a similar situation. Neither leg irons nor handcuffs were placed upon us, and we had the freedom of the gun room, which was guarded by marines. We had decent food, hammocks to sleep in, and were granted all privileges comportable with our position as prisoners.

Considering our hardships and the fact that we had been so long in irons, it is remarkable that we were all in good health. None of us had been ill in all that time, and yet many of the *Pandora's* company had been continually ailing, and more than a dozen of them had died at Timor and Samarang and Batavia. No doubt Edwards took credit to himself for our condition, but he deserved none. We were well, not because of his treatment, but in spite of it.

We had not been above an hour on board the *Hector* when I was summoned to the cabin of Captain Montague, who commanded the vessel. He dismissed the guard and bade me, in a most kindly fashion, to be seated. No mention was made of the mutiny. For a quarter of an hour he chatted with me in the courteous, affable manner he might have used toward one of his officers whom he had asked to dine with him. He questioned me at length concerning the wreck of the *Pandora,* and our subsequent adventures on the voyage to Timor. He was evidently interested in the story, but I was sure that I had not been summoned merely to entertain him with an account of our experiences. At length he opened a drawer in his table and drew forth a small packet which he handed to me.

"I have some letters for you, Mr. Byam. You may have as much time as you like here, alone. When you are ready to return to your quarters you have only to open the door and inform the guard."

He then left me, and I opened the packet with trembling hands. It contained a letter from Sir Joseph Banks, written only a few days earlier, upon his receipt of the news of the *Gorgon's* arrival. He informed me that my mother had died six weeks before, and enclosed a letter to me written the night before her death, forwarded to him by our old servant, Thacker.

I was grateful indeed to Captain Montague for the privilege of half an hour's privacy in his cabin; but there was no relief, then or later, for the desolation of heart I felt. Scarcely a day had passed, in the years since the *Bounty* had left England, that I had not thought of my mother and longed for her, and the consciousness of her love had sustained me through all the weary months of our imprisonment. There was never any question of her belief in my innocence, but she was as proud in spirit as she was gentle and kind-hearted, and the slur cast upon our good name by the event of the mutiny — above all, the fact that Bligh considered me among the guiltiest of the mutineers — was a shock beyond her strength to withstand. There was nothing of this in her letter; I had the facts, later, from Thacker, who told me that my mother's health had begun to fail from the day when she had received the letter from Bligh. I have made all possible allowances for him. He had reason to believe that I was an accomplice of Christian; but a man with a spark of humanity would never have written the letter he sent to my mother. I no more forgive him the cruelty of it now that I did when I first read it.

It was the irony of my fate that, having been blessed with the steadfast love of two women, I should now — at a time when I most needed them — be separated from my mother by death and from my Indian wife by half the circumference of the globe. Upon these two I had centred all my affections. Now that my mother was gone, I clung to the memory of Tehani more tenderly than ever before.

What might now happen seemed a matter of little consequence. I could not imagine life in England without my mother; the thought that I might lose her had never occurred to me. But when I became calmer, I realized that, for her sake at least, it was necessary to clear our name from the stigma attached to it. I must prove my innocence beyond all question.

Sir Joseph Banks came to see me only a few days after I had received his letter. My own father could not have been kinder. He had seen my mother only a few weeks before her death, and he gave me all of the small details of that visit. He remembered everything she had said, and he allowed me to question him to my heart's content. I felt immeasurably comforted and strengthened. Sir Joseph was one of those men who seem members of a race apart; who find themselves equally at home among all kinds and conditions of people. In appearance he was a typical John Bull, solidly made, with the clear ruddy complexion our English climate gives. He seemed to radiate energy, and no man could be five minutes in his presence without being the better for it. At this time he was President of the Royal Society, and his name was known and honoured, not only in England, but on the Continent as well. I doubt whether there was a busier man in London, and yet, during those anxious weeks before the court-martial, one would have thought that his only concern was to see to it that all of us were given justice and fair play.

He quickly roused me from my despairing mood, and I found myself talking with interest and enthusiasm of my Tahitian dictionary and grammar. I told him that my manuscripts had been saved from the wreck of the *Pandora* and were in the care of Dr. Hamilton, now on his way home with the rest of the *Pandora's* survivors.

"Excellent, Byam! Excellent!" he said. "There is one gain, at least, from the voyage of the *Bounty*." He had the faculty of entering with enthusiasm into another man's work, and of making him feel that there was nothing more important.

"I shall see Dr. Hamilton the moment he arrives in England. But enough of this for the present. Now I want your story of the mutiny — the whole of it — every detail."

"You have heard Captain Bligh's account, sir? You know how black the case against me appears to be?"

"I do," he replied, gravely. "Captain Bligh is my good friend, but I know his faults of character as well as his virtues. His belief in your guilt is sincerely held; yet allow me to say that I have never for a moment doubted your innocence."

"Is Captain Bligh now in England, sir?" I asked.

"No. He has again been sent to Tahiti to fulfill the task of conveying breadfruit plants to the West Indies. This time, I hope, the voyage will be successfully completed."

This was serious news for me. I felt certain that, if I could confront Bligh, I could convince him of my innocence, force him to acknowledge that he had been mistaken in jumping to the conclusion that the conversation with Christian had concerned the mutiny. With him gone, only his sworn deposition at the Admiralty would confront me, and there was no possibility of its being retracted.

"Put all that aside, Byam," said Sir Joseph. "There is no help for it, and all your desire to confront Bligh won't bring him back in time for the court-martial. Now proceed with your story, and remember that I am completely in the dark with respect to the part you played."

I then gave him, as I had given Dr. Hamilton, a complete account of the mutiny, and of all that had happened since. He allowed me to finish with scarcely an interruption. When I had done so I waited anxiously for him to speak.

"Byam, we may as well face the facts. You are in grave danger. Mr. Nelson, who knew of your intention to go in the launch with Bligh, is dead. Norton, the quartermaster, who could have corroborated your story of Christian's intention to escape from the *Bounty* on the night before the mutiny, is dead."

"I know it, sir. I had the information from Dr. Hamilton."

"Your chance of acquittal depends almost entirely upon the testimony of one man: your friend Robert Tinkler."

"But he returned safely to England."

"Yes, but where is he now? . . . He must be found at once. You say that he is a brother-in-law of Fryer, the master of the *Bounty*?"

"Yes, sir."

"In that case I should be able to get trace of him. I can learn, at the Admiralty, on what ship Fryer is now serving."

I had, somehow, taken it for granted that Tinkler would know of the need I should have for him if ever I returned home; but Sir Joseph pointed out to me the fact that Tinkler would be quite ignorant of this.

"It is not at all likely," he said, "that he will know of Bligh's depositions at the Admiralty. And it will no more have occurred to him than it did to you that your conversation with Christian could be construed as evidence against you. The chances are that Tinkler will have forgotten that Bligh overheard it. No; take my word for it, he will have no fears on your account. Not a moment must be lost in finding him."

"How soon will the court-martial take place, sir?" I asked.

"That rests with the Admiralty, of course. But this matter has been hanging fire for so long that they will wish to dispose of it as soon as possible. It will be necessary to wait until the rest of the *Pandora's* company arrive, but they should be nearing England by this time."

Sir Joseph now left me. He was to return to London by that night's coach.

"You shall hear from me shortly," he said. "Meanwhile, rest assured that I shall find your friend Tinkler if he is to be found in England."

Our conversation had taken place in Captain Montague's cabin. The other prisoners were anxiously awaiting my return to the gun room. Sir Joseph was the first visitor we had had;

in fact, we were not permitted to see anyone except persons officially connected with the forthcoming court-martial. Sir Joseph was not, perhaps, so connected, but his interest in the *Bounty* and his influence at the Admiralty gave him access to us.

I gave the others an account of my conversation with him, omitting only his opinion of the fate in store for Millward, Burkitt, Ellison, and Muspratt. These men were, he thought, doomed past hope, with the possible exception of Muspratt. Byrne was entirely innocent of any part in the mutiny, but the poor fellow had been treated as a condemned man for so long that he had more than half come to believe himself guilty. As for Coleman, Norman, and McIntosh, it was inconceivable to any of us that they would be convicted. Morrison was in a situation only less dangerous than my own, and it grieved me to think that I was responsible for it. Our delay below decks on the morning of the mutiny, in the hope of getting possession of the arms chest, was known only to ourselves, and the chances were that the story would be regarded as a fiction invented afterward to explain our absence at the time the launch put off.

We had talked of the forthcoming court-martial so often during the long passage to England that we had little more to say to each other now that the event loomed so ominously near. At times, as a relief from anxiety, we spoke of our happy life at Tahiti, but for the most part we spent our days silently, each man engaged in his own reflections; or we stood at the gun-room ports looking out at the busy life of the harbour. There were times when I was seized with a sense of the unreality of this experience, like that one feels upon waking from some dream in which the events have been more than usually disconnected and fantastic. Hardest of all to realize was the fact that we were indeed at home again, lying at anchor only a few miles from Spithead, whence the *Bounty* had sailed so long ago.

Meanwhile, owing to the kindness of Sir Joseph, we were provided with decent clothing in which to appear before the court-martial. This small diversion was a most welcome one, and to be properly clothed again had an excellent effect upon our spirits.

Ten days passed before I had further word from Sir Joseph. The letter I then received I still have in my possession, although it is now faded and worn with age. To reread it is to recall vividly the emotion I felt on the morning when it was handed to me by the corporal of the guard at the gun-room door.

My dear Byam: —

I can imagine with what anxiety you are awaiting word from me. I regret that I cannot go to Portsmouth at this time, for I should much prefer to give you my news by word of mouth. This being impossible, a letter must serve.

Upon returning to London I went directly to the Admiralty office, where I learned that Fryer is now at his home in London, awaiting summons to testify at the court-martial. I sent for him at once and learned that Tinkler, shortly after his return to England, was offered a berth as master's mate on the *Carib Maid,* a West India merchantman. The captain of the vessel was a friend of Fryer's, and as it was a good berth for the lad, offering opportunity for advancement, he accepted it.

Tinkler returned from his first voyage a year ago, and shortly afterward set out on a second one. Fryer received word, not three months since, that the *Carib Maid* was lost with all hands in a hurricane near the island of Cuba.

It would be useless to deny the fact that this is a great misfortune for you. Even so, your situation, I believe, is not hopeless. I have had a long conversation with Fryer, who speaks of you in the most friendly terms. He is convinced that you had no hand in the mutiny, and his testimony will be valuable.

Cole, Purcell, and Peckover I have also seen. They are now stationed at Deptford, awaiting summons to the court-martial. They all speak highly of you, and Purcell tells me that you yourself told him of your intention to leave in the launch with Bligh. They all know of Bligh's conviction that you were an accomplice of Christian, and it speaks well for your character among them that they all believe you innocent.

My good friend, Mr. Graham, who has been Secretary to different admirals on the Newfoundland Station these past twelve years, and who has, consequently, acted as Judge Advocate at courts-martial all of that time, has offered me to attend you. He has a thorough knowledge of the service, uncommon abilities, and is a good lawyer. He already has most of the evidences with him.

Farewell, my dear Byam. Keep up your spirits, and rest assured that I shall be watchful for your good. I shall certainly attend the court-martial, and now that my friend, Graham, has consented to go down, I shall be more at ease than if you were attended by the first counsel in England.

My feeling upon reading this letter may be imagined. Sir Joseph had done what he could to soften the blow to me, but I was under no doubt as to the seriousness of my position. I knew that, without Tinkler's evidence, my case was all but desperate, no matter how ably it might be presented. Nevertheless, I clung to hope as a man will. I resolved to fight for my life with all the energy I possessed. In one sense, the stimulus of danger was a blessing in disguise, for it kept me from brooding over my mother's death. I put out of mind every thought not connected with the approaching trial.

Sea officers, as I had been informed by Sir Joseph, have a great aversion to lawyers. I was well content, therefore, to have Mr. Graham, a Navy man himself, as my representative. Morrison resolved to conduct his own case. Coleman, Norman, McIntosh, and Byrne, who had every reason to hope that they would be cleared of the charges against them, secured the services of a retired sea officer, Captain Manly, to represent and advise all four of them; and an officer from the Admiralty, Captain Bentham, was appointed by the Crown to care for the interests of the other men.

We were visited by these gentlemen during the following week, but the first to come was Mr. Graham. He was a tall spare man in his late fifties, of distinguished bearing, and with a quiet voice and manner that inspired confidence. From the moment of seeing him I was sure that my fortunes could not be in better hands. None of us had any knowledge of court-martial proceedings, and at my request Mr. Graham permitted us to question him with respect to these matters.

"I have the morning at your disposal, Mr. Byam," he said, "and I shall be glad to be of what assistance I can to any of you."

"I mean to conduct my own case, sir," Morrison said. "I should like particularly to know the exact wording of the Article under which we are to be tried."

"I can give you that precisely, from memory," Mr. Graham replied. "It is Article Nineteen, of the Naval Articles of War, which reads as follows: 'If any person, in or belonging to the Fleet, shall make, or endeavour to make, any mutinous assembly, upon any pretense whatsoever, every person offending herein, being convicted thereof by the sentence of the Court-Martial, shall suffer death.'"

"Has the Court no alternative course?" I asked.

"None. It must acquit, or convict and condemn to death."

"But supposing, sir, that there are extenuating circumstances," Morrison added. "Supposing that a mutiny arises in a ship, as it did in ours, where a part of the company have no knowledge of any intention to seize the vessel, and who take no part in the seizure?"

"If they remain in the vessel with the mutinous party, the law considers them equally guilty with the others. Our martial law is very severe in this matter. The man who stands neuter is considered an offender with him who lifts his hand against his captain."

"But there were some of us, sir," Coleman added, earnestly, "who would gladly have gone with Captain Bligh when his party was driven from the ship into the launch. We were retained against our will by the mutineers, who had need of our services."

"Such a situation calls for special consideration by the Court and will doubtless receive it," Mr. Graham replied. "If the men so retained can prove their innocence of any complicity, they stand in no danger."

"Sir, may I speak?" asked Ellison.

"Certainly, my lad."

"I was one of the mutineers, sir. I'd no hand in starting the trouble, but like all the rest of us I had no love for Captain Bligh, and I joined in when I was asked to. Is there any hope for me?"

Mr. Graham regarded him gravely for a moment.

"I prefer not to give an opinion on that," he said. "Suppose we let the question be decided by the court-martial itself."

"I'm not afraid of the truth, sir. If you think there's no chance, I'd be obliged if you'd tell me so."

But Mr. Graham would not commit himself. "Let me advise all of you not to prejudge your cases," he said. "I have sat through many a court-martial, and, as in any civil court of law, one is not justified in forming an opinion as to a possible verdict until all the evidence is in. And so you see, young man," he added, turning to Ellison, "how mistaken I should be in attempting to tell you what I think."

The days dragged by with painful slowness. Before this time most of the men had received letters from their families. Some of them were many months old, but they were read none the less eagerly for that. With the exception of the letter received from my mother, at Tahiti, no news from families or friends had reached any of us during the more than four years we had been absent from home. Poor Coleman's family lived in Portsmouth, but he was not permitted to see them. Of all the married members of the *Bounty's* company, he was, I suspect, the only man who had remained faithful to his wife during our sojourn at Tahiti. To be prevented from seeing her and his children after all these years was a cruel blow.

July passed, and August, and still we waited.

XXI

H. M. S. DUKE

ON the morning of September 12, the ten prisoners on board the *Hector* were ordered to hold themselves in readiness to proceed to *H.M.S. Duke*. It was a grey, chilly, windless day, so still that we could hear ships' bells from far and near striking the half-hours and the hours. The *Duke* was anchored abreast of the *Hector* and about a quarter of a mile distant. Shortly before eight o'clock we saw a longboat, with a guard of marines in dress uniform, put off from the great ship's side and approach the *Hector,* and on the stroke of the hour a solitary gun was fired from the *Duke*. It was the signal for the court-martial. Our time had come.

I cannot speak of the emotions of my fellow prisoners at that solemn moment, but I know that my own feeling was one of profound relief. We had waited too long and endured too much to be capable of intense emotion — at least, that was the case with me. I felt unutterably weary, in body and mind, and if I desired anything it was peace — the peace of certainty as to my fate, whatever it might be. I remember how impatient I was to arrive on board the *Duke*. One's sense of time is largely a matter of mood, and the voyage from the *Hector* to the gangway of the larger ship, brief as it was, seemed all but interminable.

The court-martial was held in the great cabin of the *Duke,* which extended the width of the vessel, from the forward limit of the poop to the stern gallery. The quarter-deck was thronged with people, chiefly officers in full-dress uniform

who had assembled from the many ships of war in the harbour
to attend the proceedings. There were also a number of
civilians, Sir Joseph Banks among them. Dr. Hamilton, whom
I had last seen at the Cape of Good Hope, was standing with
the other officers of the *Pandora* by the bulwarks on the larboard side of the deck. Edwards was there, of course, with
his satellite, Parkin, beside him. He glanced us over with his
habitual air of cold hostility, and he appeared to be thinking:
"These scoundrels freed from their irons? What gross neglect of duty!"

On the other side of the deck were gathered the officers of
the *Bounty,* looking self-conscious and ill at ease in that company of ships' captains and admirals and rear admirals. It was
a strange meeting for old shipmates, and many were the silent
messages that passed back and forth as we looked eagerly at
each other. Mr. Fryer, the master, was there, and Cole, the
boatswain, and Purcell, the carpenter, and Peckover, the gunner. A clear picture flashed into mind of the last view we
had had of them as they looked up at us from the launch across
the widening space of blue water. Little any of us thought
then that we should ever meet again.

The hum of conversation died away to silence as the door of
the great cabin opened. Audience was admitted. The spectators filed into the room; then we were marched in with a
guard, a lieutenant of marines with a drawn sword in his hand
preceding us. We were ranged in a line by the bulkhead on
the right-hand side of the door. During the first day's proceedings we were compelled to stand, but owing to the length
of the trial, a bench was later provided for us.

A long table stood fore and aft in the middle of the cabin,
with a chair at the head for the President of the Court; the
other members sat along the sides at his right and left. A
little to the right and to the rear of the President's seat was a
small table for the Judge Advocate, and another, on the opposite side, for the writers who were to transcribe the proceed-

ings.   At still another table sat the advisors to the prisoners.
On either side of the door leading to the stern gallery, and
along the walls, were settees occupied by the sea officers and
civilians who attended as spectators.

At nine o'clock precisely, the door opened again and the
members of the Court filed in to their places.   At the order
of the master-at-arms the audience rose, and when the members of the Court were in their places, all were seated again.
The names of the twelve men who held over us the power of
life and death were as follows: —

The Right Honourable Lord Hood, Vice Admiral of the Blue,
and Commander-in-Chief of His Majesty's ships and vessels
at Portsmouth Harbour, *President*

Captain Sir Andrew Snape Hammond, Bart.
" John Colpoys
" Sir George Montague
" Sir Roger Curtis
" John Bazeley
" Sir Andrew Snape Douglas
" John Thomas Duckworth
" John Nicholson Inglefield
" John Knight
" Albemarle Bertie
" Richard Goodwin Keats

My lethargy of the earlier part of the morning left me as
I gazed at the impressive scene before me.   At first my attention was fully engaged with our judges, whose faces I examined
one by one as the opportunity presented itself.   They were,
for the most part, men in middle life, and one would have
know them anywhere, in any dress, for officers in His
Majesty's Navy.   As I looked at their stern, wind-roughened,
impassive faces, my heart sank.   I recalled Dr. Hamilton's
words: "But these men will know nothing of Christian's character, and their sympathies will all be with Captain Bligh.
You will have to prove your story of that conversation with

Christian beyond the shadow of a doubt." The only one of the twelve men who might, I thought, be willing to give a prisoner the benefit of a doubt was Sir George Montague, captain of the *Hector*.

Our names were called, and we stood before the Court while the charges against us were read. This document was of considerable length, and recapitulated the history of the *Bounty* from the time of her departure from England until she was seized by the mutineers. Then followed Bligh's sworn statement, his own account of the mutiny, a document of great interest to all of us, and to me in particular. The statement, which follows, was read by the Judge Advocate: —

I respectfully beg to submit to the Lords Commissioners of the Admiralty the information that His Majesty's armed vessel, *Bounty*, under my command, was taken from me by some of the inferior officers and men on the 28th of April, 1789, in the following manner.

A little before sunrise, Fletcher Christian, who was mate of the ship and officer of the watch, Charles Churchill, master-at-arms, Thomas Burkitt, seaman, and John Mills, gunner's mate, came into my cabin, and, while I was asleep, seized me in my bed and tied my hands behind my back with a strong cord; and, with cutlasses and bayonets fixed at my breast, threatened me with instant death if I spoke or made the least noise. I nevertheless called out so loud for help that everyone heard me and were flying to my assistance; but all of my officers except those who were concerned in the mutiny found themselves secured by armed sentinels.

I was now hauled upon deck in my shirt and without a rag else, and secured by a guard abaft the mizzenmast, during which the mutineers expressed much joy at my position.

I demanded of Christian the cause of such a violent act, but no answer was given but, "Hold your tongue, sir, or you are dead this instant!" He held me by the cord which tied my hands, and threatened to stab me with the bayonet he held in his right hand. I, however, did my utmost to rally the disaffected villains to a sense of their duty, but to no effect.

The boatswain was ordered to hoist the launch out, and while I was kept under a guard with Christian at their head, the officers and men not concerned in the mutiny were ordered into the boat. This being done, I was told by Christian: "Sir, your officers and men are now in the boat and you must go with them," and the guard carried me across the deck with their bayonets presented on every side. Upon attempting to make some resistance, one of the villains said to another: "Damn his eyes, the dog! Blow his brains out!" I was at last forced into the boat and we were then veered astern, in all, nineteen souls.

While the boat was yet alongside, the boatswain and carpenter and some others collected several necessary things, and with some difficulty a compass and quadrant were got, but no arms of any kind and none of my maps or drawings. The size of the boat was 23 feet from stem to stern, and rowed six oars. We were cast adrift with the following provision: 25 gallons of water, 150 pounds of bread, 30 pounds of pork, 6 quarts of rum, and 6 bottles of wine.

The boat was so lumbered and deep in the water that it was believed we could never reach the shore, and some of the pirates made their joke of this. I asked for arms, but the request was received with the greatest abuse and insolence. Four cutlasses were, however, thrown into the boat at the last moment, and in this miserable situation we set out for the island of Tofoa, one of the Friendly Islands, ten leagues distant from where the ship then was. This island we reached at seven o'clock the same evening, but the shore being very steep and rocky, we could find no chance of landing till the following day.

During our search for water at this island we were attacked by the savages and barely escaped with our lives, one of our number, John Norton, a quartermaster, being killed as he attempted to recover the launch's grapnel.

After considering our melancholy situation, I was earnestly solicited by all hands to take them toward home; and when I told them that no hope of relief remained for us until we came to Timor, a distance of 1200 leagues, they all agreed to live upon one ounce of bread per man each day, and one gill of water. Therefore, after recommending this promise forever to their memory, I bore away for New Holland and Timor, across a sea but little known, and in a small boat laden with 18 souls, without a single map of any kind, and nothing but my own recollection and general knowledge of the situation of places to direct us.

After enduring dangers and privations impossible to describe, we sighted Timor on the 12th of June, and on the morning of the 15th, before daylight, I anchored under the fort at the Dutch settlement at Coupang. This voyage in an open boat I believe to be unparalleled in the history of Navigation.

At Timor my boat's company were treated with the greatest humanity by the Governor and the officers of the Dutch East India Company. Here, for 1000 Rix dollars — for which I gave bills on His Majesty's Government — I purchased a small schooner, thirty-four feet long, which I fitted for sea under the name of His Majesty's schooner, *Resource*. In this vessel we proceeded by way of Surabaya and Samarang to the Dutch settlement of Batavia, where I sold the *Resource* and, with my people, embarked for Europe in ships of the Dutch East India Company.

The lists, which I herewith submit, of those who were cast adrift with me in the launch and those who remained in the *Bounty* will show the strength of the pirates.

I beg leave to inform their Lordships that the secrecy of the mutiny was beyond all conception, so that I cannot discover that any who were with me had the least knowledge of it.

It is of great importance to add that, on the night preceding the mutiny, coming upon deck during the middle watch, according to my custom, I discovered Fletcher Christian, the ringleader of the pirates, in earnest conversation with Roger Byam, one of the midshipmen. In the darkness of the deck I was not observed by these men, who were standing on the starboard side of the quarter-deck between the guns; nor had I any apprehension at that time that their conversation was not innocent. But as I approached, unseen, I saw Roger Byam shake hands with Christian, and I distinctly heard him say these words: "You can count on me," to which Christian replied: "Good! That's settled, then." The moment they discovered me they broke off their talk. I have not the slightest doubt that this conversation concerned the forthcoming mutiny.

A moment of deep silence followed the reading of Captain Bligh's statement. I was conscious of the gaze of many pairs of eyes directed upon me. No more damning statement could have been brought forward, and it was only too plain how deep an impression it had made upon the Court. How, without Tinkler's evidence, could it possibly be refuted? A sense of the hopelessness of my situation came over me. I knew that had I been in the place of any of my judges, I should have felt certain of the guilt of at least one of the prisoners.

The Judge Advocate asked: "Do you wish me to read the names on the appended lists, my lord?"

Lord Hood nodded. "Proceed," he said.

The lists were then read — first the names of those who had gone in the launch with Bligh, then of those who remained with Christian's party.   One thing that astonished me was Bligh's silence with respect to Coleman, Norman, and McIntosh.   He well knew of their desire to go with him in the launch, and that they had been prevented from doing so by the mutineers.   The barest justice demanded that he should have acknowledged their innocence; yet he made no distinction between them and the guiltiest members of Christian's party.   To this day I am unable to account for his injustice to these men.

John Fryer, master of the *Bounty,* was now called.   He had not changed in the least since I had last seen him, on the morning of the mutiny.   He glanced quickly in our direction, but there was time for no more than a glance.   He was directed to stand at the end of the table, opposite Lord Hood, and was sworn.

The Court said: "Inform the Court of all the circumstances within your knowledge concerning the running away with His Majesty's ship, *Bounty.*"

I shall give Fryer's testimony with few omissions, for it provides a clear picture of what was seen by the *Bounty's* master on the day of the mutiny.

"On the 28th of April, 1789, we tacked and stood to the south'ard and westward until the island of Tofoa bore north; then we steered west-northwest.   In the first part of the evening we had little wind.   I had the first watch.   The moon was at that time in its first quarter.   Between ten and eleven o'clock, Mr. Bligh came on deck agreeable to his usual custom, to leave his orders for the night.   After he had been on deck some little time, I said, 'Sir, we have got a moon coming on which will be fortunate for us when we come on the coast of New Holland.'   Mr. Bligh replied, 'Yes, Mr. Fryer, so it will,' which was all the conversation that passed between us.   After leaving his orders, he went off the deck.

"At twelve o'clock everything was quiet on board.   I was

relieved by Mr. Peckover, the gunner.   Everything remained quiet until he was relieved, at four o'clock, by Mr. Christian. At the dawn of day I was much alarmed, whether from the noise Mr. Bligh said he made or by the people coming into my cabin, I cannot tell.   But when I attempted to jump up, John Sumner and Matthew Quintal laid their hands upon my breast and desired me to lie down, saying, 'You are a prisoner, sir.   Hold your tongue or you are a dead man, but if you remain quiet, there is no person on board that will hurt a hair of your head.'

"I then, by raising myself on the locker, which place I always slept on for coolness, saw Mr. Bligh in his shirt, with his hands tied behind him, going up the ladder, and Mr. Christian holding him by the cord.   The master-at-arms, Charles Churchill, then came to my cabin and took a brace of pistols and a hangar, saying, 'I will take care of these, Mr. Fryer.'   I asked what they were going to do with their captain.   'Damn his eyes!' Sumner said.   'Put him into the boat and let the dog see if he can live on half a pound of yams a day.'   'Into the boat!' I said.   'For God's sake, what for?'   'Sir,' Quintal said, 'hold your tongue.   Christian is captain of the ship, and recollect that Mr. Bligh has brought all this upon himself.'

"I then said, 'What boat are they going to put Captain Bligh into?'   They said, 'The large cutter.'   'Good God!' I said, 'the cutter's bottom is almost out of her, being very much eaten with worms.'   'Damn his eyes,' Sumner and Quintal said, 'it is too good for him even so!'   I said, 'I hope they are not going to set Captain Bligh adrift by himself?'   They answered, 'No.   Mr. Samuel, his clerk, and Mr. Hayward and Mr. Hallet are going with him.'

"At last I prevailed on them to call on deck to Christian to give me permission to go up, which, after some hesitation, he granted.   Mr. Bligh was standing by the mizzenmast with his hands tied behind his back, and there were several men guarding him.   I said, 'Mr. Christian, consider what you are about.' 'Hold your tongue, sir,' he replied. 'I have been in hell for weeks past. Captain Bligh has brought all this on himself.'

"Mr. Purcell, the carpenter, had been permitted to come on deck at the same time with myself, and Mr. Christian now ordered him to have the gear for the large cutter brought up. When we came to Mr. Christian, Mr. Byam was talking with him. I said, 'Mr. Byam, surely you are not concerned in this?' He appeared to be horrified at such a thought. Mr. Christian said, 'No, Mr. Fryer, Mr. Byam has no hand in this business.' I then said, 'Mr. Christian, I will stay with the ship,' thinking that, if permitted to do so, a chance might offer for retaking the vessel. Christian replied, 'No, Mr. Fryer, you will go with Captain Bligh.' He then ordered Quintal, one of the seamen under arms, to conduct me to my cabin while I collected such things as I should need.

"At the hatchway I saw James Morrison, the boatswain's mate. I said to him, 'Morrison, I hope you have no hand in this?' He replied, 'No, sir, I have not.' 'If that's the case,' I replied, in a low voice, 'be on your guard. There may be an opportunity for recovering ourselves.' His answer was, 'I'm afraid it is too late, Mr. Fryer.'

"I was then confined to my cabin, and a third sentinel was put on, John Millward, who, I thought, seemed friendly. Mr. Peckover, the gunner, and Mr. Nelson, the botanist, were confined in the cockpit, to which place I persuaded the sentinels to let me go. Mr. Nelson said, 'What is best to be done, Mr. Fryer?' I said to them, 'If we are ordered into the boat, say that you will stay on board, and I flatter myself that we shall recover the ship in a short time.' Mr. Peckover said, 'If we stay we shall all be deemed pirates.' I told them not; that I would answer for them and everyone that would join with me. At the time we were talking, Henry Hillbrandt, the cooper, was in the bread room, getting some bread to be put into the boat for Captain Bligh. I suppose he must have heard our conversation and had gone on deck to tell Mr. Christian, as I was immediately ordered up to my cabin. I heard from the sentinels that Christian had consented to give Mr. Bligh the launch, not for his own sake but for the safety of those who were going with him. I asked if they knew who was to go with Captain Bligh, and they said they believed a great many.

"Soon after this, Mr. Peckover, Mr. Nelson, and myself were ordered upon deck. Captain Bligh was then at the gangway. He said, 'Mr. Fryer, stay with the ship.' 'No, by God!' Christian replied. 'Go into the boat or I will run you through,' pointing his bayonet at my breast. I then asked Christian to permit Mr. Tinkler, my brother-in-law, to go with me. Christian said, 'No,' but after much solicitation he permitted him to go.

"I cannot say who was in the boat first, Mr. Bligh or myself; however, we were both on the gangway together. All of this time there was very bad language made use of by the people to Captain Bligh. We begged that they would give us two or three muskets into the boat, but they would not consent to it. The boat was then ordered astern. After lying astern for some time, four cutlasses were handed in, the people at the same time making use of very abusive language. I heard several of them say, 'Shoot the dog!' meaning Captain Bligh. Mr. Cole, the boatswain, said, 'We had better cast off and take our chance, for they will certainly do us a mischief if we stay much longer.' Captain Bligh very readily agreed. There was little wind. We got out the oars and rowed directly astern. Our reason for so doing was that we should sooner be out of reach of the guns.

"As soon as the boat was cast off I heard Christian give orders to loose the topgallant sails. They steered the same course as Captain Bligh had ordered, and continued to do so for the time we saw them.

"The confusion that prevailed on board was so great, and

our attention, from that time to our arrival at Timor, so much taken up by regard for the preservation of our lives, that it was not possible for me to make any note or memorandum, even if I had had the means to do so, which I had not. This account is an exact statement of the case to the best of my recollection.

"The following is the list of persons that I observed under arms: Fletcher Christian, Charles Churchill, the master-at-arms, Thomas Burkitt, one of the prisoners, Matthew Quintal, John Millward, one of the prisoners, John Sumner and Isaac Martin. Joseph Coleman, armourer, one of the prisoners, wished to come into the boat and called several times to us to recollect that he had no hand in the business. Charles Norman, one of the prisoners, and Thomas McIntosh, another of the prisoners, also wished to come with us, but were prevented by the mutineers, who had need of their services on the ship. Michael Byrne, another of the prisoners, wished, I think, to come with us as well, but feared to do so lest the boat should be lost."

Fryer here ended his testimony.

The Court asked: "You have named seven persons who were under arms. Did you believe that these were the only persons under arms?"

Fryer: No.

The Court: What was your reason for so believing?

Fryer: From hearing the people in the boat say so, but I did not see any more, to the best of my recollection.

The Court: Inform the Court of the time you remained on deck at each of the times when you went on deck.

Fryer: About ten minutes or a quarter of an hour.

The Court: When you were upon the quarter-deck, did you see any of the prisoners active in obeying any orders from Christian or Churchill?

Fryer: I saw Burkitt and Millward under arms as sentinels.

The Court: When the launch was veered astern, did you

observe any of the prisoners join in the bad language which you say passed upon that occasion?

Fryer: Not to the best of my recollection.   I saw Millward upon the taffrail with a musket in his hand.   There was so much noise and confusion that I could not hear one man from another.

The Court: You also say that when the cutlasses were handed into the boat, very bad language was used by the mutineers. Did any of the prisoners join in it upon that occasion?

Fryer: Not to my recollection.   It was a general thing among the whole.

The Court: Did you see Thomas Ellison, one of the prisoners, upon the morning of the mutiny?

Fryer: Not at first.   Later I did.

The Court: What was he doing?

Fryer: He was standing near Captain Bligh, but I cannot charge my memory as to what he was doing.

The Court: Did he have arms in his hands?

Fryer: I am not certain whether he had or no.

The Court: Did you see William Muspratt?

Fryer: No.

The Court: When Mr. Bligh and you were ordered into the boat, did any person assist, or offer to assist Mr. Christian in putting those orders into execution?

Fryer: Yes.   Churchill, Sumner, Quintal, and Burkitt.

The Court: Were you near enough, when you heard Christian order the topgallant sails to be loosed, to know any of the people who went upon the yards?

Fryer: I saw only one, who was a boy at that time — Thomas Ellison.

The Court: How many men did it require to hoist out the launch?

Fryer: It might be done with ten men.

The Court: Did you see any of the prisoners assist in hoisting her out?

Fryer: Yes. Mr. Byam, Mr. Morrison, Mr. Coleman, Norman and McIntosh all assisted; but this was done at Mr. Cole's, the boatswain's, orders, passed through him by Mr. Christian.

The Court: Did you consider these men as assisting the mutineers or as assisting Captain Bligh?

Fryer: I considered them as assisting Captain Bligh, as giving him a chance for his life.

The Court: What reason had you to imagine that John Millward was friendly toward you at the time he was placed sentinel over you?

Fryer: He appeared to be very uneasy in his mind, as though he had taken arms reluctantly.

The Court: You say that you obtained permission for Tinkler to join the boat with you. Had he been compelled to remain in the ship?

Fryer: He had been told by Churchill that he was to stay aboard to be his servant, and came to tell me in my cabin.

The Court: In what part of the ship were the youngsters berthed?

Fryer: On the lower deck, on either side of the main hatchway.

The Court: Did you observe whether there was a sentinel over the main hatchway?

Fryer: Yes. I omitted to mention that Thompson was stationed there by the arms chest, with a musket and a bayonet fixed.

The Court: Did you consider him to have been a sentinel over the midshipmen's berth?

Fryer: Yes; over the berth and the arms chest at the same time.

The Court: Do you know that, on that day, any effort was made by any person in the ship to recover her?

Fryer: No.

The Court: What time elapsed from the first alarm to the time of your being forced into the boat?

Fryer: About two hours and a half, or three hours, to the best of my recollection.

The Court: What did you suppose to be Mr. Christian's meaning when he said that he had been in hell for weeks past?

Fryer: I suppose he meant on account of the abuse he had received from Captain Bligh.

The Court: Had there been any very recent quarrel?

Fryer: The day before the mutiny, Mr. Bligh charged Christian with stealing his coconuts.

The prisoners were now permitted to question the witness, and I was ordered to speak first. Fryer must have felt the strangeness of our situation as much as did I, myself. He had been more than kind to me during our long association on the *Bounty*, and to meet for the first time since the mutiny under those circumstances, when our conversation could be only of the most formal kind, was a strain upon the self-control of both of us. I was certain that he considered me as innocent as himself, and that he felt nothing but good will toward me. I asked three questions.

Myself: When you came upon deck the first time, and found me in conversation with Mr. Christian, did you overhear anything that was said?

Fryer: No, Mr. Byam. There was . . .

Lord Hood interrupted.

"You must reply to the prisoner's questions by addressing the Court," he said. The master therefore turned to the President.

Fryer: I cannot recollect that I overheard any of the conversation.

Myself: Had you any reason to believe that I was a member of Mr. Christian's party?

Fryer: None whatever.

Myself: If you had been permitted to remain in the ship, and had you endeavoured to form a party to retake the vessel, would I have been among those to whom you would have opened your mind?

Fryer: He would have been among the very first to whom I would have spoken of the matter.

The Court: You say that you had no reason to believe Mr. Byam a member of Christian's party.   Did you not consider the fact that when you came upon deck he was in conversation with Mr. Christian a suspicious circumstance?

Fryer: I did not; for Mr. Christian spoke to many of those, during the mutiny, who were not members of his party.

The Court: During your watch, on the night before the mutiny, did you observe Mr. Christian and the prisoner, Byam, together on deck?

Fryer: No.   To the best of my recollection, Mr. Byam was on deck during the whole of my watch, and Mr. Christian did not appear at all.

The Court: Did you speak to Mr. Byam at this time?

Fryer: Yes, upon several occasions.

The Court: Did he appear to be disturbed, or nervous, or anxious in mind?

Fryer: Not in the least.

I felt deeply grateful to Fryer, not only for the matter of his testimony concerning myself, but even more for the manner of it.   It must have been plain to all the Court that he considered me innocent.

Morrison asked: "Did you observe any part of my conduct, particularly on that day, which would lead you to believe that I was one of the mutineers?"

Fryer: I did not.

The other prisoners questioned him in turn, and poor Burkitt only made his case appear even worse than it had before, for Fryer was obliged to repeat and enlarge upon the details of Burkitt's activity as one of the mutineers.

The master then withdrew and Mr. Cole, the boatswain, was called to the stand.   His testimony necessarily covered

much the same ground; but while this was true in the case of
each of the witnesses, there were important points of difference
in their evidence. Each man had witnessed events from different parts of the ship, and their interpretation of what they
saw, as well as their recollection of it after so long an interval
of time, varied considerably.

I learned from Cole's evidence that he had seen Stewart and
me dressing in the berth on the early morning of the mutiny,
with Churchill standing guard over us. His testimony was of
melancholy importance to Ellison, and the more damaging because of the evident reluctance with which he gave it. Cole
had a great liking for Ellison, as had most of the ship's company. Nevertheless, being a man of strict honesty and a high
sense of duty, he was obliged to say that he had seen Ellison
acting as one of the guards over Bligh. He passed lightly and
quickly over the mention of his name, hoping that the Court
might not notice it. His evident struggle between the desire
to spare all of the prisoners as much as possible, and the necessity for telling the truth, was apparent to all, and won him the
sympathy of the Court but no mercy. When he had finished
he was at once probed for further information concerning
Ellison.

The Court: You say that when you were allowed upon deck,
you saw the prisoner, Ellison, among the other armed men.
How was he armed?

Cole: With a bayonet.

The Court: Was he one of the guards over Captain Bligh?

Cole: Yes.

The Court: Did you hear the prisoner, Ellison, make any
remarks?

Cole: Yes.

The Court: What were they?

Cole: I heard him call Captain Bligh an old villain.

I then asked: "When you saw Stewart and me dressing in the
berth, with Churchill standing over us with a pistol, did you

hear any of the conversation that passed between us and Churchill and Thompson?"

Cole: No, I heard nothing of the conversation. There was too much noise and confusion.

Ellison: You say that I was armed with a bayonet, Mr. Cole. Did you see me use it in any way?

Cole: By no means, lad. You . . .

"Address your replies to the Court."

Cole: He never once offered to use his bayonet. He merely flourished it in Captain Bligh's face.

At this reply I saw the hint of a grim smile on the faces of some of the members of the Court. Cole added, earnestly: "There was no real harm in this lad. He was only a boy at that time, and full of mischief and high spirits."

The Court: Do you think this in any way excuses him for taking part in a mutiny?

Cole: No, sir, but . . .

"That will do, Boatswain," Lord Hood interrupted. "Are there any further questions from the prisoners?"

Morrison: Do you recollect, when I came on deck after you had called me out of my hammock, that I came to you abaft the windlass and said, 'Mr. Cole, what is to be done?' and that your answer was, 'By God, James, I do not know, but go and help them with the cutter'?

Cole: Yes, I do remember it.

Morrison: Do you remember that, in consequence of your order, I went about clearing the cutter? And afterward the launch, when Mr. Christian ordered that boat to be hoisted out instead of the cutter?

Cole: Yes.

Morrison: Do you remember that I brought a towline and grapnel out of the main hold and put them into the launch? And do you remember calling me to assist you to hoist a cask of water out of the hold, and at the same time threatening John Norton, the quartermaster, that he should not go in the boat if he was not more attentive in getting things into her?

Cole: I have every reason to believe that he was employed in this business under my direction. I remember telling Norton that, for he was frightened out of his wits.

Morrison: Do you recollect that I assisted you when you were getting your own things, which were tied up in part of your bedding, into the boat?

Cole: I had forgotten this, but it is strictly true. I had no reason at any time to suppose that he was concerned in the mutiny.

Morrison: After I had helped you put your things into the boat, did I not then run below to get my own, hoping to be allowed to go with Captain Bligh?

Cole: I know that he went below, and I make no doubt that it was for the purpose of getting his clothes to come with us.

The Court: Did the prisoner, Morrison, seem eager to go into the boat?

Cole: None of us was eager, for we never expected to see England again. But he was willing to go, and I make no doubt he would have gone had there been room.

Burkitt then asked: "When you came aft to get the compass out of the binnacle, did not Matthew Quintal come and say he would be damned if you should have it? And you then said, 'Quintal, it is very hard you'll not let us have a compass when there's plenty more in the storeroom'? Then did you not look hard at me, and did I not say, 'Quintal, let Mr. Cole have it, and anything else that will be of service to him'?"

Cole: I know that Quintal objected to letting the compass go, though I do not remember that Burkitt said anything, but he was standing near by. The confusion was so great that it was impossible I could take notice of everything particularly.

Burkitt: During the time that you say I was under arms, do you recollect hearing me give any orders, or making use of bad language?

Cole: I only observed that he was under arms.

Millward: Can you say whether I took a musket willingly, or only because of Churchill's orders?

Cole: I do not know whether it was by Churchill's order or not. He took the musket.

The Court: Were all the people who were put into the boat bound, or were they at liberty in going into her?

Cole: They were not bound, but they marched them who were below on deck with sentinels at different times.

The Court: Were there no other arms in the ship but those in the arms chest in the main hatchway?

Cole: Not to my knowledge.

The Court: At what time did day break on that morning?

Cole: I suppose about a quarter before five, or half-past four.

The Court put many other questions to the boatswain beside those given here. He was examined closely, as Fryer had been, concerning the men in Christian's watch, those he saw under arms, my own relationship with Christian, and the like. His evidence made it plain that, although Morrison, Coleman, Norman, McIntosh, and myself all assisted in hoisting out the launch, this was done at the boatswain's orders, and could not be construed as evidence that we were of the mutineers' party.

At the conclusion of Cole's testimony, the Court adjourned for the day, and we were again conveyed to the gun room of the *Hector*. Mr. Graham came, bringing a brief note from Sir Joseph, which read: "Now you know the worst, Byam. Keep up a good heart. Both Fryer and Cole have struck excellent blows for you to-day. It is evident that their opinion of your character made an impression upon the Court."

Mr. Graham talked with me for half an hour, going over the evidence in detail, instructing me further as to the questions I should ask of the witnesses yet to be heard. He refused to give an opinion as to what he thought of my chances. "If you can, keep your mind from dwelling upon the outcome," he said. "It is not my part either to hearten or discourage you unduly, but I think it well that you have no illusions about your situation. It is grave but not hopeless. Meanwhile, be assured that I shall do everything in my power to help you."

"May I ask one more question, Mr. Graham?" I said.

"Certainly. As many as you like."

"In your heart, do you believe me innocent or guilty?"

"I can answer that without a moment's hesitation. I believe you innocent."

This heartened me greatly, and gave me reason to hope that some, at least, of the members of the Court might feel as he did.

There was little conversation in the gun room that evening. As long as daylight served, Morrison sat by a port, with his Bible on his knee, reading aloud to Muspratt, who had requested this. Ellison turned into his hammock early and was asleep within five minutes. Four men among us had little to fear. The events of the first day's hearing made it increasingly plain that Coleman, Norman, McIntosh, and Byrne were all but certain of acquittal. Burkitt and Millward paced up and down the room in their bare feet. The soft padding of Burkitt's feet was the last sound I heard before I went to sleep.

XXII

THE CASE FOR THE CROWN

At nine o'clock the following morning the hearing was resumed. As we were marched into the great cabin I noticed that it was even more closely packed with spectators than it had been the previous day. The same solemnity marked the proceedings, and Court and spectators alike attended the examination of the witnesses with the same air of absorbed interest.

William Peckover, gunner of the *Bounty*, was called in and sworn. The remarkable thing about his testimony was that he claimed to have seen but four men under arms during the whole of the mutiny — Christian, Burkitt, Sumner, and Quintal. I do not believe that he deliberately falsified his testimony. I think he must have reasoned in this way: "The mutiny took place so long ago, how can I be certain as to whom I saw under arms? I have a clear recollection of only four. The other lads shall have the benefit of the doubt. God knows they need it!" Immediately he had finished, he was questioned on this point.

The Court: How many people did the *Bounty's* company consist of?

Peckover: Forty-three, I believe, at this time.

The Court: State again how many of those you saw under arms.

Peckover: Four.

The Court: Was it your opinion that four people took the ship from nine and thirty?

Peckover: Not by any means.

The Court: Give your reasons for thinking so.

Peckover: There certainly must have been more concerned or they would not have taken the ship from us. But these are all I can say, positively, that I saw under arms.

The Court: What were your particular reasons for submitting when you saw but four men under arms?

Peckover: I came naked upon the deck, with only my trousers on, and there I saw Burkitt with a musket and a bayonet, and Mr. Christian alongside of Captain Bligh, and a sentry at the gangway, but who he was I do not remember.

The Court: Did you expostulate with Mr. Christian on his conduct?

Peckover: I did not.

The Court: Did you see Mr. Byam that morning?

Peckover: Yes. I saw him standing by the booms talking with Mr. Nelson, the botanist. Then he went below, and I did not again see him until the launch had been ordered astern.

The Court: Where was he then?

Peckover: I saw him for a moment at the taffrail.

The Court: What are your reasons for believing that Coleman, Norman, McIntosh, and Byrne were averse to the mutiny?

Peckover: When they were looking down upon us from the stern they appeared to wish to come into the boat, what slight view I had of them. I was busy stowing things in the boat, so that I remember only Coleman calling to me.

The Court: You have said that, in talking with Mr. Purcell, he said to you that he knew whose fault the business was, or words to that effect. Do you apprehend that Mr. Purcell alluded to any of the prisoners?

Peckover: No. I think he alluded to Captain Bligh, owing to the abuse so many of the ship's company had received from him.

The Court: What was the nature of this abuse?

Peckover: Many severe punishments for slight offenses, and foul and abusive language to all hands. Try as they would, neither officers nor men could ever do anything to please him.

Morrison then questioned the gunner, and brought out even more clearly, not only that he had never been under arms, but also that he had done everything in his power to supply the launch with provision and much-needed articles so that the men in her might have a better chance for their lives. Morrison conducted his case remarkably well. Unfortunately, the questions I put were to little purpose. Peckover had been officer of the middle watch on the night before the mutiny. He had seen Christian and me upon deck at that time, but had heard nothing of our conversation; nor had he heard any of the conversation that passed between Nelson and me the following morning.

Purcell, the carpenter, next took the stand. He was the same burly, heavy-jowled man whom I had heard say to Nelson on the morning of the mutiny: "Stop aboard? With rogues and pirates? Never, sir! I shall follow my commander." I had great respect for the old fellow. No one could have hated Bligh more, but there was never any hesitation in Purcell's decisions when it came to a matter of duty. His evidence was of great importance to me, but whether it helped or prejudiced my case it was difficult to say. Purcell gave the names of seventeen men whom, he stated with conviction, he had seen armed; among them, Ellison, Burkitt, and Millward. Muspratt he omitted to name.

The Court asked: "In the former part of your evidence you say that you asked Mr. Byam to intercede with Christian for the launch instead of the cutter. Why did you speak of this matter to Byam? Did you consider him one of the mutineers?"

Purcell: By no means. But I knew him to be a friend of Mr. Christian. I also knew that Christian had no liking for me and would have listened to no request I might have made

The Court: Do you believe that it was owing to the prisoner Byam's intercession that Christian permitted the launch to be hoisted out instead of the cutter?

Purcell: Yes; and had we not been given the launch none of us would ever have seen England again.

The Court: What had been the relations between Christian and Byam throughout the voyage of the *Bounty* to Tahiti and during the sojourn there?

Purcell: Most friendly.

The Court: Name any others whom you believe to have been particularly friendly with Mr. Christian.

Purcell: Mr. Stewart was one.   I can think of no others that I could say were intimate with him.   Mr. Christian was not an easy man to know.

The Court: Do you think it likely that Mr. Christian would not have divulged his plans for the mutiny to Mr. Byam, his most intimate friend?

Purcell was taken aback by this question, put to him by Captain Hammond, who sat on Lord Hood's right.   He lowered his head like an old bull at bay.

Purcell: Yes, I do think it likely.   Mr. Christian was not a man to involve his friends in trouble, and he must have known that Mr. Byam would remain loyal to his commander.

The Court: Where was Byam just before the launch was veered astern?

Purcell: I do not know.   I had seen him upon deck a few moments before, and he had told me of his intention to go with Captain Bligh.   I think he must have gone to the midshipmen's berth for his clothes.

The Court: Did you see Morrison at this time?

Purcell: No.

The Court: Do you think it possible that the prisoners, Byam and Morrison, may have feared to go into the boat and that they went below to avoid the necessity of leaving the ship?

Purcell: No, I do not.   They must have been prevented

from coming. They were not cowards as both Mr. Hayward and Mr. Hallett were . . .

Lord Hood interrupted, sternly admonishing the carpenter to reply only to the questions asked of him.

The Court: Putting every circumstance together, declare to this Court, upon the oath you have taken, how you considered Mr. Byam's behaviour, whether as a person joined in the mutiny or as a person wishing well to Captain Bligh.

Purcell: I by no means considered him as a person concerned in the mutiny.

The Court: Did you consider Morrison as a mutineer?

Purcell: I did not.

A pause followed. Lord Hood said: "The prisoners may now question the witness."

Myself: How deep in the water was the launch when the last of the people went into her?

Purcell: We had seven and one-half inches of freeboard, amidships.

Myself: Do you think others might have come into her without endangering the safety of all?

Purcell: Not one more could have entered her. Captain Bligh himself begged that no more should be sent off. When we lost Norton, the quartermaster, who was killed by the savages at Tofoa, for all our regret at the poor fellow's death we were glad to have the boat lightened of his weight. It gave the rest of us so much more chance of life.

The following morning, Friday, September 14, Thomas Hayward gave his evidence. We had awaited this most eagerly. Hayward was the mate of Christian's watch and on deck at the time the mutiny started. I, in particular, was curious to know whether his story would corroborate the account given me by Christian on the day he had called me into his cabin. Hayward made no mention whatever of having been asleep on watch at the time the ship was seized. He said that he was standing aft at that moment, looking over the side at a shark,

and that Christian had told him to oversee the vessel while he
went below to lash his hammock.

"A moment later," he went on, "to my unutterable surprise, I saw Christian, Charles Churchill, Thomas Burkitt, one
of the prisoners, John Sumner, Matthew Quintal, William
McCoy, Isaac Martin, Henry Hillbrandt, and Alexander Smith
coming aft, armed with muskets and bayonets.   On my going
forward to prevent their proceedings, I asked Christian the
cause for such an act, and he told me to hold my tongue, instantly.   Martin was left as a sentinel on deck, and the rest of
the party proceeded to Mr. Bligh's cabin.

"I heard the cry of 'Murder!' from Mr. Bligh, and heard
Christian call for a rope.   John Mills, contrary to all orders,
cut the deep-sea line and carried a piece of it to them.   Thomas
Ellison, who was at the helm, quitted it and armed himself
with a bayonet.   The ship's decks now began to be thronged
with men.   I saw George Stewart, James Morrison, one of the
prisoners, and Roger Byam, another of the prisoners, standing
by the booms.

"As soon as the launch was out, John Samuel, the captain's
clerk, John Hallet, midshipman, and myself were ordered into
her.   We requested time sufficient to collect a few clothes,
which was granted.   About this time I spoke to either Stewart
or Byam, I cannot be positive which, but I think it was Byam.
I told him to go into the boat, but in my hurry I cannot remember to have received an answer.   When I came upon deck
again I saw Ellison standing as one of the sentries over Captain
Bligh.   We were then forced into the boat.   I remember
hearing Robert Tinkler, who was not yet in the launch, call
out, 'Byam, for God's sake, hasten!'   A moment later Tinkler
himself came into the launch.   He was among the last to enter.
When we were towing astern of the ship, I saw the prisoners,
Byam and Morrison, standing at the taffrail among the other
mutineers.   They seemed well content to be there.   I remember hearing Burkitt use very abusive language, and I dis-

tinctly heard Millward jeering at Captain Bligh. This is all that I know of the mutiny in His Majesty's ship *Bounty*."

The Court asked: "You say that Burkitt used very abusive language while the launch lay astern. To whom did it seem to be addressed?"

Hayward: To the boat's people generally, I should say.

The Court: Can you recall what Millward said when he jeered at Captain Bligh?

Hayward: Yes, precisely. He said, "You bloody villain! See if you can live on half a pound of yams a day."

The Court: What number of armed men did you perceive on the *Bounty* on the morning of the mutiny?

Hayward: Eighteen.

The Court: Did you hear any of the conversation that passed between Christian and Byam with respect to having the launch in the place of the cutter?

Hayward: No.

The Court: Were you on deck during the middle watch on the night before the mutiny?

Hayward: No.

The Court: Do you know at what time the prisoner, Byam, came down to the berth on that night?

Hayward: Yes. I chanced to be awake at that time and I heard the ship's bell strike half-past one.

The Court: How do you know that it was Byam who came in?

Hayward: His hammock was next to mine on the larboard side of the berth.

The Court: Relate everything you remember with respect to Morrison.

Hayward: I remember seeing Morrison assisting to clear the yams and other supplies out of the launch before she was hoisted out, but I am doubtful whether he was at first under arms or not.

The Court: Do you mean by this that he was later under arms?

Hayward: I believe that he was, but I cannot say positively.

The Court: Did he appear to you, by his conduct, to be assisting the mutineers, or was he merely obeying the orders that were given to get the boat out?

Hayward: If I were to give it as my opinion, I should say that he was assisting the mutineers. He perhaps might wish to get the boat out to get quit of us as soon as possible.

The Court: Relate all you know of Ellison.

Hayward: Ellison was at the helm at the outbreak of the mutiny. Soon after the people had gone below to secure Captain Bligh, he quitted the helm and armed himself with a bayonet. Before going into the boat I saw him as a sentinel over Captain Bligh, and I remember him saying, "Damn him, I will be sentinel over him!"

The Court: Relate all you remember of Muspratt.

Hayward: I remember seeing Muspratt on the larboard side of the waist with a musket in his hand.

The Court: Relate all you remember of Burkitt.

Hayward: I saw Thomas Burkitt come aft, following Christian and Churchill when they went to Captain Bligh's cabin, and I saw him descend the after ladder with them. He was armed with a musket and a bayonet. After the launch was astern I saw him at the taffrail, and heard him using very abusive language to us in the boat.

The Court: Relate what you remember of Millward.

Hayward: I saw him armed as one of the sentinels, and after the boat was veered astern, I saw him at the taffrail, where he jeered at Captain Bligh, as I have said.

The Court: Have you any reason to believe that the prisoner, Byam, would have been prevented from going in the boat at the time you did, had he desired to do so?

Hayward: No.

The Court: Where was he at the time the launch was veered aft?

Hayward: I cannot say, but a moment later I saw him at the taffrail, looking down at us with the other mutineers.

The Court: Did you hear him make any remarks at that time?

Hayward: I am doubtful whether I did or not.

The Court: You have given it as your opinion that Morrison was assisting the mutineers so as to get Captain Bligh and his party out of the ship as soon as possible. In the former part of your evidence you have said that the prisoner, McIntosh, was also assisting to hoist the launch out, and that you did not look upon him as a mutineer. What is the reason for your thinking differently of them?

Hayward: The difference was in the countenances of the two. The countenance of Morrison seemed to be rejoiced and that of McIntosh depressed.

Morrison then asked: "You say that you observed joy in my countenance, and you have given it as your opinion that I was one of the mutineers. Can you declare, before God and this Court, that such evidence is not the result of a private pique?

Hayward: No, it is not the result of a private pique. It is an opinion I formed after quitting the ship, from the prisoners not coming with us when they had as good an opportunity as the rest, there being more boats than one.

Morrison: One of the boats, as you know, was badly eaten with worms. Are you certain that we might have had the other?

Hayward: Not having been present at any conference among you, I cannot say.

Morrison: Can you deny that you were present when Captain Bligh begged that the boat might not be overloaded; and can you deny that he said, "I'll do you justice, lads"?

Hayward: I was present at the time Mr. Bligh made such a declaration, but understood it as respecting the clothes and other heavy articles with which the boat was already too full.

Ellison now put a question which brought into this grimly serious trial the only touch of humour that attended it.

Ellison: You know that Captain Bligh used these words: "Don't let the boat be overloaded, lads. I'll do you justice." And you say you think this alluded to the clothes and other heavy articles in the launch. Do you honestly think that the words, "I'll do you justice," alluded to the clothes? Or did they allude to Coleman, McIntosh, Norman, Byrne, Mr. Stewart, Mr. Byam, and Mr. Morrison, who would have gone in the launch if there had been room?

Ellison scored a point here, for us, not for himself. Even the members of the Court maintained with difficulty their expressions of dignified severity.

Hayward: If Captain Bligh made use of the words, "My lads," it was to the people already in the boat and not to those in the ship.

The Court: Your opinion, then, is that Captain Bligh was not alluding to any of the people remaining in the ship?

Hayward, realizing that the Court itself considered his opinion preposterous, then acknowledged that Bligh might have been referring to those in the ship.

The malicious manner in which he had testified astonished me. This was particularly true in his evidence concerning Morrison and me. He must have known, in his heart, that we were as innocent as himself; yet he lost no opportunity to throw what doubt he could upon the purity of our intentions. Morrison he had never liked, and this ill-will was heartily returned; but my relations with Hayward on the *Bounty*, although never cordial, had not been unfriendly. I had the clearest recollection of the events of the mutiny. Hayward had never once spoken to me on that morning, and Stewart had told me that he had only seen Hayward at a distance. And yet Hayward had testified that he had told one or the other

of us to go into the boat.   The true facts were that he was so
terrified throughout the whole of this time as to be ignorant
of what he did, or said.   It was my opinion at the time of the
court-martial, and it is so still, that he arranged his recollections of what had taken place so as to put his own actions
in the most favourable possible light.   He was a man easily
dominated by others of stronger character, and I believe that
his long association with Captain Edwards, of the *Pandora,* who
considered all of us piratical scoundrels, had completely col-
oured Hayward's own opinions.

John Hallet was called next.   He was now in his twentieth
year, and I scarcely recognized the thin, frightened-looking
boy I had known on the *Bounty* in the grown man who stood
before us.   He was dressed in a handsome lieutenant's uniform
—a long-tailed coat of bright blue, with white cuffs and
lapels and gold anchor buttons.   He wore white silk breeches
and stockings, and his black pumps shone like mirrors.   As
he entered the great cabin he removed his cocked hat and placed
it under his arm, halting to make a sweeping bow to the
President as he did so.   Upon taking the stand he glanced at
us with an air that said only too plainly: "You see how I have
risen in the world?   And what are you?   Pirates and mutineers!"

His story was the briefest of any of those yet given, but it
was of grave importance to Morrison and myself.   He stated
with conviction that when the launch was about to leave the
Bounty, he had seen Morrison at the taffrail, armed with a
musket.   He also named Burkitt, Ellison, and Millward as
having been armed.   His evidence with respect to myself came
when he was being questioned by various members of the
Court.

The Court: Did you see Roger Byam on the morning of the
mutiny?

Hallet: I remember to have seen him once.

The Court: What was he doing at that time?

Hallet: He was on the platform on the larboard side, upon deck, standing still and looking attentively toward Captain Bligh.

The Court: Was he armed?

Hallet: I cannot say that he was.

The Court: Had you any conversation with him?

Hallet: No.

The Court: Do you know whether he was or was not prevented from coming into the boat?

Hallet: I do not know that he ever offered to go into the boat.

The Court: Did you hear any person propose to him to go into the boat?

Hallet: No.

The Court: Do you know any other particulars respecting him on that day?

Hallet: While he was standing as I have before related, Captain Bligh said something to him, but what, I did not hear; upon which Byam laughed, and turned and walked away.

The Court: Relate all you know of the conduct of James Morrison on that day.

Hallet: When I first saw him he was unarmed; but he shortly afterward appeared under arms.

The Court: How was he armed?

Hallet: With a musket.

The Court: At what part of the ship was he when you saw him so armed?

Hallet: It was when the boat was veered astern. He was leaning over the taffrail, calling out in a jeering manner, "If my friends inquire for me, tell them I am somewhere in the South Sea."

The Court: Relate all you know respecting Thomas Ellison.

Hallet: He appeared early under arms, and came up to me and insolently said, "Mr. Hallet, you need not mind this. We are only going to put the Captain on shore, and then you and the others may return."

The Court: Describe to the Court the situation of Captain Bligh when the prisoner, Byam, laughed and walked away, as you have described.

Hallet: He was standing with his arms bound, Christian holding the cord in one hand, and a bayonet to his breast with the other.

Upon the advice of Mr. Graham, I refrained from questioning Hallet at this time.

"This is the gravest accusation that has been made against you," he whispered, "excepting only Bligh's. Do not examine Hallet upon it now. It will be best to wait until the Court hears your defense. At that time you will have the opportunity to recall any of the witnesses you choose."

Morrison asked: "You say that you saw me armed at the taffrail. Can you declare, positively, before God and this Court, that it was I and no other person whom you saw under arms?"

Hallet: I have declared it.

Morrison: You have sworn that I did jeeringly say, "Tell my friends, if they inquire for me, that I am somewhere in the South Sea." To whom did I address this sneering message?

Hallet: I did not remark that it was addressed to anyone in particular.

Morrison: Do you remember that I did, personally, assist you to haul one of your chests up the main hatchway, and whether or not I was armed then?

Hallet: The circumstances concerning the chest I do not remember. I have before said that I did not see you under arms till after the launch had been veered astern.

The witness withdrew, and John Smith, who had been Captain Bligh's servant, was called. He was the last witness, and the only one of the *Bounty's* seamen who gave evidence. In fact, there were only three of the able seamen of the *Bounty's* company, John Smith, Thomas Hall, and Robert Lamb, who had not been of Christian's party; and of these both Lamb and Hall were dead. Smith's evidence was not of importance to any of us who were before the Court. He testified that, at Christian's orders, he had served out rum to all those under arms; also that he had gone to Captain Bligh's cabin to fetch up his clothes and other articles which were put into the launch.

This concluded the evidence given by members of the *Bounty's* company who went into the launch. Captain Edwards and the lieutenants of the *Pandora* were then called in turn, to testify as to the *Pandora's* sojourn at Tahiti when the fourteen prisoners were taken. At the sight of Edwards and Parkin, I was conscious of the same feeling of hot anger experienced how many times during the dreary months when we were in their power. Nevertheless, I must do them the justice to say that their evidence as to the proceedings at Tahiti was scrupulously exact. Edwards told how I had come off to the ship when she was still several miles out at sea, explaining who I was and giving him exact information with respect to the other *Bounty* men then on the island. He also acknowledged that the other men had given themselves up voluntarily. We should have liked to question him with respect to the inhuman treatment we had received at his hands, but this did not concern the mutiny, so we said nothing.

These were the last of the Crown witnesses, and the Court adjourned until the following day, when we were to be heard in our own defense.

XXIII

THE DEFENSE

BEING the only midshipman among the prisoners, I should, as a matter of course, have been the first to be called for my defense; but when the Court met on the Saturday morning, I requested, and was granted, permission to defer presenting my case until Monday morning. Coleman, whose acquittal was a foregone conclusion, was ready to be heard, and was therefore called. His statement was brief, and, having given it, he questioned Fryer, Cole, Peckover, Purcell, and others, all of whom testified as to Coleman's innocence, and that he had been detained in the *Bounty* against his will. The Court then adjourned.

Nearly the whole of Sunday I spent with my advisor, Mr. Graham. Captain Manly and Captain Bentham, advisors to the other prisoners, came with him, and the three groups separated to various parts of the gun room so as not to disturb one another.

I had already prepared, in writing, a rough copy of my defense. Mr. Graham went over this with great care, pointing out various omissions and making suggestions as to the arrangement of the matter. He instructed me as to the witnesses I should call and examine, after my defense had been read, and the questions I should ask each one. Hayward had testified that he had been awake on the night before the mutiny and had heard me come down to the berth at half-past one.

"This evidence is of importance to you, Mr. Byam," Mr.

Graham said. "You have told me that Tinkler went down with you at that time and that you bade each other goodnight?"

"Yes, sir."

"Then Hayward must have heard you speak. We must see to it that he acknowledges this. If we can prove that Tinkler was with you it will bear out your account of the conversation with Christian, which Tinkler overheard. Hallet struck you a heavy blow in saying that you turned away laughing after Captain Bligh had spoken to you."

"There was not a word of truth in the statement, sir," I said, hotly.

"I am sure there was not. In my opinion neither Hayward nor Hallet made a favourable impression upon the Court. But their evidence cannot be disregarded. Together, it is enough to condemn Morrison; his situation now is much more grave than it was. Did you have an opportunity to observe the actions of Hayward and Hallet on the morning of the mutiny?"

"Yes, I saw them a number of times."

"What can you say of them? Were they cool and self-possessed?"

"On the contrary, they were both frightened out of their wits the whole time, and both were crying and begging for mercy when they were ordered into the launch."

"It is extremely important that you should bring this out. When you question the other *Bounty* witnesses, you must examine each of them upon this point. If they agree with you, that Hallet and Hayward were much alarmed, it will throw doubt upon the reliability of their testimony."

It was late in the afternoon when Mr. Graham rose to go.

"I think we have covered everything, Mr. Byam," he said. "Do you wish to read your defense, or would you prefer that I read it for you?"

"What do you think I should do, sir?"

"I advise you to read it, unless you think you may be too nervous."

I told him that I had no apprehensions on that score.

"Good!" he replied. "Your story will make a deeper impression if given in your own voice. Read it clearly and slowly. You must have noticed that several members of the Court seem to be all but convinced of your guilt? It is apparent in the questions they have asked the witnesses."

"I have noticed it, sir."

"I suggest that, as you read, you keep these particular men in mind. If you do this the manner of your reading will take care of itself. It is unnecessary to remind you that you are fighting for your life. This is certain to make your words sufficiently impressive."

By this time the advisors to the other prisoners had completed their work, and they left the *Hector* with Mr. Graham. No day, in all the interminable months we had passed as prisoners, had slipped by so quickly as this one.

On Monday morning, September 17, the solitary gun boomed from the *Duke*, the signal for assembling the court-martial. We were conveyed on board with the usual guard of marines, and arrived a good half-hour before the opening of the Court. Although I had told Mr. Graham that he need have no fears about my coolness, I felt anything but self-possessed as the minutes slowly passed. As we were marched across the quarter-deck, I caught a glimpse of Sir Joseph and Dr. Hamilton among the crowd of officers and civilians waiting there. I dreaded that daily ordeal of mounting the gangway of the *Duke*, and the march, two by two, along the deck to the great cabin. We were objects of curiosity to everyone, and many of the officers stared at us as though we were wild animals. At least, so it seemed to me, but no doubt I was unusually sensitive at that time, and imagined insolence and hostility on faces which revealed nothing more than natural curiosity.

A few minutes before nine the spectators were all in their places, and on the stroke of the hour the members of the Court filed in. All in the room rose and remained standing until Lord Hood and the other officers had taken their places.

A moment of silence followed; then the master-at-arms called: "Roger Byam, stand forth!"

I rose and waited, facing Lord Hood.

"You have been accused, with others, of the mutinous and piratical seizure of His Majesty's armed vessel, *Bounty*. You have heard the Crown's witnesses. The Court is now ready to receive whatever you may have to say in your own defense. Are you prepared?"

"Yes, sir."

"Raise your right hand."

I was then sworn, and I remember how my hand trembled as I held it up. I looked toward Sir Joseph for comfort, but he sat with his hands clasped around his knee, gazing straight before him. The Court waited for me to proceed. For a moment, panic seized me. The eyes of everyone in the room were turned toward me, and their faces became a blur before my own. Then, as though it were someone else, a long distance away, I heard my own voice speaking: —

"My lord, and gentlemen of this Honourable Court: The crime of mutiny, for which I am now arraigned, is one of so grave a nature as to awake the horror and indignation of all men, and he who stands accused of it must appear an object of unpardonable guilt.

"In such a character it is my misfortune to appear before this Tribunal. I realize that appearances are against me, but they are appearances only, and I declare before God and the members of this Court that I am innocent; that I have never been guilty, either in thought or in deed, of the crime with which I am charged."

Once I was fairly started, I regained my self-control, and, bearing in mind Mr. Graham's advice, I read on, slowly and deliberately. I explained fully the conversation with Christian on the night before the mutiny, showing that it had nothing to do with that event. I then told the story of the ship's seizure as it concerned myself. I told of my conversation with Mr. Purcell and Mr. Nelson, both of whom knew that I meant to leave the ship. I told of going below, at the same time with Mr. Nelson, to fetch my clothes, preparatory to going into the launch, and how, in the midshipmen's berth, an opportunity seemed to present itself for seizing the arms chest from Thompson. I told how Morrison and I, with Friendly Island war clubs in our hands, waited for a chance to attack Thompson, and how that chance was thwarted; and how Morrison and I then rushed upon deck, only to find that we were too late to go with Captain Bligh.

"My lord and gentlemen," I concluded, "it is a heavy misfortune for me that the three men are dead whose evidence would prove, beyond all doubt, the truth of what I say. John Norton, the quartermaster, who knew of Christian's intention to leave the *Bounty* on the night before the mutiny, and who prepared for him the small raft upon which Christian meant to embark, is dead. Mr. Nelson died at Batavia; and Robert Tinkler, who overheard all of my conversation with Christian, has been lost at sea with the vessel upon which he was serving. Fortune, I realize, has been against me. Lacking the evidence of these three men, I can only say, I entreat you to believe me! My good name is as precious to me as life itself, and I beg of you, my lord and gentlemen, to consider the situation in which I am placed; to remember that I lack those witnesses whose evidence would, I am certain, convince you of the truth of every statement I have made.

"To the mercy of this Honourable Court I now commit myself."

It was impossible to guess how my words had impressed the Court. Lord Hood sat with his chin propped upon one hand,

listening with grave attention.   I glanced hastily at the others.
Two or three of them were making memoranda of points in my
story.   One captain, with a long cadaverous face, sat with
eyes lowered, and one might have thought him asleep.   I had
observed him before.   He had maintained the same position
throughout the hearing, and the same air of apparent inatten-
tion; but he was among the keenest of the questioners.   No
point that might throw light upon the events of the mutiny,
or the trustworthiness of the witnesses, escaped him.   He addressed his questions without lifting his eyes, as though he had
the witness pinned down to the table between his elbows.

Another of the captains whom I feared most sat on Lord
Hood's left, the farthest from him on that side, and the nearest
to the stand for the witnesses.   Hour after hour he sat as rigid
as though he were made of bronze.   Once he had taken his
seat at the table, only his eyes were permitted freedom of movement; his glances were keen and swift, like the thrust of a
rapier.   When I had finished, the eyes of this latter captain were
directed upon me for a moment, and, brief as the glance had
been, it chilled me to the heart.   I again recalled what Dr.
Hamilton had said at the time of our first conversation on
the *Pandora*: "There is not one of those captains who will not
say to himself, 'This is such a tale as one would expect an intelligent midshipman, eager to save his life, to invent.'"

It seemed to me, judging by the faces of the men before me,
that, with the exception of Captain Montague, each of them
was thinking those very words.   I felt utterly weary, physi-
cally and spiritually.   Then I saw Sir Joseph looking straight
at me in his kindly, heartening manner, as much as to say: "Well
done, my lad!   Never say die!"   His glance gave me new
reserves of strength and courage.

"My lord," I said, "may I now call what witnesses are avail-
able to me?"

Lord Hood nodded.   The master-at-arms went to the door
and called, "John Fryer!   This way!"

The *Bounty's* master took the stand, was again sworn, and awaited my questions.

Myself: What watch had I on the day of the mutiny?

Fryer: He was in my watch, the first watch of the preceding evening.

Myself: Had you stayed in the ship, in the expectation of re-taking her, was my conduct, from the time when you first knew me to this, in which you are to answer the question, such that you would have entrusted me with your design, and do you believe that I would have favoured it?   (I had been instructed by Mr. Graham to ask this question again.)

Fryer: I should not have hesitated in opening my design to him, and I am sure that he would have favoured it.

Myself: Did you consider those people who assisted in hoisting out the launch as helping Captain Bligh or the mutineers?

Fryer: Those without arms, as assisting Captain Bligh.

Myself: How many men, including Captain Bligh, went into the launch?

Fryer: Nineteen.

Myself: What height from the water was the gunwale of the launch when she put off from the ship?

Fryer: Not more than eight inches, to the best of my knowledge and remembrance.

Myself: Would the launch have carried more people?

Fryer: Not one more, in my opinion, without endangering the lives of all who were in her.

Myself: Did you, at any time during the mutiny, see me armed?

Fryer: No.

Myself: Did Captain Bligh speak to me at any time on the morning of the mutiny?

Fryer: Not to my knowledge.

Myself: Did you observe, on that morning, that I was guilty at any time of levity of conduct?

Fryer: I did not.

Myself: Did you see Mr. Hayward on deck during the time of the mutiny?

Fryer: Yes; several times.

Myself: In what state was he? Did he appear to be composed, or was he agitated and alarmed?

Fryer: He was greatly agitated and alarmed, and crying when he was forced into the boat.

Myself: Did you see Mr. Hallet on that morning?

Fryer: Yes; upon several occasions.

Myself: In what state did he appear to be?

Fryer: He was greatly frightened and crying when he went into the boat.

Myself: What was my general character on the *Bounty*?

Fryer: Excellent. To the best of my recollection he was held in high esteem by everyone.

The Court asked: "After the launch had left the ship, and during the voyage to Timor, was the subject of the mutiny often discussed among you?"

Fryer: No, not often. Our sufferings were so great, and the efforts necessary for the preservation of our lives so constant, that we had little time or inclination to speak of the mutiny.

The Court: Did you, during that voyage, or at any time thereafter, hear Captain Bligh refer to a conversation he had overheard between Christian and the prisoner, Byam, which took place in the middle watch on the night before the mutiny?

Fryer: I did not.

The Court: Did you, at any time, hear him refer to the prisoner, Byam?

Fryer: Yes; upon more than one occasion.

The Court: Can you recall what he said?

Fryer: On the day of the mutiny, after the launch had been cast off and we were rowing toward the island of Tofoa, I heard Mr. Bligh say, referring to Mr. Byam, "He is an ungrateful scoundrel, the worst of them all except Christian."

He later repeated this opinion several times, in much the same words.

The Court: Did anyone in the boat speak in Byam's defense?

Fryer: Yes, I did, as well as various others. But Captain Bligh bade us hold our tongues. He would allow nothing to be said in Mr. Byam's favour.

The Court: Did you at any time hear Robert Tinkler refer to a conversation between Christian and Byam which took place in the middle watch on the night before the mutiny?

Fryer: I cannot recall that I did.

The Court: Did Robert Tinkler ever speak in defense of Byam?

Fryer: Yes. He never believed him implicated in the mutiny. On the occasion I have mentioned, when Captain Bligh first accused Mr. Byam, Tinkler, forgetting himself, said, warmly: "He is *not* one of the mutineers, sir. I would stake my life upon it!" Captain Bligh silenced him instantly.

The Court: Robert Tinkler was your brother-in-law, was he not?

Fryer: He was.

The Court: He has been lost at sea?

Fryer: He has been reported lost with his ship, the *Carib Maid*, among or near the West Indies.

The Court: Were your relations with Captain Bligh cordial or the reverse?

Fryer: They were far from cordial.

Cole, the boatswain, was summoned next, and was followed by Mr. Purcell. I put to each of them the same questions I had asked of the master, and they replied to them as he had done. The questions asked by the members of the Court were much the same, and both men were examined particularly as to whether either Bligh or Tinkler had ever referred to my conversation with Christian, upon which the fact of my guilt or innocence so strongly depended.   Neither of them could remember having heard any reference made to this conversation. I had strongly hoped that Mr. Peckover, the gunner, and officer of the middle watch, might have overheard something of this conversation, but he could say only what further incriminated me, that he had seen Christian and me in conversation on the quarter-deck during that watch.

The Court asked: "At what time did you observe Christian and the prisoner, Byam, in conversation?"

Peckover: It might have been at about one o'clock.

The Court: Was it the prisoner's, Byam's, custom to remain on deck at night after the end of his watch?

Peckover: I cannot say that it was.

The Court: Was it Mr. Christian's habit to be much on deck at night, when not on duty?

Peckover: No, not as a general thing, but it was not unusual for him to come up at night to observe the state of the weather.

The Court: What, in your opinion, was their reason for remaining so long on the deck on this particular night?

Peckover: I suppose they wished to enjoy the coolness of the upper deck.

The Court: When Captain Bligh came on deck, during your watch, what did he do?

Peckover: He paced up and down for a few moments.

The Court: Did Christian and the prisoner, Byam, perceive him?

Peckover: I cannot say.   The moon had set before that time and it was dark upon deck.

The Court: Did Captain Bligh speak with Christian and Byam?

Peckover: I believe he did, but I did not hear what he said.

The Court: At what time did Byam go below to the berth?

Peckover: It may have been about half-past one.

The Court: Did Christian go below at that time?

Peckover: I cannot be certain. I believe he remained on deck.

The Court: Did you, at any time during your watch on that night, see John Norton, one of the quartermasters?

It was Sir George Montague, captain of the *Hector,* who put this question. I do not know why it had not occurred to me to ask it, or how Mr. Graham could have failed to suggest it to me. The reason may have been that Norton, being dead, seemed as out of the matter as Mr. Nelson himself, or any of the others who had died. Immediately Captain Montague had spoken I realized how important the question was.

Peckover: Yes; I saw Norton at about two o'clock.

The Court: Upon what occasion?

Peckover: I had heard the sound of hammering by the windlass, and myself went forward to see what the cause of it was. I found Norton at work upon something, and asked him what he was about at that hour of the night. He told me that he was repairing a hencoop for some fowls we had bought of the savages at Namuka.

The Court: Did you see at what work he was engaged?

Peckover: No, not clearly. It was quite dark, but I made no doubt that he was engaged as he said.

The Court: Did you have any further conversation with him?

Peckover: I told him to leave off; that there was time enough for making hencoops in the daytime.

The Court: Was not such work the business of the carpenters of the *Bounty*?

Peckover: Yes; but it was not uncommon for Norton to assist them when there was much carpenter's work to be done.

The Court: Had you ever known Norton to be so employed at night before?

Peckover: Never before, that I can remember.

The Court: Do you think it might have been a small raft upon which the quartermaster was working?

Peckover: Yes, it might have been.   As I have said, it was dark and I took no particular notice of what the object was.

The Court, particularly in the person of Captain Montague, questioned the gunner carefully on this matter, but Peckover could not remember that he had seen Christian and Norton in conversation during that evening.   Nevertheless, here was a ray of hope for me — a bit of evidence, and the only one, to bear out my story that Christian had intended to desert the ship during that night, and that he had taken Norton into his confidence.

Hayward followed on the witness stand, but for all my questioning he would not acknowledge that Tinkler had come down to the berth with me on the night before the mutiny. And yet he must have heard us bid each other good-night.   At that time we were standing within two paces of his hammock, and he had said that he heard me come in.   Hallet clung to his story that I had laughed and turned away when, as he said, Captain Bligh spoke to me.   But I could see that his sullen, insolent manner of clinging to it had made an unfavourable impression upon the Court.

My case rested here, and Morrison was next called for his defense.   He was cool and self-possessed.   His story was perfectly clear, well presented, and, I thought, wholly convincing. He confirmed my story as to the reason we had been below at the time the launch was veered astern.   Of the witnesses he called, Fryer, Cole, Purcell, and Peckover bore out all that he said, with the exception of his reason for not being on deck in time to go with the launch; for of this matter, of course, they could know nothing.   Hallet and Hayward were the only witnesses who had testified to having seen him under arms, and he forced both of them to admit that they might have been mistaken.

The Court adjourned for lunch.   At one o'clock it reassembled, and Norman, McIntosh, and Byrne were quickly heard. Their innocence had already been clearly established and, advisedly, they had made their pleas brief.

Burkitt, Millward, and Muspratt came next. The guilt of the first two was so evident that little could be said in extenuation of it. Both men had been willing mutineers from the beginning.

Ellison was the last to be heard. He had written his own defense, and Captain Bentham let it stand as it was, believing that the naïve boyish way in which Ellison had explained his actions would make the only appeal for clemency the poor lad could hope for. I well remember the conclusion of his plea: "I hope, honourable gentlemen, you'll be so kind as to take my case under consideration, as I was only a boy at the time, and I leave myself to the clemency and mercy of this Honourable Court."

By this time it was nearly 4 P.M. The Court adjourned, and we were taken back to the *Hector* to await its verdict.

XXIV

CONDEMNED

TUESDAY, the eighteenth of September, 1792, was a typically English autumn day, with a grey sea and a grey sky. It had rained during the early morning, but by the time the gun was fired from the *Duke*, assembling the court-martial, the downpour had changed to a light drizzle through which the many ships of war at anchor could be seen dimly. At length the sky lightened perceptibly, and the sun shone wanly through. The *Duke's* quarter-deck was thronged with people awaiting the opening of the Court. Sir Joseph and Dr. Hamilton were there. On the other side of the deck were the *Bounty* witnesses and the officers of the *Pandora*.

Throughout the court-martial no relatives or friends of the prisoners had been permitted to attend the hearings. Even had such permission been granted, now that my mother was dead, I had no relatives who might have come. This was a consolation to me. Whatever my fate, it was good to be certain that none of my kin was waiting that morning for the verdict that would either clear me or condemn me to death.

But as my glance went over the crowd my pulse quickened at seeing Mr. Erskine, my father's solicitor and the old friend of both of my parents. He was then well into his seventies. He had stopped with us at Withycombe many a time, and the great treats of my life, as a youngster, had been my rare visits to London with my father, when I had seen much of Mr. Erskine. He had often taken me to view the sights of London, and his kindnesses upon these occasions made them among the happiest of my boyhood recollections. For the first time since the beginning of the court-martial I was deeply stirred, and I could see that Mr. Erskine controlled his own emotion with difficulty. His association with my parents and Withycombe was so close that he seemed like a near and deeply loved relative.

Presently the door of the great cabin was opened and the spectators filed in to their places. The prisoners followed, and we stood waiting while the members of the Court took their seats. The master-at-arms called, "Roger Byam!"

I stood in my place.

The President asked, "Have you anything further to say in your defense?"

"No, my lord."

The same question was put to each of us. The spectators were then asked to leave the room, the prisoners were marched out, and the door of the great cabin closed behind us. We were taken into the waist, by the foremast. The spectators stood in groups about the quarterdeck, or walked up and down, talking together. We could hear nothing they said; indeed, a silence seemed to have fallen over the ship. There were seamen going about routine duties, but they performed them in a subdued, soundless manner as though they were officiating at church.

Mr. Graham had visited me on the previous evening. He had told me how I might know, the moment I entered the room to learn my fate, what that fate was to be. A midshipman's dirk would be lying on the table before the President. If the dirk were placed at right angles to me, I should know that I had been acquitted. If it lay with the point toward the foot of the table where I was to stand, I should know that I had been condemned.

I felt strangely indifferent as to which it might be. Presently I fell into a kind of stupor, a waking dream, in which blurred images passed over the surface of consciousness, stirring it but little more than the ghost of a breeze disturbs the surface of a calm sea.

It must have been at about half-past nine that the Court had been cleared.   When I roused myself from my reverie, an immeasurable period of time seemed to have elapsed; and indeed, the sun had passed the meridian.   I heard the ship's bells strike one o'clock.   The clouds had vanished, the sky was pale blue, and the sunlight had that golden quality which beautifies whatever it touches, giving a kind of splendour to familiar, common objects.   The *Duke's* great guns looked magical in that light, and the throng on the quarter-deck, in their varicoloured uniforms, with sudden gleams of light flashing from epaulettes or sword hilts, seemed like figures out of some romantic tale rather than officers of His Majesty's Navy.

The door of the great cabin reopened at last.   The master-at-arms appeared, announcing that audience was admitted; then I heard my name called.   The sound of the syllables seemed strange to me; it was as though I had never heard them before.

I was accompanied by a lieutenant with a drawn sword and a guard of four men with muskets and bayonets fixed.   I found myself standing at the end of the long table, facing the President.   The midshipman's dirk was lying on the table before him.   Its point was toward me.

The entire Court rose.   Lord Hood regarded me in silence for a moment.

"Roger Byam: having heard the evidence produced in support of the charges made against you; and having heard what you have alleged in your own defense; and having maturely and deliberately weighed the whole of the evidence, this Court is of the opinion that the charges have been proved against you.   It doth, therefore, judge that you shall suffer death by being hanged by the neck on board such of His Majesty's ships of war, and at such a time and such a place as the Commissioners for executing the office of Lord High

Admiral of Great Britain and Ireland, or any three of them for the time being, shall, in writing, under their hands, direct."

I waited, expecting to hear more, knowing at the same time that there was nothing more to be said. Then a voice — whose, I do not know — said, "The prisoner may retire." I turned about and was marched out of the great cabin, back to where the others were waiting.

I felt little emotion; only a sense of relief that the long ordeal was over. A true conception of all the horror and ignominy of this end was to come later. At the time sentence was pronounced I was merely stunned and dazed by the finality of it. Evidently the expression on my face told the others nothing, for Morrison asked, "What is it, Byam?" "I 'm to be hung," I said, and I shall never forget the look of horror on Morrison's face. He had no time to reply, for he was called next. We watched as the door of the cabin closed behind him. Coleman, Norman, McIntosh, and Byrne stood in a group, waiting their turns, and I remember how the others drew closer to me, as though for mutual protection and comfort. Ellison touched my arm and smiled, without speaking. Burkitt stood clasping and unclasping his huge hairy hands.

The door opened again and Morrison was marched back to us. His face was pale, but he had himself well under control. He turned to me with a bitter smile. "We must enjoy life while we can, Byam." A moment later he added, "I wish to God *my* mother were dead."

I felt a welcome surge of anger. Morrison had, unquestionably, been convicted upon the evidence of two men, Hayward and Hallet. They alone of the witnesses had testified to having seen him under arms. Having heard the evidence of the other witnesses, I had never for a moment doubted that Morrison's name would be cleared; nor, I think, had he himself doubted. I could find nothing to say to comfort him.

Coleman followed. When he came out of the courtroom

again, the guard stood to one side and Coleman walked, a free man, to one side of the quarter-deck. Norman, McIntosh, and Byrne were escorted in in turn, and as they came out the guard stood aside in each case, and they joined Coleman. Byrne was sobbing with joy and relief. The poor chap was almost blind, and groped his way to the others, his hands outstretched and the tears streaming down his face. Although their acquittal had been all but certain, now that they were actually at liberty their dazed manner and their bewilderment as to what to do with themselves would have touched any man's heart.

Burkitt, Ellison, Millward, and Muspratt were called in quick succession. All were found guilty and condemned to death. Immediately after sentence had been pronounced upon Muspratt, the spectators came out into the sunshine of the quarter-deck. We expected to see the members of the Court follow, but when the room had been cleared the door was closed again. Something, evidently, was to follow. The strain of waiting during the next half-hour was hardly to be borne.

Audience was again admitted, and the master-at-arms appeared at the door.

"James Morrison!"

Again Morrison was marched in. When he returned, he came as near to giving way to his emotion as I had ever seen him do. He had been recommended to His Majesty's mercy. This meant, almost certainly, that the recommendation of the Court would be followed and Morrison pardoned. A moment later Lord Hood came out, followed by the captains who had sat with him. The court-martial was at an end.

Muspratt looked at me in such a desolate manner that my heart went out to him. I put my hand on his shoulder, but there was nothing to be said. In the silence of the ship, I could hear the faint hum of conversation from the quarter-deck. I saw Sir Joseph, Mr. Erskine, and Dr. Hamilton stand-

ing together by the larboard bulwarks. They were not permitted to come to us at that time, a circumstance for which I
was deeply grateful.

Mercifully, we were not compelled to wait long on the *Duke*.
The guard was drawn up; we were escorted to the gangway
and clambered down the side into the longboat waiting to
convey us back to the *Hector*. Another boat was lying alongside. There were no marines in her — only six seamen at the
oars. Directly we had pushed off, we saw the freed men
descending the side to be taken ashore. We had no opportunity to bid them good-bye and Godspeed, and when their
boat put off from the side of the *Duke*, ours had almost reached
the *Hector*. Ellison stood and waved his hat, and they waved
back as they passed around the *Duke* and turned toward the
shore. A moment later they were cut off from view. I
never saw any man of them again.

During the whole time of our confinement on board the
Hector we had been treated with great kindness by Captain
Montague. We were, of course, carefully guarded, with
marines stationed in the gun room as well as outside the door,
but aside from that there had been little to remind us of the
fact that we were prisoners. Now that we had been condemned and were awaiting execution of sentence, Captain
Montague did all he could to make our situation endurable.
He granted me the privilege of being confined in a cabin
belonging to one of his lieutenants who was absent on leave.
After eighteen months of imprisonment, during which time
I had had not a moment of privacy, I was able to appreciate this
courtesy at its full value. Twice daily I was permitted to go
to the gun room for the purpose of exercise and to see the
others.

Sir Joseph Banks, the most considerate of men, did not come
to see me until the second day after we had been condemned,
so that when he did come, late in the afternoon, I was prepared
to meet him. I was then most eager to see him, and when I

opened the door of my cabin to find him standing there, my heart leaped with pleasure.

He gripped my hand in both of his, then turned to take a bulky parcel from the seaman who had brought him to the cabin.

"Sit down, Byam," he said. He laid the parcel on the small table and proceeded to remove the wrappings.

"I've brought you an old companion and friend. Do you recognize it?" he added, as he laid aside the last of the wrappings. It was the manuscript of my Tahitian dictionary and grammar.

"Allow me to say this," he went on. "I have gone over your manuscripts with great interest, and I know enough of the Tahitian language to appreciate the quality of the work you've done. It is excellent, Byam; precisely what is needed. This book, when it is published, will be of great value, not only practically but philosophically. Now tell me this: how much time would you require to put it into final shape, ready for the printers?"

"Do you mean that I may work on it here?"

"Would you care to do so?"

I was in need, heaven knows, of something to occupy my mind. Sir Joseph's thoughtfulness touched me deeply.

"Nothing would please me more, sir," I replied. "I am under no illusions as to the importance of this work . . ."

"But it *is* important, my dear fellow," he interrupted. "Make no mistake about that. I've brought your manuscripts not merely out of consideration for you. This task must be completed. The Royal Society is greatly interested, and it has been suggested to me that an introductory essay accompany the volume, in which the Tahitian language shall be discussed generally, and its points of difference to any of our European tongues pointed out. Such an essay is quite beyond me. I had only a superficial knowledge of the Tahitian speech, acquired during my sojourn on the island with Captain Cook.

and I have forgotten most of what I learned at that time. Only you can write this essay."

"I shall be glad to attempt it," I replied, "if there is sufficient time . . ."

"Could you complete it in a month?"

"I think so."

"Then a clear month you shall have. I have enough influence at the Admiralty to be able to promise you that."

"I shall make the most of it, sir."

"Do you prefer not to talk of the events of the . . . of the past week?" he asked, after a brief silence.

"It doesn't matter, sir. If there is something you wish to say . . ."

"Only this, Byam. It is needless to tell you what my feelings are. There has never been a more tragic miscarriage of justice in the history of His Majesty's Navy. I know how embittered you must be. You understand why you have been condemned?"

"I believe I do, sir."

"There was no alternative, Byam. None. All the palliating circumstances — the fact that no man had seen you under arms, the testimony as to the excellent character you bore, and all the rest — were not sufficient to offset Bligh's damning statement as to your complicity with Christian in planning the mutiny. That statement stood unchallenged, except by yourself, throughout the court-martial. Only your friend Tinkler could have challenged and disproved it. Lacking his evidence . . ."

"I understand, sir," I replied. "Let us say no more about it. What seems to me not only a tragic but a needless miscarriage of justice applies to poor Muspratt. There is no more loyal-hearted seaman afloat than Muspratt, and he is to be hung solely upon the evidence of one man — Hayward. Muspratt's testimony as to why he took arms is strictly true. It was for the purpose of helping Fryer in case he was able to form a party for retaking the ship. The instant he saw that the party could not be formed, he put down the musket."

"I agree with you, and you will be glad to know that there is still hope for Muspratt. Say nothing, of course, to the poor fellow about this, but I have it upon good authority that he may yet be reprieved."

That same afternoon, when I saw Muspratt in the gun room, I was tempted, for the first time in my life, to betray a matter entrusted to me in confidence. It would be impossible to say how badly I wanted to give Muspratt a glimmer of hope, the merest hint of what might happen in his case. I refrained, however.

Those September days were as beautiful as any that I remember. A transparent film of vapour hung high in the air, diffusing the light of the sun, so that the very atmosphere seemed to be composed of a golden dust transforming every object it fell upon. So it was, day after day, without change. The *Hector* was moored, bow and stern, and the view from my cabin was always the same, but I never tired of it. I had a prospect of the harbour looking toward the Channel and the Isle of Wight, with a great first-rate and three seventy-fours anchored not far distant. I saw boats passing back and forth, their oars dipped in gold, and the men in them seemed transfigured in the pale light. Knowing how brief a time remained to me, I found nothing unworthy of interest and attention. Even the common objects in my small cabin, — the locker, the table, and the inkwell before me, — seen in various lights at different hours of the day, I found beautiful and wondered that I had failed to notice such things before.

I was not wholly wretched at this time. A man who knows that he is to die, that his fate is fixed and irrevocable, seems to be endowed, as a recompense, with the faculty of benumbed acquiescence. The thing is there, slowly or swiftly approaching, but for the most part he is mercifully spared the full realization that it must and will come. There are moments, however, when he is not spared. Now and then, particularly at night, I would be gripped by a sense of horror that struck me to the heart. I would feel the rope about my throat, and see the faces of the brawny seamen who were waiting the order to hoist me to the yardarm; and I would hear the last words that would ever strike my ear: "And may God have mercy upon you." At such times I would pray silently for the courage to meet that moment when it should come.

Of the other condemned men, Ellison best endured the cruel waiting. He had lost his old gaiety of manner, but it was replaced by a quiet courage to face the facts that was beyond praise. Burkitt became more and more like a wild beast at bay. Every time that I was taken to the gun room for exercise I would find him pacing up and down, turning his head from side to side with the same expression of dazed incredulity on his face. He had the mighty chest of a Viking and his limbs would have made those of three ordinary men. He had never known an ache or a pain in his life save those inflicted by some boatswain's mate with a cat-o'-nine-tails. To men with such a power of life in them, death has no reality until it is at hand. Even now, I could see that Burkitt had not entirely given up hope. There was always the possibility of escape. He was narrowly watched by the guards; the eyes of one or another of them were upon him constantly.

Millward and Muspratt were sunk in moods of hopeless apathy, and rarely spoke to anyone. No one knew on what day the execution would be carried out. Not even the captain of the *Hector* would know until the Admiralty order had been received. Meanwhile, Morrison was kept in a state of what would have been, for me, the most harrowing anxiety. Although recommended to the King's clemency, there was always the possibility that mercy would be refused. The days passed and no pardon came, but Morrison was his usual calm self, and he discussed my work on the dictionary as though he

had no other interest in the world.   Had he been condemned
to die with the rest of us, Morrison would have awaited the
ordeal with the same fortitude.

Mr. Graham came to bid me farewell before leaving Portsmouth.   He told me, as Sir Joseph had done, that the Court
had no alternative in imposing sentence upon me; and,
although he did not say so directly, he gave me to understand
that I could not hope for a reprieve.   The following afternoon Mr. Erskine came, remaining until dusk, during which
time I settled my affairs and made my will.   My only living
relative was a cousin on my mother's side, a lad of fifteen who
lived in India with his father.   It was strange to think that
our old home at Withycombe and the rest of our family
fortune would go to this boy whom I had never seen.

I shall not venture to say how I would have passed those
days without work to engross my thoughts.   Once again my
dictionary proved to be the greatest of blessings, and it was not
long before I was able to give it the whole of my attention.
Every one of those manuscript pages was fragrant with Tahiti
and memories of Tehani and our little Helen.   Some of them
the baby had torn or finger-marked, and I could plainly hear
her mother's voice as she took them quickly from her, scolding
her lovingly: "Oh, you little mischief!   Is this the way you
help your father?"

Scarcely a word but brought memories thronging back.
"Tafano" — I well remembered the circumstances which added
that to my lexicon.   The sweet poignant odour of the flower
seemed to rise from the page where I had written it, and I lived
again the happy day that Stewart and Peggy and Tehani and
I had spent on the little island in the Tautira lagoon.

I worked all day long, and every day, and by the middle of
October my task was completed, in so far as the dictionary and
grammar were concerned.   I proceeded at once to write the
introductory essay, for I knew that the time remaining to me
must be short.

The strain of waiting was telling upon all of us. Although he failed to show it, Morrison must have found it hardest to bear. To me, it seemed the refinement of cruelty to keep him so long in doubt as to his fate. A month had passed, and still he received no word.

I had received several letters from Sir Joseph, but there was no mention of Admiralty news; nor did I expect any. He himself would not know the day set for the execution.

On the twenty-fifth of October, I was revising, for the fourth or fifth time, the introductory essay for my dictionary, when there came a knock at the door. Every summons of this sort brought a cold sweat to my forehead, but this one was immediately followed by a well-remembered voice: "Are you there, Byam?" and I opened the door to Dr. Hamilton.

I had not seen him since the closing day of the court-martial. He informed me that he had just been appointed surgeon to the *Spitfire*, then stationed at Portsmouth. It was one of the ships I could see from my cabin window. She was on the eve of sailing for the Newfoundland station, and the doctor had come to bid me good-bye.

We talked of the *Pandora*, the shipwreck, the voyage to Timor, and of those two monsters of inhumanity, Edwards and Parkin. Dr. Hamilton was no longer under the necessity of concealing his feelings concerning either of these men. Parkin he loathed, of course, but his opinion of Edwards was, naturally, more fair and just than my own.

"I quite understand your feeling toward him, Byam," he said; "but the truth is that Edwards is not the beast you think him."

"Have you forgotten the morning of the wreck, Doctor, when we were chained hand and foot until the very moment when the ship went down?" I asked. "That our lives were saved was due entirely to the humanity of Moulter, the boatswain's mate. And have you forgotten how later, when we were on the sand-bar, Edwards refused to give us a sail that was not in use, so that we might protect our naked bodies from the sun?"

"I agree with you there; that *was* cruelty of the monstrous sort; no excuse whatever can be made for it.   But otherwise, Byam . . .   Well, you must remember the character of the man.   He has a high sense of what he considers his duty, but not a grain of imagination — nothing remotely resembling what might be called uncommon sense.   You will remember my telling you of his Admiralty instructions?   He was ordered to confine his prisoners in such a manner as to preclude all possibility of escape, and at the same time to have a due regard for the preservation of their lives.   Captains of the Edwards kind should never be given truly responsible positions; they are fitted to carry out only the letter and never the spirit of Admiralty orders.   One can at least say this for him: he acted in accordance with what he considered his duty."

"I 'm afraid, sir," I replied, "that I can never take so lenient a view of him.   I have suffered too much at his hands."

"I don't wonder, Byam.   I don't wonder at all.   You have . . ."

The doctor was in the very midst of a sentence when the door was flung open and Sir Joseph entered.   He was breathing heavily as though he had been running, and I could see that he was labouring under great emotion.

"Byam, my dear lad!"

He broke off, unable to say more.   I felt an icy chill at my heart.   Dr. Hamilton rose hastily, and looked from Sir Joseph to me and back again.

"No . . . Wait . . . It 's not what you think. . . . One moment. . . ."

He took a stride into the tiny cabin and gripped me by the shoulders.

"Byam. . . . Tinkler is safe. . . . He is found. . . . He is in London now; at this moment!"

"Sit you down, lad," said Dr. Hamilton.   I needed no

urging. My legs felt as weak as though I had been lying in bed for months. The surgeon took a small silver flask from his pocket, unscrewed the top, and offered it to me. Sir Joseph sat in the chair at my table and mopped his forehead with a large silk handkerchief. "Will you prescribe for me as well, Doctor?" he asked.

"Please forgive me, sir," I said, handing him the flask.

"Good heaven, Byam, don't apologize!" he replied. "Necessity knows no laws of deportment." He took a pull at the flask and returned it to the surgeon. "Damn fine brandy, sir. I'll wager it has never done better service than here, this day. . . . Byam, I came from London as fast as a light chaise would bring me. Yesterday, at breakfast, I was glancing through my *Times*. In the shipping news I chanced to see an item announcing the arrival of the West Indiaman *Sapphire* with the survivors of the crew of the *Carib Maid,* lost on a passage between Jamaica and the Havannah. I need not tell you that I left my breakfast unfinished. When I arrived at the dock I found the *Sapphire* already discharging her cargo. The *Carib Maid* people had gone ashore the evening before. I traced them to an inn near by. Tinkler was there, on the point of setting out to the house of his brother-in-law, Fryer. Like the other *Carib Maid* survivors, he was still dressed in various articles of clothing furnished by the *Sapphire's* company. He looked the part of a shipwrecked mariner, but I gave him no time for excuses. I bundled him into my carriage and carried him straight to Lord Hood. As luck would have it, the Admiral was in Town; he had dined with me the night before. Tinkler, of course, was in the greatest bewilderment at all this. I said nothing of my reason for wanting him — not a word. At half-past ten Lord Hood and I were at the Admiralty with Tinkler between us, dressed just as he had come ashore, in a seaman's jersey and boots three sizes too large for him.

"Now what has happened, or what will happen, is this:

Tinkler will be examined before the Admiralty Commissioners, who alone have the power to hear his evidence. By the grace of God and my copy of yesterday's *Times,* that evidence cannot be impeached as biased or prejudiced. Tinkler knows nothing of the court-martial. He has not seen Fryer, and he does not know that you are within ten thousand miles of London. I left him at the Admiralty, in proper charge, and came in all haste to Portsmouth."

I could think of nothing to say. I merely sat, staring like a dumb man, at Sir Joseph.

"Will the court-martial be reconvened tc pass upon this evidence?" Dr. Hamilton asked.

"No, that cannot be done; it is unnecessary that it should be done. The Admiralty Commissioners who will receive Tinkler's evidence have the power, in case the new testimony warrants it, of reversing the verdict of the court-martial in Byam's case, and completely exonerating him. We shall have their decision within a few days, I hope."

My heart sank at this. "Will it require days, sir, for the decision to be made?" I asked.

"You must bear up, lad," Sir Joseph replied. "I understand, God knows, how hard the waiting will be; but official wheels turn slowly."

"And my ship, the *Spitfire,* sails to-morrow," said Dr. Hamilton, ruefully. "I shall have to leave England without knowing your fate, Byam."

"Perhaps it's just as well, Doctor," I replied.

Sir Joseph opened his mouth to speak, and then gazed blankly at me.

"Byam, I'm afraid I've made an unpardonable mistake! The realization has only this moment come to me! Good God, what have I done! You should have been told nothing of all this until the decision of the Commissioners has been given!"

"Not at all, sir," I replied. "You shan't be allowed to condemn yourself. You have given me reason to hope. Even though the hope prove unfounded, I shall be none the less grateful."

"You truly mean that?"

"Yes, sir."

He gave me a keen, scrutinizing glance. "I see that you do. I am glad I came." He rose. "And now I must leave you again. I shall go back to London at once. I must be there to expedite matters as much as possible for you." He shook my hand. "If it is good news, Byam, Captain Montague shall receive it for you by messenger riding the best horses that ever galloped the Portsmouth road."

XXV

TINKLER

SIR JOSEPH BANKS carried my completed manuscripts back to London with him. Having finished my work, I asked permission to take up my quarters in the gun room again, and returned the same evening. The strain of waiting was less hard to endure in company. I told only Morrison of Tinkler's return; it would have been cruel to have informed the others, men deprived of all hope of life.

Morrison's Bible proved a resource to all of us during those last days. It was the same copy he had carried with him on the *Bounty,* and had been preserved even through the wreck of the *Pandora.* We read aloud, in turn, to the others, and we continued for hours so as to prevent ourselves from thinking of what was soon to come. Millward and Muspratt had aroused themselves from their stupor of despair. My liking and respect for these men increased greatly at this time. Tom Ellison had never for a moment lost his courage. It was a bitter thought that this lad, who had not an ounce of harm in him, was to lose his life as the result of a boyish indiscretion, at a time when he was most fitted to live. Only Burkitt remained as he had been from the day when sentence was pronounced. Except for brief intervals at mealtime, he paced up and down, hour after hour. Occasionally he would sit down for a moment, his head between his hands, staring dully at the floor; then he would lift his great shaggy head and glance around the room as though he had never seen it before, and a moment later spring to his feet and resume his pacing.

On the morning of October 26, we watched the *Spitfire* getting up her anchors. It was a windless day, and boats' crews from the *Hector* and the *Brunswick* were sent to assist in towing her out of the harbour. We saw, or thought we saw, Dr. Hamilton standing on the poop as the ship moved slowly out toward Spithead. Whether or not it was the surgeon, we knew that he was thinking of us that morning as we were thinking of him and wishing him Godspeed.

We welcomed every diversion, however slight; not a ship's boat crossing our line of vision escaped us. We criticized the way her men handled the oars, and conjectured as to where she was going and why. And every time the door of the gun room opened, every time the guard was changed or food was brought, I felt the cold chill about my heart that every condemned man must have known. Many a time during those weeks did I wish that the Admiralty Commissioners might have stood in our places for one day. The needless cruelty inflicted upon six men, prolonged during a period of more than a month, gave me a disgust for official routine which I retain to this day.

On the Sunday afternoon, Morrison was reading aloud to the rest of us. It was a cold day of drizzling rain, and Morrison was sitting close to one of the ports, holding his Bible on a level with his eyes that he might benefit by what dim light there was. All of us, excepting Burkitt, were gathered around him as we listened to that most beautiful of all the Psalms: —

The Lord is my shepherd; I shall not want.

Morrison read on in his clear musical voice, choosing those psalms that had comforted many generations of men in time of trouble. Of a sudden he halted in the midst of a sentence, and turned his head quickly toward the door. In so far as I remember we had heard nothing, — no sound, no voice, no tread of feet, — and yet we rose together and stood waiting, our eyes turned in the same direction. Burkitt stopped short and looked from the guards to us and back again. "What's up?" he asked, hoarsely. There was no need to reply. The door opened and a lieutenant of marines entered, followed by the master-at-arms and a guard of eight men.

It was all but dark in the room and we could scarcely distinguish the faces of the men who had entered. The master-at-arms carried a paper in his hand. He crossed to one of the ports and held it up to the dim light.

"Thomas Burkitt — John Millward — Thomas Ellison."

"The prisoners named step forward," the lieutenant ordered.

The three men moved to the centre of the room. Handcuffs were snapped upon their wrists, and they were placed in the centre of the guard, four men in front and four behind.

"Forward, march!"

They were gone in an instant without a word of farewell being said. Morrison, Muspratt, and I stood where we were, and the door was closed and locked once more. A moment later, as we peered from the ports, we saw one of the *Hector's* cutters put off from the gangway, and in the last grey light of the autumn afternoon we could distinguish the three shackled men on a thwart astern. Moored abreast of the *Hector* and about four hundred yards distant was *H.M.S. Brunswick.* We saw the cutter pass under her counter and disappear.

The anxiety of the night that followed is painful to recall. Morrison, Muspratt, and I made no pretense of sleeping. We sat by one of the ports, now and then peering out into the darkness toward the *Brunswick,* talking in low voices of the men who had gone. We knew well enough that it was their last night of life. The fact that we had been left behind gave us reason to hope that their fate was not to be ours. My heart went out to poor Muspratt, whose anguish of mind may be imagined. I did not dare hint, even now, at what Sir Joseph had told me concerning him, but I was glad that Morrison encouraged him to hope.

"Your case has been taken under consideration, Muspratt; I am sure of it," he said. "I have never doubted that it would be. The fact that we have been left here proves that there is something in the wind concerning us."

"What do you think, Mr. Byam?" asked Muspratt.

"That Morrison is right," I replied. "He has been recommended to the King's clemency. The Court's appeal on his behalf must have been granted. You and I have been left here with him. Don't you see, Muspratt? If they intended to hang us, we would have been sent to the *Brunswick* with the rest."

"But maybe they want to hang them first? Or what if they're going to hang us on the *Hector*?"

So we talked the night long, and God knows it was long. We considered every possibility, every conceivable reason for our separation from the others. And the minutes and the hours dragged by, and at last the darkness was suffused with the ashy light of dawn, through which the huge mass of the *Brunswick* grew more and more distinct.

Our guard was changed with the watch, at eight bells. No news came. One of the few prohibitions imposed upon us — and a quite just one — was that we should not speak to the guards, so we had no means of knowing what news was current on the ship. At nine o'clock, Morrison, who was standing by a port, turned and said, "They've run up the signal for punishment on the *Brunswick*."

On all British ships, eleven o'clock in the morning was the hour for inflicting punishment. We had no doubt as to whom the *Brunswick's* signal concerned. Ellison, Burkitt, and Millward had but two hours to live.

At half-past ten we saw one of the *Hector's* longboats, filled with seamen, put off to the *Brunswick*. Boats from other vessels in the harbour followed; the men in them, we knew, were being sent to witness the execution. Muspratt remained at the port, gazing toward the *Brunswick* as though fascinated by the sight of her lofty yards. Morrison and I paced the room together, talking in the Indian tongue of Teina and Itea and other friends at Tahiti, in a desperate attempt to occupy our minds. It was getting on toward the hour when Captain Montague entered, followed by the lieutenant who had come the night before. A glance at the captain's face told us all we needed to know, but if there was still doubt in our minds it was banished when the lieutenant ordered the guard to dismiss. The men filed quickly out, glancing back at us with friendly smiles. Captain Montague unfolded the paper in his hand.

"James Morrison — William Muspratt," he called.

The two men stepped forward. Captain Montague glanced at them over the top of the paper he held, a kindly gleam in his blue eyes. He then read, solemnly: —

"In response to the earnest appeal of Lord Hood (Admiral of the Blue, and President of the Court-Martial by which you have been tried, convicted, and condemned to death for the crime of mutiny on His Majesty's armed transport, *Bounty*), who, by reason of certain extenuating circumstances, has begged that you may not be compelled to suffer the extreme penalty prescribed by our just laws, His Majesty is graciously pleased to grant to you, and each of you, a free and unconditional pardon."

"Roger Byam."

I took my place beside my two comrades.

"The Commissioners for executing the Office of Lord High Admiral of Great Britain and Ireland, having received and heard the sworn testimony of Robert Tinkler, former midshipman of His Majesty's armed transport, *Bounty*, are convinced of your entire innocence of the crime of mutiny, for which you have been tried, convicted, and condemned to death. The Lord's Commissioners do, therefore, annul the verdict of the Court-Martial as it respects your person, and you stand acquitted."

Captain Montague then stepped forward and shook each of us warmly by the hand.

"I have no doubt," he said, "that three loyal subjects have been spared to-day for further usefulness to His Majesty."

My heart was too full for words. I could only mutter, "Thank you, sir!" but Morrison would not have been Morrison had he not been prepared even for such a moment as this.

"Sir," he said, earnestly, "when the sentence of the law was passed upon me, I received it, I trust, as became a man; and if it had been carried into execution, I should have met my fate, I hope, in a manner becoming a Christian. I receive with gratitude my Sovereign's mercy, for which my future life shall be faithfully devoted to His service."

Captain Montague bowed gravely.

"Are we now at liberty, sir?" I asked, doubtingly.

"You are free to go this moment if you choose."

"You will understand, sir, that we desire, if possible, to avoid . . ."

The captain turned to the lieutenant. "Mr. Cunningham, will you see to it that a boat is ordered at once?"

Captain Montague accompanied us to the upper deck, and a few moments later we were informed that the boat was waiting at the gangway. As I bade farewell to the captain he said, "I hope, Mr. Byam, to have the pleasure of meeting you again soon, under more fortunate circumstances." We climbed hastily down the side, and the midshipman in charge of the boat's crew gave orders to push off. We were in no position to enjoy the sweetness of those first moments of freedom. Six bells had struck while we were waiting on deck. Within two cables' lengths of us lay the *Brunswick*, her lofty masts and yards clearly outlined against the grey sky, and on our way to the wharf at Portsmouth we had to pass directly under her carved and gilded stern. Three men on her upper deck were standing at the very brink of death. Well we knew what was happening there. We sat with averted faces. We drew away from her, the seamen pulling at their oars steadily and in silence, but I saw that their eyes were all turned in the same direction, toward the tall ship now astern.

Of a sudden a great gun broke the silence with a reverberating roar. Against my will I turned my head. A cloud of smoke half hid the vessel, but as it billowed out and drifted slowly away I saw three small black figures suspended in mid-air, twitching as they swayed slowly from side to side.

Captain Montague had given me a letter from Sir Joseph, written at the Admiralty immediately after the decision of the Commissioners was known. He had taken inside places for us on that night's London coach. As a postscript he had written: "Mr. Erskine expects you at his house. You must not disappoint the old gentleman, Byam. You will want to see no one for several days; I quite understand that. When you have had the time you need alone, will you send me word? I have something of importance to communicate."

Nothing could have been more characteristic of Sir Joseph than this postscript. With all his bluff, hearty, manly qualities, he combined the delicacy and thoughtfulness of a woman.

The three of us were too shaken in mind for conversation — too sore in spirit, too bewildered at the change in our fortunes. We sat gazing out at the fields of home gradually fading from view as the autumn evening closed in. Opposite me in the coach there was a vacant place, and it remained unoccupied all the way to London, which we reached at daylight the following morning. But for me, all through the night, Tom Ellison sat there. I heard his laughter, his cheery voice. I saw him peering eagerly out of the window, missing nothing, enjoying everything, engaging in conversation the old gentleman who sat next to me. "Yes, sir, we 've been away from home five long years, lacking one month. If you've ever been a sailor you'll know what this journey means to us. . . . What's that, sir? . . . No, no; much farther than that. Ever hear of an island called Tahiti? Well, that's where we've been. If you was to dig a hole straight through the earth you'd come out somewhere near it."

Sea Law. Just—yes; just, savage, and implacable. I would have given the whole of the Articles of War and all those who wrote them to have had Tom Ellison sitting, in the flesh, opposite me in that seat in the London coach.

It saddens me to think of our brief, casual farewells. There was reason for this. We three had been together so long, it was inconceivable that we could drift apart. We stood outside the booking office at the Angel, St. Clements, Strand, watching foot passengers, carts, chaises, and hackney coaches passing by. Morrison and I were both well provided with money, he by his family and I by Mr. Erskine, but Muspratt, we knew, had not two ha'pence to rub together in his pocket. His home was in Yarmouth, where he had lived with his mother and two younger sisters. Morrison was bound to the North Country.

"See here, Muspratt," he said, "how are you off for rhino?"

"Oh, I'll manage, Mr. Morrison," he replied. "I've ridden shanks' mare to Yarmouth before now."

"And your mother's waiting for you there? He's not to ride shanks' mare this time, eh, Byam?"

"That he is not!" I replied, heartily. We pressed five pounds each upon him, and it did our hearts good to see the expression of amazement and delight on Muspratt's face. We shook his hand warmly and he hurried away at once to book his seat in the Yarmouth coach. We stood looking after him as he made his way down the crowded street. He turned and waved to us from the corner, and disappeared.

"Well, Byam?" said Morrison. I gripped his hand.

"God bless you, lad!" he said. "We must never lose track

of each other." A moment later I was alone, among strangers, for the first time in five years.

I could not have wished for a kinder, more considerate host than Mr. Erskine, my father's old friend. He had long been a widower, and still lived, with three elderly servants, in the house in Fig-Tree Court, near the Temple, where I had last visited him on my way to join the *Bounty*. The silence of that well-ordered house, where I had no appointments to keep and might do as I pleased from morning till night, was as healing to my spirit as the breath of the sea to a man at the end of a long illness. I wandered about the quiet streets in the vicinity of the Temple, or sat for hours by the window in my pleasant room overlooking Fig-Tree Court, where scarcely a dozen passers-by were to be seen in the course of an afternoon. And I thought of nothing. I had to accustom myself by degrees to the business of living — to the very thought that the gift of life was still mine to enjoy. Meanwhile, I was scarcely more animate than the two old trees that cast faint shadows on the pavement in the wan autumnal sun.

I had gone for my usual walk that day. When I returned, at five o'clock, Mr. Erskine had not yet come in, but Clegg, his butler, met me in the hallway.

"There's a gentleman waiting to see you, sir. He's in the library."

I took the stairs three at a time. I knew that my letter would bring him at the earliest possible moment. I flung open the door. There was Tinkler, standing with his back to the sea-coal fire.

Mr. Erskine was engaged that evening. At least, he sent word by Clegg to that effect; but my belief is that, upon coming home and learning that Tinkler was there, he had retired to his own room for no other reason than that we might have the evening together, alone. We had dinner in the library, in front of the fire. There was so much to be said that we scarcely knew how or where to begin. Tinkler had not yet recovered from his astonishment at the manner in which he had been pounced upon and kidnapped by Sir Joseph Banks.

"Remember, Byam, that I still thought of you as being somewhere on the other side of the world. When I had returned from my first voyage to the West Indies, I had heard that a ship, the *Pandora*, had been sent out to search for the *Bounty*. That was the extent of my information about you, and months had passed since that time. I had heard nothing of Edwards's return, and not a word of the court-martial. I had come ashore the previous evening, in clothing borrowed from men on the *Sapphire*, the ship that had rescued us. Another time I'll tell you the story of the *Carib Maid* and how she was lost. Only ten of us survived, — the other boats were lost, — and there we were at an inn about a stone's throw from the dock where the *Sapphire* was berthed. I'd had a glorious breakfast of eggs and bacon, and was just on the point of setting out for my brother-in-law's house when a fine carriage and pair drove up, and before I could say How-do-you-do or God bless me I found myself inside, sitting opposite Sir Joseph Banks.

"I had never laid eyes on him until that moment. He gave not even a hint of what he required of me, but I imagined that it must, somehow, concern the *Bounty*. 'Possess your soul in patience, Mr. Tinkler,' he said. 'I shall see to it that Mr. Fryer is notified of your arrival. I will merely say this, now: Mr. Fryer will strongly approve of my taking you in charge in this high-handed fashion.' With that I had to be content. Sir Joseph gave some instructions to his coachman and we drove westward at more than a smart clip. Presently we stopped before a very splendid house. Sir Joseph leaped out, strode up to the door, vanished, and ten minutes later out he came again with Admiral Hood in tow! Naturally, I was more mystified than ever, but I felt highly flattered at having two such guardians. We drove straight to the Admiralty.

"I shan't go into the details. Sir Joseph and the Admiral left me in charge of a Captain Maxon — Matson — some such name. He was a very courteous, pleasant, and vigilant companion, and did n't let me out of his sight for a moment. I spent the rest of that day, the following night, and until ten o'clock the next morning in his company. We told each other the stories of our lives, but all I gathered from him as to the business in hand was that it concerned the *Bounty*.

"Promptly at ten that morning, I was taken before the Board of Admiralty Commissioners. Picture me, still dressed in the cast-off clothing of three men, standing before that august assembly! I was sworn, and then graciously permitted to sit down.

" 'Mr. Tinkler, will you please to inform the Commissioners of anything you may know concerning Roger Byam, former midshipman of His Majesty's armed transport, *Bounty*.'

"You can imagine, Byam, how the mention of your name affected me. I felt a cold shiver of apprehension running with considerable speed up my spine and on to the roots of my hair. I had by no means forgotten how often Bligh had damned you as a piratical scoundrel without permitting any of us to say a word in your defense. Believe me, I had tried; and the second time I attempted it I thought he meant to throw me out of the boat. Now I thought, 'By God, old Byam 's caught! He 's in trouble, here or somewhere.' I looked from one to another of the Commissioners for a hint of what was expected of me.

" 'Do you mean, sir, concerning his present whereabouts?' I asked.

" 'No. Perhaps the question was a little vague. You are quite naturally mystified. We wish to know the particulars, if you recall them, of a conversation said to have taken place on the quarter-deck of the *Bounty* between Mr. Fletcher Christian and Mr. Byam on the night previous to the mutiny on that ship. Did you overhear such a conversation?'

"I remembered it at once, and it was at that moment, Byam, that light began to dawn upon me.

" 'Yes, sir,' I replied; 'I remember it quite well.'

" 'Reflect carefully, Mr. Tinkler. A man's life depends upon what you shall now depose concerning that conversation. Take as much time as you need to collect your thoughts. Omit no smallest detail.'

"The whole business came clear to me, Byam. I knew then precisely what was wanted, and you may thank God that my memory is as yet unimpaired by old age. But here's the extraordinary thing: from the night when you and Christian were talking between the larboard guns on the quarter-deck until the moment when I stood before the Commissioners, I'd forgotten the immensely important fact that Bligh had overheard a part of what you said. Would n't you think that might have stuck in my mind? There's a reasonable explanation, of course: during the boat voyage to Timor, and afterward, old Bligh never once, to my knowledge, explained why he considered you of Christian's party. We all believed that the reason was your failing to appear on deck before the launch was veered astern. And we knew that Christian had spoken to you a number of times on the morning of the mutiny. Furthermore, you were Christian's friend. That was more than enough to make the old rascal damn you straight out.

"You may believe that I took my time in proceeding. I told the story from the moment when we went on deck together during Peckover's watch. I'd forgotten nothing. I even told them how I'd confessed to you that I was one of the culprits who had stolen Bligh's invaluable coconuts. I told them how I lay down to take a caulk between the guns just before Christian came along and engaged you in conversation. But above everything, Byam, thank heaven and Robert Tinkler for this: I remembered how Bligh came up at the very moment you were shaking Christian's hand, when you said, 'You can count on me.'

"The Commissioners sat leaning forward in their chairs. One old fellow sat with a hand cupped behind his ear. On his behalf I spoke with particular slowness and distinctness. 'Mr. Christian replied: "Good, Byam," or "Thank you, Byam," I cannot be certain which, and they shook hands upon it. At this moment Mr. Bligh interrupted them; they had not heard him approach. He made some remark about their being up late, and . . .'"

"'That will do, Mr. Tinkler,' I was told. I was ushered out of the room, and . . . well, old lad, here we are!"

"You know, Byam," Tinkler went on, after a moment of silence, "I've often wondered whether that affair of the coconuts was not the actual cause of the mutiny. Do you remember how Bligh abused Christian?"

"I'm not likely to forget that," I replied.

"I can recall Bligh's very words: 'Yes, you bloody hound! I *do* think so! You must have stolen some of mine or you would be able to give a better account of your own!' What a thing to say to his second-in-command! I more than half believe that was what goaded Christian to desperation. What do you think?"

"Let's not talk of it, Tinkler," I said. "I'm sick to death of the business."

"Forgive me, lad. Of course you are."

"But I'd like nothing better than to hear about your voyage in the launch to Timor."

"I'll say this, Byam: in that situation, Bligh was beyond all praise. He was the same old blackguard, and he ruled us with an iron hand, but, by God, he brought us through! I don't believe there's another man in England who could have done it."

"What prevented him and Purcell from murdering each other, cooped up as they were in a small boat?"

"It was a near thing, a very near thing. Matters came to a head at a small island on the Great Barrier Reef. We were

in a desperate situation and had put in there for the night.
I've forgotten how the dispute started, but I remember Bligh
and Purcell standing on a sandy beach facing each other like
a couple of old bulls. We were damn near dead of hunger and
thirst, but these two still had fight in 'em. Bligh made a stride
to the boat, took two of our four cutlasses, and handed one to
the carpenter. 'Now, sir,' he said, 'defend yourself or forever
hold your peace!' The rest of us scarecrows stood looking on;
we were too wretched to care what might happen. And
Purcell backed down. He apologized. That was the only
time there was ever a question of Bligh's authority."

"Do you remember Coupang, Tinkler?"

"Coupang! That heaven on earth! Let me tell you how
we came in. It was about three in the morning . . . but wait
a minute! How about filling my glass? As a host, Byam,
you leave something to be desired."

And so it went the night through.

XXVI

WITHYCOMBE

I HAD spent a week at Fig-Tree Court when I sent Sir Joseph the message he had asked for. I supposed that he wished to see me for some reason connected with my Indian dictionary, and now that the first numbness of mind succeeding my acquittal had passed, I looked forward with pleasure to the interview; and it would give me an opportunity to ask whether I might render any services to him, or to the Royal Society, upon my return to the South Sea.

The death of my mother had severed my last tie with England, and I had been through so much that all ambition, all a young man's craving for a life of action, seemed dead in me. I may, perhaps, be excused for my feeling of bitterness at this time. English faces seemed strange to me, and English ways harsh and even cruel. I longed only for Tehani and the tranquil beauty of the South Sea.

It was my intention to inform Sir Joseph of my plan to leave England for good. I was possessed of ample means to do as I pleased — even to purchase a vessel, should that prove necessary. Ships would be sailing from time to time for the newly formed settlement at Port Jackson, in New South Wales, and, once there, I might find it possible to buy or charter a small ship to take me to Tahiti. I knew that, for my mother's sake, I could not leave England without paying a visit to Withycombe, and I both dreaded and longed to see our old house, so filled with memories.

Sir Joseph's reply to my message was an invitation to dinner on the same evening, and I found him in company with Captain Montague, of the *Hector*. We discussed for a time the events taking place in Europe, which pointed to an early outbreak of war. Presently Sir Joseph turned to me.

"What are your plans, Byam?" he asked. "Shall you return to the Navy, or go up to Oxford, as your father hoped?"

"Neither, sir," I replied. "I have decided to return to the South Sea."

Montague set down his glass at my words, and Sir Joseph looked at me in astonishment, but neither man spoke.

"There is nothing, now, to keep me in England," I added.

Sir Joseph shook his head slowly. "It had not occurred to me that you were considering Tahiti," he said. "I feared that, in your present state, you might intend to give up the sea for the seclusion of an academic career. But the islands . . no, my lad!"

"Why not, sir?" I asked. "I am free of obligations at home, and I should be happy there. Saving yourself and Captain Montague and a handful of other friends, there is no one in England I wish to see again."

"I understand — I understand," Sir Joseph remarked kindly. "You have suffered much, Byam; but remember, time will heal the deepest wounds. And remember another thing: if I may say so, you *have* obligations, and weighty ones."

"To whom, sir?" I inquired.

My host paused, thoughtfully. "I see that it has not even occurred to you," he said. "It is a delicate matter to explain. Montague, suppose I leave it to you?"

The captain sipped his wine as if pondering how to begin. Presently he looked up. "Sir Joseph and I have spoken of you more than once, Mr. Byam. You have obligations, as he says."

"To whom, sir?" I asked once more.

"To your name; to the memory of your father and mother. You have been imprisoned and tried for mutiny, and though you were acquitted and are as innocent as Sir Joseph or myself, something — a little unpleasant something — may cling to your name. *May* cling, I say; whether or not it shall, rests with you. If you choose to follow some career ashore, or, worst of all, decide to bury yourself in the South Sea, men will say, when your name is spoken of: 'Roger Byam? Yes, I remember him well; one of the *Bounty* mutineers. He was tried by court-martial and acquitted at the last moment. A near thing!' Public opinion is a mighty force, Mr. Byam. No man can afford to disregard it."

"If I may speak plainly, sir," I replied, warmly, "damn public opinion! I am innocent, and my parents — if there is a life beyond death — know of my innocence. Let the others believe what they will!"

"You were a victim of circumstance and have been hardly used," said Captain Montague, kindly. "I understand very well how you feel; but Sir Joseph and I are right. You owe it to the honourable name you bear to continue the career of a sea officer. War is in the air; your part in it will soon silence the whisperers. Come, Byam! To speak plainly, I want you on the *Hector*, and have saved a place in the berth for you."

Sir Joseph nodded. "That's what you should do, Byam."

I was still in a nervous condition as the result of my long imprisonment and the suspense I had been through. Captain Montague's kindness moved me deeply.

"Uncommonly good of you, sir," I muttered. "Indeed I appreciate the offer, but . . ."

"There's no need for an immediate decision," he interrupted. "Think over what I have said. Let me know your decision within a month. I can hold the offer open until then."

"Yes, take your time," said Sir Joseph. "We'll say no more of it to-night."

Captain Montague took leave of us early; afterward Sir Joseph led me to his study, hung with weapons and ornaments from distant lands.

"Byam," he said, when we had settled ourselves before the

fire, "there is a question I have long desired to ask you. You know me for a man of honour; if you see fit to answer, you have my word that I will never divulge the reply."

He paused. "Proceed, sir," I said; "I will do my best."

"Where is Fletcher Christian — can you tell me?"

"Upon my word, sir," I replied, "I do not know, nor could I hazard a guess."

He looked at me for a moment with his shrewd blue eyes, rose briskly, and pulled down a great chart of the Pacific from its roller on the wall. "Fetch the lamp, Byam," he said.

Side by side, while I held the lamp, we scanned the chart of the greatest ocean in the world. "Here is Tahiti," he said. "What course was the *Bounty* steering when last seen?"

"Northeast by north, I should say."

"It might have been a blind, of course, but the Marquesas lie that way. The Spaniard, Mendaña, discovered them long ago. Rich islands, too, and only a week distant with the wind abeam. See, here they are."

"I doubt it, sir," I replied. "Christian gave us to understand that it was his intention to seek out an island as yet unknown. He would not have risked settling on a place likely to be visited."

"Perhaps not," he replied, musingly. "Edwards touched at Aitutaki, I believe?"

"Yes, sir," I replied, and as I glanced at the dot of land in the immense waste of waters, a sudden thought struck me. "By God!" I exclaimed.

"What is it, Byam?"

"I must tell you in confidence, Sir Joseph."

"You have my word."

"I told you that I could not even hazard a guess, but I had forgotten one possibility. After the mutiny, when we were sailing eastward from Tofoa, we raised a rich volcanic island not marked on any chart. It lies to the southwest of Aitutaki, distant not more than one hundred and fifty miles, I believe.

We did not land, but the Indians came out in their canoes, and seemed friendly enough. I questioned one man in the language of Tahiti, and he told me the name of the place was Rarotonga. The mutineers were eager to go ashore, but Christian would have none of it. Yet, when he left Tahiti for the last time, he must have thought of this rich unknown island, so close to the west. If I were to search for Christian now, I should go straight to Rarotonga and be pretty sure of finding him there."

Eighteen years were to pass before I learned how mistaken I was in this opinion. Sir Joseph listened attentively. "That's interesting," he said. "Captain Cook had no idea there was land so close to Aitutaki. A high island, you say?"

"Two or three thousand feet, at least. The mountains are rugged and green to the very tops. There is a broad belt of coastal land; it looked rich and populous."

"The very place for them! Is the island large?"

"Nearly the size of Eimeo, I should say."

"Gad, Byam!" he exclaimed, regretfully; "I'd like to report the discovery. But have no fear — the secret is safe with me. . . . Christian . . . poor devil!"

"You knew him, sir?"

He nodded. "I knew him well."

"He was my good friend," I said. "There was provocation, God knows, for what he did."

"No doubt. It's strange . . . I had supposed that Bligh was his best friend."

"I am sure that Captain Bligh thought so, too. . . . I've a sad task ahead of me. I promised Christian that I would see his mother if ever I reached England."

"His people are gentlefolk; they live in Cumberland."

"Yes, sir; I know."

Sir Joseph rolled up the chart. I glanced at the tall clock against the wall. "Time I was getting home, sir," I said.

"Aye, bedtime, lad. But one word before you go. Let me

advise you, most earnestly, to consider Captain Montague's offer. You are sore in spirit, but that will pass. Montague and I are older men. We know this sorry old world better than you. Give up the idea of burying yourself in the South Sea!"

"I'll think it over, sir," I said.

Day after day I put off my visit to Withycombe. I dreaded leaving the quiet old house in Fig-Tree Court, and when at last I took leave of Mr. Erskine I had already been to Cumberland and back on Christian's errand. Of my interview with his mother I shall not speak.

On a chill winter evening, with a fine rain drizzling down, I alighted from the coach in Taunton, and found our carriage awaiting me. Our old coachman was dead, and his son, the companion of many a boyhood scrape, was on the box. The street was ankle-deep in mud, with pools of water glimmering in the faint gleam of the lamps. I stepped into the carriage, and we went swaying down the rutty, dimly lighted street.

The faint musty smell of leather was perfume to me, and brought back a flood of memories — of rainy Sundays in the past when we had driven to church. Here, in the door, was the pocket into which my mother used to slip her prayer book, nearly always forgotten until we were about to enter our pew. I could hear the very tones of her voice, humorous and apologetic: "Oh, Roger! My prayer book! Run back and fetch it, dear." And there seemed to linger in the old coach the fragrance of English lavender, which she preferred to all the scents of France.

The rain fell steadily, and the horses trotted on, splashing through pools, slowing to a walk on the hills. Tired with my long journey from London, I fell into a doze. When I awoke, the wheels were crunching on the gravel of the Withycombe drive, and ahead of us I could see the lights of the house. For a moment, five years were blotted from my mind; I was returning from school for the Christmas holidays, and my mother would be listening for the carriage, ready to run to the door to welcome me.

Thacker was standing under the portico, and the butler and the other servants — a forlorn little group, it seemed to me. Never, save on that night, have I seen tears in Thacker's eyes.

A few moments later I was seated alone in the high-ceilinged dining-room, filled with shadows and memories. The candles on the table burned without a flicker, and in their yellow light our old butler moved noiselessly about, filling my glass and setting before me food that I ate without knowing what it was. It had been my privilege to dine here on Sundays, as a small boy, and on other evenings to come in to say good-night when my father and mother were at dessert — a good-night enriched by a walnut, or a handful of raisins or Spanish figs. Here I had dined with my mother, after my father's death; here Bligh had dined with us on that night so long ago. Save for him and his letter my mother might be opposite me now. . . . I rose and went upstairs.

In my father's study, high up in the north wing, I stretched out in a long chair under the chandelier. His spirit seemed to fill the place: his collection of sextants in the cabinet, the astronomical charts on the wall, the books in their tall shelves — all were eloquent of him. I took down a leather-bound volume of Captain Cook's *Voyages,* but found it impossible to read. I was listening for my mother's light footstep in the passage outside, and her voice at the door: "Roger, may I come in?" At last I took up a candle and made my way along the hallway, passing the door of my mother's room on the way to my own. Into her room I dared not go that night. I fancied her there, as I had seen her a hundred times in the past, reading in bed, with her thick hair tumbled on the pillow, and a candle on the table at her side.

West winds, blowing off the Atlantic, made that December a warm and rainy month, and I took many a long walk along the muddy lanes, with the rain in my face and the wind moaning through the leafless trees. A change, so gradual as to be almost imperceptible, was coming over me; I was beginning to realize that my roots, like those of my ancestors, were deep in this West Country soil. Tehani, our child, the South Sea — all seemed to lose substance and reality, fading to the ghostliness of a beautiful, half-remembered dream. Reality lay here — in the Watchet churchyard, in Withycombe, among the cottages of our tenants. And the solid walls of our old house, the order preserved within, through death and distress, brought home to me the sense of a continuity it was my duty to preserve. Little by little my bitterness dissolved.

Toward the end of the month my decision was made. It cost me dear at the time, but I have since had no cause to regret it. I wrote to Captain Montague that I would join his ship, and enclosed a copy of the letter in a longer one to Sir Joseph Banks. Two days later, on a grey windless morning, I stood under the portico, waiting for the carriage which was to take me to Taunton to catch the London coach. The Bristol Channel lay like polished steel under the low clouds, and the air was so still that I could hear the cawing of the rooks from far and near. Two fishing boats were working out to sea, their sails hanging slack, and the men at the sweeps. I was watching them creeping laboriously toward the Atlantic when I heard Tom's chirrup to the horses, and the sound of wheels on the drive.

XXVII

EPILOGUE

I JOINED Captain Montague's ship in January, 1793, and hostilities broke out in the following month, the beginning of our wars with the allied nations of Europe — the stormiest and most critical period of British naval history, which was to culminate, after twelve years of almost constant actions, in the great sea fight off the coast of Spain. I had the honour of fighting the Dutch at Camperdown, the Danes at Copenhagen, and the Spanish and French at Trafalgar, and it was after that most glorious of victories that I was promoted to the rank of captain.

Throughout the period of the wars I had many a dream of being stationed in the Pacific upon the establishment of peace, but a sea officer in time of war has little leisure for reflection, and as the years passed my longing to return to the South Sea grew less painful, and the sufferings I had endured less bitter in memory. It was not until the summer of 1809, when in command of the *Curieuse*, a smart frigate of thirty-two guns, captured from the French, that my dream came true. I received orders to set sail for Port Jackson, in New South Wales, and thence to Valparaiso, touching at Tahiti on the way.

I had on board a half-company of the Seventy-third Regiment, sent out to relieve the New South Wales Corps; the remainder of the regiment had gone ahead, on board the ships *Dromedary* and *Hindostan*. Four years before, through the influence of Sir Joseph Banks, Lord Camden had appointed Captain Bligh governor of New South Wales; now the notorious Rum Rebellion had run its course, and a new governor, Colonel Lachlan Macquarie, had been sent to take charge of the troubled colony. Accusing Bligh of harsh and tyrannical misuse of his powers, Major Johnston, the senior officer of the New South Wales Corps, and a Mr. MacArthur, the most influential of the settlers, had seized the reins of government and kept Bligh a prisoner in Government House for more than a year.

During the long voyage out, by the Cape of Good Hope and through Bass Straits, Bligh was often in my thoughts. For his belief that I was one of the mutineers, and my sufferings as a prisoner, I had never blamed him at heart. But the letter to my mother, which had certainly been the cause of her death, was another matter. I had no desire to affront him in public, yet I knew I could never take his hand. He had played the part of a brave captain in the wars; at Copenhagen, Nelson had congratulated him on the quarter-deck of the *Elephant*. But now, as his career was drawing to a close, the history of the *Bounty* was repeating itself, and Bligh was once more the central figure in a mutiny. I had no means of determining the justice of the case, but the fact was strange, to say the least.

We left Spithead in August, and it was not until February, 1810, that the *Curieuse* entered the magnificent harbour of Port Jackson, and cast anchor in Farm Cove, exchanging salutes with the three British ships of war moored close by — the *Porpoise*, the *Dromedary*, and the *Hindostan*. While we were making all snug, a boat put off from the latter ship, bringing her captain, John Pascoe, on board. Pascoe had had the honour of serving as Nelson's flag-lieutenant at Trafalgar, and was an old friend of mine. It was a hot day of the antipodean summer, and a blistering sun shone down from a cloudless sky. I ushered my guest into the cabin, where it was cooler than on deck, and ordered the steward to make a pitcher of claret punch. Pascoe sank down on a settee, mopping his face with a large silk handkerchief.

"Whew! I'll wager hell is no hotter than Sydney just now!"
he exclaimed. "And, by God, their climate is no hotter than
their politics! What have you heard of all this in England?"

"Only rumours; we know nothing of the truth."

"The truth is hard to get at, even here. No doubt there is
justice on both sides. The rum traffic has been the ruin of
the colony, and it was in the hands of the military officers.
Bligh perceived the evil and attempted to stop it, using the
same famous tact and consideration which brought on the
Bounty mutiny. As governor, he was invested with far
more power than the King enjoys at home, but his only means
of enforcing it was the Rum Puncheon Corps, as they are
called. You know at least the result: Bligh a prisoner in
Government House, and the administration in the hands of
Major Johnston, a puppet for Mr. MacArthur, the richest
settler in the colony. A pretty mess!"

"What will happen now?"

"The Seventy-third stays here and the Corps returns to
England. Johnston, MacArthur, and Bligh will have it out
at home. Colonel Macquarie, whom I brought out, remains
as governor."

Pascoe was eager for news from home, and we gossiped for
a time. Presently he rose. "I must be pushing off, Byam,"
he said: "Bligh has ordered us to sail this afternoon."

When I had taken leave of him at the gangway, I ordered a
boat and went ashore to arrange for the debarkation of the
troops, and wait upon the governor. It was indeed a fiery day,
and as I trudged up the path that led to Government House I
sank ankle-deep in dust. The anteroom in which I was asked
to take a chair was dark and cool.

"His Excellency is occupied for the moment, Captain Byam,"
said the A.D.C. who received me. He bowed and sat down to
continue his writing, and next moment, from beyond the
closed door, I heard a strident voice raised angrily. In an
instant I felt myself twenty years younger, transported as if

by magic to the deck of the *Bounty* on the afternoon before the
mutiny. The same harsh voice, unchanged by a score of years,
rang out in memory, as if repeating the words which had
goaded Christian to madness: "Yes, you bloody hound! I *do*
think so. You must have stolen some of mine or you would
be able to give a better account of your own. You're
damned rascals and thieves, the lot of you!"

The voice in the cabinet ceased and I heard the deep, conciliatory murmur of the governor. Then Bligh broke out
again. His grievances had lost nothing in the two years he
had brooded over them.

"Major Johnston, sir? By God! The man should be taken
out and shot! As for MacArthur, I took his measure the first
time I laid eyes on him. 'What, sir?' I said, 'are you to have
such flocks of sheep and cattle as no man ever heard of before?
No, sir! I have heard of you and your concerns, sir! You
have got five thousand acres of the finest land, but, by God,
you shan't keep it!' 'I have received the land by order of the
Secretary of State,' replied MacArthur, coolly, 'and on the
recommendation of the Privy Council.' 'Damn the Privy
Council!' said I, 'and the Secretary of State, too! What have
they to do with me?'"

Again I heard the deep conciliatory murmur of the Governor's voice, interrupted by Bligh's strident tones: "Sydney,
sir? A sink of iniquity! A more depraved, licentious lot of
rascals don't exist! The settlers? God save the mark!
They're worse than the convicts — the very scum of the earth!
You must know how open I am to mercy and compassion, but,
by God, sir, such qualities are wasted here! Rule them with
a hand of iron! Rule them by fear!"

There was a scraping of chairs and the door was flung open.
A stout burly man in captain's uniform stood in the doorway,
his face purple with emotion and heat. Without a glance at
me, he strode truculently across the room, while the A.D.C.
sprang up and hastened to open the outer door. Captain

Bligh gave him neither word nor glance as he brushed past. Next moment he was gone. The tired young A.D.C. closed the door, and turned to me with a faint smile. "Thank God!" he murmured devoutly, under his breath.

We came in sight of Tahiti on a morning in early April, passing to the north of Eimeo with a fine breeze at west by north. But the wind chopped around to the east as we approached the land, and we were all day long working up to Matavai Bay. My lieutenant, Mr. Cobden, must have had some inkling of what was passing in my mind, for he and the master saw to it that I was disturbed by no detail of the working of the ship.

Communication with Tahiti was all but impossible in those days, and not once, during the twenty years that had passed since I had embraced Tehani in the *Pandora's* sick bay, had I had word of her, or of our child. In 1796, having learned that the ship *Duff* was to sail for Tahiti with a cargo of missionaries, — the first in the South Sea, — I had been at some pains to make the acquaintance of one of those worthy men, and received his promise to search out my Indian wife and child, and send me word of them when the ship returned to England. But no letter came back to me. In Port Jackson, I had met and talked with some of these same missionaries, and told them of my orders to visit Tahiti and report on the condition of the people. Their accounts of the island were of a most melancholy nature. Considering their lives and those of their wives and children in danger, the missionaries had embarked for Port Jackson on a vessel providentially lying at anchor in Matavai Bay. They had spent twelve years on Tahiti, learned the language (they were kind enough to say that my dictionary had been of the greatest aid to them), and worked unremittingly at their task of preaching the Gospel. Yet not a single convert had been made. War, and the diseases introduced by the visits of European ships, had destroyed four fifths of the people, I was

told, and the future of the island appeared dark indeed.   As
for Tehani, not one of the worthy missionaries had ever heard
of her, nor set foot on Taiarapu, where I supposed her still to
reside.

As my ship approached the land on that April afternoon,
Tahiti wore the green and smiling aspect I remembered so well,
and it was hard to believe that an island so fair to the eye could
be the scene of war and pestilence.   A flood of memories overwhelmed me as Point Venus came in sight, and One Tree Hill,
and the pale green of the shoal called Dolphin Bank.   Yonder
was the islet, Motu Au, opposite Hitihiti's house; close at hand
I saw Stewart's shady glen, and the mouth of the small valley
where Morrison and Millward had resided with Poino.   And
closer still was the mouth of the river in which I had first met
Tehani, so long ago.   I was only forty years old, — robust and
in the prime of life, — yet as I conned the frigate through the
narrow passage I knew so well, I had the feeling which comes
to very old men, of having lived too long.   Centuries seemed
to have elapsed since I had looked last on the scene now before
me.   I dreaded setting foot on shore.

It was strange as we dropped anchor to see that no canoes put
out.   A few people were discernible along the beach, watching
us apathetically, but they were pitifully few beside the throngs
of former days, and where once the thatched roofs of their
dwellings had been clustered thick under the trees, there was
scarcely a house to be seen.   Even the trees themselves had a
withered, yellow look, for, as I was to learn, the victorious
party had hacked and girdled nearly every breadfruit tree in
Matavai.

At last a small patched canoe put out to us with two men on
board.   They were dressed in cast-off scraps of European
clothing and were no more than beggars, for they had nothing
to exchange for what we gave them.   They addressed us in
broken English.   I was pleased, when they spoke together in
their own tongue, to find that I understood pretty well what

they said. I inquired for Tipau, Poino, and Hitihiti, but received only shrugs and blank stares in reply.

It lacked an hour of sunset when my boat's crew landed me on Hitihiti's point. I ordered them to await my coming on the Matavai beach, and turned inland alone, at the very spot where the surgeon had stumped through the sand twenty years before. Not a human being was to be seen, nor could I find a trace of my *taio's* house. The point, formerly covered with a well-kept lawn, was now grown over with rank weeds, and the path leading to the temple of Fareroi, once trodden by countless feet, was scarcely discernible. On my way to the still reach of river where I had met Tehani, I halted at sight of an old woman, squatting motionless on the sand as she gazed out to sea. She looked up at me dully, but brightened when she found that I addressed her in her own tongue, though haltingly. Hitihiti? She had heard of him, but he was dead long since. Hina? She shook her head. She had never heard of Tipau, but remembered Poino well. He was dead. She shrugged her shoulders. "Once Tahiti was a land of men," she said; "now only shadows fill the land."

The river was unchanged, and though the bank was overgrown with vegetation, I found my way to my seat among the roots of the ancient *mapé* tree. The noble tree stood firmly rooted and flourishing, and the river ran on with the same faint murmuring sound. But my youth was gone, and all my old friends dead. For a moment anguish gripped me; I would have renounced my career and all I possessed in the world to have been twenty years younger, sporting in the river with Tehani.

I dared not think of her, nor of our child. I had resolved to sail to Tautira on the morrow and dreaded what I might discover there. Presently I rose, crossed the river at a shallow place, and walked toward One Tree Hill. The groves of breadfruit trees which had once provided food for innumerable people were now hacked, yellow, and drooping; in place of scores of neat Indian cottages, only a few filthy hovels were to be seen; and where a thousand people had lived only twenty years before I met scarce a dozen on my walk.

Proceeding down the eastern slope of One Tree Hill I soon reached Stewart's glen where I had passed so many happy hours. There I sat me down on a flat stone, close to the spot where his house had once stood. Not a trace of the house remained, nor of the garden he had tended with such care, though I found what I took to be the remains of one of his rockeries for ferns. Stewart's bones, overgrown with coral, lay mingled with the *Pandora's* rotting timbers on a reef off the Australian coast. Where was Peggy? Where was their child? The sun had set, and the shadows were deepening in the glen. Sadly I rose and made my way over the steep rocky trail that led to Matavai.

Next morning I took the pinnace and a dozen men and sailed around the east side of Tahiti Nui to Taiarapu. The eastern coast seemed in a more flourishing state than Matavai, and I was agreeably surprised to find that Vehiatua's former realm had not been desolated by war. But pestilence had done its work, and scarce one man was to be found where five had lived in my time. As we approached Tautira, I strained my eyes for the sight of Vehiatua's tall house on the point. It was gone, but presently I perceived with emotion that my own house, or one like it, stood on the spot where I had lived. The boat grounded on the sand, while a score of people, with brighter faces than those of Matavai, stood on the beach to welcome us. I scanned their countenances while my heart beat painfully, but there was no man or woman I knew. I dared not ask for Tehani, and the missionaries in Port Jackson had informed me that Vehiatua was dead, so, telling my people to bargain for a supply of coconuts, I set off in search of someone known to me. The little crowd of Indians stopped by the boat. I was glad to be left alone.

I took the well-remembered path, and before I had walked

halfway to the house I met a middle-aged man of commanding presence, who halted at sight of me.   Our eyes met, and for an instant neither spoke.

"Tuahu?" I said.

"Byam!" He stepped forward to clasp me in the Indian embrace.   There were tears in his eyes as he looked at me. Presently he said, "Come to the house."

"I was on my way there," I replied, "but let us stop a moment where we can be alone."

He understood perfectly what was in my mind, and waited with downcast eyes while I mustered up courage to ask a question his silence answered only too eloquently.

"Where is Tehani?"

"*Ua mate* — dead," he replied quietly.   "She died in the moon of Paroro, when you were three moons gone."

"And our child?" I asked after a long silence.

"She lives," said Tuahu.   "A woman now, with a child of her own.   Her husband is the son of Atuanui.   He will be high chief of Taiarapu one day.   You shall see your daughter presently."

Tuahu waited in considerate silence for me to speak.   "Old friend and kinsman," I said at last, "you know how dearly I loved her.   All these years, while my country has been engaged in constant wars, I have dreamed of coming back.   This place is a graveyard of memories, and I have been stirred enough. I wish to see my daughter; not to make myself known to her. To tell her that I am her father, to embrace her, to speak with her of her mother, would be more than I could endure.   You understand?"

Tuahu smiled sorrowfully.   "I understand," he said.

At that moment I heard a sound of voices on the path, and he touched my arm.   "She is coming, Byam," he said in a low voice.   A tall girl was approaching us, followed by a servant, and leading a tiny child by the hand.   Her eyes were dark blue as the sea; her robe of snow-white cloth fell from her shoulders in graceful folds, and on her bosom I saw a necklace of gold, curiously wrought like the sinnet seamen plait.

"Tehani," called the man beside me, and I caught my breath as she turned, for she had all her dead mother's beauty, and something of my own mother, as well. "The English captain from Matavai," Tuahu was saying, and she gave me her hand graciously. My granddaughter was staring up at me in wonder, and I turned away blindly.

"We must go on," said Tehani to her uncle. "I promised the child she should see the English boat."

"Aye, go," replied Tuahu.

The moon was bright overhead when I reëmbarked in the pinnace to return to my ship. A chill night breeze came whispering down from the depths of the valley, and suddenly the place was full of ghosts, — shadows of men alive and dead, — my own among them.

THE TRILOGY OF THE "BOUNTY"

CHARLES NORDHOFF and James Norman Hall began in 1929 their preliminary work upon an historical novel dealing with the mutiny on board *H.M.S. Bounty*. It was at first anticipated that one or both of the authors would have to journey to England and elsewhere to collect the necessary source material, but, upon the advice of their publishers, this research was delegated to competent English assistants. With their painstaking help, the archives of the British Museum were searched through, as well as the rare-book shops and the collections of prints and engravings in London, for all procurable material dealing not only with the history of the *Bounty*, but also with life and discipline in the British Navy during the late eighteenth and early nineteenth centuries. With the generous permission of the British Admiralty, photostat copies were made of Bligh's correspondence and of the Admiralty records of the court-martial proceedings. Copies of the *Bounty's* deck and rigging plans were also secured, with special reference to the alterations made for her breadfruit-tree voyage; and a British naval officer, whose interest in these matters had been aroused, then proceeded to build an exact model of the vessel.

Books, engravings, blueprints, photostats, and photographs were finally assembled and sent to the publishers' office, where the shipment was checked, supplemented with material collected from American sources, and forwarded to its final destination, Tahiti, the home of Nordhoff and Hall.

THE TRILOGY OF THE "BOUNTY"

The *Bounty* history divides itself naturally into three parts, and it was the plan of the authors, from the beginning, to deal with each of these in a separate volume, in case sufficient public interest was shown in the first to justify the preparation of the trilogy.

Mutiny on the Bounty, which opens the story, is concerned with the voyage of the vessel from England, the long Tahiti sojourn while the cargo of young breadfruit trees was being assembled, the departure of the homeward-bound ship, the mutiny, and the fate of those of her company who later returned to Tahiti, where they were eventually seized by H.M.S. *Pandora* and taken back to England for trial. The authors chose as the narrator of this story a fictitious character, Roger Byam, who tells it as an old man, after his retirement from the Navy. Byam had his actual counterpart in the person of Peter Heywood, whose name was, for this reason, omitted from the roster of the *Bounty's* company. Midshipman Byam's experience follows closely that of Midshipman Heywood. With the license of historical novelists, the authors based the career of Byam upon that of Heywood, but in depicting it they did not, of course, follow the latter in every detail. In the essentials relating to the mutiny and its aftermath, they have adhered to the facts long preserved in the records of the British Admiralty.

Men against the Sea, the second narrative, is the story of Captain Bligh and the eighteen loyal men who, on the morning of the mutiny, were set adrift by the mutineers in the *Bounty's* launch, an open boat but twenty-three feet long, in which they made a 3600-mile voyage from the scene of the mutiny to Timor, in the Dutch East Indies. Captain Bligh's log of this remarkable voyage, a series of brief daily notes, was, of course, the chief literary source of this second novel. The voyage is described in the words of one of those who survived it — Thomas Ledward, acting surgeon of the *Bounty*, whose medical knowledge and whose experience in reading men's sufferings would qualify him as a sensitive and reliable observer.

Pitcairn's Island, the concluding story, is, perhaps, the strangest and most romantic. After two unsuccessful attempts to settle on the island of Tupuai (or Tubuai, as it is more commonly spelled in these days), the mutineers returned to Tahiti, where they parted company. Fletcher Christian, acting lieutenant of the *Bounty* and instigator of the mutiny, once more embarked in the ship for an unknown destination. With him were eight of his own men and eighteen Polynesians (twelve women and six men). They sailed from Tahiti in September 1789, and for a period of eighteen years nothing more was heard of them. In February 1808, the American sealing vessel *Topaz,* calling at Pitcairn, discovered on this supposedly uninhabited crumb of land a thriving community of mixed blood: a number of middle-aged Polynesian women and more than a score of children, ruled by a white-haired English seaman, Alexander Smith, the only survivor of the fifteen men who had landed there so long before.

The story of what befell the refugees during the eighteen years before the arrival of the *Topaz* offers a fitting conclusion to the tale of the *Bounty* mutiny. As the authors have said, in their Note to *Pitcairn's Island,* the only source of information we now have concerning the events of those years is the account — or, more accurately, the several discrepant accounts — handed on to us by the sea captains who visited Pitcairn during Smith's latter years. It is upon these accounts that their story is based.

Those who are interested in the source material concerning the *Bounty* mutiny will find an exhaustive bibliography of books, articles, and unpublished manuscripts in the Appendix to Mr. George Mackaness's splendid *Life of Vice-Admiral William Bligh,* published by Messrs. Angus and Robertson, of Sydney, Australia. Among the sources consulted by

Nordhoff and Hall were the following: "Minutes of the Proceedings of a Court-Martial on Lieutenant William Bligh and certain members of his crew, to investigate the cause of the loss of H.M.S. Bounty"; A Narrative of the Mutiny on Board His Majesty's Ship "Bounty," by William Bligh; A Voyage to the South Sea, by William Bligh; The Life of Vice-Admiral William Bligh, by George Mackaness; Mutineers of the "Bounty" and Their Descendants in Pitcairn and Norfolk Islands, by Lady Belcher; The Mutiny and Piratical Seizure of H.M.S. "Bounty," by Sir John Barrow; Bligh of the "Bounty," by Geoffrey Rawson; Voyage of H.M.S. "Pandora," by E. Edwards and G. Hamilton; Cook's Voyages; Hawkesworth's Voyages; Beechey's Voyages; Bougainville's Voyages; Ellis's Polynesian Researches; Pitcairn Island and the Islanders, by Walter Brodie; The Story of Pitcairn Island, by Rosalind Young; Descendants of the Bounty Mutineers, by Harry Shapira; Captain Bligh's Second Voyage to the South Seas, by I. Lee; Sea Life in Nelson's Time, by John Masefield; Life of a Sea Officer, by Raigersfield; New South Wales Historical Records; Pitcairn Island Register Book; Memoir of Peter Heywood; Adventures of Johnny Newcome, by Mainwaring.

DATE DUE			

GAYLORD 234

PRINTED IN U S A

Free Public Library
Colusa, California

RULES

1. Books may be kept two weeks and may be renewed once for the same period, except 7-day books and magazines.

2. A fine of four cents a day will be charged on each book which is not returned according to the above rule. No book will be issued to any person incurring such a fine until it has been paid.

3. All injuries to books, beyond reasonable wear, and all losses shall be made good to the satisfaction of the Librarian.

4. Each borrower is held responsible for drawn on his card and for all fines accruing or

FC 96